P9-DFE-833

PRAISE FOR
**THE *NEW YORK TIMES* BESTSELLING
BIBLIOPHILE MYSTERIES**

"Suspenseful, intelligent mysteries with a sense of humor. . . . Kate Carlisle never fails to make me laugh, even as she has me turning the pages to see what's going to happen next."
—Miranda James, *New York Times* bestselling author of the Cat in the Stacks Mysteries

"Another superb entry. . . . Quirky characters and an intriguing cookbook with a fabulous history add to the fun. Highly entertaining."
—Carolyn Hart, *New York Times* bestselling author of the Death on Demand Mysteries

"Saucy, sassy, and smart—a fun read with a great sense of humor and a soupçon of suspense. Enjoy!"
—Nancy Atherton, *New York Times* bestselling author of the Aunt Dimity Mysteries

"Fun and funny . . . delightful."
—Lorna Barrett, *New York Times* bestselling author of the Booktown Mysteries

"A delicious, twisty tale."
—Julie Hyzy, *New York Times* bestselling author of the White House Chef Mysteries and the Manor House Mysteries

continued . . .

OTHER BOOKS BY KATE CARLISLE

Bibliophile Mysteries
Homicide in Hardcover
If Books Could Kill
The Lies That Bind
Murder Under Cover
Pages of Sin
(a Penguin Special e-book)
One Book in the Grave
Peril in Paperback
The Cookbook Conspiracy
The Book Stops Here

Fixer-Upper Mysteries
A High-End Finish
This Old Homicide
Crowned and Moldering

Ripped from the Pages

A Bibliophile Mystery

Kate Carlisle

AN OBSIDIAN MYSTERY

OBSIDIAN
Published by New American Library,
an imprint of Penguin Random House LLC
375 Hudson Street, New York, New York 10014

This book is a publication of New American Library. Previously published in an
Obsidian hardcover edition.

First Obsidian Mass Market Printing, May 2016

For more information about Penguin Random House, visit penguin.com.

ISBN 978-0-451-41601-8

Printed in the United States of America
10 9 8 7 6 5 4 3 2 1

Penguin
Random
House

*For cheering me on like no one else can,
this one's for you, Pam.*

Chapter 1

"Won't this be fun?" My mother squeezed me with painful enthusiasm. "Two whole months living right next door to each other. You and me. We'll be like best girlfriends."

"Or double homicide victims," my friend Robin muttered in my ear.

Naturally, my mother, who had the ultrasonic hearing ability of a fruit bat, overheard her. "Homicide? No, no. None of that talk." Leaning away from me, she whispered, "Robin, sweetie, we mustn't mock Brooklyn. She can't help finding, you know, dead people."

"Mom, I don't think Robin meant it that way."

"Of course she didn't," Mom said, and winked at Robin.

Robin grinned at me. "I love your mom."

"I do, too," I said, holding back a sigh. Mom had a point, since I did have a disturbing tendency to stumble over dead bodies. She was also right to say that I couldn't help it. It wasn't like I went out in search of them, for Pete's sake. That would be a sickness requiring immediate intervention and possibly a twelve-step program.

Hello, my name is Brooklyn, and I'm a dead-body magnet.

Robin's point was equally valid, too, though. My mother and I could come very close to destroying each other if Mom insisted on being my BFF for the next two months.

Even though she'd raised her children in an atmosphere of peace and love and kindness, there was a limit to how much of her craziness I could take. On the other hand, Mom was an excellent cook and I could barely boil water, so I could definitely see some benefit to hanging around her house. Still, good food couldn't make up for the horror of living in close proximity to a woman whose latest idea of a good time was a therapeutic purging and bloodletting at the new panchakarma clinic over in Glen Ellen.

I focused on that as I poured myself another cup of coffee and added a generous dollop of half-and-half.

A few months ago, my hunky British ex–MI6 security agent boyfriend, Derek Stone, had purchased the loft apartment next door to mine in San Francisco. We decided to blow out the walls and turn the two lofts into one big home with a spacious office for Derek and a separate living area for visiting relatives and friends. Our reliable builder had promised it would only take two months to get through the worst of the noise and mess, so Derek and I began to plan where we would stay during the renovation. I liked the idea of spending time in Dharma, where I'd grown up, but live in my parents' house? For two months? Even though there was plenty of room for us? Never!

"It would be disastrous," I'd concluded.

Derek's look of relief had been profound. "We're in complete agreement as usual, darling."

"Am I being awful? My parents are wonderful people."

"Your parents are delightful," he assured me, "but we need our own space."

"Right. Space." I knew Derek was mainly concerned about me. He'd be spending most weeks in the city and commuting to Sonoma on the weekends. His Pacific Heights office building had two luxury guest apartments on the top floor, one of which would suit him just fine.

I could've stayed there with him, of course, but that

would've meant renting studio space at the Covington Library up the hill for my work. This would entail packing up all my bookbinding equipment and supplies, including my various book presses and a few hundred other items of importance to my job. Those small studio spaces in the Covington Library basement, while cheap, were equipped with nothing but a drafting table and two chairs, plus some empty cupboards and counters.

I'm a bookbinder specializing in rare-book restoration, and I was currently working on several important projects that had to be delivered during the time we would be away from home. The original plan of staying with my parents, while less than ideal, would've allowed me access to my former mentor's fully stocked bookbinding studio just down the hill from my parents. Abraham Karastovsky had died more than a year ago, but his daughter, Annie, who lived in his house now, had kept his workshop intact. She'd also given me carte blanche to use it whenever I wanted to.

For weeks, Derek and I had tossed around various possibilities, including renting a place somewhere in the city. That seemed to be the best alternative, but at the last minute, we were given a reprieve that made everyone happy. My parents' next-door neighbors, the Quinlans, generously offered up their gorgeous French-style cottage for our use. They were off to Europe for three months, and we were welcome to live in their home while they were gone.

We offered to pay them rent, but all they required from us was that we take good care of their golden retriever, Maggie, and water their plants. When Mom offered to take care of the plants (knowing my tendency to kill them), it was too good a deal to pass up. I was hopeful that sweet old Maggie and my adorable kitten, Charlie (aka Charlemagne Cupcake Wainwright Stone, a weighty name for something so tiny and cute), would become new best friends.

So last weekend, Derek and little Charlie and I had moved out of our South of Market Street loft and turned it over to our builder, who promised to work his magic for us.

And suddenly we were living in Dharma, next door to my parents, in a lovely two-story French-style cottage that was both elegant and comfortable. The floor of the wide foyer was paved in old, smooth brick, giving the space a natural, outdoor feeling. The spacious living room was more formal, with hardwood floors covered in thick area rugs and oversized plush furniture in browns and taupes. Rustic wrought-iron chandeliers hung from the rough-hewn beams that crisscrossed the vaulted ceiling. The sage-toned kitchen was spectacular, with a twelve-foot coffered ceiling, a pizza oven, and a wide island that provided extra space for food preparation as well as seating for six. Off the kitchen was a small library with built-in bookshelves, a wood-burning fireplace, and two overstuffed leather chairs. I could already picture the two of us sitting there reading books each night by a cozy fire.

And in every room on the ground floor, dark-wood-paneled French doors opened onto an interior patio beautifully landscaped with lush plants and flowers.

Once we were unpacked and exploring the kitchen, Derek and I watched Maggie and Charlie sniff and circle each other for a few minutes. Finally, they seemed to agree that they could live in peace together. At least, I hoped so. Maggie ambled over to her bed and settled herself down on the fluffy surface. Charlie followed right behind her, clambered up and perched directly on Maggie's big paw. Maggie stared at the tiny creature for a long moment, and I prepared myself to whisk the cat away. But then Maggie let out a heavy sigh and closed her eyes. Charlie snuggled up against the big dog's soft, warm fur and was asleep several seconds later.

Derek and I exchanged smiles. I had a feeling we would all be very happy here.

And now here I was, sitting in my mother's kitchen on a bright Monday morning, drinking coffee with Robin and listening as my mother tried to brush past the fact that I did indeed have an alarming tendency to come upon dead bodies in the strangest places. Luckily, that wasn't likely to happen in Dharma anytime soon.

As I watched Mom bustle around her sunny kitchen, I wondered how I'd ever thought I could avoid seeing her every day simply because we weren't together in the same house. Not that I minded visiting with her on a regular basis. I joked about it, of course, but in truth, my mother was great, a true original and a sweet, funny woman with a good heart. All my friends loved her. She was smart and generous. But sometimes . . . well, I worried about her hobbies. She'd been heavily involved in Wicca for a while and recently had been anointed Grand Raven Mistress of her local druidic coven. Some of the spells she had cast had been alarmingly effective. She would try anything once. Lately she'd shown some interest in exorcisms. I didn't know what to expect.

I supposed I didn't have much room to criticize Mom's hobbies, given that my own seemed to revolve around crime scenes.

"Do you want some breakfast before we leave?" I asked Robin. We'd made plans to drive over to the winery this morning to watch them excavate the existing storage cave over by the cabernet vineyards. It would eventually become a large underground tasting room. Cave tastings were the hottest trend in Napa and Sonoma, and our popular Dharma winery was finally jumping on the bandwagon.

Robin pulled out a kitchen chair and sat. "I already had breakfast with Austin. He had to be on-site at seven."

"Derek left the house about that time, too. I thought he'd be driving into the city today, but he decided to hang around to watch the excavation."

"Austin was so excited, he could barely sleep last night." Robin lived with my brother Austin, with whom she had been in love since third grade. She and I had been best friends since then, too, and I loved her as much as any of my three sisters. I didn't get to see her as often as I used to when she was living in San Francisco, but I knew she was blissfully happy with Austin, who supported her sculpting work and was clearly as much in love with her as she was with him.

Austin ran the Dharma winery, and my brother Jackson managed the vineyards. My father did a great job of overseeing the entire operation, thanks to his early experience in the business world. Decades ago he'd turned his back on corporate hell and gone off to follow the Grateful Dead. Ironically, these days, Dad and four other commune members made up the winery's board of directors. He was also part of the town council, but this time around he loved all of that business stuff. It probably helped that Dad had always been remarkably laid-back and still was. I sometimes wondered if Mom had cast a mellow spell on him.

I checked the kitchen clock. It was already seven thirty. The cave excavation was scheduled to begin at eight. "I'll just fix myself a quick bowl of cereal, and then we'll go."

Robin glanced at Mom. "Becky, are you coming with us?"

"You girls go on ahead," she said, pulling a large plastic bin of homemade granola down from the cupboard. "I want to put together a basket of herbs and goodies for the cave ceremony. I'll catch up with you later."

"What cave ceremony?" I asked as I poured granola into a bowl and returned the bin to the cupboard.

She looked at me as though I'd failed my third-grade spelling test. "Sweetie, we have to bless the new space."

"Oh." I shot Robin a wary glance. "Of course we do."

Robin bumped my shoulder. "You haven't been away so long that you'd forget about the sacred cave ceremony."

"I've been busy," I mumbled. She was teasing me,

but still, I should've known that my mother would want to cast a protection spell or a celebration spell to commemorate the groundbreaking of our winery's newest venture.

I could picture Mom doing a sprightly interpretive dance to the wine goddess. She would chant bad haiku and sprinkle magic sparkles on the heavy tunneling machines and equipment. It would be amazing, and the heavy equipment would turn our dark storage cave into a large, magical wine-tasting space where all would be welcome.

"Oh, sweetie," Mom said, hanging a dish towel on the small rack by the sink. "While you're here, you should go to lunch at the new vegan restaurant on the Lane. They serve a turnip burger that is to die for."

I swallowed cautiously, hoping I didn't lose my breakfast. "I'll be sure to check that out, Mom."

She glanced at me and laughed. "Oh, you should see your face. Do you really think I'd be caught dead eating something so vile?"

"I . . . Okay, you got me." I shook my head and chuckled as I carried my bowl to the sink. "I was trying to remember when you turned vegan."

"I tried it once for a day and a half and vowed never again. And even then, did I ever serve my children turnips? No, never."

"You're right and I appreciate it. But I haven't seen you in a while. I was afraid maybe you'd turned into Savannah." My sister Savannah was a vegetarian now, but she'd gone through several austere phases to get there, including a few months when she would only eat fruit that had already fallen from the tree.

"No, I was just pulling your leg."

I smiled at her. "You still got it, Mom."

"I sure do." She grabbed me in another hug, and it felt good to hold on to her. "Oh, Brooklyn, I'm so happy you're here."

"So am I."

She gave me one last squeeze, then let me go. As I washed out my cereal bowl, she left the kitchen.

"Let's get going," Robin said after I put my bowl away in the cupboard. "I don't want to miss anything."

"Wait a second, girls," my mother called from her office alcove off the kitchen. She walked out, holding two tiny muslin bags tied with drawstrings, and handed one to each of us. "I want you both to carry one of these in your pocket," she said, her expression deadly serious. "It'll keep you safe."

"That is the coolest, scariest piece of equipment I've ever seen," Robin said.

I had to agree. We both stared at the monstrous excavation machine that was parked at the mouth of the storage cave, waiting to roll into action. They called it a road-header, and it was huge, weighing more than sixty tons (I'd overheard Dad gushing about its weight to Derek while they were standing around having a manly conversation about heavy equipment), and was as large as the biggest bulldozer I'd ever seen.

Extending at least fifteen feet out in front of its tank-like body was a medieval-looking articulated arm, or boom, at the tip of which was a large steel ball covered in clawlike spikes. As the machine rumbled forward, the ball rotated fast enough to tear its way through hard rock, slowly creating a tunnel. That was the theory, anyway. It hadn't started working yet. When it did, there would be dust and noise and, possibly, earthquakelike shaking. It would all be worth it when the tasting cave was completed. I could barely wait for that day.

It had always made sense to use caves for wine-barrel storage. Sonoma tended to get hot in the summer, and underground storage was the cheapest and most efficient way to maintain a constant temperature, which was vital to the health of the wine.

But over the past few years, many of the local wineries

had expanded on the idea and had brought the actual wine-tasting experience into the caves. I'd done a tour of some of the tasting caves in the area, and they were beautiful, unique spaces. Some were rustic; others were elegant. One low-ceilinged, tunnel-like cave I'd visited in Napa had been excavated by hand during the days of the gold rush. You could still see the uneven spike marks on the dark stone walls made by the workers' hammers and pickaxes.

Several wineries in the area had built luxurious private dining rooms within their caves. Another offered a complete spa experience. There were waterfalls and unusual lighting and nooks and crannies to explore. One local tasting cave featured an underground library. And there was always wine.

And finally, wine-cave tasting was coming to Dharma. We already had a number of storage caves on the property, but none was big enough to use as a fully functioning tasting room. The most spacious of the storage caves was located on the opposite side of the parking lot from the current tasting room. Once the cave excavation was completed, the current tasting room would be redesigned to use for private dinners and special events.

The wide double doors at the entryway to the storage cave were made of thick wood and arched to fit the cavelike opening. With the doors opened, the passageway was broad enough to allow a truck or a forklift to drive through. The interior was dark and cool and roomy enough to hold the hundreds of oak barrels that stored the wine until it was bottled.

The barrels had been moved into the fermentation barn and to other parts of the winery to avoid possible damage from the heavy equipment that would be used to expand the cave. Geologists had already tested the hard ground above the existing cave and had approved the digging.

A crowd was beginning to gather as Robin and I

planted our folding chairs on the blacktop a safe distance from the storage-cave entrance. We were drinking coffee and sharing cookies and snacks with at least fifty other commune members who were also here to watch the show.

I spied my father standing with Derek next to a massive piece of equipment. My two brothers and a couple of others were there, too, deep in conversation. They all wore hard hats and looked very manly while kibitzing with the excavation company's owner, a tall, good-looking, gray-haired man named Stan.

We had been warned that there would be a tremendous amount of dust flying and the noise would be impossible to endure without earplugs or, better yet, headphones that covered our ears completely. A while ago, Stan and his men had walked through the crowd, passing out headphones and protective goggles to anyone who wanted them.

The crowd's chatter subsided abruptly, and that was when I noticed Guru Bob walking toward the group of men. Guru Bob, otherwise known as Robson Benedict, was the avatar, the spiritual leader of the commune. My parents considered him a highly evolved conscious being, and, having known him for most of my life, I couldn't disagree. He was the reason my parents had gathered up their six small children and moved us all to Sonoma so many years ago when Guru Bob summoned them. Back in the day, he had purchased sixteen hundred acres of rich Sonoma farmland and had chosen this spot to establish his Fellowship for Spiritual Enlightenment and Higher Artistic Consciousness.

The commune members began growing grapes that first year, and, ten years later, with the winery thriving and lots of members' shops, restaurants, and B and Bs doing well, Guru Bob decided to incorporate our little community. He suggested we call the new town *Dharma*, which means "law" in Eastern philosophy.

But the word meant much more than that, according

to some philosophies. When the world was first created, it was said to have emerged from chaos. As the gods stabilized the mountains and separated earth from sky, they created harmony and stability—*Dharma*. In Buddhism, the word referred to cosmic law and order. Other disciplines translated it to mean "to live in harmony with the law."

Guru Bob chose to interpret the word as the Sikhs and others had: "To follow the Path of Righteousness." That idea appealed to his followers as well, and the town of Dharma was born.

Oh, and while Guru Bob was a fun name we kids liked to use, I would never have called him that to his face. It would have been disrespectful. Funny thing, though—I'd always had the feeling he knew we called him Guru Bob and didn't mind at all.

After five minutes of serious discussion, Guru Bob waved to the rest of us and walked away, heading off toward the center of town. I knew the reason he left wasn't that he didn't have an interest in what was going on. It was more that he'd put reliable people in charge of the job and he didn't want them to think he was watching over their shoulders or micromanaging. He would show up later to see how things turned out, trusting that everything had gone according to plan.

The buzz of voices rose once again.

"I'm getting excited," Robin said.

"So am I."

She gave me a look. "You sound surprised."

"I guess I was trying to be blasé about it, but this is really fun."

"It is. And I already told you how psyched Austin is to get started."

"My dad is, too."

She laughed. "He's been talking about building this tasting cave since before I moved back up here. At least a year ago."

"I know." I sipped my coffee. "So it's about time we

did it. It seems like every winery in the county has a tasting cave now."

She smirked. "And we must keep up with the trends."

I nodded, although I knew that keeping trendy wasn't the only reason the winery had finally chosen to carve out a larger space for the tasting rooms and additional barrel storage. The plain fact was that underground storage saved money. Temperatures in our existing caves didn't vary much from the recommended sixty-two degrees, which was ideal for making and storing wine. Dad had mentioned that they planned to build an interior waterfall to add to the natural humidity. Solar panels installed on the hillside above the caves would collect energy to be used for lighting the cave space and for pumping out excess moisture.

There was only one small tunnel built under the vineyards that led from one storage cave to another. More would be added, and they would be upgraded, widened, and modernized with better drainage in the floors and a thicker layer of shotcrete added to the walls for improved insulation. Shotcrete was a concretelike material applied using high-velocity hoses so that it dried quickly and covered every inch of the cave wall.

It was amazing how much cool information you could pick up from hanging around my father for a few hours. I'd learned that the winery committee had also approved plans to build a freshwater lake on the other side of Ridge Road that would eventually provide irrigation for the entire vineyard and winery. The plan was for Dharma to become self-sustaining and energy independent within five years.

A few of the men began walking toward us, away from the cave entrance where the heavy roadheader was ready to spring into action. Derek grinned as he approached, and my stomach did a little twist. There was something about a gorgeous man smiling at me that gave a boost to my day. Especially when that man was Derek Stone. The hard hat was an added treat.

"Having fun?" I asked.

"I'm having a fantastic time," he said, his British accent sounding even sexier than usual. Maybe it was the worn jeans or the heavy work boots he was wearing. Then again, he sounded sexy in a business suit, too.

I handed him my coffee mug. He took a sip and handed it back to me. "Thanks, love." Then he moved behind my chair so he wouldn't block my view, and we all waited for the show to begin.

A few seconds later, the sound of a loud, powerful engine erupted, and anyone who wasn't wearing a headset immediately fumbled to get one on. A cloud of thick dust erupted from the cave doorway and filled the air. I adjusted my goggles to watch the roadheader extend its claw arm deeper into the storage cave, where I imagined it clawing its way through the thick stone. A Dumpster-sized vessel rolled out on a track, carrying a pile of broken-down gravel that was dumped off to the side. I figured that pile would be massive by the time the job was done.

On the drive over, Robin had explained that the initial excavation would take several long weeks, possibly a few months. It all depended on the thickness and resistance of the stone.

But barely five minutes after the digging began, the earsplitting noise suddenly stopped. One of Stan's men, the one who was spotting for the driver, came running out of the storage cave.

"We've broken through some sort of wall," he explained loudly to my father and the other men. He didn't sound happy about it.

I looked up at Derek and saw him frowning. The experts had determined that most of the ground under the hillside was solid rock and heavily compressed soil. What did he mean, *We've broken through*? Was the dirt and stone beneath the vineyards less solid than the geologists had thought?

Dad, Derek, Austin, Jackson, and a few others went

running toward the cave, where the roadheader had come to a complete stop. I glanced at Robin and without saying a word, we both jumped up and went running after them. No way were the boys going to have all the fun.

Eighteen narrow inches separated the massive road-header from the sides of the storage-cave door, so we were able to slide past and enter the cool, dark space.

The dust was just clearing as Robin and I joined Derek and the others at the far end of the room where they stared at a jagged, gaping hole in what had been a solid stone wall a few minutes ago.

It looked broken, like an egg that was dropped and cracked open. Fissure lines radiated out from the large gash in the middle of the wall.

"We don't know how stable the walls are," Austin said to the small crowd, "so I'd like everyone to leave the cave for their own safety."

The commune members walked away, whispering quietly to one another. No one knew what this new development would mean to the tasting room plans, never mind the structural viability of the underground space.

I was too curious to leave. I noticed Robin wasn't going anywhere, either. But I sort of wished we'd both been given hard hats to wear. In lieu of that, I stuck my hand in my pocket to make sure my mom's little herb packet was still there. It was probably silly, but I felt better carrying it.

Derek flicked on a small flashlight and studied the open gash. About two feet wide and about four feet off the floor, it was just low enough that I could climb up and through it if I were brave enough. Was there some space back there? A tunnel, maybe? There had to be something.

Thanks to the beams from Derek's flashlight, I could see that the wall itself was at least four inches thick.

I moved closer and touched the grainy surface. "Is this concrete?"

"Looks like it," Derek said, exchanging a look with me. A wall of concrete meant that it was manmade. The excavation crew must have thought the concrete had been applied to the surface of the storage-cave walls and figured that behind the concrete were natural rock and packed earth.

"Can you see inside the hole?" I asked.

"Barely," he said, aiming the light directly into the hole in the wall. He leaned his head inside to take a look.

I held my breath. What if some wild creature was living in there? I shoved my hand back into my pocket and touched that small bag of herbs again. It gave me the oddest sense of well-being.

"Idiot," I whispered under my breath. "It's just some weeds in a bag." But I continued to rub the thin muslin packet anyway, hedging my bets while briefly considering slipping it into Derek's pocket.

Derek pulled his head back and handed the flashlight to Austin, who leaned in to take a look. "Holy Mother."

"What is it?" Robin demanded.

"You've got to see it for yourself."

"Let me see," I said, sounding like a typical younger sister. But Austin handed me the light without comment. I took another deep breath, not knowing what to expect. What in the world could survive in such a small, airless space?

I stuck my head inside to take a look for myself.

"Can you see well enough?" Derek murmured in my ear as I swung the small beam of light around.

I had to blink a few times before I could make out what I was looking at. The light beam didn't illuminate the entire space, but instead landed on small objects that were indecipherable at first. Slowly, though, things began to take shape. "What in the world?"

"What is it, Brooklyn?" Robin asked.

"It's a whole bunch of . . . stuff. Different things. Furniture. A big inlaid wood wardrobe with a beautifully beveled mirror built into its front door. There's an antique table with a fancy candelabra on it. A bookshelf with lots of things on all the shelves. Silver candlesticks. A silver teapot. At least, they look like silver from here." I leaned in farther. "There's more over in this corner. Another table with some small statuary. A couple of busts. I can't tell who they are. There are two bronze horses. Oh, the horses are bookends. And there are books." I flashed Derek a quick smile, then returned to scan the space. "A glass-fronted cabinet. It's got some more silver pieces inside. Another set of candlesticks and . . . is that another silver pitcher? On a tray of some kind. It all looks like hammered silver. It must be a set."

"And there're some gold pieces over there," Austin said, pointing. He towered over me and was able to gaze around without my blocking his view.

Robin, shorter than me by almost six inches, asked Austin to give her a boost up. I stepped aside so she could take a look.

"Here you go, baby," he said, holding her by the waist and easily lifting her up to see through the opening.

Derek handed the flashlight to Austin, and he held it steady as she took a look around. "It's an old curio cabinet."

"Can you see the silver inside?" Austin asked.

"Yes. It all looks beautiful."

"Do you see the bookends?" I asked.

"Yes. And books, too."

"I know," I said, grinning. "How cool is that?"

Robin slid back down. "It figures you'd see books before anything else."

"Books and possibly artwork," Derek said, taking the flashlight back and aiming it in another direction.

I got closer and found what he was looking at, a spot along the interior wall where several rolled canvasses stood leaning against the curio cabinet like drunken soldiers.

I moved away so Dad could take a look. After a minute, he stepped back, and Jackson took his turn.

"What is all this stuff?" I asked. "What's going on here?"

Derek shook his head. "I have no idea."

"It's a treasure trove," Dad said. "Just got to figure out where it came from."

"I wish we had a better light," I muttered.

At that moment, Stan walked up and handed me and Robin our own hard hats.

"Thanks." I put the rigid plastic hat on my head and felt safer instantly.

Then Stan pulled a long black industrial-strength flashlight from his tool belt and handed it to Derek. "Maybe this will help."

"Thanks, mate." Derek pushed the button on the heavy foot-long torch, and the powerful light filled the room.

"Like night and day," I said, smiling at Stan. "Thanks."

He nodded and strolled back outside. A man of few words.

Derek aimed the big flashlight's beam into the interior space.

"We need to get this wall knocked down," Dad said.

"Just what I was thinking," Jackson said, glancing toward the front of the cave. "I'll go talk to Stan."

I stretched up on my toes and poked my head farther through the opening. Derek continued holding the flashlight above my head. "Wow, over there in the other corner. It's another full-sized dresser with a mirror. There's a wooden box on top of it that looks like a jewelry box."

Derek turned the beam toward the left to allow me a better glimpse.

"It's beautiful," I said. "Looks French. Inlaid wood and lots of ormolu." I was able to recognize the finely gilded decorative detailing along the edges of the piece, thanks to Guru Bob, who had an antique desk in that style that I'd admired for years. He'd been kind enough to describe the history of the design to me.

"Pricey," Dad said.

"It's definitely worth a lot," I murmured.

"But what's a fancy dresser doing in a cave?" Robin wondered aloud. "And a curio cabinet? And silver candlesticks?"

"And books," I added.

"Good question," Austin said, his tone turning suspicious. "The sooner this wall comes down, the better."

I continued to scrutinize the dresser, too fascinated by our discovery to care how utterly bizarre it was that these amazing treasures were hidden behind a solid wall of concrete inside the winery storage cave. "That's definitely a jewelry chest on top of the dresser. It's the same inlaid pattern as the dresser. I wonder if there's anything inside."

"Jewels, of course," Robin said, grinning.

Something caught my eye on the dresser. "Oh, there's a silver tray with one of those old-fashioned silver combs and a hairbrush on it. It's pretty."

"I'm sure it's pretty," Robin said, "but it's still kind of weird."

"You're right," I said, and shivered a little. "It's like somebody lives in there."

I moved out of the way, leaving Derek alone to continue examining the odd crevice. He angled the flashlight in different directions, casting light onto every inch of the space. He scanned the low ceiling and ran the beam along the rest of the walls.

I was curious to see what other bounty we would find in there, so I peeked around Derek to take another look. Seconds later, I let out a piercing shriek.

"What is it?" Austin demanded, crowding me as I tried to push away from the wall.

Robin patted my shoulder. "Knowing Brooklyn, she probably found a dead body."

Her words barely registered as I pointed a shaky finger at what I saw on the floor close to the wall.

Derek aimed the beam where I'd indicated and muttered an expletive. He stepped back from the hole in the wall, turned off the flashlight, and wrapped his arm around my shoulders.

Robin's smile faltered. "Derek?"

"You were right, Robin," Derek said, giving me a soft squeeze of sympathy. "This cave has just turned into a crime scene."

Chapter 2

In seconds, Derek and Dad had the men rounding up pickaxes and sledgehammers in order to take down the rest of the wall.

I was shuffled out of the cave and barely had time to deal with another dead-body encounter.

Stan and his men backed the huge roadheader out of the enclosed space to give everyone more room. Stan ran and grabbed his own sledgehammer and joined the workers. Concrete dust was soon billowing out of the large storage cave. I was concerned for the men, of course, since it was getting hard to breathe, but I knew Derek wouldn't stop until he could step right into that inner room. I would've grabbed a pickax and gone to work on the wall myself, but I was certain I would just be in the way. As soon as the air cleared, though, I was going to jump in and find out who that dead person was. I had other questions, too. Where had all those beautiful treasures come from? And at what price?

One of Stan's men jogged over with a handful of cheap filter masks.

"Will those help?" Robin asked.

"It'll keep some of the larger particles from getting into their lungs," he said.

Larger particles? So the smaller ones would get

through? That was not a good answer. Robin and I exchanged worried looks as the man ran into the cave to hand out the masks.

Less than two minutes later, Derek and Austin stumbled out, covered in dust. Jackson, Stan, Dad, and one other man followed a few seconds later.

I rushed over to Derek, who was ripping the mask away from his mouth. "Are you all right?"

"I'm fine," he said, slapping the dust off his shirt. "But Stan was starting to wheeze, so I thought we'd better take a break. We'll wait for the dust to settle before we go back in."

"Okay. I don't want anyone to get sick from breathing that stuff."

"Nor do I," he muttered as he bent over to shake more dust out of his hair. "I think we'll be all right."

I scuffled back a few feet to avoid being enveloped in the powdery cloud he'd just created. I was getting worried. Hadn't people died from breathing the dust inside old caves? Didn't I remember hearing something about archaeologists breathing the dust of mummies' tombs? Didn't they carry strange viruses?

I guess my mind was going a little wacky while I waited for the okay to go back inside. After another half hour, I was ready to scream. I'd always thought I was a patient person, but apparently I was wrong because I was beyond anxious to get in there and figure out who had died in the cave. Everyone else was standing around, chitchatting and hacking up particles and brushing off more dust. Didn't anyone else feel the same urge I felt? Where did all that furniture come from? The silver, the art, the books. The body. Didn't anyone want answers?

"I'm going in," I declared, and began to walk toward the cave.

"Hold on," Derek said, grabbing my hand.

"Why?" I demanded, prepared to battle against Derek's innate urge to protect and defend.

He grinned. "Because I'm going with you."

"Okay." I calmed down a smidgen. "Good. We've waited long enough. We need to check out that cave and call the police."

"In that order," he murmured, clearly resolved to survey the scene of the crime before raising the alarm. He picked up the flashlight and joined me.

Much of the dust had settled, but we stirred more up with every step we took. I coughed as some of it got into my throat, and I wondered how Derek and Dad and the others had withstood it for the thirty minutes they'd been in here breathing that stuff.

When we got to the back wall, I could see how much work the men had done earlier. The opening into the hidden room was bigger now, almost the size of a small doorway, about three feet wide by five feet high. Eighteen inches still remained along the bottom of the wall, which meant we had to step carefully over the small barrier.

"Good job," I said, beaming at Derek.

"The men were on a mission."

I smiled at his words. He made it sound like he was leading his troops off to war. I ducked my head and stepped over the stone lip. Once on the other side, I was able to stand without crouching. I had expected the enclosure to feel damp or stuffy, but the air was clean and I detected a mild floral scent. It was also slightly larger than I'd thought, maybe fifteen feet long by twelve feet across, the size of a typical bedroom.

Derek joined me inside the small enclosure, flipped on Stan's flashlight, and pointed the beam toward the floor.

That was when I saw the body again.

Although he was facedown, he was obviously a man, and he was pressed up against the wall as though he'd sought out a secure resting place. I figured that was why we hadn't seen him at first. We had been diverted by all of the treasures surrounding him.

He wore an old-fashioned brown suit and had short,

dark hair. On the ground near his right arm was a well-worn brown leather suitcase.

"I wonder if he got trapped here during the 'ninety-seven earthquake," Dad said.

I glanced up. Dad stood on the other side of the barrier, but he had poked his head in so he could watch us. Austin and Robin were crowded around him. Jackson had gone back to work in the winery, and the rest of the men must have either lost interest or needed to return to their jobs as well.

"That's almost twenty years, Jim," Derek said, touching the dead man's neck and studying the change in color. "This man's skin looks and feels as if he died a few hours ago."

"Maybe the absence of air helped preserve him," I said.

"What're you saying? You think he was mummified?" Austin's wry tone gave a clear indication of his opinion of my theory.

I was used to getting snarky comments from my big brothers, so I just shrugged. "Anything's possible."

"Yes," Derek said, "but let's see if there's a more practical explanation."

"Like maybe he actually died a few hours ago," Dad suggested. "Except I don't see how that's possible."

"Nor do I," Derek said.

"Derek, did you notice how clean the air was when you first stepped inside here?"

He looked at me from across the man's body. If he hadn't detected it before, he took notice now, breathing in deeply through his nose. "Very fresh. And there's something else."

"A light floral scent, right? I was thinking it might be coming from the dresser. The owner probably used sachets in the drawers. That's what it smells like to me, anyway."

"I can smell it, too," Robin said, and I gave her a grateful smile. So I wasn't going crazy.

Derek handed me the flashlight to hold while he continued to search the man's clothing for identification.

My attention was drawn to the small leather suitcase on the other side of the body. "Can we open that?"

"I don't suppose he'll complain if we do," Derek said, interrupting his search to move the suitcase away from the dead man.

I set the flashlight down on the ground with the beam pointing to the ceiling. It diffused the light, but we had enough to see what we were doing. The brass latches were old-fashioned as well, but Derek got them unhooked and spread the suitcase open. Inside was a neatly folded stack of men's clothes packed next to a small black toiletries bag. Laid on top of the clothing was something I had not expected to see.

"It's a book," I whispered.

"A book?" Austin laughed. "Doesn't that just figure?"

"It sure does," Dad said.

Derek's lips twisted in irony as he handed me the book. "Might as well examine it. This could provide as many answers to this puzzle as anything else in this room."

"Stranger things have happened." I aimed the flashlight's beam at the book's leather cover and read the title: *Voyage au Centre de la Terre* by Jules Verne.

Journey to the Center of the Earth.

Is it totally geeky to admit that my fingers were tingling just touching it? It was covered in three-quarter morocco leather with gilding on the spine. The boards were marbled. I opened it to the title page to see the date: 1867. It was written in French. On the same page was a fanciful illustration of a view into a prehistoric world, and I was hopeful that there would be other illustrations within.

This was not the time or place to study it more fully, but as soon as we were finished here, I was going to run straight to Abraham's studio and inspect this book from cover to cover. Meanwhile, I clutched it for dear life and reluctantly returned my gaze to the body.

"We can go through the rest of the suitcase later," Derek said, turning back to the dead man. "Right now, I'd rather find out who this poor fellow is and what he's doing here."

I stared at the man's suit jacket, which fit his body well, although it was longer than most men wore their jackets these days. The shoulders were padded, and the waist was narrow.

"I'm no fashion maven," I said, stating what everyone in my world thought was obvious, "but I think that style and the shade of brown are from the forties or fifties."

I heard Robin snicker, and I shot her a smile. She was the one who knew fashion and had always been willing to share her best ideas with me.

"You're right, love," Derek said, pondering the situation. After a moment, he said, "I'd like to photograph the body before we turn him over. Can you stand up and hold the flashlight steady?"

"Sure." I stood and set the book down on the dresser nearest the wall, then picked up the flashlight and focused the beam of light directly on the dead man. Derek pulled out his phone and began snapping photographs from every possible angle.

After at least twenty clicks, he stopped and slid the phone back into his pocket. "That should do it."

"Good." I knelt down beside him. "Does he have a wallet or ID on him?"

"Not in his back pockets. I hope to find something in his suit pockets, but we'll have to turn him over to find out."

"Let's do it."

He looked up at my brother. "Austin, can you give me a hand?"

"Sure thing." My brother stepped into the space and knelt down next to Derek. Together they carefully rolled the man over onto his back while I held the flashlight.

"How did he get in here?" Austin wondered aloud, studying the man's face. "He looks like he died just a little while ago."

"And not from natural causes," I muttered as my stomach began to churn. "That's a lot of caked blood on the side of his head."

"And there's a bullet hole in his chest," Derek said flatly, pointing out the frayed hole in the lapel.

"No earthquake did that," Dad conceded.

Derek scowled. "No, a killer did that. We'd better call the authorities."

Before calling the sheriff's department to report a murder from who-knew-how-long-ago, Derek searched the man's pockets thoroughly and held up his findings: a French passport and a business-sized envelope.

I was surprised when Derek slit open the envelope and pulled out its contents. He was often a stickler for following the rules, but since he'd come from the world of clandestine law enforcement in England, I knew he preferred to find the answers on his own.

"What is it?" I asked.

"A ticket," he said, holding up a rectangular piece of paper for everyone to see. "He's booked passage from New York to Southampton on the *Queen Mary*."

"The *Queen Mary*," Robin echoed. "The ocean liner?"

"Yes. It's dated April 12, 1946."

We all needed a moment to figure that one out.

Staring down at the body, Austin scratched his head. "That's, like, seventy years ago."

"Brilliant," Robin said, patting his arm. "But we just agreed that the guy looks like he died a few hours ago."

"He does," I said, "but his clothes are more in line with the date on that ticket. Like I said, the nineteen forties or fifties."

Robin shook her head slowly. "This is weird."

"Maybe he's an actor," Dad suggested, "and died wearing a costume."

"And the ticket is a prop?" Robin said.

"Or some kind of souvenir," I said.

Austin shrugged. "That makes as much sense as anything else, I guess."

"Derek, what does the passport say?"

Derek opened the passport and read the name. "'Jean Pierre Renaud.' And the name on the passenger ticket is the same."

"That's pretty elaborate for a theatrical prop."

"It is," Derek said. "I don't believe this man was an actor, nor do I believe the ticket is a prop."

"So you believe he died here seventy years ago?" I asked. "That's awfully hard to swallow."

"It's a mystery." Derek stood and brushed more dust off his trousers. "However, if it is a case of mummification, the body will begin to decompose rapidly at this point. The authorities need to get here as quickly as possible."

"I contacted them," Dad said. "They won't be here for another forty minutes or so." He reached into his pocket for his cell phone. "I'm going to call Robson, too."

Yes, I thought. Guru Bob would certainly want to know about this. I glanced up at Derek. "I know I mentioned it first, but seriously, how in the world could this body have been mummified? Wouldn't you need to remove the organs and coat it in resin or something?" I vaguely recalled those details, thanks to a museum presentation I'd attended during a high school field trip.

He aimed the flashlight around the space. "This wall had to have been built within hours of the man's death. Once that was done, as you were correct to suggest, a lack of air, combined with this cold, dry space, helped preserve him."

"Truly bizarre," Robin murmured.

Guru Bob walked into the cave barely ten minutes

after Dad called him. Everyone stood in silence, watching his reaction to what we'd discovered.

He was clearly upset by the presence of the body. We'd all been shaken, but Guru Bob seemed to take it more personally. A man had been murdered in Dharma. His home. His sanctuary.

The mood was so somber, it felt as though we were attending a memorial service. And in a way, we were.

Guru Bob had always been as careful as one could be to keep too much negativity from touching Dharma. I knew it firsthand because I'd once brought a visitor to Dharma who turned out to be a cold-blooded killer. Guru Bob didn't blame me, of course, but I would never forgive myself for being so clueless.

"He is French," Guru Bob murmured. It was a statement, not a question.

"Yes," Derek said. "According to the passport I found in his pocket, his name is Jean Pierre Renaud."

Guru Bob flinched at the name. It was a subtle reaction, but I saw it. Did he recognize the name? Or was he simply reacting to the fact that evil had visited Dharma once again?

But if this man had died here seventy years ago, Dharma hadn't even existed yet. The winery hadn't existed. Who owned this land back then?

"Did you know him, Robson?" I asked.

He paused for a moment, and I wondered if he would answer me. Finally he nodded. "He was a friend of my grandfather."

It was my turn to flinch. I had not been expecting that answer. I recovered quickly and gazed around the enclosure. "Are these his things?" I asked.

"I do not know, gracious." Guru Bob often used the endearment, hoping to encourage the person to show a bit of grace.

He turned to Derek. "I would like you to find out as much as you can about this man and these items. How did such a collection wind up in our caves?"

"I'll be glad to look into it."

Guru Bob nodded his appreciation. "I suggest you talk to my cousin Gertrude." He smiled. "Although, officially, she is my first cousin once removed. And you must not call her Gertrude. She goes by Trudy. I believe she could be of some assistance."

Derek gave me a curious look, and I realized he'd never met the amazing Trudy.

"I'll introduce you," I said with a smile.

After Guru Bob left, I spent a few minutes strolling alone through the vineyards, silently reflecting on everything that had happened in the last few hours. I was a little ashamed to admit that the most appalling part hadn't been the discovery of the cave itself or the wondrous treasure hidden behind those thick walls. It wasn't even the fact that a man may have been murdered there and left to rot for seventy years. No, for me the worst part was that *I* had been the one to find the body.

I hated to be so self-centered and I promised the sentiment would last for only a minute, but right then and there, it was all about me. Why me?

I felt a strong, protective arm on my shoulders, and I turned and leaned against Derek.

"Don't despair, darling," he murmured.

"Me? Despair?" I tried to smile. "How did you know?"

"It's a completely rational reaction. Especially when it happens to you with such frightening regularity."

"It's not fair." I sounded whiny. That would stop in a minute, too.

"No, it's not." He wrapped his arms around me. "I'm just relieved that this one won't be pinned on you."

"Thanks a lot."

He chuckled, and we continued walking along the rows of thick, healthy plantings. The cabernet grapes were plump and dark, and the leaves were beginning to curl and turn orange, a sure sign that autumn was closing in on us. It was my favorite season in wine country, harvest time. I looked up at Derek and realized that this would be his second harvest since we'd been together. Wow, time had sure flown by since he first chased me up here. Back then, he'd been fairly certain I was a murdering vixen who'd killed my mentor for some horrific reason he couldn't quite come up with.

Ah, memories.

A full hour later, two detectives pulled into the parking lot. Derek and I waited to greet them and lead the way to the storage cave. They introduced themselves as Detectives Phil Gordon and Hannah Parrish from the Sonoma County Sheriff's Department, and they were so pleasant, it was almost scary. I was accustomed to the good-hearted mockery dished out by Detective Inspector Lee of the San Francisco Police Department, so it was a shock to be treated respectfully by these law enforcement officers. A shock, but one I welcomed.

It probably helped when Derek mentioned his bona fides: British Royal Navy commander, ten years in British intelligence with MI6, and now president and CEO of Stone Securities, his company that provided security to the wealthiest people and most precious artwork on the planet.

"And what do you do, Ms. Wainwright?" Detective Parrish asked politely.

"I'm a bookbinder," I said.

"That sounds fascinating."

"You have no idea," Derek murmured.

Twenty minutes later, we were joined by another detective, this one from the Coroner's Unit, and an assistant from the same department.

Once we were gathered around the hole in the wall of the cave, Derek and I explained what had happened here. It quickly became clear to the sheriff's people that this was going to be an unusual case. Yes, it was a homicide. That much was obvious. But as far as determining who the killer might be, Detective Gordon admitted that for the first time in his experience, figuring out "who" wasn't as important as first figuring out "when."

"Probably the best thing to do," Detective Parrish said, "is transport the body over to our Forensics Pathology group in Fairfield. They'll be able to determine the time of death."

"Or rather, the *year* of death," Detective Gordon amended.

"Yeah, weird," Parrish muttered as she stared at all the odd and beautiful furnishings shoved into this small space.

She reminded me of Robin, not just because she kept uttering that word, but because she was petite and pretty, with dark brown hair and a fun attitude—in spite of the circumstances.

The coroner's small staff quickly took charge of Jean Pierre Renaud's body. They completed a cursory examination inside the cave and then carried him outside and into their van in under an hour.

Derek gave them both his phone number and requested that he be kept in the loop if they found out anything. Everyone from the sheriff's department promised "Commander Stone" they would do so.

I had to admit, it was pretty great to have a big hunky commander on my side. And I knew it would make Guru Bob happy to be kept informed of the details, too.

Parrish and Gordon did a cursory search in and around the small chamber. They contacted their crime scene techs to find out how soon they could get there to dust for fingerprints and collect any trace evidence they could find.

While the detectives waited for the CSI team to arrive, they rounded up the witnesses who'd seen the inside of the room or actually been inside, namely me, Derek, Robin, Austin, Dad, and Jackson.

I told Detective Parrish everything that had happened that morning: what I'd seen, what I'd smelled, what we'd assumed or theorized about the body and the ticket and the passport. Other than that, I didn't know much.

"I didn't even know that space existed until this morning," I said, wishing I'd held on to my coffee mug from earlier. "And I have no idea how that furniture and all those expensive items got there."

"Somebody here must know," she said.

"I guess. It's possible that some original members of the commune were storing stuff in there and the cave got sealed up somehow. My dad mentioned that there was a big earthquake up here a few years ago. That might've done it. I mean, that's not what killed Mr. Renaud, but that might explain how his body was trapped there."

It still didn't make sense, but I wasn't about to say that out loud. An earthquake would've had to have occurred more than fifty years ago, and it would've buried Renaud in rubble along with damaging all the furniture and treasures.

I also wasn't about to mention Guru Bob's reaction to seeing Renaud dead on the floor. I didn't feel comfortable talking about Guru Bob to the detective, as nice as she was. That Renaud had been a friend of Guru Bob's grandfather certainly had plenty of relevance, but I quickly decided to leave it to Guru Bob to enlighten the police. Maybe that made me a bad citizen, but I refused to involve Guru Bob until I talked to him about it.

And that reminded me that I'd completely forgotten about his cousin Trudy. I wanted to talk to her as soon as possible.

Trudy's was another name I didn't intend to bring up with the cops. I liked Detective Parrish, but my loyalty remained with Guru Bob and Trudy, who were like family to me.

Detective Parrish gave me an intense look. "Bottom line, Ms. Wainwright. Do you think there's something in that chamber that precipitated Mr. Renaud's death?"

I considered her question. "I have no idea. If he was killed some seventy years ago, I'm not sure there's anyone alive who might know what happened in there."

I felt another twinge as I remembered the Jules

Verne book. I'd have to add that to my list of omissions, because there was no way I would mention that I'd taken it from the room. And I had to say, I didn't feel an ounce of guilt about it.

Okay, that was a lie. If I was breathing, I was pretty much guilt-ridden. I lived with it. But that didn't mean I was going to give up the book. From my earliest days of working with rare books, I'd been instructed that if all else failed, I was to *save the book*. Earlier, I'd tucked it under a blanket in the trunk of my car for safekeeping. Now, as Detective Parrish finished her questioning, I started to wonder if the book could possibly have anything to do with the murder of Mr. Renaud. I doubted it, although I wasn't sure why. I'd dealt with plenty of rare books that had incited murderous intentions.

Not that I would mention that fact to Detective Parrish, either. Most law enforcement officials rolled their eyes whenever I was silly enough to suggest that *a simple book* might be the perfect motive for cold-blooded murder. It gave me no pleasure to count how many times I'd been right.

Chapter 3

Later that afternoon, Derek hung out with my dad and brothers, drinking wine and discussing the cave within the cave and all the stuff we'd found inside its walls. I was anxious to study the Jules Verne book, so I gave Annie a quick call just to let her know I'd be using Abraham's studio. She was glad to hear from me and said I was welcome anytime, so I fished the book out from the trunk of my car and walked down the hill to Abraham's house.

I figured that if the brown suitcase was Mr. Renaud's, and he was a friend of Guru Bob's grandfather, then Guru Bob would want this book for his library collection. And if that was the case, it would need quite a bit of cleanup work before I would feel good about handing it over to him.

Even though it was obviously a rare book—I could tell by looking at the binding, the title page, and the date of publication—it had apparently belonged to a rambunctious young boy, based on the childish scrawls I'd noticed on a few pages. I would have to examine the book more closely before I would know if I could get rid of the scrawls and still maintain the book's integrity.

As I strolled along the sidewalk of the treelined road on which my parents had lived for more than twenty years,

I had to smile at the hodgepodge of home styles that made up our friendly little enclave. It was typically American for our own rambling, craftsman-inspired ranch home to live in harmony with the Quinlans' two-story French cottage next door and the Westcotts' modified Tudor across the street behind a sheltering copse of oak and pine trees.

Two doors down, the Farrell family had a cool-looking California bungalow, and next door to them, the Barclays had built their house in the prairie style because of their affection for Frank Lloyd Wright. Carl Brundidge, the commune lawyer, lived in a contemporary steel-and-glass showpiece that somehow fit perfectly nicely next door to the "midcentury modern," which was how Mr. Osborne described his home, otherwise known as a good old 1950s house complete with plastic flamingoes in the garden. Years ago, he had built a geodesic dome workshop in the backyard to keep his hippie vibe alive. Next door to the Osbornes were the Howards, who lived in a glorious three-story Victorian gem. And near the bottom of the slope was Abraham's imposing Spanish colonial mansion.

Guru Bob had always encouraged his followers to do their own thing when it came to choosing their style of house. Once the winery became successful and people started making money, neighborhoods like ours popped up all over Dharma. Visitors to the area couldn't quite wrap their brains around the fact that all these beautiful homes and shops and upscale restaurants belonged to commune members. It went against their ingrained image of what a "commune" should look like.

When I reached Abraham's house, I opened the side gate, skirted the pool and patio, and continued across the lawn to the studio he'd built for his bookbinding business.

I stared at the locked door and realized that I hadn't been back here since Abraham's death. At the time, yellow crime scene tape had crisscrossed the entrance, blocking my way. I had hesitated, but had finally torn it off to get into the room. I'd been a suspect in Abraham's murder, so ripping away the tape probably wasn't the smartest thing I could've done, but I'd come up here on a mission to find a clue to his murder. And I'd found it, even though I didn't know it at the time.

Now I let out a breath, unlocked the door, and stepped inside—and realized how completely unprepared I'd been for the overwhelming sensations that bombarded me.

I could smell Abraham in here. I could hear his voice and see his ink-stained fingers from the letterpress projects he often took on in addition to the bookbinding. The scent of leather mingled with the musty fragrance of old paper. An odd waft of peppermint almost brought me to my knees.

This room held his essence.

No wonder his daughter, Annie, had left it as it was when he died.

I managed to stay on my feet, but decided to grab a high stool and sit for a minute as a barrage of memories assaulted me. I'd grown up in this room. Abraham was a huge part of my world. He was my teacher, my friend, my confessor, my taskmaster. I'd dreamed of being a bookbinder just like him ever since I was eight years old, when I watched him bring back to life a beloved book that my horrid brothers had tried to destroy. It was nothing short of miraculous to me.

I could still see him standing by the book press, wearing his black leather apron over an old white shirt with the sleeves rolled up to his elbows. He was a big, strong, barrel-chested man who had no trouble at all tightening the huge brass book press down onto a newly rebound masterpiece.

I'd watched him do it so many times that I'd figured it was easy. What a shock it had been to find out how difficult that sucker was to use. Of course, I was only eight years old at the time. To this day, I thought of

Abraham's muscular arms whenever I struggled to press a book.

I pulled the stool over to the center worktable where I set down the Jules Verne book. Then I had to go through every drawer in the cluttered room to find Abraham's standing magnifying glass. After ten minutes, I finally found it jammed in a cupboard with his punches and brushes and a myriad of other tools. He'd always been kind of a slob, although he preferred to call himself an unfettered free spirit.

Under the magnifying glass, the Jules Verne book looked even worse than I'd originally thought. I could see every little flaw along its spine and knew I would have to reconstruct it. The six raised bands had become flattened from years of handling, and all the elaborate gilding had faded away. The crown of the spine was tattered and splitting away from the front hinge. The morocco leather was in decent condition overall, but the two leather corners on the front cover had begun to fray along the edges and would need to be replaced. I anticipated using all new leather on the spine and corners rather than trying to match what little was worth saving.

Opening the front cover, I could see that the marble endpapers were in remarkably good condition with no chips or tears. The pattern was a beautiful blend of dark blue and burgundy swirls and eddies. The flyleaf—those first few blank pages of a book—was another story. On the front flyleaf, a child had signed his name across the page in bold blue ink.

Anton Benoit.

The back flyleaf had suffered much worse abuse. Here, Anton had scrawled a long message using rust-colored ink. At the end of the message there was a date, *le 6 avril 1906*, and a place, *La Croix Saint-Just, France*. And there were two childish signatures scrawled at the bottom, *Anton Benoit* and *Jean Pierre Renaud*.

Jean Pierre: The name of the dead man. He'd been a young boy when he signed his name to this page. What had brought him all the way from France to California? And what had he been doing here that got him killed? How did he know Guru Bob's grandfather?

What the heck did it all mean?

The rust-colored ink was uneven and hard to read. Thick and blotched in some spots, scratchy and thin in others, and in a few places, it faded altogether. I stared at it through the magnifying glass for a long time, holding the book closer to the lens to figure out what it was about the ink that bothered me. Abruptly I figured it out and dropped the book in disgust.

"Blood," I said. "Ew."

Since I'd grown up with brothers, I knew it made perfect sense that two boys, probably nine or ten years old, would want to cut their skin open and draw their own blood to use as ink.

I shook my head. "Idiots."

The date and the boys' names were about the extent of my ability to translate the page of French. The scratchy handwriting didn't help, but after staring at the immature penmanship for another minute, I thought I could make out the first phrase, *Nous promettons solennellement*.

"We promise . . . solemnly?" I shrugged. "Close enough."

It sounded like the two boys were pledging an oath or something to each other.

I tried to recall my high school French, but it wasn't coming back to me. Some years ago, I'd memorized a bunch of French phrases for a trip to Paris. Unfortunately, nowhere in the boys' message did it say anything about where to find *les toilettes*, so that didn't help, either.

Reminding myself of the book's subject matter, I wondered if maybe Anton and Jean Pierre had pledged to make their own journey to the center of the earth. Since I had lived with two brothers, this sounded like something a couple of boys might vow to do after reading an enthralling adventure story.

But did they really have to destroy the value of this book by writing all over it? Yes, of course they did. Children were notoriously dangerous to the health of a fine book.

I made a mental note to ask Derek to translate the French words for me, and then moved on to study the inner pages. The paper was thick and white with some foxing throughout. The occasional instance of reddish brown spots was to be expected on a book this old. Fortunately, there were no more scrawled writings from Anton or Jean Pierre on any other pages.

I did a quick survey of the rest of the book and discovered an old piece of notepaper folded and wedged between two pages, marking the beginning of chapter forty-five. At first I thought it was a bookmark, but when I unfolded it, I found a diagram with a list of numbers and more words written in French. Again, my pitiful schoolgirl French didn't help. I would have to show this to Derek, too. Naturally, he spoke flawless French among the other hundred or so languages he seemed to know.

The big school clock on the studio wall ticked off the time. That old thing had to be thirty years old, I thought fondly, realizing I'd spent over two hours here. I had to go home and get ready for dinner with Austin and Robin, so I found a short stack of soft cloths in one of Abraham's drawers, used two of them to wrap around the book for protection, and slipped the book into my tote bag.

Walking home took longer because it was all uphill, but I made it back in time to take a quick shower and dress for dinner. Derek had a glass of wine waiting for me. "Thank you. This is nice."

"I thought we could relax for a few minutes." We sat on the comfortable couch in the Quinlans' living room. Derek had placed a plate of crackers and a small triangle of softened Brie on the heavy wood coffee table. "Did you have a chance to examine the book?"

"Yes," I said, "and I was hoping you'd look at it, too. I'm in need of your translation skills."

"I assume the book is written in French."

"It is," I said, smiling. "But you don't have to translate the book for me."

"Good, because I'm fairly certain you can pick up an English version somewhere."

I gave him a look as I swirled my wine and took a taste. "What I hope you'll translate are the notes I found inside the book."

"Notes?" he said, intrigued. "I'll be happy to look them over first thing tomorrow. Do they explain everything that happened in the cave?"

I chuckled. "If only. No, the one in the book was written by two little boys long before the cave incident. And get this, they wrote it in blood."

Derek laughed, knowing my squeamishness around blood. "You must've loved discovering that."

"It's not funny. It's gross."

"That's because you were never a little boy."

"Nice of you to notice."

"I've definitely noticed." He sat back and stretched his arm across my shoulders. "Boys like to do gross things. I thought you knew."

"I do. The note made me think of Jackson and Austin as kids. They probably would've done something like that. Disgusting creatures."

"Young boys are morbidly fascinated by blood. My brothers and I tried to stab or slice one another up at every opportunity."

"Oh God. And your poor mother had to put up with five of you."

"She loved every minute of it. We were angels."

"I can't wait to hear her version of the story."

He shrugged. "She might use another term to describe us."

"The word *hooligans* comes to mind," I said, laughing.

He grinned. "I suppose that's more accurate."

I took another sip of wine. "This is awfully good."

"It's the five-year-old pinot noir we tasted today. I begged your brother for a bottle to bring home."

I rested my head on his shoulder. "My hero."

"It's the least I could do, knowing you were hard at work the entire afternoon."

I sat forward, spread some cheese on a cracker and handed it to him, and then made one for myself.

"Thanks, love."

I finished my cracker and took a sip of wine. "Have you heard anything from the detectives?"

"Not yet. The crime scene lads showed up after you left. They dusted for prints and scoured through everything. We'll have to wait and see what they turn up."

"I don't know what they can tell us. It's not like they'll arrest anyone, right? The man died seventy years ago. Nobody living here now was around back then."

He swirled his wine distractedly. "So it would seem."

"You don't sound convinced."

"I'm not." He paused, weighing his words. "Don't you find it odd that Robson's grandfather knew the dead man?"

I frowned. "I suppose. But I was mostly concerned about Guru Bob because he looked so sad."

"Yes, he did." Derek nodded thoughtfully. "According to your father, Robson—Guru Bob—moved up here only about twenty-five years ago. That was when he bought all this property and started the Fellowship. But if the dead man's passport and passenger ticket are to be believed, Jean Pierre Renaud has been lying dead in that cave for close to seventy years. So where does Guru Bob's grandfather fit into those two scenarios? Was it just a coincidence?"

Knowing Derek as well as I did, I knew he didn't believe in coincidences. "You don't actually think that Guru Bob is lying, do you?"

"I believe he's got more integrity than anyone I know,

but in this case . . ." Derek shook his head. "Let's allow it to play out a bit more before jumping to any conclusions."

I thought about it for a minute. "My parents must've repeated that Guru Bob story at least a hundred times. He came up here, bought a tract of land, and then we all moved up. We lived in Airstream trailers for the first year, which was torturous, but Mom and Dad assured us that all our sacrifices would be worth it. And then we started growing grapes, and you know, the rest is history."

Derek smiled. "Yes, practically legendary."

"Maybe it's the legend that's wrong," I said slowly. "Maybe Guru Bob never said anything either way, but everyone assumed that he bought the property right then and there. But what if he didn't? What if the land was always in his family?"

Derek finished the last sip of wine and set his glass on the table. "You mentioned that you'd introduce me to Robson's cousin Trudy. Can we do that tomorrow?"

"Absolutely. You'll get a kick out of her. And she'll know plenty of their family history."

"I had no idea he had relatives living nearby," Derek said as we took our glasses and cheese plate into the kitchen.

"Trudy's the only one I know of, and she's lived here longer than we have. She doesn't mingle much with the commune folks, although she's good friends with my mom. She always helps with the harvest, and she shops in town. You might recognize her when you see her."

We finished cleaning up, refilled the animals' water dishes, and then took off to meet Robin and Austin at Arugula, my sister Savannah's restaurant on the Lane in downtown Dharma. It was less than a mile away, and we found a parking place easily enough.

The Lane—more formally known as Shakespeare Lane—had become a destination point over the last few years with its upscale shops and fabulous restaurants as well as the Dharma winery just up the road. B and Bs

were beginning to sprout up all around town, and there
was a small luxury hotel and spa at the far end of the
town center. My sister China had a popular yarn and
weaving shop, Warped, on the Lane, and now Savannah's
restaurant was here and very successful. Our family was
well represented on the Lane and at the winery, where
my father and brothers worked.

I could tell something was bothering Robin the minute we walked in. They had already been seated at the
table but stood when they saw us. I gave her a hug, and
I was pretty sure I heard her growl, sort of like a bear.

I flashed a wide-eyed look at Derek, who had also
noticed her mood.

I moved around to Austin and whispered, "What's
up with Robin? What did you do?"

He laughed and grabbed me in a hug. "She'll be fine."

"Men are so naive," I said, patting his shoulder. But
he was still grinning, so I figured he preferred to stay
clueless.

I sidled up to Robin. "What's bugging you?"

She bared her teeth. "Men."

"Ah. Okay, then. How about some wine?"

"Definitely."

We waited patiently in silence while the waiter
opened the bottle. Austin took a sip and approved it,
and our glasses were filled. The waiter walked away,
and Austin said, "I'd like to propose a toast."

As we all raised our glasses, I noticed a blinding flash
of light and set my glass down. "What is that? What're
you wearing?"

"Nothing," Robin barked. "Drink your damn wine."

"Nothing?" I burst out, shoving my chair back. "There's
a gigantic diamond ring on your finger. What do you mean,
nothing?"

"Hello?" Austin said. "I'm in the middle of making a
toast."

Robin glared at Austin, then reluctantly thrust her

arm out so that I could see the ring. I grabbed her hand and stared at the most gorgeous diamond ring I'd ever seen. "That's a Tiffany setting."

Her look at me dripped with suspicion. "I'm wondering how you know that, but yeah, he went to Tiffany."

"It's spectacular," I said. "And it looks beautiful on you."

She shook her head in dismay. "Can you imagine anything less practical? Tiffany! It's two and a half freaking carats! How am I supposed to wear this thing around Dharma? We live out in the country, for God's sake."

"It's the *wine* country," Austin said, laughing. "We shop at Dean and Deluca."

She ignored him. "I'm a sculptor. I can't wear this while I'm working. What were you thinking? You should've bought me a pair of earrings or something."

"Fine," Austin grumbled, then extended his wineglass. "A toast, to the woman who has agreed to be my wife. I am the happiest man in the world." He clinked glasses with Derek and slugged down a big gulp of wine.

"Aww." I jumped from my chair, misty eyed, and rounded the table to squeeze Robin in a hug. "I'm so thrilled. So happy for you."

"I don't know why," she groused, refusing to hug me back. "I should've told him no. He's such a goofball."

"You're wearing his ring," I said softly, hugging her again. "You said yes. You love him and he loves you. I'm so proud of him and so glad he finally wised up."

"That's what you think." But her tone was lighter, and I felt her chuckling as she hugged me back.

"We'll be sisters for real," I whispered.

"Oh." She pressed her hand to her lips, and her eyes filled with tears.

And my work here was done.

Derek stood and gave Austin a hearty handshake and a slap on the back. "Congratulations, mate."

"Thanks, Derek. I'm a lucky man."

"You are indeed."

I don't know why it surprised me to hear the sincerity in Derek's voice. I knew he was crazy about my family and Robin, so that wasn't the issue. Maybe it was because we'd never discussed marriage before. And why would we? We'd only known each other . . . I did the math and felt a little dizzy. We'd been together almost two years. Time had flown by. And when he bought the loft next door to mine and was the one to suggest that we merge the two together, I knew he was committed to me. I suppose I had always assumed that he simply wasn't interested in marriage. Otherwise, surely he would have proposed to me by now. Although honestly, I'd never given it that much thought. I was perfectly happy with our relationship as it was.

Savannah came out of the kitchen with a bottle of champagne for the table, and we all celebrated the engagement in style. Less than a year ago, Robin, who had been living in San Francisco at the time, was being threatened by some guys in the Russian mafia, so she'd moved up here for a while to be safe. That was when Austin had made it clear that he wanted her to stay. She had. And they'd been living together ever since.

Despite the delicious food, wine, and celebratory atmosphere, we ended the evening early because everyone had plans for the next day.

The next morning, after a breakfast of coffee, scrambled eggs, and bagels, Derek moved to the desk in the family room and began translating the pledge and the note I'd found inside *Journey to the Center of the Earth*. I opened all the curtains to let the sun pour into the room and then pulled up a chair next to him to see how he was coming along. It took him less than ten minutes to translate what was scrawled in the rust-colored ink over the back flyleaf.

"They were blood brothers," Derek explained. *"Frères du sang."*

"Sang," I mused. "Like sanguine. Bloodred."

"Exactly." He took a sip of coffee and then read what

he'd translated. "'We solemnly pledge this oath in blood to be comrades, friends, defending each other until the day we die. Together we will find the volcano that holds the portal that leads to the center of the earth, and we will share equally all the treasure we find there. So help us God. Signed, Anton Benoit and Jean Pierre Renaud.'"

I smiled. "I figured they were planning a trip to the center of the earth. That was the basis for the pledge."

"That, and friendship."

My smile faded as I remembered Guru Bob's words. "Do you think Anton killed his friend?"

"I have no idea."

"Jean Pierre's body was surrounded by treasures of another sort."

"Yes." Derek was deep in thought as he perused the page again. "I think a talk with Robson's cousin Trudy is our best first step in getting to the bottom of what happened to Monsieur Renaud."

I checked the clock. "She's probably at church right now, but we could go over there in an hour or so."

"Good."

He started to push away from the desk, but I stopped him. "I have one more thing for you to look at."

He sat down. "Another note in the book?"

I opened the book and pulled out the paper I'd found wedged between the pages.

"Ah, an actual note," he said, unfolding the piece of paper. "I thought you were referring to something else written in the book."

"No. This looks like it was written by someone else."

He stared at the squiggly diagram. A few seconds later, he turned the page on its side, and then flipped it to the other side. "It looks like a map."

"A map," I said, gazing at the odd design. "I didn't think of that. I just saw the list of numbers and words on the side and hoped you'd translate them."

"I'd be glad to." He studied it for another minute.

"You're right that it was written by a different person, and I'm fairly certain that person was an adult, not a child."

"I didn't spend enough time studying it," I said, taking the paper from him. I'd taken some handwriting analysis classes to help me with authenticating signatures in books, which was an occasional part of my job.

I handed the note back to Derek. "It's definitely more mature. I wonder if it was written by one of the two boys, now grown up."

"If not, the next question is, how did it get into this book?"

"Good question," I said, frowning.

"These numbers here might indicate distance. Either in meters or footsteps. We won't know until we try to follow what it says."

"Where do we start?"

He grinned. "I haven't gotten that far in the translation. Guess I'd better get busy."

"Okay, I'll wash the breakfast dishes while you figure it out."

A few minutes later, I was putting the clean dishes away, and Derek joined me at the kitchen counter. "The starting point is at a spot he calls *l'arbre souhaitant*. Translated, it means 'wishing tree.'"

"Oh." I perked up. "The Wishing Tree. You've seen it. That beautiful old oak tree growing in the grassy circle at the entrance to the winery. The roots are so big and thick that they grow above the ground and surround the base of the tree in massive gnarly knots. Water collects in the nooks and crannies and pockets of the roots like little pools, and for as far back as I can remember, it's been a tradition to toss pennies into the pools and make wishes."

"Isn't that fascinating?" he said, and grabbed my hand. "Shall we go on a treasure hunt?"

Chapter 4

Before leaving the house, Derek ran next door to get the key to the winery storage cave from my father. Then we drove over to the winery and managed to find a parking place in the crowded lot. Even this early in the day, Sundays in wine country could be challenging with so many people driving up from the Bay Area. It was especially busy this close to harvest time.

"There's the tree," I said, pointing to the beautifully gnarled oak that some claimed had been standing in that place for more than three hundred years.

"I've seen it so many times," he said. "I had no idea I could've been making wishes all along."

"Now that you know, you won't be able to stop yourself."

The tree was immense. Its heavy limbs, twisted and dark and covered in moss, reached sixty feet in all directions. Some were so old and thick that they skimmed the ground. The knobby branches used to remind me of a wicked witch's crooked fingers, stretching out to snap up the next child who came too close. Of course I didn't believe that anymore, but it always gave me a little chill when I got close enough to make a wish.

Derek gazed up through the lush, leafy branches. "Up close, it's so much bigger than I realized."

I pressed my hand against the rough trunk. "When we were young, my three sisters and Robin and I would stand on either side of the trunk and try to join hands. It was too big for us to make it."

Derek pulled some change from his pocket. "It's fitting that we make a wish first."

"Oh, that's a nice idea." I took two pennies from him and tossed them into the small pool of water near where I was standing. My wishes always started out simple, but quickly grew complicated. I liked to squeeze in a sub-wish or two, and I wasn't sure if that disqualified my main wish or not.

This time I wished for good health for everyone in my family, but then I added names to the list, like my neighbors in San Francisco and my friend Ian and a few others. They were like family, so that counted, right? Then, as always, I tagged on a wish for world peace.

"Is it safe for the tree when its roots grow above ground?" Derek wondered aloud.

"Apparently most of its roots extend down at least forty feet, so it's not as shallow as it appears."

"That must be how it's survived for so long. In England we have oaks that have been standing since the time of King Henry the Eighth and before. They always seem so majestic, as if they have stories to tell and are only waiting for someone to listen."

I squeezed his hand, pleased that we shared the same sort of daydreams. "I know just what you mean."

"I know you do, love." He took a look at the piece of paper he'd used to write out the instructions in English. I'd asked him to copy it because I didn't want to bring the original notepaper with us. It belonged with the book.

After studying his notes, Derek glanced around, checked the sky for the position of the sun, and pointed toward the storage cave we'd excavated yesterday. "Starting here, we take one hundred forty-seven steps in a northeast direction."

"Is that it? No jogging off this way or that?"

"No, just one straight shot, according to the instructions. Although there are landmarks noted along the way."

"Should be interesting," I said, letting go of his hand. "Okay, you lead the way and I'll follow you."

He took my hand back. "I say we ought to walk side by side so we can both count. In case I lose track."

I smiled at him, knowing he wouldn't lose track. But I appreciated that he thought I'd be helpful. "All right."

"Let's go." We headed in the northeast direction he'd indicated, until we'd crossed the parking lot. I counted steps under my breath.

Derek stopped abruptly and consulted his notes. "At thirty-seven footsteps, we should be directly in front of a hedgerow."

"A hedgerow. You mean, like a row of bushes?" I looked around and pointed. "There are some on the other side, over by the tasting rooms."

"That's the wrong direction. Perhaps there were hedgerows here all those years ago."

"Maybe. Are you sure we went in the right direction?"

"Yes. Let's keep going."

We continued in a straight line until we reached number seventy-eight. "Stop here." He gazed around. "There should be a circle of rosebushes here. Red ones, for red wine."

"All the roses were moved to the other side of the vineyard a few years ago to accommodate the flow of people taking the tour. I'm afraid the bushes were getting trampled."

He frowned and stared at the instructions.

"But I'm pretty sure they used to be right in this area," I added.

"Ah. We'll go with that, then." We started up again, and this time we made it all the way to the arched double doors of the cave. Unfortunately, the entry was masked off with yellow construction tape, blocking our way.

"I guess this was necessary," I said, "but it's going to

be a turn-off for the visitors. They'll think something awful happened here." I briskly waved that statement away. "I mean, something awful *did* happen here, but you know what I mean. The bright yellow isn't exactly subtle."

"True," he said dryly, "but the construction tape was preferable to the detectives' crime scene tape."

"Oh, wow. They wanted to put up crime scene tape? Okay, I'll go along with the construction tape."

"Excuse me. Is this where the body was found?"

I blinked and turned. Two women in their sixties stood a few feet away, wearing jeans, sweatshirts, and sneakers. They were staring with excitement at the cave entrance.

I gave Derek a quick glance, then said, "I, um, yes, that's what I hear."

"That's so cool!" the one woman said, and turned to her friend. "I can't wait to buy some of their wine."

"Let's get over to the tasting room," the other said, and they walked away briskly.

"So much for the news being bad for business," I murmured. "That was weird. How did the word get out so quickly?"

"I can't say, but perhaps that explains the heavy crowds today."

"I thought it was because it's so close to harvest time."

It wasn't about the harvest, though, because that same basic "Where's the body?" scenario was repeated by three more visitors before I was finally able to flag down Jenny, one of the winery workers.

"Would you mind guarding the entrance while Derek and I take another look inside? I'll call Austin and let him know where you are."

"Okay, sure," she said easily.

I warned her that people might want to know if this was where the body was found.

She waved her hand blithely. "Oh, we've already had dozens of people asking about it. Austin said to tell them, yes, a body was found near here. But if they want more info, we should send them to see the manager."

"Sounds reasonable."

I used my cell to call my brother to tell him that Derek wanted to go back into the cave to check on something. Since it was Derek, Austin didn't have a problem with the plan. I was such a clever sister.

"Be careful," Austin added. "And tell Jenny she should stay out there until you're finished."

I relayed the message to Jenny, who was perfectly happy playing traffic cop while Derek and I tore off enough of the tape to allow us to get the door opened and slide inside.

A few steps inside the cave, we found the light switch and turned it on. In the small alcove the guys used for an office, Derek found one of the flashlights that had been left there yesterday and took it in case we needed it.

"It's so quiet in here," I said, then winced. "Oh darn. I hope you kept count of your footsteps."

"I did. We hit number one hundred two at the edge of the entrance."

"So we've got forty-five steps to go."

We both counted steps as we walked slowly through the cave in the same northeast direction. At the wall between the cave and the inner chamber, we hit one hundred thirty-three.

"I'm getting a bad feeling about this," I muttered.

"Let's carry on." Derek stepped over the barrier, and I followed. We were able to take another ten steps until we stopped directly in front of the French wardrobe with the beautiful beveled mirror I'd admired on our first visit to the cave.

"I can't believe it's a dead end," I said, smacking my palm against the side of the wardrobe. "We only needed to take four more steps. Maybe whoever made that map had smaller feet than you. We should start over and go in a slightly different direction."

"I think we wound up exactly where we should have," Derek said, his gaze focused on the wardrobe.

Trying to read his mind, I turned and stared at the well-appointed antique. It was at least seven feet tall and five feet wide with the large mirrored door in the center and two smaller doors on either side. I glanced back at Derek. "What are you thinking?"

"I think we should move this piece of furniture."

"You think there's something behind it." It wasn't a question, and I wasn't about to argue with one of Derek's hunches. The fact that the thing had to weigh hundreds of pounds was immaterial.

"Let's do it."

With Derek doing most of the actual lifting and me huffing and puffing while trying to angle the piece away from the wall, we managed to move it almost two feet.

When we stood to survey the result, it took a second or two for me to comprehend what we'd uncovered: a narrow, arched entry into a deeper cave.

"Another cave?" I whispered.

"Would you prefer to go first, or shall I?" Derek asked, switching the flashlight on.

I stared at the hole in the wall and imagined all the slimy, slinky creatures that might be crawling around back there. With a slight shiver, I stepped aside. "After you."

He slipped around the dresser and disappeared into the space beyond.

"Derek?"

"Are you coming?" His voice echoed out from the enclosed space.

"You bet I am." Creepy crawlies notwithstanding, I wasn't going to let him go in there without me. Love did weird things to people.

I could see the occasional flashlight beam bouncing off the inner walls and felt a little better about stepping into the unknown.

Derek glided the beam around the room, and I followed

the light, trying to get my bearings. This space was slightly larger than the outer chamber and the ceiling just high enough for Derek, who was more than six feet tall, to stand without stooping.

"Look at this," he said, focusing the beam of light on the far wall to our left.

"Oh my God," I whispered.

"Indeed," he said.

If I'd thought the outer chamber was filled with lovely treasures, this space put that one to shame.

Leaning against the walls were paintings of various sizes, still in their beautifully gilded, rococo-style frames. Next to these, I counted sixteen canvas rolls that I thought also might be paintings.

A massive oak table held at least twenty finely bound books, as well as more silver candlesticks, goblets, and urns. There were a number of small bronze or marble statues of various objects: an angel cupping the cheek of a woman; two lovers; a horse; a naked discus thrower; a woman curled up and weeping; a matching set of cherubs mounted on marble bases and each holding a gold candelabra. I counted three large marble busts of important-looking men. Off to the side were stacks of wooden crates that held a number of cases of wine. Two large wooden wine barrels stood on the other side of the table. Derek tried to move one of them and was able to do so easily. "This one is empty."

"Where in the world did all of this come from?" I wondered aloud. "It must be worth a fortune."

"A very large fortune," Derek mused, still scanning the flashlight across the treasures we'd found.

I walked over to where the canvas rolls stood and unrolled one of them at random. It was a painting of a dancing woman in the style of Renoir, with bright, bold colors in an outdoor setting. A fun-loving group of partygoers surrounded the woman, and a buxom barmaid carried a tray of drinks in the background. The canvas was almost four feet high by at least five feet wide. It couldn't be a Renoir, could it? If not, it was an excellent forgery.

"Derek, look at this."

"I'm looking at this." He turned and showed me a small framed painting of the Madonna and Child. It was stunning, only about eighteen inches tall by thirteen or fourteen inches wide. The Virgin's face was pale and lovely with soft brown eyes and a tiny cleft in her chin. Her reddish hair curled softly as it streamed over her shoulders. The child was adorably plump, with a headful of curly brown hair, wise eyes, and a knowing smile. Their delicate golden halos seemed illuminated from within. The frame was ornately carved and gilded.

"It's as beautiful as any Botticelli I've ever seen."

Derek frowned. "Yes, isn't it?"

"You don't honestly think it was painted by—"

"I do, actually," he murmured. "Or someone equally gifted."

I was in no position to argue with Derek, who had been responsible for the security of some of the most expensive artwork on earth. I gazed from the serene Madonna to the vibrant painting in my hands. "We'd better call Guru Bob. He'll know what to do."

"I confess I have no idea what to do."

It might've been the first time I'd ever heard Guru Bob admit to being clueless. I couldn't blame him. All of these priceless objects hidden away in caves for decades? On Dharma winery land? It defied explanation.

He walked around the cavernous space, taking his time and studying each piece. He was casually dressed in soft khaki trousers and a white dress shirt with comfortable-looking loafers. For him, that was casual since I rarely saw him in anything other than a suit and tie.

I walked with him, shining the flashlight on each piece. Guru Bob took my arm and wound it through his companionably. We stopped to watch as Derek unrolled each canvas.

I couldn't say if any of the paintings were originals, but I could honestly claim that we were in the midst of great works painted in the style of Renoir, Monet, Chagall, and, perhaps, Botticelli.

"Tell me, Brooklyn," said Guru Bob. "Have you any theories that might explain where this extraordinary treasure came from?"

I hesitated for a moment, then spoke. "We found a book inside the suitcase that belonged to Mr. Renaud."

He tilted his head slightly. "A book?"

"Yes. *Journey to the Center of the Earth*, by Jules Verne. I, um, took it. I didn't want the police to have it. They don't always appreciate the fragility of a rare book."

He smiled and tightened his hold on my arm. I interpreted the action as a sign of approval.

"Anyway," I continued, "inside the book was a pledge written in French and signed by two boys. There was also a piece of notepaper left inside the book. It was written by an adult, also in French. On the note was a map, and that's how we found our way into this part of the cave."

"From a map you found in the book?" He looked frankly stunned.

"Yes." I gave Derek a quick look and noticed he was listening to every word. "Derek translated the map's instructions, and they led us from the Wishing Tree directly into this part of the cave. Well, actually, we were stopped at the fancy wardrobe in the outer chamber, but Derek had the bright idea of moving it, and, sure enough, it was covering up this small opening. And that's how we found this room."

"Astounding." Guru Bob glanced over at Derek.

"It certainly is," Derek said.

"It seems you took your own journey into the center of the earth," Guru Bob said. "How resourceful of you."

"I didn't even think of that," I said, grinning at Derek.

"Thank you both for being so tenacious." He gave my arm a light squeeze and nodded to Derek. "I will be grateful for any more information you come across that might provide an answer to this remarkable puzzle."

He turned and stared again at the items scattered around the room.

"Does anything look at all familiar?" Derek asked.

"Sadly, no," Guru Bob said. He turned back to me. "You said the pledge was written by two boys, and they signed their names."

"That's right."

"Do you remember what their names were?"

"Of course," I said. "They were Jean Pierre Renaud and Anton Benoit."

He inhaled suddenly, as though he'd received a punch in the stomach. Guru Bob rarely showed emotions unless they were positive ones, but right now he looked completely flummoxed and not happy about it.

"You knew them," Derek said softly.

Guru Bob sighed. "You may recall my telling you that Jean Pierre Renaud was a friend of my grandfather."

"Yes, of course," I said, and Derek nodded.

Guru Bob sighed. "My grandfather was Anton Benoit."

Chapter 5

"Like many families, mine had its secrets," Guru Bob admitted after we'd left the darkness of the cave for a picnic table under an oak tree near the tasting room. Derek and I sat together facing Guru Bob. I hoped he didn't feel as if we were interrogating him, but it felt like that to me.

"My father rarely spoke of his parents or their life in Sonoma. Never liked to talk about growing up working in the vineyards, except to say that it was not for him. He moved our family to San Francisco when I was barely a teenager."

"What was your grandfather like?" I asked.

"He died before I was born, so I never knew him."

"I'm sorry."

"Thank you, gracious. I do know that when my grandfather and uncles reached the United States, they changed the family name of Benoit to the English version of the name, and that is how I came to have the last name of Benedict."

He pronounced the name Benoit as *Ben-wah*.

Derek leaned forward. "And you had no idea that the hidden chamber with all that artwork and furnishings even existed?"

"No idea at all." He shook his head, looking almost

ashamed. I hoped that wasn't the case, but he was clearly unhappy about the discoveries inside the caves, especially the body of Mr. Renaud. "I feel so inadequate, unable to answer your simple questions. As I said, my father was not forthcoming when it came to discussing my grandfather, or much else for that matter. You have not talked to my cousin Trudy yet, have you?"

"Not yet."

"She is your best hope for finding the answers. She is actually my father's cousin and twenty years older than I. She moved here with the rest of the family when she was a child. I will let her know you plan to visit her."

"Do you think she knew what was inside the cave?" Derek asked.

"No," he said, shaking his head for emphasis. "Absolutely not. Trudy is wonderfully impulsive and would never have been able to keep it a secret."

He was right about that. His cousin was a generous free spirit who loved life and people. She would've wanted to share all that bounty with others.

"Who lived on this land before the commune bought up all the property?" I asked.

"It belonged to my grandfather and his brothers. As they died off, their children inherited the land. Two of them returned to France and another one died, until Trudy and my father were the only ones left. When my family moved to the city, Trudy stayed and leased the land to a few local farmers, until I came back years later and asked to take it on. She was more than happy to relinquish all that responsibility, and the commune continues to pay her a monthly dividend."

"Then we'll talk to Trudy," I said.

Derek told Guru Bob that he planned to take pictures of the objets d'art and send them to his contacts at Interpol in case they'd been reported stolen by their owners.

"If more damage was done, it is best to find out sooner

than later," Guru Bob said, agreeing with Derek's plan.
"There has been too much secrecy. Even Trudy has never
been willing to share stories of what happened to her
during the war, but I have a feeling she will open up to
Derek if she knows that it is part of a bigger mystery."

"I'm sure she will," I said, confident of Derek's pow-
ers of persuasion.

Guru Bob's frown softened into a smile. "My cousin
does love her mysteries. And she has always had a soft
spot for the British."

"Trudy is so excited to meet you," Mom said to Derek
the next day as he drove across town to meet Guru Bob's
cousin—or first cousin once removed, to be precise.
"And you'll love her. She's a sweetie pie."

"I'm looking forward to meeting her, too," he said.

I'd given Mom the front seat while I sat in back with
a pretty pink bakery box on my lap.

Trudy lived a half mile on the opposite side of the
Lane from us, on a pretty, hilly street lined with syca-
more trees and California bungalows of every color and
size. Hers was painted pale blue with white trim, and the
wide front porch held a set of cheerful white wicker chairs,
perfect for relaxing on warm fall afternoons.

Trudy was smiling as she greeted us at the door, wearing chic slim jeans and a pretty green sweatshirt over a
preppy blue-collared shirt. She was as tall as I was, about
five feet eight, and her hair was a beautiful shade of light
reddish brown.

I introduced her to Derek, and she took his arm, pulling him into the house. "I've heard all about you. You
saved our Brooklyn's life."

"She's saved my life as well, on more than one occasion."

"Isn't that sweet? I like you so much already." She
turned and beckoned me and Mom to follow. "Come
in, come in. Amelia, is the tea ready?"

"Yes, yes," groused Trudy's companion, Amelia, as

she fluffed up the pillows on the sofa in Trudy's living room. "What do you think I've been doing?"

I had never seen Amelia in a good mood, but Trudy seemed to take her companion's curmudgeonly attitude in stride. The woman was in her forties and wore a drab blue plaid dress that hung down to her calves, with a gray cardigan buttoned all the way up. Her hair was dirty blond tinged with gray and it hung in straggly clumps to her shoulders. She was a complete contrast to Trudy's brightness, cheery attire, and attitude.

I vaguely recalled that the two of them had met in the hospital when Trudy was laid up with a broken leg—or was it a fractured hip? Amelia needed a job, and Trudy hired her to be her cook, housekeeper, and general companion. Or something like that. I would have to get the complete story from my mother later.

"Wonderful," Trudy said, clapping her hands. "We'll have tea momentarily. And, Amelia, will you look at what Brooklyn brought? Our favorite cookies from Sweet Nothings."

"Sugar cookies?" Amelia asked, entrenched frown lines digging across her forehead.

"Yes, sugar cookies," I said. "They're my favorite, too. Melt in your mouth." I handed her the box, and as she grabbed it, she almost grinned. That is, she bared her teeth at me, and I was willing to take that as a smile.

"Can I help you with anything?" I asked, following her into Trudy's charming country kitchen.

"No," Amelia said curtly, pointing toward the living room. "Go sit down, and I'll bring everything out shortly."

"Okeydokey." I could take the hint. I headed back to the front room, where Trudy was clutching Derek's arm as she led him around the frilly room and showed off some of her favorite tchotchkes. The room was full of them: a glass hummingbird hanging off a lampshade; a Belleek porcelain bell; a tiny cloisonné pillbox in the shape of a lady's handbag; and lots of books, along with dozens of framed photographs on every surface.

Mom was seated at one end of the pale green striped brocade sofa, so I took one of the overstuffed pale rose chairs and watched Trudy charm Derek. Apparently Trudy's soft spot for the British coincided with a soft spot for handsome men. And who could blame her?

Amelia walked in and placed a large silver tray on the French provincial coffee table, then left the room. She had managed to squeeze a pot of tea, a small platter of cookies, cups, saucers, utensils, and little napkins onto the tray.

Amelia showed no signs of returning, so I scooted forward in the big chair. "Shall I pour?"

"Would you, dear?" Trudy said as Derek delivered her to her place at the opposite end of the sofa from Mom. "And I'll be happy to answer any questions your Derek wishes to ask me."

Derek sat in the other chair and flashed me a quick smile as I began to pour tea into cups. I placed a small cookie on the side of each saucer and handed them to Mom, Derek, and Trudy.

"Thanks, sweetie," Mom said.

"There are more cookies on the platter," I said, although I'd counted three missing and eyed the doorway to the kitchen, where I knew Amelia was scarfing them up. I didn't mind. I just hoped she would remember to smile at me next time.

"How long have you lived in Dharma, Trudy?" Derek asked once he'd taken his first sip of the hearty English blend.

"I moved here as a small child," Trudy said. "I was barely seven years old when we left our village in France and boarded the ocean liner for America. That was in the fall of 1944."

"That must've been a treacherous time to travel," he commented.

"Indeed it was, but being a child, I saw it as a grand adventure."

"Why did you leave?" I asked.

She stared at her cookie before taking a ladylike bite. "It was critical that we leave. We lived just over four miles from Oradour-sur-Glane. The massacre there took place in June, and we were afraid that at almost any moment, the same would be done to our village."

"Where did you live?" Derek asked.

"La Croix Saint-Just. North of Oradour, along the River Glane."

"Near Limoges?" Derek asked.

"That's the nearest large city, twenty miles southeast."

He smiled. "I know the area."

"*Très bien!* Very good." Trudy laughed. "Goodness, can you believe I still slip into French if I'm not paying attention?"

To my untrained ear, her French sounded perfect, even though she'd lived in Sonoma for close to seventy years, if my quickie calculations were correct.

"What happened in that town near you?" I asked.

Derek answered, his gaze steady on me. "The Nazis gathered all of the women and children into the Catholic church, locked the doors, and began looting the village."

"The men were rounded up and herded into several area barns," Trudy continued stoically, "and killed by machine gun. Then the Nazis gassed and bombed the church with all those people inside and set fire to the rest of the town."

"Oh my God," I whispered.

"It was said to be in retaliation for some of the villagers' collaborating with *la Résistance*."

Mom reached across the sofa and squeezed Trudy's hand. "I'm so sorry."

"Very few escaped," Trudy said, and then turned to Derek. "So you're aware of this ugly moment in French history?"

Derek nodded. "I attended some low-level NATO

meetings near Limoges a few years ago and spent a day walking through Oradour-sur-Glane. It was heart-breaking."

"Yes, it is still. Even though I was a child, I can't remember being so frightened before or since."

There was a moment of troubled silence, and then Derek asked, "Can you tell us about your father?"

"Yes, of course." She smiled. "Luc Benoit was born in La Croix Saint-Just, but to tell his story, I must begin with his father, my grandfather, Christophe Benoit, who was born and raised in the town of St. Emilion."

My eyes grew wide. "St. Emilion?"

"Yes. It is known for its Bordeaux wines. You've heard of it?"

I almost laughed at the understatement. "Yes, I've heard of it." St. Emilion was world-renowned for its pre-mier red Bordeaux wines. Every schoolkid in Sonoma had heard of St. Emilion.

"Grandpapa grew up working in his father's winery, but on a high school trip to Limoges, he met and fell in love with my grandmother, Belle. She was from La Croix Saint-Just and had no intention of moving to St. Emilion no matter how important Christophe's winery was."

"She was a hometown girl," Mom said in complete understanding.

"Precisely," Trudy said, smiling as she nodded. "So what else could my grandfather do but move to La Croix Saint-Just and marry her? They had four sons, one of whom was my papa, Luc. His brother Anton was Rob-son's grandfather. Grandpapa Christophe had only ever known winemaking, so he brought with him a satchel of old-growth vines from St. Emilion and planted them in the rich soil of La Croix Saint-Just."

"How did that work out?" I wondered aloud.

"Oh, he became very successful, possibly because he was one of the few winemakers in the area."

"He would've been very popular," Mom agreed.

Derek set his empty teacup and saucer on the coffee table. "What can you tell us about his brother Anton?"

"Uncle Anton was the oldest of the four boys and very smart," she said. "They sent him to the Université de Poitiers to study medicine."

"Anton was a doctor?" I asked.

"Yes, a medical doctor by profession." She chuckled lightly. "But he was a born academic. My grandfather used to say with much affection that Anton would rather have been teaching medicine than practicing." She took a quick sip of tea before continuing the story. "Uncle Anton worked in a small clinic a distance from town until it closed, and then he became more involved in the family winery. He turned out to be excellent at winemaking because of his ability to apply biology and chemistry to the blending of the wines."

"When did he decide to come to this country?" I asked.

"It was the war," she said, her eyes unfocused as though she were recalling those days. "The Germans marched into Paris in 1940. I was too young to remember much, but I have since heard the stories repeated by my parents and grandparents."

"It had to be a horrific time," Mom said, reaching for the teapot to pour us all more tea.

"It was. By 1942, the French winemakers were fearful of having their precious vineyards burned and their wines stolen by the Nazis. My father and Uncle Anton and their two brothers began bricking up their caves and ripping out the vines so the Nazis couldn't destroy them."

I frowned. "But if they were ripping out their own vines, weren't they destroying them anyway?"

"No, no, I misspoke," Trudy said, holding her teacup steady for Mom to refill it. "The men took the ancient vines out carefully by the roots and packed them in small burlap bags with the dirt still surrounding the root ball. They hid these inside wine barrels and sent them to all parts of the world, wherever they had friends or acquaintances in the winemaking business. This way, the vines could be replanted surrounded by the dirt that had always nurtured them. The *terroir*." She looked at me. "You are familiar with the term?"

"Yes," I said, remembering my days conducting tastings at the winery. "*Terroir* is everything that gives a certain wine its specific characteristics. The dirt, the climate, the microclimate, the geological conditions. All of these affect the taste of the wine. Even other plants growing in the area will lend flavor to the wine. *Terroir* can include the type and location of a particular oak tree used to make the barrel in which it's aged, or the yeast added during fermentation."

I realized everyone was staring at me, and I winced. "Sorry. I tend to go off on the subject."

"No, no, I find it fascinating," Trudy said. "And very true. The winemakers had a need to protect their *terroir* as well as their vines, so they collected the dirt, too. And many cases of bottled wines, of course. They distributed them to those friends around the world for safekeeping."

"But you still weren't safe," Derek prompted.

Even though I knew the outcome, I was sitting on the edge of my seat. "Your parents must've been scared to death."

"It was a dark time," she said, frowning. "When the massacre occurred at Oradour, our village fathers called a town meeting. Uncle Anton suggested that everyone gather their most treasured belongings together and hide them in one safe place."

"Did they all agree?"

"Yes. The blacksmith had a false door in the floor of his shop, and they intended to hide everything in the space underneath. But then my uncle Jacques was caught by the Nazis for being part of the Resistance. We were afraid he would be tortured. He escaped, but he and his brothers decided that our entire family had to leave immediately to avoid certain death at the hands of the enemy. The men of my family used up every connection they'd ever had to get us out of the country."

"Did they leave everything with the blacksmith?" I asked.

"No. Uncle Anton, as the oldest, was in charge, and he suggested that he and my uncles collect the most valuable belongings of everyone in the village and take them out of the country with them. When the war was over, Anton would be responsible for bringing it all back safe and sound.

"Everyone agreed that this was the best solution, so for several nights, people came by our house and left the most beautiful artwork and statues and gold coins and jewelry and silver pieces. Even some furniture. The father of one of my school friends claimed to be related to the French kings. He and the men carried several exquisite pieces of furniture into our house. I remember seeing a dresser with a mirror and a vanity table. All very fancy."

At the mention of the furniture, I exchanged a glance with Derek.

"How did you get everything out of the country?" he asked.

"By the will of God," she said. "And pure luck. The small items were placed inside the wine barrels and covered in dirt. The biggest items were shipped to a company in San Francisco that Uncle Anton knew of, and he planned to take possession of them when we arrived. Those larger crates were marked as furniture. And, of course, much of it was indeed furniture."

"That must've taken some time to arrange." I was completely enthralled by her tale.

"The clock was ticking," she said. "My mother was so nervous in those days. I didn't know why until a few years later when I was finally able to understand what we'd been through."

"So everything was packed up, and that was when you left."

"We had to sneak out of the village and travel at night.

Along the way we were assisted by many kind people. I was miserable and frightened, but I didn't dare complain."

"Because you might've been discovered."

"Yes," she said flatly. "We finally made it to the coast and traveled across the channel to Southampton, England. Then by boat to New York and then by train to California. The wine barrels traveled with us. It was a harrowing journey every step of the way, because we never knew when we might be stopped and searched. My father and uncles had to carry an enormous amount of cash because they didn't know when or where they might have to pay off an official."

"How awful for them," Mom murmured. "And all of you."

"Isn't it?" Trudy said, shaking her head. "Even when we arrived at the little train station in Petaluma, safe at last, my mother refused to let a porter take her suitcase. She was afraid she wouldn't get it back."

"Your poor mother," Mom said. "She had to worry about her children, too."

"Yes," Trudy murmured. "I had a younger brother, Olivier. He returned to France after the war and died a few years ago."

"I'm sorry."

"Thank you. He was a dear old thing, and his wife was lovely. They're both gone now. I remember how Ollie and I used to practice our English together every day on the boat." She seemed lost in thought for a moment but then perked up. "When we arrived in San Francisco, we collected our shipments of furniture and everything else we'd sent ahead. My father and uncles bought three cars and a truck, and we all drove out here to Sonoma."

Derek smiled calmly, even though I could tell he was anxious to get back on track. "Once they knew you were all safe, did your parents arrange to take everything back to the villagers?"

Trudy's expression was not happy. "I don't believe

so, not right away. The war was still raging back home. But to be honest, I have no idea when or how they sent the items back. My parents never spoke of it."

"They never said anything about the villagers' belongings?" I asked, not quite believing what she'd said.

"When we first arrived, they talked about it. And they told us stories. We were growing older, and I think they wanted us to know some of our history. But one day, they just stopped talking about it. All of it. The artwork. The harrowing details of the trip we'd taken. The war. Even our old village in France. My parents never spoke a word about any of it again."

"Not a word?" Mom echoed in puzzlement.

"Not as far as I knew."

"Do you have any idea why?" I asked.

"No. I was still a child and didn't think to ask. I assumed my father and uncles had taken care of everything, but they never said. I decided that they simply didn't like to dwell on the past. But I wish I knew what happened. There were so many beautiful things, I would like to know that they all made it back to their rightful owners and that our French village was peaceful again. I have so many questions."

Derek and I exchanged another glance, and he reached for Trudy's hand. "We might be able to give you some of the answers you're looking for."

She trembled visibly. "What do you mean?"

"I mean, we know where the treasures are. We can take you to see them, Trudy."

She waved him away with a tired smile. "Oh, I'm too old to travel."

"You don't understand," I said, laughing. "They're only a mile away. In the wine cave."

"It's simply too much to comprehend," Trudy said. "It all looks so familiar, and yet, it's—it's . . . Oh, there's the Greniers' family portrait. Good heavens, they're all so young." She gazed at the framed oil painting for a long moment, then turned to stare at herself in the pretty gold-leaf mirror attached to a rococo vanity table. "This belonged to my girlfriend from so many years ago, Nanette Allard."

"It's beautiful," I said.

"Isn't it? I always envied her for having so many nice . . . Oh!" She inhaled so suddenly, I thought she might faint.

"Are you all right?"

"What is it?" Derek asked. "Do you remember something else?"

Trudy let out a faint trill and flitted over to the bookshelf, where she grabbed a small white marble sculpture of a bird and clutched it tightly to her bosom. "It's my missing bookend!"

She closed her eyes and simply breathed for a moment. Then she held it out for us to see. "It's a quail. I can't believe it. I haven't seen this since I was seven years old."

"It was yours when you were young?" Derek asked.

She laughed. "The set actually belonged to my father, but he gave it to me because I loved carrying it around the house. One of the set disappeared shortly after we moved here, and I was bereft. But here it is."

"Amazing," Mom said.

"I still have its mate on my mantel at home. Well, not its mate, exactly. The one I have at home is a kitten, but it's similar in size and style to this one." She turned it this way and that. "It's charming, isn't it?"

"Beautiful," I repeated, taking the sculpture when she offered it. As Trudy said, it was a quail, and its head, half of its body, and one outstretched wing were beautifully carved while the rest of its body was still encased in the small block of marble. I handed it to Derek.

"It's so simple," he said, "and yet it manages to show so much emotion and strength. The way it's carved as though it's poised to fly free from the marble reminds me of Rodin's style."

"I think so, too." Trudy let out a happy sigh. "This

was done by nobody in particular and isn't worth much money, of course. But it has lots of sentimental value."

I noticed Derek's eyebrow quirk up. Did he disagree with her? Did he believe the piece might be a more important work than Trudy thought? I'd thought of Rodin, too, when I held the little sculpture. I loved his work and had enjoyed touring his museum in Paris, but I couldn't remember whether he'd ever sculpted small animals like that. Unbidden, an old news story sprang to my mind, about the Musée Rodin in Paris discovering a number of fake sculptures in other exhibitions around the world. The article mentioned a way to tell if a Rodin sculpture was an original. Knowing Derek, I suspected he already knew how to tell.

"All these fantastic paintings," Mom said as she scanned the artwork leaning against the walls. "I can't believe they've been hiding in here all these years."

"Someone went to a lot of trouble to keep them hidden," I said.

"But why?" she asked. "Everything is so beautiful. Why not share it with the world?"

"Perhaps there was an earthquake," Trudy said. "I can't imagine my father or my uncles purposely barricading this space, but an earthquake might've made it inaccessible."

"Quite possibly," Derek said, although I knew he was only saying it to placate her. We had already decided that an earthquake would've destroyed most of the valuables hidden in these chambers. There would've been rubble and stones and earth blocking the way, not smooth cement walls.

But I played along. "Yes, anything could've happened." I didn't want Trudy to worry that her family members might've done something devious. But how else could this be explained?

I glanced at Mom, who took the hint. "It's getting late. If you don't mind, I'd better go home and start dinner."

"Oh goodness," Trudy said, checking her wristwatch.

"Amelia is going to scold me for being gone so long without calling."

Amelia would scold her? Sadly, I believed it and wondered if Trudy couldn't find a more pleasant companion than that sourpuss.

I led the way out of the chamber, through the storage cave, and out to the pathway that led to the parking lot.

In the car, Trudy held her quail sculpture in her lap, and we chitchatted about the awesome discovery all the way back to her house.

Derek left the motor running while he walked Trudy to her door. Once she was safe inside, Derek returned, and we took off for our side of town. I leaned forward from the backseat and touched Mom's shoulder. "Did you know any of that stuff about Guru Bob?"

"You mean that he was French? I had no idea!"

"No, I mean did you know that his family already owned this property long before we moved up here to join the Fellowship?"

She frowned. "I suppose he did. Your father and I always thought he came here and bought the property on his own."

"So Dad didn't know, either?"

Mom's shoulders dropped fractionally. "Neither of us had any idea that Robson's family owned this property." But Dad had been known to keep secrets from Mom in the past. For her own good, he'd said at the time. Her eyes narrowed with purpose. "I'll find out exactly how much your father knows when I get home."

"Go, Mom."

"Not that it should be any big deal," she argued with herself. "Robson doesn't have to tell us every detail of his life."

"True."

Then she frowned. "In fact, I'm trying to remember exactly what he *did* tell us. Maybe we all just assumed he'd purchased the land around that same time."

"Maybe."

"I'll get back to you on that."

I caught Derek watching me in the rearview mirror and grinned. He always had too good a time watching me spar with my mother.

He pulled into Mom's driveway and came to a stop.

"I'd like to return to the caves tomorrow," Mom said as she was climbing out of the car. "The space needs a spiritual cleansing."

Normally I would've rolled my eyes and tried to discourage her, but seeing as how a murder had occurred in that small cave, and lord only knew what had happened in the larger one, I figured it might actually do some good if she went ahead and cleaned it up a little, spiritually speaking.

"I'll go with you," I said.

"I'll take you both there," Derek said. "The potential value of the treasure in those caves is phenomenal, and that much money can make people do crazy things. I think we'd be wise to follow the 'safety in numbers' adage for the time being."

"I couldn't agree more," Mom said, beaming at him. "See you kids tomorrow."

Once Mom was gone, I pounced on Derek. "Do you honestly think that sculpture might be a real Rodin?"

He glanced at me sideways before backing out of my parents' driveway and pulling into the Quinlans'. "How dare you read my mind."

"It wasn't that hard," I said, chuckling. "The expression on your face made it obvious."

"It's sad," he lamented. "I used to be so mysterious. Inscrutable."

I laughed. "You're absolutely sphinxlike most of the time, but I suppose I'm getting used to you."

"The Rodin connection makes sense, though, don't you think?" Derek said as he unlocked the side door into the kitchen. "Trudy's from a prominent French family that goes back several generations. They had a winery that was popular in the area. Who's to say they didn't commission a work by Rodin at some point?"

I was momentarily distracted as canine Maggie trundled over to greet us and feline Charlie pounced on my foot. As I washed out Maggie's bowl and filled it with fresh water, I remembered what we were talking about. "It's two works," I said. "Remember the quail's mate is on Trudy's mantel?"

He stooped to pick up Charlie and nuzzled her soft neck. "Did you happen to see it when we were there?"

"No." I smiled. "There was so much other stuff to see."

"Isn't that the truth? Her home is quite like a miniature museum in and of itself."

"I agree. I'd like to visit her again to get a look at that other sculpture she was talking about."

"Yes, let's arrange that." He took out his phone and punched in a quick note to himself.

I hung up my purse on a hook by the back door and sat down at the kitchen table with my phone. "No time like the present," I said, and Googled *Rodin sculptures*. It brought me to the site of the Musée Rodin, and I scrolled through the photographs. I saw plenty of old men with their jowls and wrinkles, and beautiful women of all shapes and sizes. There were lovers embracing and angels avenging, but no charming little animals.

I reported my findings to Derek.

"It probably wasn't sculpted by Rodin, but I'd be willing to guess that it's from the same era. It's a stunning piece."

"I think so, too. And speaking of notable Frenchmen, I never would've guessed that Guru Bob was French, would you?"

"He's so well dressed and speaks so formally, I always figured he was English."

I laughed. "If only that weren't true, I'd be able to say something rude."

Derek leaned back against the kitchen counter and

folded his arms across his chest. "We British are exceedingly polite, as you well know."

"And yet"—I glanced around—"I've been home for three minutes, and I don't see my glass of wine anywhere."

He slapped his forehead in mock dismay. "Butler's night off, love. I'll get right on it."

My cell phone rang at that moment, and I glanced at the screen. I chuckled as I answered the call. "Hey, Mom. Long time no see."

"Hello, sweetie," she said, speaking quietly. "Can you and Derek come over right now? Robson is here and would like to talk to all of us together. It's important."

Chapter 6

"I have been contacted by a number of media outlets," Robson said as soon as we were all gathered in my parents' large, comfortable living room. "They are asking for details and interviews."

"They've already heard about the treasure in the cave?" I frowned, trying to figure out how the word got out. "That was fast."

"No, gracious," he said. "Not the treasure. They have only asked about the body that was found."

"Oh, that makes sense." I shot Derek a quick glance. "They probably heard the news from someone at the sheriff's department."

"Perhaps." Guru Bob stood in front of my parents' dark wood and tile-framed fireplace with his hands clasped behind his back. He was a tall, fair-haired man who never seemed to age, but for the first time I noticed streaks of silver in his hair. It only made him appear more distinguished, I decided. In his present stance, he resembled an admiral handing out difficult assignments to his closest allies.

"Brooklyn, dear," he continued, "I would appreciate it if you and Derek would agree to meet and speak with the media people who show up seeking information. Given your firsthand knowledge of the situation, you will be the best spokespeople for the winery and the Fellowship."

I gave Mom a quick look, and she nodded her encouragement. I couldn't figure out why.

"I'm happy to talk with them of course," I said. It was a lie. I hated the idea of schmoozing with the press. But I wasn't about to turn down a personal request from Guru Bob. "But wouldn't you rather have one of your lawyers do it?"

"To put it plainly, no," he said, smiling for the first time since we'd arrived. "The lawyers know nothing of the circumstances. And have you ever noticed that they have a tendency to get lost in the weeds? If you understand my meaning of that term?"

I smiled. "I do."

"It is a colorful phrase that certainly fits in this instance." He glanced at Derek. "Now that you have talked to Trudy and know more of the background of my family and what brought them to Dharma, I believe you will be prepared to handle anyone who comes asking questions."

"I appreciate your confidence," Derek said, leaning forward to rest his elbows on his knees. I recognized the move to mean he was pondering something deeply. "But, Robson, even though we've talked to Trudy and we know a lot more than we did when we first opened up the walls of the cave, we're missing quite a bit of information. Is there anything more you'd like to share with us?"

"I wish I could tell you more," Robson said, sounding frustrated, which was alarming since he rarely showed negativity. "Frankly, I would prefer it if you could limit your conversation with the press to the topic of Mr. Renaud's body. How he was found. Where you found him. Details about the excavation itself. Those sorts of things. I believe the news media will find those unpleasant details appealing."

"No doubt," Derek said. "But I don't believe they'll

be satisfied with our bare-bones explanation. A good reporter will want to investigate exactly what happened to Mr. Renaud and how he ended up inside a walled-up cave."

Guru Bob lifted his shoulders philosophically. "I fully expect that my family history and the recently discovered artwork will become fodder for some. I don't expect you to lie about it. Trying to prevaricate will only make matters worse."

"On that we agree," Derek said. "That's why I want to be absolutely sure we have all the facts before we stumble into something we know nothing about."

Guru Bob nodded calmly. "Of course."

"I can handle the press," Derek said, "but I refuse to allow Brooklyn to be a target for some reporter's misdirected sense of truth and justice."

"I can handle it," I said, even though I shivered at the thought.

Guru Bob took a long moment to consider his words and finally said, "I will have a few more things to disclose as soon as our last guest arrives."

I glanced at Mom, who shook her head, meaning that she was as clueless as I was of the identity of our missing guest.

"Please rest assured," Guru Bob continued. "Neither of you will be hung out to dry, as they say. I am the leader of this Fellowship, first of all, and second, it is my family's story that will be exploited. If any backlash or unexpected disclosure occurs, I will step forward and deal with it."

"I don't think it'll come to that," Derek said, sitting back and sounding a lot calmer than he had a minute ago. "I'm sure we'll be able to handle it with no problem. But I appreciate your willingness to come to our rescue if necessary."

Robson nodded. "You and Brooklyn have come to my rescue on more than one occasion, so if I ever have the opportunity to return the favor, I will." He scanned the room, meeting each of our gazes one by one. "It is lowering to realize that for all these years, this dark secret was festering right here in our midst. I should have had at least an inkling, but I did not. That troubles me." He shook his head. "And the fact that it is connected to my family hurts my heart."

"You can't blame yourself," I said quickly. "It all happened before you were born."

His sudden smile was luminescent. "Your defense of me is like a balm, gracious. I appreciate everything you are doing for the Fellowship and for me." He looked at Derek. "Both of you. I am grateful."

If I didn't change the subject to something less emotional and more tangible, I would burst into tears. "Robson, how many news outlets have you heard from?"

"Close to two dozen," he said. "I have made a list of their names and contact numbers."

Two dozen? I blew out a breath. "Have you considered hiring some extra security for the caves?"

"I have indeed."

There was a knock on the front door, and Mom hurried to answer it.

Guru Bob showed a hint of a smile. "Timing is everything."

As Mom led the visitor into the living room, she wore a big broad grin. And then I saw why.

"Gabriel," I whispered.

He winked and almost took my breath away. "Hey, babe."

I dashed over to grab him in a hug. "I haven't seen you in forever. How are you?"

"I'm better now." The man was too devastatingly handsome for his own good, and his dark eyes gleamed with devilish intent. With his arm still slung over my shoulders, he scanned the room. "Greetings, everyone."

"Hello, mate." Derek strolled over and gave him a hearty handshake.

Gabriel smacked him on the back. "Good to see you, man."

I glanced from one man to the other. They were both extraordinarily hot, and I knew from experience that being in the same room with them could be hazardous to a girl's ability to speak in complete sentences. While both men exuded strength and masculine self-confidence, Derek was smoother, more sophisticated, and deliberate. Gabriel was more likely to shoot from the hip. He was—and always would be—a *bad boy*.

I beamed at Guru Bob. "Your extra security?"

He chuckled. "Who else would I call?"

Gabriel had saved my life almost two years ago when I was about to be attacked in a noodle shop on Fillmore Street in the city. At the time, I thought I'd lucked out that this tall, dark, and gorgeous stranger had walked into the shop at that precise moment, but it turned out that he'd been following me—for reasons I would discover much later.

I'd never quite figured out if he was a good guy or a thief, a gun for hire or a solid citizen. Maybe all of the above. I knew he could be deadly, but that didn't matter. He had saved my life more than once, and, like Derek, he would always be a hero to me.

He went by only one name: Gabriel. Like the archangel. I figured a guy that tall, dark, and dashing probably didn't need more than just the one name. Gabriel had a knack for finding whatever it was you needed. His business card read DISCREET PROCUREMENT.

As usual, today he was dressed all in black, from his black suede bomber jacket down to his boots. The color suited him just fine. He had made a temporary home for himself here in Dharma, and I knew he'd been working on some kind of security system for Guru Bob.

He pulled a chair in from the dining room and sat down. "So, what's all the hubbub about?"

"Hubbub?" I had to laugh. "Nothing much. Just a dead body that's been perfectly preserved for almost seventy years in a hidden cave under the vineyards,

surrounded by a treasure trove of artwork and goodies
that looks like something from a museum heist."

His lips twisted into a smile. "Sounds like fun."

I sat down next to Derek. "Did you know he'd be
here?"

"I had my suspicions," he said, his eyes twinkling.
Besides being the two most gorgeous men I'd ever seen
in real life, Derek and Gabriel had become good friends
and had worked or consulted with each other on a few
high-profile top secret security cases over the past year.
I didn't know many of the details, which was probably
just as well.

A discreet cough from Guru Bob brought us all back
to attention.

"Now that Gabriel is here," he said, "I will share
more information with you. And I have an additional
request. It is your choice completely whether you wish
to accept it or not."

"What is it?" I asked, concerned at the way he'd
phrased it.

Gesturing with his hand, he singled out Derek and
Gabriel. "I would appreciate it if you two would accom-
pany me to Frenchman's Hill tomorrow. I must talk to
some people about what was found in the caves."

"Absolutely," Derek said without hesitation.

Gabriel gave him a thumbs-up. "No problem."

I had every intention of going with them, but I would
mention it later.

"What do the Frenchman's Hill folks have to do with
the caves?" Mom asked casually, but I could hear the
edge in her voice. Was she worried about more secrets?

I'd gone to high school with a few kids from Frenchman's Hill, and they all had one thing in common: they
were French, duh. Their families had traveled to Sonoma
from France over the past half century, settling on farmland about five miles northwest of Dharma. The area
had come to be known as Frenchman's Hill.

Coincidence that so many French families had moved to the area? I thought not. Especially after hearing Trudy's stories earlier.

"It is a long story," Guru Bob said easily, taking a seat in the lyre-back chair nearest the fireplace. "If you can spare me a few more minutes?"

"Absolutely," I said. I wasn't going to miss this.

"Wait." Dad jumped up from his chair. "Since nobody's going anywhere, I've got a bottle of wine I'd like you all to try. It's a Meritage blend I'm experimenting with."

"Good idea, Jim," Guru Bob said. "We should enjoy a glass of wine as we talk."

"Thanks, Dad," I murmured as he filled my glass. He gave me a wink and turned to pour wine into Derek's glass. Dad had always had a wonderful way of defusing tension, often by changing the subject to wine, one of his favorite topics.

I swirled my wine and stared at the streaks coating the sides of the glass and slowly dripping down. These streaks were known as *wine legs*, and some wine lovers thought that the slower the legs moved, the better the quality of wine. I'd learned that it had more to do with alcohol content and good old gravity, but it was fun to zone out while watching them slide down into the liquid.

Once Dad finished pouring the wine and was back in his chair, Guru Bob began his story.

"I have a vivid memory of an incident that happened when I was ten years old. I was helping my father in the vineyards when three men approached him. They told him they were new to the area and were looking for Anton Benoit or one of his brothers. The men had recently moved to Sonoma from the village of La Croix Saint-Just, where Anton was raised."

I nodded. We had learned that from Trudy earlier that day.

"The three were trying to track down Anton," Guru Bob said, "to retrieve their family's belongings from him. My father was furious. He wanted to know why they were accusing his father of theft. The men quickly tried to defuse his anger, admitting that they were still learning English and had used the wrong phrasing."

"Did they explain themselves?"

"They did, and my father calmed down. I cannot remember all the details of their conversation, but despite their smiles and pleasantries, I know in my heart that they believed my grandfather was guilty of thievery."

I wasn't about to doubt Guru Bob's emotional memory. The man could pick up on an emotion so subtle, you wouldn't even know you were feeling it until he mentioned it.

The three men told Guru Bob's father how, during the war, their families had entrusted Anton with their most valuable heirlooms and he had taken them to America, promising to return them after the war. Everyone in the village had been desperate to keep their precious belongings out of the hands of the Nazis.

It was the same basic story we'd heard from Trudy earlier that day.

"My father was sympathetic," Guru Bob said, "but he insisted he had no idea what the men were talking about. They tried describing some of the artwork and furnishings, but my father could only shake his head. He was clueless. He even invited the men into his home, but they did not find what they were looking for."

"You told us that your grandfather died before you were born," I said, thinking back to our conversation at the picnic table the day before.

"That is right. I never knew him. Marie, my grandmother, though, lived until I was well into my teens, and she was wonderful."

"I'm glad you knew her, Robson," Mom said.

"I am, too." He smiled. "So now we are all caught up-to-date. You know about my family, and you know about the treasures. Soon others will find out. It remains for me to immediately seek out those French families and explain that their belongings are safe, after all."

"Do you know if any of the three men still live here?" Gabriel asked.

"I never saw them again. My father was not interested in working the land, so shortly after that, we moved to San Francisco. The land was never sold, though, so when I grew up, I was able to reclaim all of it."

"And none of your other relatives wanted the land," I said.

"Yes. As I explained yesterday, some of them returned to France. A few have died. Trudy was the only one who stayed. She has always loved it here."

I tried to do the math. My family moved here when I was eight, so that was about twenty-five years ago. "So when you reclaimed your land and started the Fellowship, the people of Frenchman's Hill had already been here for years."

"Yes. And all this time, I have kept tabs on the families living here. Back then, they were all from La Croix Saint-Just, but more recently, others have moved here from different areas. Only two of the original families decided to return to France after a few years. The others stayed and have thrived. They grow grapes, of course, and a few years ago, they created a cooperative through which they sell their grapes to the local wineries. Recently they opened their own tasting room and continue to do quite well."

"I've been to their tasting room," Dad said. "They're doing good work."

"Do you think they all moved here to find their family treasures?" I asked. "Wouldn't they have approached you on more occasions than that one time in the vineyard?"

"They have not," Robson said. "I cannot say why. Perhaps my father's anger quelled their suspicions."

Derek frowned. "And now you're going to tell them that their suspicions were justified."

"And that their raison d'être for moving here in the first place is about to pay off," I added.

"Should be fascinating," Gabriel said, chuckling. "I assume you want us there for extra muscle?"

"I do, if you would not mind." Guru Bob looked around the room, shaking his head. "One never knows how a person will react to such shocking news."

"I'm happy to tag along," Derek said. "Although I can't imagine you'll have many complaints after you tell them they're about to get back their priceless artwork and treasures."

"I hope it will be a positive visit, but I will not be surprised if we experience a confrontational moment or two."

Did I mention that Guru Bob never used contractions in his speech? It probably sounded odd to an outsider, but I was so used to it, I rarely noticed. He had once explained that it kept him consciously aware of his speech. He was all about being conscious and aware in each moment.

I was anxious about the visit to Frenchman's Hill tomorrow and was more determined than ever to go along for the ride. If nothing else, I might get a chance to say hello to one or two of my old high school friends. And it would be interesting to see how well the French folks took the good news.

Early the next morning, Derek drove to Frenchman's Hill with one contact name from Guru Bob. He had managed to track down a Monsieur Georges Cloutier and had requested a meeting with him and others who had emigrated from La Croix Saint-Just. Derek gave no clue as to the topic of the meeting except to assure him that it would be to the group's benefit. Monsieur Cloutier knew Guru Bob by reputation and was intrigued enough to make some calls and offered his home for the meeting at one o'clock that afternoon.

Before Derek left, I'd told him that I planned to drive over to the winery. I knew he didn't want me going into the caves alone, but it was important that we start an inventory of everything in there. It was the responsible thing to do. Derek had said he would try to meet me there later. I knew it was because he thought I was afraid to go into the cave alone, but I assured him that I wasn't.

"All right, love," he said. "But just in case." And he gave me an extra tight hug and kiss before he left.

Now, in the privacy of my car, I could admit to being more than a little freaked-out about going inside the cave all by myself. It was one thing to tramp around with a big hunky guy like Derek, or one of my brothers, but all alone? In the dark? With spiders?

My shoulders jerked as chills shot across them. I was not looking forward to this, but it had to be done.

I pulled into the lot and parked, grabbed my legal pad, a fold-up stool I'd borrowed from my mom, and the heavy flashlight Derek had given me. As I walked to the storage-cave entrance, I was surprised to see Gabriel approach.

"Hey, you," I said, giving him a one-arm hug. "Are you here to start setting up the security system?"

"Something like that," he said with a sideways grin, cryptic as always.

"Have you been inside already? Seen the stuff in there? It's pretty awesome, isn't it?"

"Haven't seen anything yet, but I know it's really dark in there."

I stared at him for a long moment. "Derek asked you to meet me here."

"Why would he do that? You're a big girl. You can handle this."

"That's right. I can." I unlocked the wide double doors of the storage cave.

He shrugged. "I'm just here to make sure you don't steal anything."

I laughed all the way to the back wall.

Once we'd climbed inside the chamber, Gabriel took a long look around. "What a haul," he said after a few minutes.

"It's impressive, isn't it?"

"Yeah. Now I see why Robson wants some extra muscle when he visits Frenchman's Hill."

I frowned at him. "You think they'll be angry?"

"If any of this stuff was stolen from your family, wouldn't you be?"

"I see your point, but I hope they won't take it out on Guru Bob. That wouldn't be fair."

"Emotions get in the way of reason sometimes."

"Too true," I said. With that, I continued writing down what I found. My organizational skills were outstanding, but there was so much to figure out. I finally divided my list into sections: furniture; silver; paintings; small sculptures; larger sculptures and busts; jewelry; and miscellaneous.

After I'd been working for ten minutes, Gabriel told me some of his guys had arrived, so he'd be outside working on the security system.

"I'm fine," I assured him.

"Okay, but keep in mind I'm only a piercing scream away."

I laughed again and waved him off. For the next two hours, I sifted through jewelry boxes and unrolled canvas paintings, writing down everything I saw and describing it all in detail. I took pictures of things, thinking it would help to have some visuals when I finalized my list.

Despite my brave words, it was still a little creepy exploring the dark chambers by myself with just the big flashlight for illumination. But I survived. When I got home, I transferred what I had so far on my inventory list onto a computer document. Then I printed my photos out on glossy photo paper.

I was home by noon to meet Derek, and a few minutes before one o'clock, we pulled up in front of the home of Monsieur Cloutier. Gabriel parked right behind us, with Guru Bob in the passenger seat of his sleek black BMW. Monsieur Cloutier's wife answered the door and introduced herself as Solange. She was a petite, dark-haired woman with a ready smile, and she led us out to the terrace, where a number of men and women were standing around a long table filled with platters of food.

"Did you prepare all this?" Guru Bob asked Solange. "On such short notice?"

"Oui, monsieur," she said, smiling with pride as she waved us toward the table. *"C'est pour vous. S'il vous plaît,* sit. Sit. Enjoy."

"What a lovely and generous way to welcome us to your home," he said, taking her hand in both of his. "You will be joining us?"

"Oui, in a moment." She gave him another smile and scurried back into the house.

As soon as the men saw Guru Bob, they all approached. It was reassuring to see them recognize him as the patriarch of Dharma and treat him with respect.

We were introduced to everyone. Besides the Cloutiers, there were four men and two women. Their ages ranged from early eighties to midtwenties.

One old man, Gerard, said, "We came to Sonoma in 1952, Felix, Simon, and I, with our families. Alas, our friend Simon died years ago, but my friend Felix is still with us."

"I am indeed," a wiry, gray-haired man said, chuckling as he took hold of the arm of a younger man, pulling him forward. "This is Henri, Simon's son. He is head of his household now."

Henri appeared to be in his midfifties. He was a big friendly bear of a man with red hair and a ruddy complexion. Felix smacked him several times on the shoulder, his pride in the younger man obvious.

The first man, Gerard, extended his arm toward one of the women helping to set the table. "And that is my wife, Beatrice." She smiled and waved at us.

"And that pretty one there is Henri's wife," Felix said, pointing to the third Frenchwoman in attendance, who was presently carrying yet another platter to the table.

The woman glanced up at Felix's words and smiled indulgently.

"That is my Sophie," Henri said proudly.

The twelve of us drifted toward the table and eventually took seats, chatting about the weather and predicting whether this would be the best grape crop in history or not.

It was a beautiful fall day, and the Cloutiers' terrace overlooked the vineyards. I felt instantly at home since my parents' home had a similar view of rolling green hills covered in rows and rows of grapevines with the occasional oak tree spreading its branches in every direction.

Dining with all of these strangers was only awkward for a moment until we began to help ourselves and pass the platters to others. Everyone was smiling as we shared the food. It all looked fantastic. Slices of rare roast beef, grilled artichokes, roasted peppers in olive oil, caprese salad with fresh tomatoes and basil, grilled sausages with sautéed onions and peppers, arugula salad sprinkled with chunks of goat cheese and orange slices, asparagus in vinaigrette, and a yummy-looking quiche.

There was wine, too, of course, and by the end of the meal, we were a jolly group. Madame Cloutier began to clear the table, and Gabriel carried platters into the house. The other two women helped, and soon I could hear giggling and chatting going on inside. Minutes later, several ladies returned carrying platters of pastries sprinkled with powdered sugar. Homemade beignets!

As soon as the rest of the women and Gabriel came back outside and sat down, Monsieur Cloutier signaled that it was time to get down to business and offered Guru Bob the floor.

He began by thanking the Cloutiers for their hospitality and hoped that all of us would always be good neighbors to one another.

"We all have something in common," he continued, looking around the table, meeting the others' serious gazes. "Either we or our forefathers traveled here from La Croix Saint-Just. Some came to escape certain death. A few were on a quest for a better life. But most of you came in search of something you thought had been stolen from your family. I am here today to right a wrong."

Several of the men exchanged glances with one another but said nothing.

Guru Bob appeared to brace himself as he announced, "My grandfather was Anton Benoit."

There were a few gasps, followed by a brief silence.

"Felon!" Henri shouted suddenly, and pushed his chair back from the table. He stood and scowled at Guru Bob as he spewed a stream of French insults.

Both Derek and Gabriel stood immediately.

Guru Bob's expression remained calm.

"Henri, *s'il vous plaît*," Felix said with a world-weary wave of his hand. "Be patient. Let our guest explain himself."

Henri's jaw was clenched as he appeared to weigh his odds with Derek and Gabriel. He was bigger than both of them, but it wasn't from muscle. He had to realize his chances of defeating either one of them in a fight were close to nothing.

Not that I expected Derek or Gabriel to lay one finger on Henri. They were only here for intimidation purposes. I hoped.

"Henri," Felix chided, "it is too nice a day to quarrel."

"Coquin," the big man muttered, causing Felix to roll his eyes. Henri made a show of doing the old man a favor by sitting, but it was obvious to me that he'd done so because of Derek and Gabriel's clear intention to take him on if necessary.

Derek and Gabriel sat as well. Madame Cloutier refilled Gabriel's wineglass, and he winked at her. Despite their friendly interaction, the tension around the table was now as thick as the grilled sausages we'd just eaten.

"I never met my grandfather," Guru Bob said when

he had the attention of the group again. "But I heard the stories of his escape from France and how he took all of the villagers' belongings with him for safekeeping. I assumed, wrongly, that everything was returned after the war. Recently, though, I found out how wrong I was to assume such a thing."

"Blaireau," Henri muttered.

Gabriel stood, looked at Henri, and raised an eyebrow. "Dude."

Henri gave an ill-tempered shrug. *"Désolé."*

It was a poor apology. I tried to recall some of the French words my sister had taught me while I was visiting her in Paris, but *blaireau* didn't come to mind. I had a feeling it wasn't a compliment. But why was this guy insulting Guru Bob? Didn't he get that the man was bringing him good news?

"Brooklyn, dear," Guru Bob said, leaning forward to grab my attention. "Do you have the photographs?"

"I do." I pulled them out of the bag I'd set beside my chair and handed them to him.

Gabriel, instead of sitting down again, walked a few feet away from the table and leaned his back against the outside wall. From that position he had an excellent, unobstructed view of the whole table and the still-grumbling people. He folded his arms across his chest and watched the interactions from there.

"We recently excavated one of our storage caves to expand its size," Guru Bob explained. "Behind what we thought was a solid stone wall we discovered a chamber that had been sealed off for the past seventy years. Inside we found the body of a Frenchman. Jean Pierre Renaud. Did you know of him?"

Felix laid his head in his hands. He muttered a few words in French, then glanced up, his eyes wet with tears. "He was a friend. When I arrived here and sought him out, I couldn't find him. So I thought perhaps he'd moved away and lived a good long life elsewhere."

"I am sorry for your loss," Robson said. "The sheriff's department is investigating, and I will be happy to pass along any information I receive from them."

He nodded. *"Merci."*

Guru Bob took a deep breath and let it out. I could tell this wasn't easy for him. And I had a feeling it was only going to get worse.

"We discovered a number of other items behind the stone wall. I'd like you to see them." He passed a few photographs to his left, a few to his right, and a few to the people sitting across the table. The looks on their faces ran the emotional gamut from devastation to delight.

"Gerard, look," Beatrice whispered. "It is my father's escritoire."

"The Botticelli," Solange cried. Tears formed in her eyes, and she pressed a hand to her lips.

I didn't dare look at Derek, but I knew what he was thinking. It really was a Botticelli painting! My next immediate thought was, *Gabriel needs to beef up the winery security right away.*

"These are my mother's candlesticks," Henri said, slapping the photograph with the back of his hand. "She died of a broken heart, knowing she would never see her beautiful things again."

"While my words cannot possibly ease the pain you feel, please know that I am truly sorry." Guru Bob's compassion for the other man was clear in his voice.

"That's not good enough." Henri fumed for a moment, sniffing loudly like an angry bull about to strike. But one sharp glance from Felix had him gritting his teeth. He sat back in his chair, and his breath slowed. Was he trying to chill out? I hoped so. The man was a loose cannon.

But abruptly he stood again and focused on Guru Bob. "My friends think I'm wrong to direct my anger toward you, sir. But I look at you, and I see a man whose family has been in possession of our most precious heirlooms for several generations. All that time, we had nothing. So how are we to be made whole again? Will you simply return our trinkets and that will be that? No. You owe us more. Your family owes us more. Perhaps we should pay them a visit and see what appeals to us."

Sophie grabbed hold of her husband's arm. "Henri, no!"

Felix made a guttural sound of contempt, but Henri ignored both of them and continued talking. "I may not have the money or means to take you on personally, sir, but suppose I call the newspapers and tell them my story. How much is it worth to avoid negative publicity?"

Guru Bob was able to maintain his usual Zen-like calm throughout the diatribe, but Gabriel was seething and asked, "Are you talking about blackmail, Henri?"

Alarmed, I exchanged a glance with Derek, who was quick to address the cooler heads at the table. "You're all free to seek whatever counsel you wish in this matter. However, I'll caution you that the more publicity you seek regarding these valuable objects, the greater the possibility of break-ins and thefts."

"Ah, *écoutez*, Henri," Felix chided. *"Réfléchissez avant de parler à nouveau."*

I leaned closer to Derek. "What did he say?"

He whispered in my ear, "He told Henri to listen and think before he speaks again."

"Good. He's a hothead."

Guru Bob stood once more to address everyone at the table. "Again, I am very sorry to have caused you pain. All I can do to mitigate your years of suffering is to return everything as quickly as possible. I would ask that you each make a list of the items your families gave to my grandfather. As quickly as I receive your lists, I will see that your belongings are delivered back to you with all speed."

"Merde," Henri said with a guttural snarl. "You can take that freaking list and shove it." He glared at his friends around the table. "How can we trust him? I say we go over there and take what belongs to us."

"You need to mellow out, friend," Gabriel said, walking up behind him. "You take one step onto Dharma winery property and you'll be looking trouble right in the eye."

Derek took my hand and nodded discreetly at Guru Bob. We stood, and Derek handed Monsieur Cloutier a business card. "Please call me if you need anything."

"Merci, Monsieur Stone," he murmured.

Guru Bob bowed his head briefly to Solange. "Thank you for your warm hospitality and wonderful food. I look forward to welcoming you into my home in the future." He pulled Monsieur Cloutier aside for a brief, private word.

I thanked Solange, then turned and smiled at the others. "It was lovely to meet all of you."

I could hear Henri grumbling still, trying to incite his friends to challenge Guru Bob. We were close to the front door when I heard footsteps pounding after us.

"You are the grandson of a thief!" Henri shouted. "Why should we take your word for anything?"

Two of the Frenchmen grabbed hold of him, giving us time to walk swiftly out of the house, slip into our cars, and drive away.

Chapter 7

"We have to make sure Guru Bob's okay," I said, trying not to wring my hands as we raced away from Frenchman's Hill.

Derek reached over and took hold of my hand. "I've already planned to follow them home."

"You're the best."

"Yes, I am."

I laughed as he knew I would. But he could tell I was still tense, so he squeezed my hand lightly. "Things will be fine, love."

My jaw clenched. "That guy was so angry."

"Henri has all the qualities of a real troublemaker, but you must've noticed that the others weren't backing him up."

"I did, and I was grateful for that. But even if Henri doesn't incite any more discord, it was still difficult to watch him attacking Guru Bob."

"Yes, it was," Derek said with a pensive frown. "But Guru Bob handled it well."

"He did. I just hope he won't feel guilty about it."

"He won't," Derek said. "He'll take action."

I squeezed his hand. Sometimes he said the best things.

Derek pulled to a stop at the curb, right behind

Gabriel's BMW. I jumped out of the car and followed Guru Bob halfway up the walkway leading to his elegant Queen Anne Victorian home at the top of the hill. "Robson."

He paused and turned, looking surprised to see me. "Brooklyn, is something wrong, dear? You seem upset. What happened?"

"That man called you names and accused you of horrible things. I just wanted to make sure you're all right."

"I am fine." He peered at me for a long moment. "You must not suffer on my behalf, gracious."

"I'm not." I frowned at myself for lying. "Well, maybe a little. I didn't like the way Henri spoke to you."

Guru Bob sighed and touched my shoulder to console me. "Henri is in pain. I did not take his harsh words to heart, and you must not, either."

"I'll try not to."

He pressed his lips together in thought. Finally he said, "My grandfather was a complicated soul. I never met him, but I had hints of him in my own father, who was a good man but not a happy one."

"I'm sorry."

Lost in his own thoughts, he didn't acknowledge my comment. "I wonder, did Anton take the treasured items strictly to help his friends and neighbors in the village? Was his purpose always altruistic? If so, why did he betray them in the end? Or did he? If he truly had no conscience, would he not have sold off the pieces? Or brazenly displayed them in his own home? He did neither. He hid them away in a cave. What does it mean?"

"I don't know," I whispered.

"And the body in the cave." It was almost as if Guru Bob had forgotten I was there. He was talking to himself, trying to work through many thoughts. "We must be asking ourselves, did Anton Benoit kill another man?"

"No," I said. "Absolutely not. I don't believe that."

His focus returned to me, and he smiled. "You have

more confidence than I, gracious. Remember, I did not know my grandfather."

"If he was yours, he was a good man."

"Someday we might know the truth."

I flailed my arms out. "Now I'm worried about you all over again."

He reached out and held my shoulders, and in an instant I felt reassured. "You are an angel and a bright light in my life. Because you and Derek are here with us in Dharma, I know that all will be well."

"We'll make sure of that," I promised. "We've got your back."

He pressed his hands together in what I called his *Namaste* pose, as though he were praying. Then he bowed slightly. "Good-bye, dear."

I lifted my hand in a wave. "Bye."

He walked a few steps, then turned and grinned. "And thank you for having my back."

I laughed softly and jogged back to the car.

An hour later, Gabriel showed up at our place with a six-pack of beer. I opened a bag of pretzel sticks, and we sat down at the kitchen table to commiserate.

"Well, that went well," he said after popping open three bottles and handing them out.

"Oh, just peachy," I said. "That guy Henri is going to burst a blood vessel one of these days."

Gabriel shook his head. "Dude's got some anger-management issues to work out."

"In some ways, I can't blame him," Derek said. "But he can't go around threatening Robson. He doesn't realize who he's dealing with."

I chuckled. "I think he might've gotten a clue after seeing you guys flex your muscles a few times."

"We do what we must," Derek said with a shrug.

Gabriel just chuckled and grabbed a handful of pretzels.

I told them what Guru Bob had told me earlier when we were standing in front of his house.

"Sounds like he's not sure if his grandfather killed Jean Pierre Renaud," Gabriel said.

"That's what it sounded like to me, too," I said. "But I can't imagine anyone related to Guru Bob actually killing someone, especially his best friend from childhood."

"It's hard to picture," Gabriel agreed.

I frowned into my beer. "You know how Guru Bob can present something as though it's a riddle to be solved? That's what it sounded like when he talked about his grandfather."

"Then we'll just have to solve the riddle," Derek murmured.

"Yes, but we also have to keep him safe in the meantime."

"We will, darling." He pointed his beer bottle at Gabriel. "From what I've seen, Gabriel's got almost all of Dharma wired into his security systems."

Gabriel winked at me.

"Okay, good." I took a quick sip of my beer before getting up to pull a triangle of creamy Brie out of the refrigerator. I arranged it on a plate with some water crackers and set it on the table.

"Perfect," Derek said.

"We needed more sustenance than pretzels," I said.

"Thanks, babe," Gabriel said, and reached for a cracker.

"I have a question," I said as I sat down again. "What does *blaireau* mean? Henri called Guru Bob a *blaireau*."

Gabriel grinned. "Literally, it's French for *badger*."

"A badger?" I shook my head, baffled. "What kind of an insult is that?"

"Have you ever seen a badger? Not a pretty animal."

I chuckled. "You have a point."

Derek said, "I believe Henri was calling Robson's grandfather a *blaireau*, not Robson himself."

"Oh." I thought about it. "Yeah, maybe."

"It's like calling someone a dweeb or a moron," Gabriel explained.

"In England, we prefer the term *plonker*," Derek said. "Means the same thing. Dimwit, idiot."

"I like plonker myself," I said. I tried to recall all of Henri's insults. "He also said something like *coquin*. What does that mean?"

"Rascal," Derek said, shrugging. "Scalawag."

"For real?" I was puzzled. "As fired up as Henri was, that's an awfully weak slur."

"There were women present," Gabriel surmised. "If he'd used stronger terms, the men would've kicked his ass."

"I wanted to slap him," I said, my fists bunching up at the memory. "I mean, *rascal* isn't the worst expletive in the world, but how dare he say anything like that to Guru Bob. It's not his fault his grandfather never gave that stuff back. And hey, Guru Bob went over there to let those people know their stuff was still safe and they could have it anytime. So gee, Henri, maybe you should've said, *Thank you, Badger*, instead of calling him all those rude names."

Gabriel snorted while Derek leaned over and gave my hand a comforting stroke. "Robson deliberately put himself in that role, darling. He knew what was coming, even predicted there would be some confrontations. I'd say we got off easy if Henri was the only one attempting to stir up trouble."

"There'll be more," Gabriel warned.

"I agree," Derek said soberly. "The others might have longer fuses, but a few of them will end up taking potshots, too."

I let out a little moan at the thought of more clashes with the French families. "The sooner we get rid of all that stuff, the better."

"Agreed." Derek drained his beer. "I didn't care for Henri threatening to go to the newspapers, either."

I turned to Gabriel. "How do you plan to protect the

caves from Henri and rude reporters and any other troublemakers who come along?"

"The usual way," he said nonchalantly. "Satellite technology, surveillance drones, big guys with guns."

I rolled my eyes. "Okay, you don't have to tell me. I shouldn't have asked."

Derek bit back a smile. "I think he just told you, love."

I frowned at the two of them. "Drones? Are you kidding?"

Gabriel shrugged. "They work. It's a good way to keep an eye on things. I've also installed motion sensors that'll activate closed-circuit cameras."

"You've already installed them?"

"Babe," he said, and left it at that.

"Right. Of course you have. You know what you're doing. But drones? Wow." I took a long sip of beer. Times had changed.

"Brooklyn," Derek said as he tossed his beer bottle in the plastic recycling crate, "we've got to return those calls from the media people who want information."

I winced. "With everything else going on, I forgot all about that."

"We'll split up the list. You call half and I'll call half."

"That'll help ease the pain."

He smiled. "And while I'm thinking about it, I'd like to get those photos you showed to the French folks. I want to scan them and send them to Interpol in case any of the items have been reported stolen."

I pulled the pictures from my purse and handed them to him. Gabriel was smart enough to take off then, and after he'd left, Derek and I discussed our strategy for dealing with the media. I wanted to make sure we had our stories straight in order to present a united front for the sake of the Fellowship and for Guru Bob.

"Not that he has anything to hide," I said quickly. "I mean, none of us does. We just happened to find Mr. Renaud's body. And thank goodness, the sheriff's detectives are convinced that nobody living here today could've killed him. End of story."

"We both know it's not the end of the story," he said.

"No, of course not, but we're not going to discuss anything about the artwork and furnishings we found, right?"

"That's right," he said as he cleared the table. He wrapped the remaining cheese in plastic wrap and stuck it in the fridge. "At least, not during this first round of calls. It'll come up eventually, though."

"Sooner than we think," I muttered.

"Now that the French families know, it's only a matter of time."

"And who can guess what fresh hell they'll stir up." I folded the paper with Guru Bob's notes, tore it neatly in half, and handed Derek one of the sheets. "Here are your names. I guess we should get started."

"All right. I'll make my calls in the office." He studied my face. "Something's bothering you."

He knew me too well. I held up the paper with the list of names. "I'm concerned that one of these guys on the list will try to turn the story into another Robson Benedict exposé."

"You still feel the need to protect him."

"I do," I said, unsure how to explain my feelings. "He's . . . vulnerable. It's because he has so many followers and they're all thriving up here. People can be weird about that. It's as if they don't approve of all this positivity. They don't understand it."

"I see your point. He'd be a good target for some unscrupulous reporter."

"It's happened before," I said. "Every few years, some reporter will get a bug up his butt to do an in-depth story on the Fellowship. They rehash old newspaper articles and conflate us with other so-called spiritual groups that have been in trouble with the law. They attack his character and refer to Dharma as a cult." I glared at Derek. "You must know how ridiculous that is."

"Of course I do."

I sighed. "Of course you do."

He pulled me up out of my chair and wrapped his arms around me. "We can't worry about things that might not happen. As long as we're prepared to tell the truth about what we saw, how we found the body, and then direct any other questions to the sheriff's office, we'll get through this with little or no fuss."

"No fuss, no worries."

"That is to be our mantra," he said, planting a soft kiss on my forehead. "I'm hopeful we can handle most of these phone inquiries within the next few days, but some of the reporters are going to want to come up here for interviews. Let's try to put them off until next weekend."

"They'll want to come sooner," I said, sitting back at the table.

"We have a perfectly legitimate reason to hold them off. This is a spiritual community, and the members aren't available at the spur of the moment."

"True enough. We should arrange to have them all come here at the same time and do a press conference. Say, at two o'clock next Saturday afternoon."

"It might be better to do it the following Tuesday or Wednesday instead. It's so busy here on the weekends. We don't want to draw more of a crowd than we can handle."

"Good thinking. I'd hate to draw a huge crowd of bystanders while we're talking about the caves and the body and all that."

"Exactly. Now, how do you feel about telling the reporters a small white lie? We can be vague about it, but we'll let them know that, say, a week from Wednesday at two o'clock is the first time the commune members will be available to talk."

"That's a long time from now."

"I think we'll need the time to prepare for this."

"You're probably right. It's not like I've ever given a press conference before." I wrote down the time and date, but then stopped. "There's nothing to keep them from coming up to the winery anytime they want to."

"They're welcome to do so, but they won't get the information they need for their stories until Wednesday at two o'clock."

"Okay. And just in case, I'll have Mom spread the word that nobody should talk to reporters until the official press conference a week from Wednesday." I stared across the table at him. "Are you okay with spending more time up here than you thought you would?"

"That's the best thing about being the boss," he said, grinning. "I can do what I want most of the time. The office won't be overly busy this week, so I should be able to handle things by phone. I'll work a few hours each morning and check in every afternoon."

"I don't want you to feel obligated."

"Darling." He reached across and squeezed my hand. "This is important to me, too."

"Thank you."

"And if something comes up that I can't handle by phone, I'll simply drive into the city for a few hours."

"Okay, then I won't worry about you, either."

"Please don't," he said. "I promise I won't let myself fire me."

I smiled at that. He picked up his list of names and went off to the office while I sat back down at the table to make the calls.

Forty minutes later, I was just finishing up my last call when he came back and joined me at the table.

"How did you do?" I asked after disconnecting the call.

"I spoke with eight of the people on my list. A few of them weren't happy about waiting so long, but they'll all be here a week from Wednesday. I left messages with the other four to call me back. How about you?"

"I'm waiting on two callbacks. Everyone else was willing to go along with our time frame, especially when I suggested that they could contact the sheriff's department for more information in the meantime. It was almost too easy."

"That can't be good," he said, looking amused.

"I know. Something's bound to go wrong."

I had followed Derek's advice, explaining to each reporter that Dharma was a private spiritual community and that nobody would be available to talk to them until the agreed time. It may have been a white lie, but I didn't care. It would give us some bit of control over the proceedings.

For a number of hours over the next two days, I hid myself away inside the cave and finally managed to finish my inventory. I was indebted to Gabriel and Derek, who fashioned a light tree in each of the chambers. So my eyesight was saved, and in the end, I had a list of several hundred items. I had no idea how many families might've entrusted their precious items to Guru Bob's grandfather, but I hoped they would be happy to get them back.

Altogether I counted twenty-two pairs of silver candlesticks of various sizes and shapes; six more elaborate candelabra sets (I considered them candelabra if they held at least four candles each), two of which featured golden winged cherubs at the base; fourteen marble or bronze busts of various people, including Voltaire, Victor Hugo, two of Cardinal Richelieu, several of other unnamed French dignitaries, and four anonymous beautiful women. There was also a bust of Benjamin Franklin, who apparently was adored by the French, along with an elaborate marble bust of Louis XIV. I knew which Louis it was only because it was engraved on a plaque below the statue.

There were seven pieces of large, expensive furniture, including three dressers with mirrors, the large wardrobe that had blocked the passageway into the deeper cave, an escritoire, and the whimsical rococo-style vanity table with tufted chair and mirror that had belonged to Trudy's childhood friend Nanette. There

were also several smaller tables fancy enough that some
families must have worried that they might be taken by
the Nazis.

In total, there were twenty-seven pieces of fine artwork, ten smaller works still in frames, including the
Botticelli *Virgin and Child*, and the rest rolled up, most
notably, the Renoir-like café scene and the excellent
portrait of the Grenier family that Trudy had identified
on her first visit to the caves.

There were thirty-two assorted animal sculptures
small enough to fit in my hand. These included horses
and birds and a puppy. I counted Trudy's quail in this
group. I listed ten more small sculptures of various sub-
jects: three sets of lovers sculpted in marble; five bronze
angels; and the discus thrower and weeping woman I'd
noticed the first time I stepped inside the cave.

I found forty-one finely bound books, most of them
written in French. I hadn't been able to study the books
before, but once I was alone in the cave for those long
hours, I took the opportunity to thoroughly check them
out. One of the villagers must have been a devotee of the
poet Rainer Maria Rilke because there were beautiful
first edition copies of *Letters to a Young Poet* and the
Duino Elegies. There was also a remarkable rare copy
of *Alice's Adventures in Wonderland*, or rather, *Aven-
tures d'Alice au pays des Merveilles*. It had a striking
bright blue cloth cover with gilded images of Alice on
the front cover and the Cheshire cat on the back. The
book had been translated into French in 1869, and it
made me smile to think of the poor translator trying to
convert all of the wonderfully illogical conversations that
were scattered throughout the book.

The other books included French classics by Victor
Hugo, Gustave Flaubert, and several by Alexandre
Dumas. All of them were in good condition and some
were even excellent. I estimated the value of the collection
of books at about two hundred thousand dollars, but that
was just off the top of my head. And that wasn't including

the fourteen family Bibles, which all had thick leather bindings and elaborate family histories written within their pages.

Among the silver pieces were four complete silver tea sets and eight silver water pitchers. There were three Sèvres urns and six Meissen figurines. Within the eight jewelry boxes I found twenty-four pieces of expensive jewelry, including six diamond rings; three simple necklaces with diamond pendants; one lovely emerald and gold necklace; three red-jeweled necklaces (these were ruby or carnelian or garnet; I couldn't say for sure), two with silver settings and one with gold; four assorted diamond bracelets; six silver bracelets; and one art-deco-style chinoiserie enamel bracelet with a gold setting.

When I arrived home, I added all of these to the growing list on my computer, then printed out two copies. And then hoped that my items matched those on the French families' lists, because if there were any discrepancies on my part, I was afraid there might be an open revolt on Frenchman's Hill.

I'd honestly thought that by controlling the time, place, and circumstances of the press conference, we'd be able to skate easily through the next week or so. But I was sadly mistaken.

By the following Tuesday, word of the treasures in the caves had spread across the world. We had no idea who had started the rumors—I suspected our friends at the sheriff's department gave the information to any reporters who happened to call, or perhaps Henri had followed through on his threat to contact the local newspaper— but Guru Bob reported that he'd received inquiries from several more Bay Area television stations, six Southern California newspapers, and another four reporters from the East Coast. Online news magazines were clamoring for photos and interviews. Two Los Angeles–based entertainment channels were sending camera crews up to film around Dharma and the winery. They agreed to be here for our Wednesday afternoon session.

I figured Derek and I could handle the press and the rumors, but when Guru Bob received the telephone call from the current mayor of La Croix Saint-Just, he insisted it was time for us to regroup and summoned us to his hilltop home for a meeting. The most recent calls from reporters had nothing to do with the body in the cave. It was all about the expensive heirlooms. Poor Mr. Renaud, forgotten for seventy years, was again being ignored in favor of the alluring treasure trove.

Robson greeted Gabriel, Derek, and me at the front door and led the way into his beautiful sitting room with the wide bay-window view of the hills and vineyards of Dharma. After serving us coffee and allowing us to get comfortable, he hit us with the news. "The mayor called to let me know that he is representing the families who still remain in the village. He warned me that a few of the citizens are discussing reparations."

"That's hostile," I muttered. "Maybe they've been contacted by Henri."

Guru Bob shrugged. "They are unhappy."

"That's not your fault! You're not the one they should be threatening."

Guru Bob reached over and patted my arm. "Your fierceness is one of my secret weapons, Brooklyn."

"Sorry, but it burns me up to hear people blaming you."

"What do they think they'll get in terms of compensation?" Gabriel wondered aloud.

"I doubt it will come to that," Robson said. "The mayor was very accommodating, despite the veiled threat he issued at the beginning of our conversation. He will e-mail us a list of the items belonging to each of the village families. Everyone will get back what is owed to them."

"Good," I said. "The sooner everything is distributed, the better."

"The mayor might've calmed down," Derek said, "but the families may still feel affronted. Have you contacted your lawyers?"

"In an abundance of caution, I have. They are researching the matter."

"It's blackmail," I grumbled.

Derek gave a subtle nod of agreement. "The lists of lost items from the mayor and from the Frenchman's Hill families will have to be compared and contrasted with Brooklyn's inventory. There may be some unclaimed items. We should come up with a plan for all of it."

Guru Bob aimed his gaze at me. "Brooklyn's inventory?"

"Yes," I said, trying not to squirm. "I thought it was important to write down everything we found in the caves. Once we get the families' lists, we can do that comparison Derek mentioned."

"That is wonderful," Robson said. "Thank you, Brooklyn."

I smiled. "I figured I might as well put my list-making obsession to good use."

Derek exchanged a subtle glance with Robson. "She's quite organized. It extends to everything in the house, right down to the spice cupboard."

"Despite a deep-seated inability to cook," I said, and shrugged.

Guru Bob beamed at me. "All things in good time."

Derek was desperately trying to hide his smile as he quickly changed the subject. "I think we should consider hiring expert appraisers, maybe from one of the auction houses, in case there are any discrepancies to deal with. They'll be able to trace the provenance of some of these items if there are disputes."

"That's a good idea." I stood to pace since I could think better on my feet. "What if some of the families have died off? Or maybe one of them came by something illegally. I mean, there are some priceless heirlooms in that cave. I've already done a preliminary examination of the books and they alone are worth a few hundred thousand dollars, just at first glance."

Derek nodded thoughtfully. "I still wonder how these families from a small French village came into possession of some of those works of art."

"Trudy said that one of her young friends claimed that her father was descended from Louis the Fourteenth and that's how the family owned one of their dressers. A reputable auction house would be able to prove it one way or another." I frowned. "The Botticelli is a complete mystery to me."

"I share many of those same concerns," Robson said, glancing from Derek to me. He took a sip of coffee and set the cup down slowly. "So this morning I contacted an art appraiser with whom I have worked in the past. He will be here next Monday and will require access to the caves."

"I'll be happy to give him the guided tour," Derek said. "Unless you'd rather do it."

"I prefer to have you do it, if you would not mind. I think it best if I avoid entering the cave unless accompanied by some of our own people."

I bristled at the implication: that others would think Guru Bob wasn't to be trusted.

He smiled at me as if he knew what I was thinking—which he probably did. "I will arrange to have Mr. Garrity meet me at the outer door of the storage-cave entrance, where I will introduce him to you."

"Sounds good." They decided on a time, and Derek typed it into his phone calendar.

I knew that the art appraiser wouldn't be the only one demanding access to the artwork. "Have you considered moving everything out of the caves and into a more accessible space? It would have to be secured, of course."

"It is a good question." Robson turned to Gabriel. "You are the security expert. What do you think?"

Gabriel considered for a few seconds before shaking

his head. "We're better off leaving everything in the caves. There's only one way in and out so it's easier to guard. I've got the entire area locked up and fortified with more security than any bank in town."

"That's true enough," I said. "Never mind my question. It was just a momentary thought."

"I appreciate hearing any momentary thoughts you may have," Robson said, making me smile.

Derek tapped his fingers on the arm of his chair, a sure sign that his brain was moving ahead at lightning speed. "What would you say to the idea of taking a number of photographs of the artwork, blowing them up to poster size, and displaying them in the town hall?"

I thought about it for a moment. "But why display photographs of the items rather than wait for folks to give us a description of their possessions? Wouldn't that give someone a chance to claim an item that wasn't theirs?"

Derek shifted in his chair, crossing one leg over the other. "One reason to do so is to prove to the Frenchmen that we're being completely transparent about the treasured items we found. Essentially, we're telling the world about the discovery we made. And by the time the exhibit begins, we will have received all of their lists of lost items, so I don't think we'll run into a problem with cheating or larceny."

"I guess you're right," I said after considering his explanation. "And since reporters will be spreading the word around the country anyway, we could have something concrete to show people who come up here hoping to get a look at the caves and the treasure."

"I can guarantee those reporters will not be allowed to set foot inside the caves," Gabriel said.

I nodded. "Good."

"It would also help us get out in front of the story," Derek said. "We could advertise the exhibit from here to the Bay Area and give it an intriguing name to draw more attention to it."

"Something like The Hidden Treasures of La Croix Saint-Just? And then a subtitle with something to do with escaping the Nazis during the Second World War."

"Excellent, darling," Derek said with a grin.

"I'm not sure why, but I'm starting to love this idea." I gazed fondly at Derek. "I had no idea you had such PR and marketing savvy."

"Hidden depths," he said with a humble shrug, making me laugh.

My smile faded. "The only problem is that it's sure to attract a lot of looky-loos to Dharma."

He flashed a wry grin. "Looky-loos earn their name because they look with no intention of buying. But that won't happen in this case. Anyone driving all the way up to Dharma to see the exhibit will wind up spending the day here. They'll tour the poster display and follow it up with a visit to the winery."

"And they'll shop and have lunch on the Lane," I added. "What do you think, Robson?"

He had been listening to us toss ideas back and forth. Now he said, "There must be a greater purpose to the exhibit."

"There is," Derek said, all seriousness now. "This is how we publicly demonstrate full disclosure. The French families think we're hiding something from them, but we're not. We'll take pictures of everything exactly as we found it, including the caves themselves."

"And it'll be educational and historical, too," I added.

"All right," Robson said after a moment of consideration. "And once we have received the families' lists of belongings, I would like them to be given a tour of the caves. It is only fair that they see things as we found them."

Derek nodded. "I'll call Monsieur Cloutier to make sure, but I'm confident we'll have their lists in hand within another day or two and can schedule a tour this weekend."

"The sooner, the better," Robson said, warming up to the idea. "It is most important that we relieve the families' apprehension. That is my biggest concern."

"All of this will help address that," Derek said with conviction.

I turned to Derek. "I thought of another issue. What if the families balk at the idea of having their personal items photographed for the exhibit?"

He pondered that one. "I considered that, too, but I don't believe it's for them to decide. We're documenting a moment in history. We found this cache on winery property and are detailing it for posterity." He turned to Robson. "Do you agree?"

"I do."

"Then all that's left to do is iron out a few more details," I said. "Would you like me to organize things, or would you rather appoint someone else to do it?"

"You are my number one choice, Brooklyn dear," Robson said with a grin.

"Lucky me," I said, smiling back at him. "Do you want us to check in with you on each aspect, or shall we just run with it?"

"I trust you to do everything to perfection."

Now I laughed out loud. "We'll see how that works out."

As we gathered our things and stood to leave, Derek said, "Can you give us a bit more information about this art appraiser?"

"His name is Noland Garrity," Robson said, walking with us down the wide hall toward the front door. "I will be sure to let him know that the books are to be appraised by Brooklyn."

"Oh," I said, touched by his words. "Thank you, Robson. I'll wait to see if any of them are left behind once the families have claimed their possessions."

"So what's this appraiser guy like?" Gabriel asked.

Robson gave a mild shrug. "A curmudgeonly sort, but he is very good and very discreet. He worked for many years at Sotheby's auction house in New York and Christie's in Beverly Hills. Now he is a freelance appraiser and author."

"Sounds legitimate," Derek said. "I presume it won't be necessary to run his name through Interpol?"

Guru Bob chuckled. "No. He is quite reputable."

I watched Derek's nonreaction as he reached for the doorknob, and I knew without a doubt that he would run Garrity's name through Interpol anyway. Because that was how he rolled.

I spent the drive home making notes as Derek and I discussed everything involved in pulling this crazy idea together.

"We can get a bunch of dramatic statements from people who've been inside the caves," I said. "We've got you and Trudy, my mom and dad, and Robin and my brothers. Oh, and Stan, from the excavation company. He can talk about it from his own point of view and make it sound like an adventure." I grew more excited as I wrote down the names.

"Are you comfortable delegating some of the tasks to others?"

"Oh yeah. I think I'll ask my mom to be in charge of gathering everyone's stories. We can write them out on cards and post them on the walls along with the photographs. Like they do in art museums."

"Good idea," Derek said as he braked for the traffic light before turning onto Shakespeare Lane. "Trudy can give a historical perspective, telling how her family escaped the Nazis and traveled here. And if any of the French folks are interested in contributing, they can each tell their own personal story."

I gazed at him. "Can we pull this all together before next Wednesday when the reporters show up?"

"Why not?"

I stared at him. "Yes. Why not?" Glancing down at my list, I wondered aloud, "Will the reporters be satisfied with photographs instead of being given a tour of the caves?"

"They'll have to be, since they won't be allowed inside the caves under any circumstances."

"Good," I said. "Because letting them go inside would be a really bad idea."

"If we entertain them well enough, they'll go away satisfied."

"Entertain them?" I stared at my list. "Do you think we need music at the town hall?"

"If you'd like," he said, "but I was referring to someone giving a guided tour of the exhibit. Someone with a lot of enthusiasm."

"A docent or two?"

"Trudy would enjoy doing that, I think."

I grinned. "She would be perfect. And so would you."

"Me?" He did a double take, looking at me as if I'd grown a second head. "Absolutely not."

"But they'll love you. It's the British accent. We Yanks are suckers for it."

He rolled his eyes. "No." The light turned green, and he proceeded slowly through the intersection.

I wrote his name down. "You'll be great."

"No."

"Oh, I just realized that Robin can take the pictures. She's a fantastic photographer."

"She does have a wonderful aesthetic style," he agreed.

"I'll contact her." I added it to my list. I was going to be busy for the next few days, but I wouldn't be alone. I planned to call every member of my family and everyone else I knew in Dharma to help me out. With barely one week to pull this together, I would need all the help I could get.

Late the next morning, Trudy answered the door seconds after Mom rang the bell. "Becky and Brooklyn. What a nice surprise."

"I hope you don't mind us dropping in," Mom said. "But we were in the neighborhood, and I thought, let's see if Trudy is home."

"I love spontaneity. And to tell the truth, I'm happy to see you because you've saved me a phone call." She swung the door wide open, allowing us room to come inside. "Amelia, look who's here."

If the horrified expression on the woman's face was any indication, Amelia didn't share Trudy's love of spontaneity.

"I suppose they'll want tea or something," Amelia muttered as she stomped off to the kitchen.

"That would be lovely, thank you, Amelia," Trudy called. She turned and smiled at us. "It's as if she reads my mind."

"She must be such a joy to live with," I said, biting my tongue. It's not that I enjoyed antagonizing Amelia, but her sour reaction made our impulsive visit even sweeter.

In truth, our visit wasn't impulsive at all. I wanted to see the matching bookend that Trudy had told us about the other day in the cave. Mom had agreed to be my partner in crime—well, not crime, so much as equivocation— and we had memorized our lines well.

Two hours earlier, Derek and I had accompanied my mother into the caves to watch her perform her sacred cleansing ceremony. My ears were still ringing from her enthusiastic whoops, and I could still smell the white sage smoke in my hair. Mom had outdone herself, invoking the cave goddesses to keep the place safe. I firmly believed that the cave would last another thousand years with or without Mom's help, but it couldn't hurt to add some extra insurance. Mom was, after all, the powerful Grand Raven Mistress of the Celtic Goddess Coven of greater Sonoma County. She was not to be messed with.

After the ceremony, Derek drove off in the opposite direction to meet with Monsieur Cloutier to arrange a tour of the caves for any of his community who wanted to participate.

Now Trudy led the way into the living room, and we sat around the coffee table. There was an open storage box on the table filled with photos and letters and memorabilia.

"Did we catch you at a bad time?" Mom asked.

"Oh no," Trudy said, waving her hand breezily. "I've just been going through some of my aunt Marie's old letters and photos."

"Oh, your aunt Marie is Robson's grandmother," I said, then realized I was stating the obvious. But now I was even more interested in seeing some of those letters.

"That's right," Trudy said. "She gave this box to me years ago, mainly because so many of these letters were from my mother."

"That was thoughtful of her," Mom said.

"She was a sweet lady," she said.

"What was your mother's name?" I asked.

"Camille." She smiled fondly. "I've always loved that name."

"It's a charming name," Mom said.

"Yes." Trudy sighed. "After touring the caves the other day, I was feeling sentimental about my family, so I pulled these out to read and reminisce."

"What a good idea." Mom smiled as she glanced inside the box and lifted a short stack of letters wrapped with a faded blue ribbon. She held it close to her nose and sniffed. "Oh, Brooklyn, look at this wonderful old paper."

To an outsider, it probably looked odd to be sniffing a bunch of letters, but my mom knew and appreciated that I was addicted to anything having to do with old paper and books—the look of it, the feel of leather and paper in my hands, the smells. I took the stack of letters from my mother, ran my fingers across the surface of the paper, and felt its thickness. Then I took a deep breath, absorbing its scent. "Oh, I love it. So musty and evocative of a time long ago. And this is a beautiful, high-quality paper."

"Isn't it?" Trudy said.

"Oh gosh, I'm being presumptuous." I'd just invaded

her home and helped myself to her mother's precious letters. "I'm sorry, Trudy."

But Trudy was fascinated. "Not at all. I never thought about it, but of course you would appreciate old paper. Please look at anything that strikes your fancy."

But I returned the stack of beribboned letters to their place inside the box and sat down again. "People really knew how to write letters back in the day."

"They did," Trudy said. "My mother's letters are pages and pages long. She turned every little trip on the train into an adventure filled with funny events and news and odd tidbits. I can hear her voice as I'm reading."

"That's the true gift of letter writing," Mom said.

Trudy held up a faded pink envelope. "I was just trying to read this one when you knocked on the door. It's from Aunt Marie to my mother, but it's in a language I can't figure out."

"It's not written in French?" I asked.

"No." Trudy chuckled. "I have a feeling it's some sort of hybrid language the two of them made up when they were in school. They were girlfriends from a very early age and attended a convent school near Limoges. For hundreds of years, the nuns taught the ancient languages, Latin, Medieval French, Coptic, some sort of ancient Hebrew, among others."

"That must've been challenging."

"You would think so, but according to my mother, the students used to take it in stride. My mother and aunt would use a combination of those languages in their letters to each other so nobody else could understand what they wrote."

I smiled. "Little girls like to keep their secrets."

"Most definitely." She handed the pink envelope to me. "You might find this one interesting, Brooklyn. Not the letter itself, but the paper is unlike anything else in the box."

I looked at the envelope and frowned. "There's a stamp but no address written on it."

Trudy looked mildly concerned. "Oh, I didn't realize. . . ."

"It's probably explainable," I murmured. "She might've slipped another letter inside a new envelope." I rubbed the notepaper between my thumb and forefinger. The finish felt like satin, and I wondered where it had originated. I looked more closely and could make out part of a watermark. "May I take this with me for a day or two? I would love to track down this papermaker."

"Certainly." She nodded eagerly. "You've stirred my curiosity."

"Yes. Mine, too." I slipped the letter into my purse, knowing this wasn't the time to delve into its secrets. But now I was anxious to study it and hoped I could grab some time tonight before or after dinner. My friends and family were used to my getting geeky over things like this.

"Oh," Trudy said, suddenly remembering. "I was going to call you later today."

"That's right. You said something when we first arrived."

Trudy reached for a smaller piece of paper on the side table. "I have a favor to ask you, if you don't mind."

"Not at all," I said.

She hesitated as Amelia toddled in at that moment with a tray holding a small pot of tea and several mugs. Setting it down on the coffee table, Amelia made a show of rubbing her nose and glaring at Trudy's box of letters. "So much dust," she muttered.

I glanced at the tray and noticed there were no cookies being served. This time, though, Amelia was nice enough to pour the tea into our cups and pass them around. I thanked her profusely, and she gave me a glower that was meant to make me cower. Instead, I smiled and winked at her. She huffed and puffed and stomped off to the kitchen.

What were we talking about? I had to think for a minute. "Sorry, Trudy. You had a favor to ask?"

"Yes." She waved the piece of paper she'd been

holding. "I received a phone call this morning from the granddaughter of an old friend. She told me the oddest thing. She read a brief story in her local newspaper about the treasure in the caves. It reminded her that I live in the area, and she asked if I would like to have a visitor for a week. Of course I was delighted to say yes."

"That'll be fun for you," Mom said.

"Won't it? After we finished our phone call, she sent me the sweetest e-mail." She waved the piece of paper again, and I assumed it was the e-mail from the girl. "She's a darling thing, but I'm concerned that she'll be bored staying here. I'm not as spry as I used to be, and I think she might appreciate meeting some people closer to her own age."

"Why would she be bored?" I said. "You're wonderful company."

"Aren't you a dear." Trudy sighed. "But she's so much younger than me. She's closer to your age, Brooklyn, and I was hoping you'd be willing to take her to lunch one day while she's here. And if the two of you get along, perhaps some evening you and Derek can take her out and introduce her to some more friends. I would pay for your meals, of course."

"Don't be silly," I said. "I'll be happy to meet her for lunch." I didn't mention how ridiculously busy I'd been lately because I figured I still had to eat lunch, right? So why not do a favor for Trudy and by extension, Guru Bob?

"When does she arrive?" Mom asked.

"Next week, on Wednesday."

I tried to visualize my calendar. Wednesday was our big press conference with all the reporters. "I'll come by on Thursday and take her to lunch, if that works for you."

"It's perfect. I'm so grateful."

"It's no problem at all," I said.

"What's her name, Trudy?" Mom asked.

"Elizabeth Trent."

"Elizabeth is one of my favorite names," Mom said fondly. "A classical, solid name for a woman."

Her comment was interesting, considering she'd named her girls Brooklyn, Savannah, China, and London, after the cities in which we were conceived or born. But I wasn't about to bust her chops in front of Trudy. I'd save it for the drive home.

Trudy handed the e-mail to Mom to read, while I glanced around the room, trying to be nonchalant. I couldn't see the sculpture anywhere, but there were so many objects on every available surface, including several small shelves affixed to the walls that held fancy commemorative teacups and such. I turned in my chair to search again, scanning the shelves on either side of the fireplace and the mantel. And there it was! The marble piece I'd been hoping to see.

Now that Trudy had rediscovered the missing twin bookend, she had cleared a minuscule section in the middle of the mantel, slightly hidden behind a cloisonné vase, to show off the creamy white bookends. Between them they held a small collection of nicely bound books.

"Oh, I just noticed your bookends!" I said, my voice rising two octaves. Did that make me sound a little phony? Probably, but Trudy was too polite to say anything. "May I see them?"

"Of course," Trudy said. "Pick them up and hold them. They love being touched."

I smiled at her words because it was the same way I felt about books. I crossed the room and stared at the twin pieces.

"Don't they look wonderful together?"

"They do," I murmured, and carefully lifted the piece that had been carved into a kitten. Its lighthearted features and frisky front paws were fully formed and ready to strut away from the block of marble. But its little back paws and tail were still encased in marble, their outlines carved in bas-relief.

"This is delightful," I said.

"I love them so much," Trudy said, and her eyes glazed in reminiscence. "My father had no choice but to give me the set because I refused to leave it alone. I always had them in my room."

"I don't blame you."

Mom set Elizabeth's letter down on the table. "Your friend's granddaughter sounds like a wonderful, thoughtful girl. I hope I'll have a chance to meet her while she's here."

While Mom chatted with Trudy, I pulled my phone out of my pocket and surreptitiously snapped a photo of the marble kitten to show Derek later. I doubted the sculptures had been created by Rodin, simply because the subject matter was so lighthearted, but I had no doubt that they were worth a lot more than Trudy thought they were. Glancing around, I'd bet there were a lot of things in this room that were worth more than she thought. It was just hard to tell because of the overwhelming amount of stuff on display.

My shoulders stiffened all of a sudden, and I glanced up to see Amelia watching me from the kitchen doorway. Her eyes were narrowed and suspicious. Was she going to snitch on me and tell Trudy I'd snapped a picture? I smiled and waved, but inside, I felt the temperature plummeting. Rubbing my arms, I wondered what was wrong with that woman.

A sudden image flashed through my mind of Henri the angry Frenchman threatening Guru Bob the other day. He had mentioned Guru Bob's family in his threats, and that meant Trudy. Did Henri know her? They lived within a few miles of each other. It would be easy enough to find out where she lived. Would Henri consider hurting her or stealing from her?

While I was still feeling the biting chill of Amelia's stare, another thought occurred to me. Did Henri know Amelia? What were the chances of those two ever meeting? Was that what Henri had implied when he mentioned getting closer to Guru Bob's family? Would he use Trudy's companion to gain access to Trudy's expensive art objects? What did we know about Amelia, after all?

My mind was spinning, and I forced myself to brush the thoughts away. Just because Amelia was unpleasant didn't mean she hung out with all the other people I considered equally hostile. It wasn't as if they met weekly at the local Cranky People's Club, right? At least, I hoped not. Besides, Amelia seemed completely devoted to Trudy.

I glanced around, trying to be subtle as I checked to see if the windows were wired or if a security company decal was visible anywhere. Did Trudy have an alarm system? I couldn't tell and this wasn't the time to ask her, but as soon as I got to my car, I planned to call Gabriel to find out.

Chapter 8

"Trudy's house isn't part of the Dharma security grid," Gabriel told me.

Security grid? I wasn't exactly sure what he was talking about. "So she doesn't have any kind of alarm system set up?"

"Not that I know of. Is there a problem?"

"I'm worried about her," I said. "She has some valuable things in her house, but mostly I'm nervous about her safety after hearing what that hothead Henri said the other day."

"He did threaten Robson's family," Gabriel conceded, "but at the time I thought he was just blowing off steam. Maybe not, though."

"If he's pushed to the limit and makes good on his threats, he'll come after Trudy. Robson doesn't have any other relatives around here that I know of."

"I'll talk to him. After everything that's gone down lately, he'll want Trudy's home to be secured."

"Thank you," I said, relieved.

"You got it, babe."

A moment later, we hung up and I started the car. I glanced at Mom, sitting in the passenger seat. "I have a question. What's with Amelia?"

Mom sighed. "I know she's odd, but she's very devoted to Trudy."

"Do you know the story? How did they meet?"

"They met in the hospital when she was laid up with a broken leg."

"Okay, so Trudy needed help getting around on crutches, so she hired her. That's understandable, I guess."

"No, sweetie," Mom said. "Amelia was the one with the broken leg. Trudy offered her a place to stay until she was back on her feet."

"Really?" That was a surprise. "So Trudy was the good Samaritan, not the other way around."

"If you know Trudy, it makes sense, doesn't it?"

I nodded. "Trudy is a wonderful, generous person."

"She still volunteers at the hospital. Amelia drops her off and waits for her in the car."

I laughed in surprise. "She just sits outside? She won't go inside and volunteer, too?"

"No."

"She's a piece of work," I said, shaking my head.

"I know it might not be obvious, but Amelia has been very good for Trudy."

"I don't see how. She's just so . . . mean."

"She's fiercely protective."

"You say tomato . . ." I sighed, turning onto the highway. "Have you known Amelia a long time? I don't remember seeing her around town before she moved in with Trudy."

"Amelia was never a member of the Fellowship, if that's what you mean. But then, neither was Trudy. I don't actually know how long Amelia's lived in the area, but I can't remember a time when she wasn't around. She used to run a house-cleaning business with Harmony Byers."

"Harmony Byers? Crystal and Melody's mother?"

"Yes." She saw the look on my face and added, "Harmony's a lot more sedate than her two girls."

"Thank God for that." It was a good thing we were stopped at a light, or my shock might've caused me to run the car into a side ditch. I'd gone to school with Crystal Byers. She and her sister, Melody, were two scary little peas in a pod, to say the least. The *very* least.

"Is Amelia an Ogunite?" I asked, almost afraid to hear the answer. The Byers family belonged to the Church of the True Blood of Ogun, a local religious group whose zealous members lived a few miles away in an area known as the Hollow. Their religion taught them to honor the creative spirit of the earth, but some of their adherents took that credo to a whole new level when it came to living off the land. To put it bluntly, they were gun-toting survivalists likely to shoot first and ask questions later. They were also brazen evangelists who insisted on spreading the message of Ogun to anyone standing within earshot.

If Amelia was an Ogunite, it might explain why she was so hostile to me. I'd run afoul of some church members in the not-too-distant past.

"I think Amelia might've dabbled in church philosophy a bit," Mom said. "Or maybe she just pretended to do it for Harmony's sake. But it didn't take, and I have a feeling that was why the partnership broke up."

"Lucky for Amelia," I muttered. I waited for traffic to clear before turning onto the Lane. "I can't imagine anyone being happy to work with the Byers for any length of time."

"Who can say? It might've been her broken leg that made it impossible for her to clean houses. When Trudy met Amelia in the hospital, I understand she was a pitiful sight. Trudy brought her home, fixed her up, and gave her a job."

"Trudy is a good person," I said again, because especially in this case, it bore repeating.

"Much better than any of us." Mom and I exchanged smiles. The truth was, Mom was also one of the most caring people in the whole world.

"I'll be interested to meet Trudy's friend Elizabeth,"

I said, then remembered Mom's conversation with Trudy. "And speaking of Elizabeth, I hear you like that name. I believe the words you used to describe it were *classical* and *solid*."

Mom's smile was smug. "If you believed me, then so did Trudy."

I frowned as I came to the Stop sign at Vivaldi Way. "So you were just handing her a line?"

"Of course not. We were having a civilized chat. Elizabeth *is* a lovely name. It's just not to my taste. But I was determined to say whatever it took to keep the conversation going so that you could do what you had to do."

I rarely gave my mother marks for subtlety, but once in a while she surprised me. "Good work, Mom."

She flashed me a sly smile. "Just doing my job."

That night, Derek and I enjoyed a quiet dinner outside on the deck with grilled steaks, baked potatoes, and a salad, my favorite meal. Sweet Maggie lounged contentedly at our feet under the table, but we kept Charlie inside the house because I was afraid she'd be the perfect snack for the red hawks that flew over the hills.

I told Derek how Mom and I had dropped in on Trudy, and I described the kitten sculpture I'd seen. "It looks so lifelike, I expected it to start prancing around like Charlie would, frisky and adorable. And it's beautifully sculpted. It may not be a Rodin, but I imagine it's worth a lot of money."

"I'm sorry to say I didn't even notice it the first time we were there," he said. "I'd like to see it."

"I didn't see it that first time, either, probably because her house is jammed with so many baubles and goodies." I gazed at him for a second, then smacked my forehead. "I can't believe I forgot I took a picture."

He chuckled as I jumped up, grabbed my phone, and scanned the photograph. "Here it is. The lighting's not that great, but I think you can get the general idea."

He studied the photograph and slid his fingers across the screen to enlarge it several times. "I'd like to see it in person, but your photo-taking skill is not bad."

"Thank you, considering I took it while Amelia was glaring at me from her kitchen hideout."

He glanced up at me. "Why?"

"She's just weird." I set the phone aside and continued eating dinner. "By the way, I talked to Gabriel about installing a security system at Trudy's house. I'm concerned about Henri's threats."

"She doesn't have an alarm on her house?"

"No, and after looking around again today, I'll bet some of her so-called tchotchkes are more valuable than she realizes. Many of them are old family heirlooms, so she might not have any idea what they originally cost."

He chewed a mouthful of steak as he considered that. "I was thinking that very thing when we were there the other day. But I didn't know her home wasn't hooked into the Dharma grid."

I paused with my fork in midair. "What exactly is the Dharma grid?"

"Robson asked Gabriel to set up a wide-area security system to protect anyone in the commune who felt that their property might be vulnerable. It also covers Robson's home, of course, and the winery, the school, the art museum, and a number of the shops and restaurants on the Lane."

I frowned. "Is this a result of that ugly incident that happened last year?"

He hesitated, but then confessed, "Yes."

"So it's all my fault."

"No, it's not." Derek grabbed hold of my forearm and gently squeezed for reassurance. "It's the fault of those friendly neighbors who turned out to be murdering psychopaths."

"I suppose." I set my fork down. "But I'm the one who brought them into our world."

"I refuse to let you beat yourself up over this," he said firmly. "It was time to raise the level of security around here anyway. The times are changing."

"You can say that again," I muttered. "Gabriel's probably got drones flying by, watching all of us."

"Yes, he does, love." He pointed to the sky. "Be sure to smile."

"Very funny." But the joke did improve my attitude. So did a sip of the full-bodied cabernet we were drinking. After savoring it for a moment, I returned to my baked potato. But then I remembered something else. "Trudy was going through some old letters of her mother's, and I took one of them with me. I want to try to track down the papermaker, but it would be fun if you could translate the contents."

"I can try," he said between bites. "Couldn't Trudy translate it for you?"

"No. She thinks it's some hybrid of schoolgirl medieval French and Latin or something. It was a letter from her aunt to her mother, and they probably wanted to keep the contents a secret."

He smiled. "I'm intrigued. Let me give it a whirl after dinner."

Once we were finished with dinner and dessert—homemade gelato from my sister Savannah's restaurant—I washed the dishes, and Derek put them away. Then I found Trudy's letter and showed it to him.

"The paper's beautiful, isn't it?" I said.

"Yes. Unusually thick. It almost has a satin finish, which seems odd to me because it's so old."

I nodded. "Some old vellum appears satiny to the look and to the touch."

He turned it over a few times, studying it.

"As I said, I'm mainly interested in the paper, but I really hope you can read this language. It would be fun to give Trudy the translation."

He sat down at the kitchen table and pulled the letter

out of the envelope. After one glance at the paper, he held it up to the light instead of reading it. "That's a curious watermark."

"I thought so, too. That's how I'm hoping to trace the source of the paper." The watermark on the letter was hard to discern at first because of the writing that covered the page. But I was able to distinguish it on the back side. It was a row of stylized turtles at various intervals, and every few inches, the word *Charente* appeared.

I had learned to make watermarks while taking classes in papermaking years ago. There were several ways to do it, but the most common was to take thin wire and bend it into the shape you wanted, affix the wire to a drum—these were called dandy rolls and looked like large rolling pins—and roll the drum over the paper. Where the wire hit the paper, it created a slight indentation. You might not be able to see it unless you held it up to the light.

The process was more complicated than that, especially when it came to mass production, but that was the easiest way to explain it.

"Charente," Derek murmured.

"Yes," I said. "It sounds French, doesn't it? I figured it's the name of the paper company that made the stationery. But the design is unusual and artistic enough that it could also be the name of the papermaker himself. Or herself."

Derek glanced up. "It's also the name of a river in southwestern France."

"Is it? Well, maybe that's where they made the paper."

He nodded absently as he studied the page. "Perhaps."

"I want to get a better look at that mark." I jogged back to the bedroom where I had stashed my set of portable bookbinding tools. Pulling out my magnifying glass, I returned to the kitchen and sat down to study the paper more closely.

"I don't recognize the language," Derek said. "There

are a few French prefixes here and there, but they're mixed up with Hebrew symbols and it's all nonsensical. At least to me."

"I'm bummed." There were so few languages he couldn't translate at least partially. "Should I ask Gabriel?"

"Certainly, but I'm not sure he'll have any better luck with it."

I scrutinized the handwriting more closely. "I guess I could ask my bibliophile chat group."

"Good idea," he said. "And describe the watermark to them, too. They always come up with interesting theories."

"That's why I thought of them." I pushed my chair back and stood.

"There is one more thing," he said, looking up at me.

"What's that?"

"The letter wasn't written by a schoolgirl. That is an adult's handwriting."

As Derek watched the late news in the family room surrounded by Maggie and Charlie, I sat alone at the desk in the Quinlans' office with my computer logged onto my online bibliophile chat group. They were in the middle of a chat about foxing, a favorite topic of bookbinders because those pesky brown spots were a perennial problem with old books.

The chat group was full of eclectic and brilliant minds, so after first apologizing for interrupting their conversation, I described the watermark and the quality of the paper and asked if anyone was familiar with it.

"It's most likely French," I added. "And probably made in the nineteen forties or fifties."

I was immediately bombarded with comments, mostly from people thanking me for changing the subject. Nobody liked talking about the heartbreak of foxing, but we couldn't help ourselves.

A few of my online friends were intrigued and promised they'd look into it and get back to me.

To thank them, I mentioned that I'd found a beautiful French edition of *Journey to the Center of the Earth* and regaled them with the childish blood oath I'd discovered on the flyleaf. The chatter picked up, and the conversation veered off into horror stories of books damaged by children.

A while later I was about to sign off but decided to throw them one more question. It wasn't exactly related to bookbinding, I explained to the group, but it was part of the letter I was researching.

I typed out the first paragraph of the letter and then asked, "Does anyone recognize this language? Our current theory is that it's a mashup of several extinct languages, including, possibly, medieval French. I appreciate any help you can give me."

I received six comments, but only one of them was helpful. Claude, a genius of a librarian from Maryland, suggested that the letter might've been written in Chouadit, an extinct Jewish language once spoken in southern France.

"The word *Chouadit* means *Jewish* in the old Judeo-Provençal language of the area," Claude wrote. "There might be some Aramaic thrown in there, too. I won't get your hopes up, but give me a day or two to work on the translation itself, and I'll let you know what I come up with."

I thanked Claude profusely, wished everyone else a good evening, and signed out of the group. I made a quick detour over to Google the word *Charente*. It turned out to be a region near Limoges as well as the name of the river that ran through the area.

Charente was also the name of a small stationery shop in San Francisco. I stared at the screen, imagining Marie Benoit traveling into the city for the day and coming across the shop. For sentimental reasons, she would want to buy a little something in the store, and so she chose a pretty package of stationery.

My imagination could get carried away sometimes.

"You're smiling," Derek said.

"Oh, I didn't realize you were standing there." I rubbed my eyes. I'd been staring at the computer for the past hour.

"I snuck up on you."

"I'm glad. It was time to quit." I shut down the computer. "And yes, I'm happy. I think I've worked out the stationery question, and the people in my chat room are the smartest people in the world. I'm lucky they let me play with them."

"You're not exactly a lightweight yourself," Derek said with a laugh. "Are you ready for bed, love?"

I yawned. "I didn't think I was, but all of a sudden I'm exhausted."

He pulled me up from my chair, and I went willingly.

By Saturday morning, we had received a complete list of heirlooms from every family involved, including those still living in France. I had cross-checked their lists with my inventory and came across at least six discrepancies. Luckily, there were more treasures listed on my inventory than the families had claimed. I figured that some people had died before they'd informed their heirs that they'd given a valuable family keepsake to Anton for safekeeping. Each of the unclaimed items would have to be given extra attention by Noland Garrity.

There were also a few instances where I might've mislabeled something. For instance, one person had listed a set of hammered silver candelabra. I remembered seeing a set of hammered silver candlesticks that held two candles each. Would one of those be considered a candelabra? Technically, I didn't think so, but maybe that was what they'd always called it. It was a small detail, but I wanted to return to the cave to make sure I wasn't mistaken.

Once I'd worked out that inconsistency, I walked over to Mom's house to see how she was coming along with the job of tracking down everyone who'd been inside the cave and getting their personal stories recorded for the upcoming exhibit. She was compiling the stories at that very moment and would be printing them out on heavy card stock. Later, the cards would be mounted on the walls of the exhibit.

She had also lined up volunteers to work in the exhibit room and outside with crowd control. Mom had been putting together events in Dharma for years, and it was pretty obvious from whom I'd inherited my organizational gene.

After talking to Mom, I drove over to the caves to meet Robin, who had agreed to take photographs of some of the most interesting items I'd inventoried inside the cave.

I considered myself the art director and presented my ideas and concepts to Robin, and I expected her to transfer my creative vision to film.

Robin laughed a lot, mostly at me as I tried to give her advice on how to take a picture. She basically considered me a nuisance, but to my credit, I handled the lighting, a piece of cake since Derek and Gabriel had set up the light trees. I borrowed two clamp lights from Austin's garage and readjusted them strategically for each shot. It was hard work, but worth it.

As we drove to her favorite printer in Santa Rosa, I gave Robin due credit. "Your photos are going to turn out absolutely fantastic."

"Thanks. Wait till you see what a great job this printer does."

The next day, we dashed back to Santa Rosa to pick up the poster-sized prints. Robin was right about the printer. The simple posters had been transformed into artwork. Now I was getting excited.

While Mom was herding the volunteers and Robin and I were racing back and forth from Santa Rosa, Derek led the group from Frenchman's Hill into the caves. That night as we ate dinner, I tried to get Derek to share some crazy stories with me, but he insisted there was nothing to tell.

"They were on their best behavior," he said, sounding almost disappointed. "Maybe Felix had a long talk with everyone, and they realized that Robson is not their enemy. They were all gracious and thankful and thrilled to see everything. I felt like a tour guide with a bunch of happy people."

"I'm shocked. Even Henri was well behaved?"

"Perfectly," he admitted after taking a sip of wine. "The most traumatic thing that happened was that some of them broke down in tears. I can't blame them, since there is so much family history and pain involved in all of this."

"And it's all mixed up with the war."

"Exactly. It was quite dramatic, but all good."

"I'm especially glad Henri didn't give you any trouble."

"Not a bit," Derek said. "In fact, they've all promised to come to the winery for the Pre-Harvest celebration next week."

I had to laugh. Basically, wine-country people would dream up almost any excuse to get together and taste wines. The annual Pre-Harvest celebration was Dharma's official kickoff to harvest season, and it was always a fun-filled day of wine tasting, along with loads of great appetizers and munchies brought in by the local chefs, including my sister Savannah.

"That should be interesting," I said. "I wonder if Madame Cloutier could be talked into bringing some of those amazing beignets with her."

"Let me just make a phone call," Derek said with a determined grin.

I beamed at him. "That's my hero."

Monday morning, I arrived at the town hall to find a squadron of volunteers standing by to hang the posters and mount the quote cards that Mom had already designed. The day before, Robin had laid out a structure for the room itself that would give each photograph its own space and lighting. As a professional sculptor, she was used to mounting art exhibits, so within hours, she had all the posters hanging on the walls and on columns around the room.

Another volunteer with some creative ability had designed a program to hand out to visitors. A different group of commune volunteers agreed to work outside with the crowds, giving directions to visitors and handing out the programs. Mom and Robin and Trudy would act as docents, answering questions and telling their own stories of their brief adventures inside the caves.

And I tried really hard, but Derek still refused to play the docent.

I wondered a few times if we were crazy to devote this much time and energy to the town hall exhibit. But the result would show the Frenchmen that Guru Bob was being completely aboveboard, and it would give the visiting reporters something to look at instead of the actual treasures inside the cave. Those were our two main purposes, and I prayed we would be successful. But beyond that, the exhibit would be a wonderful new activity for visitors and locals to experience.

I glanced around and found Robin deeply involved with a few of the more artistic types as they put the final touches to the overall layout and positioning of the posters. I knew I wasn't needed, so I let her know I was going and then rushed off to join Derek at the storage cave, where he was scheduled to meet Guru Bob and Noland Garrity, the appraiser.

While parking the car, I noticed a handsome older man talking to Guru Bob by the rounded doors leading to the storage cave. Derek was there, too, but he was more involved with studying the security box than with the conversation going on next to him. The stranger—I assumed it was Noland Garrity—was tall, just a few inches shorter than Derek and Guru Bob, who were both more than six feet tall. As I approached, I thought it was pretty great to see three tall, handsome men gathered together in one spot.

"Here is Brooklyn," Guru Bob said, sounding relieved to see me. As soon as I was close enough, he introduced me to the appraiser. "Brooklyn Wainwright, this is Noland Garrity. I've hired him to assess the items we found in the cave."

"Hello, Mr. Garrity." The man didn't smile as I shook his hand. In his white polo shirt, khaki trousers, and highly polished brown penny loafers, he was dressed for going to the country club rather than skulking through caves.

Guru Bob added, "Noland, I trust you will benefit from Brooklyn's insight and positive energy."

With that odd statement, Guru Bob bid us good-bye. That was when I noticed Mr. Garrity surreptitiously wiping his hand on his trousers—the hand he'd just used to shake mine.

I won't take it personally, I thought, and turned to watch Guru Bob walking briskly across the parking lot. Where was he off to in such a hurry? On the other hand, it was a good sign that he trusted us with his appraiser, and I smiled at Noland Garrity. "Did Robson describe some of the treasures we found? You won't believe how amazing it is."

"Yeah, that's great. Look, I don't have all day," he said, squinting up at the bright blue sky. "And why is it so damn hot up here?"

I exchanged a puzzled look with Derek. His eyebrow shot up in response. It couldn't be more than seventy degrees outside on this gorgeous fall day. What was Garrity complaining about? Maybe he was just one of those people who always complained and were never really happy. If so, I really hoped his visit would be a short one.

And what was with his brusque attitude? Was he angry about something? Could he be angry at Guru Bob for leaving him here with us? I hoped he would mellow out once he was able to get a look at all the treasures.

Derek turned away from us to lift the cover of the security box and tap a series of numbers on the keypad. When a buzzer sounded, he used his key to unlock the dead bolt on the doors. "Right this way."

Once inside the cool storage cave, Garrity grunted in dismay. "Where are you taking me? It's filthy dirty in here."

Maybe I'd been working too hard lately, because I had little patience for this man. Guru Bob had to have told him that he was going to be inside a wine cave. And, as caves went, this one was pretty much pristine. And well ventilated. I glanced around. Yes, the cement floor was swept clean, and the wine barrels were in a perfectly straight line against the walls. The cavernous space was well lighted. What was he complaining about?

"And what's that awful smell?" he asked, sniffing and looking around.

"That's the smell of expensive red wine," I said, biting my tongue not to add, *And you'll never taste a drop of it, as God is my witness.*

"Good thing I don't drink."

Aha! There was one more reason to hate him. And it was probably the reason why he was so unlikable. After spending less than five minutes with the appraiser, I was pretty sure I knew why Guru Bob had rushed off. What I wanted to know was, why did he hire him in the first place? *Curmudgeonly* didn't begin to describe Noland Garrity.

Derek continued walking to the end of the big room where the excavated hole had been enlarged. I noticed a step stool leading up to the opening and realized that sometime during the last few days, Derek had placed it there to help the people from Frenchman's Hill climb over the eighteen-inch ledge and step down into the chamber.

At the opening, Derek stopped and turned to Garrity. "I hope you're not claustrophobic, because this space we're about to enter is small and the air is a bit stale. I assure you the air is clean, but the space has been sealed up for about seventy years."

Garrity pressed his white handkerchief to his mouth and nose. "I can barely breathe already, and you're saying it'll be worse?"

"Yes, because it's a smaller enclosure. But there's plenty of air. You won't suffocate," he added dryly.

"Is that supposed to be some kind of a joke?"

"Not really," Derek said. "On the positive side, the artwork and furnishings have been sealed up as well, so their condition hasn't deteriorated."

"I'll be the judge of that."

"Indeed," Derek said affably. I didn't know how he managed to stay so upbeat. I was ready to strangle the jerk.

"Here we go," Derek said, and easily stepped over the wall.

"Wait a minute," Garrity said, stopping at the wall. He bent over the low ledge, trying to get a look at where he was about to venture. All of a sudden he began to wobble and couldn't quite right himself. "Whoa."

"Mr. Garrity, are you all right?"

"Uhh . . ."

Was he having a heart attack? I grabbed him by his belt and yanked him back from the cave opening.

He stumbled, then righted himself. It took him a few long seconds to recover his dignity, and, once he did, he gave me a look of pure contempt. "How dare you grab me like that?"

"The way you were moaning and swaying, I thought you were going to pass out."

"Look at my shirt. It's filthy." He slapped the white polo shirt to get the dirt out, but he only made it worse.

And I thought Amelia was crabby. This guy could give her lessons. I couldn't believe I'd thought he was handsome only minutes ago. Just went to show that my mother was right again. *Handsome is as handsome does.* This guy was the poster boy for that old cliché.

On his second try, he managed to make it over the wall and into the chamber. "What in the world?" His voice echoed in the small chamber. "Are there rats? It smells moldy back here."

"No, it doesn't," I said, stepping easily into the space. "It's actually very clean, and there are no rats anywhere. My mother swept every inch of it two days ago. And if you dare say one word about my mother, I will smack you—"

"Darling, Mr. Garrity would never say anything about your mother, now would you, Mr. Garrity?" Derek said, trying to calm me down while subtly warning Garrity to shut his piehole if he didn't have anything nice to say.

Garrity ignored him. "When Robson told me there was a cave, I didn't think I'd actually have to climb into it. He lied to me."

"Robson doesn't lie," Derek said, his tone deceptively mild.

The man lifted one weary shoulder. "Whatever."

I knew Derek was generally more patient than I was, but how could he tolerate this man? My respect and admiration for Derek's tolerance were growing to biblical proportions.

Ignoring the appraiser, Derek maneuvered around the small enclosure, flipping on the set of lights he'd mounted onto the five-foot light tower at the far end of the chamber. I noticed that unlike on the day Robin and I took pictures, the extension cords were tucked safely along the bottom edges of the cave. Derek had been very busy when I wasn't looking.

With the lights illuminating everything, Garrity

couldn't help but glance around. "So this is it? This is what I crawled into a cave to see?"

"There's more to see in the next chamber," Derek said. "The entry is directly behind the wardrobe."

He uttered an expletive. "You can't possibly expect me to drag myself even deeper into this pit. It's filthy. I won't do it."

"That's fine, then," Derek said, his English accent brisk and to the point. Grabbing my hand, he said, "Let's go, darling." We took turns climbing over the wall and back into the larger storage area.

"Where do you think you're going?"

Derek half turned. "We're going home. You've made it quite obvious that you aren't interested in seeing the artwork and objects inside the cave. I'm sure Robson will be happy to take back the check he wrote you."

"For God's sake, I didn't mean it literally."

"Yes, you did," Derek said amiably. "So we're leaving, and I expect you to follow because I'm not leaving you in here alone."

"You don't have to be so sensitive about it."

"I'm not sensitive at all," Derek said in an even tone. "I'm complying with your wishes."

As we walked away, Garrity shouted, "Wait, damn it. Don't be so stupid."

"Don't be so stupid?" I stopped and turned. "What is wrong with you?" My jaw was clenched so tightly, I could barely think straight. "Do you think we have nothing better to do than listen to your whining all day? Honestly, you have done nothing since you got here but complain and make insulting remarks about my friends and family. If you think we're going to put up with that for one more minute, you're as crazy as I think you are."

I stared up at Derek, and he winked at me. Okay, maybe I hadn't been as eloquent as I wanted to be, but I'd meant every word. Could Derek possibly be enjoying this jerk's antics?

"All right, all right. Don't get your panties in a twist." Garrity waved his hand, dismissing me. "If you think it's so important, I'll look at the rest of the cave."

"Hey, you're not doing us any favors. You're the one getting paid to be here."

Derek quickly clutched my arm, knowing I was furious. I'd been taking Krav Maga classes with my neighbor, and I was ready to attack. He was probably smart to hold me back.

"Does this mean you'd like to see what else is in the cave?" Derek asked with a reasonableness that astounded me.

"Fine," Garrity said. "Yes, I want to see what's in the cave. Happy now?"

"That's all you had to say," Derek said, and led the way back to the wall. With great reluctance, I followed behind them both.

Once inside the chamber, Derek said, "Look around all you want."

Garrity was already scanning the items, trying not to look impressed. He pulled out a notebook and began writing. Finally he murmured, "I suppose this is an interesting collection, but it's nothing extraordinary."

"Robson may have explained that—"

"I need complete silence while I work."

"Then why don't you shut up?" I muttered.

He turned and stared at me, affronted. "You've got a mouth on you."

Derek bared his teeth in a semblance of a grin. "She does, as well as a mean left hook. Careful you don't set her off even worse."

Garrity frowned thoughtfully and went back to studying the art objects and making notes.

We were silent for another five minutes until Mr. Garrity said, "This can't be everything."

"No," Derek said patiently. "As I explained earlier, the entry to the second chamber is behind the wardrobe."

Garrity rolled his eyes.

If only Derek had brought his gun with him, I'd shoot the damn fool in the foot. But then he wouldn't be able to walk out of here. No, I would have to shoot him in the arm because there was no way I was going to be stuck dragging this whiner all the way out of the cave.

Who was I kidding? I would never point a gun at a living creature, but this guy was sorely trying my long-held peacenik values.

"It's right this way." Derek continued speaking as if Garrity hadn't said a word. "Follow me."

He slipped easily behind the large piece of furniture and disappeared into the space beyond.

"Wait. Where'd you go?"

"This way," I said, and followed Derek into the darkness. Garrity plodded behind me.

I no longer cared how much Robson admired the man's work. I refused to be nice to this guy. I didn't give a fig how brilliant an appraiser he was. How could Derek stomach the insufferable man? I didn't care if he knew art. I wanted him to go away. But now I couldn't walk out of the cave because I refused to leave Derek alone to deal with him.

Derek had set up another light tree in this space to make it easier to see the details of the artwork and other items.

In the second chamber, Noland's expression finally registered enough awe to satisfy me. When he noticed me watching him, he yawned and shrugged as if suffering from existential ennui. But he couldn't pull it off. The artwork was simply too remarkable.

After a half hour of silent observation and note taking, he turned to Derek. "I'll need complete access to these rooms if I'm to do a competent job of appraising the work. Do I get the key from you?"

"I assure you you'll have complete access." Derek handed him his business card. "Just call my cell anytime you want to look at something and I'll arrange an escort for you."

"An escort?" Garrity let loose a scornful laugh. "No, no. That's not how I work. I'll require the security code and a key to the doors so I can come and go at my own pace."

"I'm afraid that won't be possible," Derek said, and bared his teeth in a rakish smile. "That's not how I work."

Chapter 9

By Wednesday morning, our remarkably professional-looking exhibition of The Hidden Treasures of La Croix Saint-Just was ready to be presented to the world. The subtitle of the exhibit was How One French Village Saved Its Legacy from the Nazis. That gave it a wine-country spin with the added jolt of the Nazi connection.

Within two hours of its opening, there was a line of curious visitors winding out the door and down the steps of the town hall. Mom, Robin, and Trudy, along with their exhibit staff and crowd-control volunteers, were all doing an amazing job.

I stuck around to hear people's reactions, and they were glowing, thank goodness. Everyone was intrigued with the story of the French family shipping their fellow villagers' treasured heirlooms out of the country and escaping the dreaded Nazis in the middle of the night.

At one o'clock, Derek picked me up, and we drove to Dharma's city hall for the big press conference scheduled for two o'clock that afternoon. On the drive over, we discussed our strategy again. Derek was to give a brief introduction, and I would talk about what we'd found in the cave; then we would take their questions. He insisted it would go smoothly, but I was nervous.

We parked in the city hall parking lot and stayed in the car to finish discussing what we would say. Our strategy was simple: tell the truth. Before we took any questions, we would start with the story of how we found the body in the cave and estimate how long the man had been there—omitting the name of the victim, of course. Any questions beyond the basics, even if we knew the answers, would be referred to the sheriff's department.

Next, we would discuss how we'd inadvertently found the second cave—omitting the discovery of the map on the notepaper inside *Journey to the Center of the Earth*. I insisted on this because I didn't want anyone coming after the book. In my experience, people were more than willing to kill over a valuable book. And that reminded me that I hadn't yet gone online to appraise its worth.

Finally, we would suggest to everyone that they attend the Treasures photographic exhibit at the town hall. Because there was no way in hell any of these reporters would be allowed to step one foot inside the cave if Derek had anything to say about it.

"Are you ready for this?" Derek asked.

"Sure. Do you want to embellish anything, or just give them the straight scoop?"

"There's no way you can possibly embellish anything, so please don't try."

"Why can't I embellish things?"

"Because you're a rotten liar."

"Thanks a lot." I smacked him in the arm.

He patted his heart. "I say it with love."

"I know I get a little tongue-tied and turn beet red when I'm dancing around the truth, but this is different. I can pull this off."

"There's nothing to pull off. We simply tell the truth." He quickly added, "But not the whole truth."

I grimaced. "See, this is where I get hung up. What part do we leave out?"

He grabbed my hand and kissed it. "You're scaring me to death."

"Come on. Tell me what *not* to say."

"All right." He sighed. "They already know about

the dead body in the cave, of course, but they don't know that Robson's grandfather was the man's best friend—and we're not going to tell them."

"Right."

"They don't know about the book we found, with the two boys' signatures. They don't know that you found a map in the book that led us to find even more priceless objects. They don't know about Henri threatening Robson."

I nodded. "Right. Got it. Let's do this."

It was Derek's turn to look uneasy. "You should probably wait in the car."

"No way. I'm going to be awesome. Don't worry."

Shaking his head, Derek gazed out the window toward the city hall steps where the members of the press were assembling. "I suppose we ought to get out there."

I leaned forward to get a better look. "It's a bigger crowd than I expected."

"Yes." He pointed to a car parked at the end of the aisle from us. "And someone from the sheriff's department is here, too."

"Good. I'm glad you called them."

He glanced back at me. "Are you ready?"

"As ready as I'll ever be."

He sighed. "If you insist on coming along, just feign laryngitis. I'll do the talking."

I slugged his arm again, and he was smirking as we climbed out of the car to greet the press.

"We'll take a few questions now," Derek said after we'd both presented our stories and descriptions and thoughts about the body and the things we'd seen inside the caves. I'd counted thirty reporters and camera operators while Derek was talking, and they'd been respectfully silent during our presentation. Now they began shouting and waving their arms.

"Can you tell us more about the victim in the cave? How old was he?"

"Does he have a name?"

"Exactly how did he die?"

Derek gave a quick answer to each question, and I referred them to the sheriff's department for further information on the dead man. Derek then pointed to a good-looking young guy in the front row whose arm was raised in the air. "Yes, go ahead."

"Josh Atherton, *Antiquities Magazine*," he said, and smiled brightly at us both. "Thank you, Mr. Stone, Ms. Wainwright. Wow, this has been really fascinating. I wonder, do you have any idea how long ago the cave was sealed up?"

Derek spoke. "Based on the identification found on the victim, we estimate that the cave was sealed approximately seventy years ago."

"A quick follow-up if you don't mind," Atherton rushed to say. "Specifically, what identification did you find?"

"The police found the man's passport," Derek said carefully. "Apparently there was something else found on his body that gave the investigators a more specific date to work with. You'll have to contact them for more information."

More questions were blurted out, and we answered as many of them as we could. I was surprised by how many reporters asked about the murder victim since that information was available in the sheriff's records, which were open to the public.

I was finishing up an answer when a tall woman with spiky red hair interrupted. "Why won't you allow people to go inside the cave?"

Derek stepped to the microphone. "Our excavators and geologists have suggested that until we have completed the work that was interrupted, it's safer to restrict the number of people passing through. Beyond that, the cave is private property and contains many items of great value. Don't you agree it would be foolish to allow free access to the public?"

Many in the crowd shrugged in acquiescence, but I noticed a few reporters scowling, as though they were angry at us for considering them part of the general public.

Josh Atherton raised his hand again, and I pointed to him. "Mr. Atherton."

He beamed at me when I said his name. "Thank you so much. Let me preface my question by explaining that my readers truly enjoy being drawn into another world. So I was hoping you would describe what you felt when you first walked into the cave. I assume it was dark. Were you afraid? Did you notice the smells, the sights, the sounds? Do you recall the temperature?"

"It was musty and dark," I said, recalling the first time I walked into the cave. "At first I was excited and overwhelmed. I wanted to get in there and see everything. And I wasn't alone, so I was sharing the moment with others who were equally excited. But since then, I've gone there by myself, and I must admit, it's eerie. Silent. Cold. I'm reminded that this place was sealed off from the world for decades. Why? To hide a dead body? To protect those beautiful rare objects? I almost feel as though I shouldn't be there. But it's also thrilling, a punishment and a reward. The sublime and the . . ." I chewed on my lip, suddenly aware of my blathering. "Well, it's hard to explain."

"It's a weighty question," Derek said, noting my uneasiness. "Perhaps we'll end it there. Thank you all very much."

"And while you're in Dharma," I added hastily, "do take advantage of the photographic exhibit at the town hall over on Shakespeare Lane. You'll see pictures of the beautiful artwork we're talking about, and they'll answer a lot of your questions."

The crowd broke up slowly. I made eye contact and smiled at Detective Parrish, who was surrounded by reporters. Others stood chatting with one another and comparing notes. Derek signaled to the tech guy who had set up the podium and microphones. "We're done here, Willy. Thanks a lot for your help."

"No worries, man."

Derek grabbed my hand, and we walked quickly back to the car.

"Should we rescue Detective Parrish?" I asked.

He glanced over at the crowd gathered around the woman. "If she needs to talk, she knows where to find us."

"I like her. I feel bad for throwing so many questions her way."

"I like her, too, but this is part of her job. That's why she came here today."

"I guess that's true." I took one more look at the detective. She seemed perfectly calm as she was peppered with queries.

Once seated inside the car, Derek turned to me. "Are you all right? That last question was a bit personal."

"It took me by surprise. I'm still a little dazed."

"I was surprised you answered it."

"I was, too." I buckled my seat belt. "He was so nice, and the question seemed genuine. I'm afraid my answer sounded peculiar. I hope he doesn't write about how bizarre I am."

"It wasn't bizarre; it was honest." Derek started the engine and slid the stick shift into reverse. "Are you familiar with that magazine?"

"*Antiquities?* No. But I'm going to look it up."

"That's my girl."

That night we had reservations at Umbria, our favorite Italian restaurant on the Lane. We arrived early, so Derek waited at the bar while I dashed across the street to say hello to my sister China at Warped, the yarn and weaving shop she owned.

I spotted China with six ladies gathered around the giant loom at the back of the store. She waved but didn't come over, so I figured she was in the middle of a class. I took the time to wander around admiring the beautiful

yarns and threads and designs she had on display. Several
sets of brightly colored place mats were stacked on
a shelf, and a number of intricate wall hangings were
draped along one wall. A dowel hanging from the ceiling
held beautifully crocheted wool scarves. Dozens of balls
of colorful yarns were tossed into baskets and placed
around the shop. I was drawn to a small, fluffy woven
doggy bed on a side shelf and wondered if Charlie the
kitten would like to sleep in something warm and cozy
like that.

My sister was so talented, I thought wistfully. She was
an incredible textiles artist and a beautiful mother. But
then, all of my sisters were talented in one way or another,
and I included myself. Not that I could weave or cook,
but when it came to making or taking apart a book, I
knew what I was doing. Although I had to admit I often
wished I had the talent to cook something more than a
boiled egg. Heck, I even screwed that up sometimes.

But hey, I also had a talent for finding dead bodies,
although that wasn't anything to stand up and cheer
about. I realized I was squeezing a ball of midnight blue
alpaca yarn as if it were a stress toy and quickly dropped
it into a nearby basket.

"Oh, hey. Hi."

I whipped around to see Josh Atherton, the reporter,
standing a few feet behind me. "Oh, hi. It's Josh, right?"

"Yeah," he said. "Wow, I'm thrilled that I ran into you."

I checked to see if China was free yet. "I just stopped
by for a minute."

He glanced around, looking a little awestruck. "This
is such an amazing place. I mean, wow, so many great
colors and patterns. Does the owner make all these
things?"

"Yes, she does."

"Wow," he said again, and I wondered if I was making him nervous. "The stores up here are so full of cool
stuff. Awesome." He turned in a circle, taking it all in,
but then appeared to be embarrassed by his gushing,

if his pink cheeks were anything to go by. "Sorry, I get distracted sometimes."

"I don't mind at all," I said, smiling. "This is my sister's store, and I happen to think it's fabulous."

"Oh." He grinned and gazed around again. "That makes it even cooler."

I chuckled.

He scratched his head, still embarrassed. "Anyway, thank you so much for answering my question earlier. I hope it didn't make you uncomfortable. I could tell you gave a heartfelt response."

"It was honest," I admitted. "But I don't usually bare my soul in public like that."

"I live for those moments." He grinned again, and I noticed he had dimples in his cheeks. He wore a thin, navy cashmere V-neck sweater over a white button-down shirt and blue jeans. His dark blond hair was a bit scruffy, and he wore wire-rimmed glasses. He was ridiculously cute.

He shoved his hands into his pockets. "I would love to set up an appointment to talk to you further. I promise I won't take up too much of your time, but I'd like to write an in-depth story on this discovery."

"I'm not the person to talk to. I can point you toward people who are more connected to the discovery."

"But I can tell you have a real emotional connection to that cave."

I shook my head. "Not really."

He smiled again. "You're being modest, but I understand." He pulled a card from his pocket and handed it to me. "Here's my cell number if you change your mind. I'm staying in the area this week, and I would consider it an honor if you called."

I glanced down at his card, then back at him. "I'll think about it."

"I hope so. Thanks again." He shook my hand heartily and walked out of the store.

"Who was that cutie pie?" my sister whispered.

I whipped around and gave her a hug. "I didn't realize you were finished. How are you?"

"Great. I've missed you. I was wondering when you'd come in to see me."

"I'm sorry I didn't come by sooner, but we've been running around forever, dealing with the cave treasures and getting the exhibit prepared."

She smiled. "You and Derek always cause such excitement when you come to Dharma."

I laughed. "Oh yeah, excitement is one word for it. Look, Derek is waiting for me over at Umbria, but can we get together for lunch sometime this week?"

"Absolutely. I'm dying to tell you about London's latest claim to fame."

"Oh no. Is she having triplets?"

China laughed. Our youngest sister, London, was always doing something that was so much more fabulous than any of us had ever done. For instance, when China's darling baby, Hannah, was born, London used the occasion to announce that she was pregnant with twins. We loved London to death, but we also enjoyed giving her grief.

London, who had been named after London, Ontario, Canada, where my mother went into labor after a Grateful Dead show, never minded our teasing. As the youngest, she was used to it.

Rather than name their children lovely, classic, *solid* names, as my mother had described *Elizabeth's*, my parents had chosen to name us after the cities in which we were either conceived or born. Because my parents had been rabid Grateful Dead fans, most of those cities were places in which the revered band had once performed. The one exception was my sister China, who was born after a protest march at the Naval Air Weapons Station at China Lake, out in the Mojave Desert.

I promised China I would call her in a few days and grabbed her for a hug good-bye, then jogged across the street to Umbria, where I found Derek in the middle of a Primitivo wine flight. Wine flights had been popular for years and were a good way to learn more about the different types of wines. A bar or winery would offer three half glasses of either the same wine from different vintages, or three red wines of varying color or richness, or three of the exact same wine that had been stored in three different types of oak barrels. Places were always coming up with new themes for their wine flights. It was a fun way to figure out how to distinguish one wine from the next.

The last time we'd visited Dharma, my father had been raving about the Primitivo grapes he had planted. They were said to possess the exact same genetic characteristics as Zinfandel, but the wines tended to be different in color, richness, and levels of earthiness. It made sense, of course, given what we already knew about the *terroir*.

Derek stood when he saw me approaching and pulled out a bar stool for me. "Darling, you're just in time to rescue me from this diabolical bartender."

"You poor thing." I sat down and smiled at the man behind the bar. I'd known him for years. "Hi, Lance."

"Hey, Brooklyn. We just added this Primitivo wine flight to our list. Would you like to try it?"

"Not tonight, thanks. I'll just help Derek with his."

I took a sip of the lightest of the three wines in the order. It was an old-vine Zinfandel from a vineyard up in Geyserville. "I like that."

"I thought you would." Lance handed me the second glass. "This is the Primitivo. It's from Abruzzi in Southern Italy."

I held up the glass and admired the color, then took a sip. "This is spicier than the first one."

"I thought so, too."

I took another small sip and savored it. "I'm getting a hint of toasted almond."

"Very good, love. I tasted more vanilla than almond."

"That's the oak you're both tasting," Lance explained. He handed me the third glass. "Here's the Barbera."

I swirled the wine, feeling only slightly pretentious. But since this was wine country, I was hardly alone. "This color is beautiful. It's the deepest of the three."

"As it should be," Derek said.

"This is the kind of wine that stains my teeth."

"We'll only have a sip or two."

I smiled and took that sip and tasted its light, sour-cherry essence. "Strange that it's so dark in color, but light in flavor."

"That's what makes it a perfect everyday wine," Lance said. "Except for the unfortunate teeth-staining part."

After a few more sips of the three wines, our hostess arrived and Derek paid the bar bill. As soon as we were seated at our table, I started to tell Derek about running into Josh Atherton. But before I could get a full sentence out, we were interrupted by our waiter, who approached with two fresh glasses of red wine and set them in front of us.

"We didn't order these," Derek murmured to the waiter.

"From the gentleman and lady over there," he said, pointing.

We turned and saw two of the reporters from our press conference at city hall. They were easy to recognize because they both had red hair and freckles. The man was short and heavy and wore denim overalls with a Hawaiian shirt, while the woman was almost six feet tall and wore a bright yellow jumpsuit with turquoise high-top tennis shoes. She was the spiky redhead who had asked the question about access to the caves. Together they were the oddest, brightest, most interesting-looking couple I'd seen in a while. And for someone living in San Francisco, that was saying a lot.

They were watching us eagerly, and since it was too late to refuse the wine, we smiled and held up our glasses in a toast. The two grinned at each other and came to our table.

"We just wanted to say a quick thank-you," the woman said, extending her hand. "I'm Darlene Smith."

"And I'm Shawn Jones," the man said. We all shook hands.

Darlene grinned. "We have a popular Bay Area news blog called Alias Smith and Jones. Not exactly original, but we've gotten a lot of mileage out of it."

"It's clever," I said. "I've heard of it."

"It's got a pretty good following, if I do say so myself," Shawn said.

"Listen," Darlene said. "We won't take up your time, but we wanted to thank you for recommending the photo exhibit. You were right—it answered a lot of questions. So . . . thanks."

"You're welcome," I said politely. "I'm glad it helped."

"Was that your mother working there?" Shawn asked. "With the blond ponytail? You two look a lot alike. Pretty."

I gave him a questioning look. "I'm not sure . . ."

Darlene rolled her eyes and elbowed Shawn in the ribs. "Dude, you sound like a stalker." She turned back to me. "Don't listen to him. We met a lovely woman named Becky, and she told us her daughter had given a press conference at city hall. We figured it was you."

"Ah." I smiled tightly, wondering what in the world my mother had told them. They were, after all, reporters, and easy to talk to, it seemed. "Yeah, that's my mom."

"She's a kick in the pants," Shawn said, rubbing his side where Darlene's elbow had made contact. "And a real beauty, just saying. She was doing the whole tour guide thing and working in a lot of her own opinions and thoughts about the caves. I wrote it all down. Really great stuff."

"I hope so." But inside I was thinking, *Oh dear, I can't wait for the exposé.*

"We're interrupting your dinner," Darlene said suddenly, nailing her partner with another elbow to the rib cage. "Let's go, Shawn. Just wanted to thank you guys again."

"You're welcome," Derek said. "Thank you for the wine. Very kind of you."

Darlene leaned closer to me and said, "Oh, honey. That voice of his makes me want to swoon." Then she pulled Shawn away and waved over her shoulder. "Great to meet you two!"

Derek and I stared at each other for a full thirty seconds before we could speak again.

No doubt about it, we were going to need more wine.

Chapter 10

By the time I left to meet Trudy's friend Elizabeth for lunch on Thursday, I'd heard from four people who had been approached by Josh Atherton for interviews. According to China, who called me first thing, he was so nice, she couldn't say no.

His questions were good ones, too. More penetrating and insightful than the usual, "What would you do with the treasure?" According to China, most of the reporters had been asking the same litany of questions.

"And Josh is awfully cute," she added. "I was thinking I might set him up with Annie."

Annie, Abraham's once-estranged daughter, had met her father just before he died. A month after that, her mother had passed away from a long illness. Annie had decided to move to Dharma to regroup and start over, thanks to so many of Abraham's friends welcoming her as they would a beloved family member. She moved into Abraham's beautiful home, and, months later, she opened an upscale kitchenware shop on the Lane and business was booming. Annie had made a place for herself here.

"Josh is pretty cute," I agreed. "But don't forget he's a reporter and he's looking for ways to boost his story. I wouldn't get too close to him until the story's been written and published. And frankly, I doubt he'll stick around once that happens."

"Well, he's nice and Annie's lonely, so maybe I'll drop a hint or two."

I smiled as I hung up the phone. China was a much more open, generous person than I was. Of course, I'd seen the seamier side of life and no longer had the ability to openly trust people as she did. And didn't that make me sound like an old warhorse? I hated the thought that living in the city might've made me more cynical than my sisters who'd remained in the wine country.

Talking to China reminded me that I hadn't been over to see Annie at her store yet. It would be easy to drop by after lunch and say hello. I'd already been to the house to use Abraham's workshop this week, so I really needed to make the effort to see her in person and thank her.

China's phone call also reminded me that I wanted to look up Josh's credentials. Especially if he was going to go out with Annie, whom my mother considered an adopted daughter. I went online and checked the *Antiquities* Web site. The magazine came out bimonthly and had an extensive online presence. Josh was a senior editor and wrote several articles for each issue as well as a blog column once a week for the Web site.

I clicked onto a few of his articles to get an idea of his style. His personality seemed to come through in the narrative, which was completely accessible and entertaining. I wasn't used to that in an academic journal. To compare, I checked a few of his colleagues' works and found them much drier. They were a little more educational, but not fun at all. Some were downright boring.

It was good to know that Josh was exactly who he claimed to be. But I still wouldn't rush to recommend him as a date for Annie—not that my opinion would keep China from doing so.

I pulled up in front of Trudy's and saw her standing on the front porch with an attractive woman about my age. They were waiting for me, I realized, and I wondered if they'd come outside to avoid dealing with Amelia.

Maybe I was projecting, but I was still grateful to avoid the grumpy woman.

"Hi," I said, strolling up the walkway.

"Oh, Brooklyn, you made it," Trudy said, pressing a hand to her chest. Had she been nervous that I wouldn't?

I took a quick glance at my wristwatch. I was right on time. Was she that anxious to get rid of Elizabeth? Or was Amelia making life difficult for her?

The other woman bounced down the steps and extended her arm to shake my hand. "Hi, I'm Elizabeth Trent. It's so nice to meet you."

"I'm Brooklyn Wainwright. It's good to meet you, too."

I liked her immediately because of her open smile and obvious warmth. Elizabeth Trent was just plain beautiful, with long black hair, intelligent brown eyes, and olive skin. She was my height, and she wore khaki cargo pants with a white blouse and brown flats. It was uncanny how similar our outfits were—tan jeans, white blouse, and brown flats. What were the chances?

I started to walk up to the porch, but Trudy waved me away. "You girls go on now. No need to stick around and keep me company."

"Okay," I said, "but I'll stop to visit with you on the way back."

"You're a sweet peach. Now go have a good time. And thank you again, Brooklyn. I know Elizabeth will enjoy herself with you."

We both waved and climbed into my car. Elizabeth gave me a look of sheer appreciation. "Thank you so much. Trudy is wonderful, but it's nice to get out and meet people."

Driving off toward the center of town, I asked, "And how's Amelia handling things?"

"Oh." Elizabeth paused. "She seems nice."

I burst out laughing. "She's a toad, but she's a good

companion for Trudy. At least, that's what my mother keeps telling me."

Elizabeth was openly relieved to hear me say what she was probably thinking. "She's friendly enough with Trudy, but I'm definitely not one of her favorites."

"Trust me. Compared to her feelings for me, she's probably deeply in love with you."

She shook her head. "I seriously doubt it."

"Oh, Amelia has no favorites. Ever. About anything or anybody." We shared a few Amelia stories, and by the time we reached the Lane and parked, we were laughing like old friends.

As we walked down the sidewalk, I pointed out spots of interest, such as the park surrounding the town hall at the end of the Lane, the in-town tasting rooms for some of the local wineries, and a few of the better restaurants, notably, my sister's Arugula.

Elizabeth gazed into each of the store windows as we passed and finally stopped to look at the items on display in the pottery shop window. "I'm going to have to devote an entire day to shopping. These stores are calling my name."

"They do that to me, too."

"The whole town is so pretty." She pointed to the row of shops across the street, one of which was China's Warped. "I love the vines growing on the buildings and all the old stone and brick facades. It's got a real old-world charm."

"I agree. If you have time after lunch, I thought we'd go over to the town hall, and I'll show you our new exhibit."

"I'd like to see it."

We walked past another few stores and stopped at the corner. "We're going to lunch across the street. I hope you like Mexican food."

"I love it," she said. "I can't get decent Mexican food where I live."

"That's a tragedy." We crossed the street and walked into El Diablo. "Here we are."

"The Devil," she said with a laugh. "What a great name."

We walked into the cool, dark restaurant. The hostess took us to a comfortable booth where a waiter appeared with chips and salsa.

Elizabeth grabbed a chip, dragged it through the salsa, and took a bite. "This salsa is fantastic."

"Everything's good here. It may be a little early, but if you like margaritas, they serve the best in the world."

"I'd love one, but I probably shouldn't indulge at lunch." She brightened. "Maybe I'll come back for dinner."

I grinned. "Excellent plan."

She crunched down on another crispy, salty chip and sighed. "I'm in heaven."

Once we'd placed our orders, Elizabeth said, "Thank you again for playing tour guide. I really appreciate it."

"It's no problem. I'm having a good time." I took a sip of water and leaned back against the classic tuck-and-roll vinyl fabric of the booth. "So, where are you living that you can't get good Mexican food? I need to know so I don't go there."

She laughed. "I live in a small town in Michigan, in the upper peninsula. I know they have some good Mexican restaurants in that part of the world, but not in my town."

"Were you born and raised there?"

"Not really. I was a navy brat, so I grew up all over the place. Even spent two years in Sicily."

"We have a naval base in Sicily?"

"Yes, we do. It was fun living there, but being a kid, I naturally whined about going home to Michigan most of the time. And once I got home, I couldn't wait to leave again."

"No wonder I can't place your accent."

"It's because I'm a mutt," she said. "I even affected

an Italian accent for years after we left Sicily. I was such an annoying child."

"I'm pretty sure we were all annoying children."

"Absolutely," she said. "It's the role of children everywhere to annoy adults."

I smiled. "We sound so cynical."

"Maybe that's why we're getting along so well."

Chuckling, I grabbed another chip, dunked it into the salsa, and popped it into my mouth. "So your grandmother and Trudy were old friends?"

"Yes, my grandparents spent their honeymoon here and returned every year for vacation. At some point, Grandma Reenie met Trudy, and they became friends. After that, they corresponded and got together every year. Grandma died last year, and I haven't been very good about contacting her old friends."

"You can't be expected to do it all right away."

"I guess not." Idly, she dragged the edge of one chip through the salsa and seemed to study the pattern it made. "I had a hard time for a while. I think I fell into a depression, although I didn't recognize it at the time. Grandma was my only living relative, and we were really close."

"I'm so sorry." I already liked Elizabeth. Knowing that she'd been alone and hurting made me feel for her. "Is Reenie your grandmother's nickname?"

"Yes, short for Irene."

"Was she Irish?"

"Can you tell?" Elizabeth laughed. "She was my mom's mother. Mom was Irish down to her toes, with beautiful strawberry blond hair and a peaches and cream complexion." She brushed her hand over her head of dark hair. "Naturally, I take after my dad."

"Your hair is gorgeous."

She laughed. "I wasn't fishing for a compliment, but thank you."

There was a short pause, and we both reached for the chips.

Elizabeth sighed. "I've been doing better lately, contacting Grandma's old friends around town. And then I heard on the news that they found that treasure here, and I recalled that Trudy lived nearby, so I gave her a call. And it was the best thing I could've done. She reminds me of my grandmother in so many ways."

"That's wonderful. I hope you two have a great visit."

"I think we will. We're going champagne tasting tomorrow."

I laughed. "How fun."

I recommended a few good champagne houses, and we settled into an easy conversation over *poblano chiles rellenos* and *tacos al carbón*.

After lunch, we walked over to the town hall in the middle of the park. On the way, I explained that we'd decided to take pictures of the artwork and items we'd found in the caves and display them for anyone interested in the story. "Not only is the discovery historically important, but there are also a lot of families with a vested interest in keeping these items safe. So we decided to keep everything locked up in the storage caves and created this exhibit for the families and the community to enjoy in the meantime."

"It's fascinating," Elizabeth said. "It sounds like you were dealing with a lot of disparate parties."

"Yes, and some of them are very unhappy." I was thinking of Henri as I said it, but a picture of Noland Garrity sprang to mind and almost ruined my afternoon.

"I should think the owners would be overjoyed at the discovery."

"Well, there's a dispute over whether the items were actually stolen or just accidentally hidden away for some seventy years."

Her eyes were focused on something in the distance. "I'll be interested to see the photographs."

"Here we are." I led the way up the wide steps of the town hall and into the exhibit space.

"Amazing," Elizabeth whispered. She gazed around

at the impressive display, walked to the ends of each
aisle to check what was there, and then headed straight
for the group of pictures detailing the *Dancing Woman*
painting, the one I thought had been painted in the style
of Renoir. She stared at each one of the photos for a
long time and seemed to have forgotten I was there. I
was fine with that, just happy to know that someone
could be so engrossed in the exhibit.

I left her alone and wandered over to the next row,
where the photos of the furniture were hanging. I loved
the details of the inlaid wood that Robin had managed
to capture with her camera and my excellent lighting.

"It just figures you'd be here."

I turned and found Noland Garrity glaring at me. I
couldn't think of anything pleasant to say, so I waited
for him to speak.

"This isn't art," he said derisively. "It's a pitiful
excuse. I get nothing out of it. I need access to the caves,
and if I can't obtain keys from your boyfriend, I'll go
directly to Robson myself."

"Robson is a busy man," I said, trying for the equanimity I'd seen Derek display. "If you need access,
Derek will assist you. Just call his cell number. He made
it clear, he's available whenever you are."

"I just called him, and he can't be there until three
o'clock. What am I supposed to do until then?"

I checked my watch. "It's two thirty. I think you'll
live till three." So much for equanimity. I couldn't help
the snarky comment. What was this guy's problem? I
wanted to smack him.

"You have been nothing but rude and sarcastic and—"

"Good-bye, Mr. Garrity." I said it quickly and
walked away before he could insult or threaten me any
further because I would have to pound him into sand
if he did. For the next ten minutes I skimmed the outer
edges of the room until I saw him walk out the door. I
breathed more easily.

What a crank! I didn't care if he knew everything

there was to know about art. He was a horrible man who didn't have a clue about how to get along with people. I just prayed that he didn't treat Guru Bob the way he treated me.

I would have to remember to ask Derek to check with Interpol soon. If nothing in the caves had been reported stolen, we wouldn't need Mr. Garrity's services anymore.

But I knew Robson wouldn't get rid of the odious man until he had done a complete and thorough appraisal of everything found in the cave. Robson had expressed concern that in the case of a family member dying and leaving no heirs, we would have to dispose of the heirloom somehow. The most equitable way to handle it, we decided, was to sell the item to a museum or reputable collector and divide the proceeds among the remaining families. For that to be done fairly, an appraiser had to establish its value.

"Hey, you."

I jolted, still nervous that Garrity might sneak up on me. But this was Robin, so I relaxed instantly.

"Hi!" It was always good to see my best friend, and now I'd have a chance to introduce Elizabeth to her as well. I gave her a big hug and shook off the residual effects of Noland Garrity. "Are you working here today?"

"Not today. I brought Austin and Jackson in to see the photos."

"That's great. I know they'll love them."

My brothers were only a step or two behind Robin, and deep in conversation, probably discussing dirt or something equally captivating.

"Hi, guys."

"Hey, Brooks," Jackson said, giving me a one-armed hug. I always got a kick out of seeing Jackson after having him gone for so long. He'd spent ten years doing some job he never talked about that kept him out of the country. Once he was back home, Guru Bob enlisted him to travel for the Fellowship and the winery for two more years. Again, the reasons for all that travel weren't mentioned, at least not to my mother and me. Apparently, Jackson was good at keeping secrets. In any case, he was home for good now, and my family was glad of it. For the past year, he'd been managing the vineyards and doing a great job.

I stared at the two men I'd grown up with and couldn't help but admire them. They were both tall and good-looking, with dark blond hair like my dad. Today Jackson wore a faded denim jacket over a black T-shirt with black jeans and boots, the original cowboy hunk. Austin was dressed a bit more in the "Sonoma style" with his chambray shirt tucked into a pair of well-worn jeans. And boots. Either way, they were both pretty hunky, if I did say so myself.

"What're you doing here, Brooks?" Austin asked.

"I'm showing a friend of Trudy's around town. We had lunch at El Diablo, and now we're checking out the exhibit. I'll introduce her to you when she's finished admiring Robin's photos."

Austin glanced around the room. "Man, this is great. The photos are fantastic." He wrapped his arm around Robin's waist. "You rock, Robbie."

"Thanks, honey." Robin beamed, and the twosome wandered off to admire more of Robin's work.

I looked around for Elizabeth but didn't see her. There were three more aisles of photographs, so there was plenty to look at. I figured I'd catch up with her in a few minutes.

I thought of something and turned to my brother. "Do you want to join Derek and me for dinner tomorrow night? I thought we'd take Elizabeth to Arugula."

Jackson gave me a sideways glance. "This isn't some kind of a setup, is it?"

I was taken aback. "No." I started to laugh. "I wouldn't do that to you."

"You'd be amazed to know how many people would."

"Uh-oh. So now that Austin's spoken for, you've moved to the top of the eligibility list?"

"Exactly," he drawled. "So don't try it."

"I didn't even think of it. She's in town for only a few days, and Trudy wants her to meet people in hopes that she'll visit more often."

"Sounds reasonable," he admitted.

"I'm going to ask China and Beau to join us, and Robin and Austin, too. I thought we could make it a party. But I understand if you'd rather not."

He frowned, probably because he realized he was misjudging my intentions. "Yeah, okay, I'll join you."

"Great. Tomorrow night at seven."

"I'll be there." Jackson walked over to the first photograph on the aisle in front of us. "Robin did a good job with these."

"I think so, too. The lighting is awesome, isn't it?"

He grinned at me. "I take it you helped with the lighting?"

"Yeah."

"Well then, the lighting is phenomenal."

I heard a sharp intake of breath and turned to see Elizabeth, staring wide-eyed across the room.

"Oh, there you are, Elizabeth," I said as I went over to her. "I wanted to introduce you to my brother."

She was trying to swallow, and I wondered if she was about to choke on something. I grabbed her arm. "Are you all right?"

But she couldn't speak. Worried, I glanced back at Jackson.

But he was gone.

"What the heck?" I scanned the room to see where he'd wandered off to, but I didn't see him anywhere.

Now, that was weird.

I turned back to Elizabeth. "Did you see where he went?"

She gulped convulsively, still unable to speak.

I grabbed her arm. "Are you going to be sick? What's wrong?"

She finally shook herself out of whatever state she'd fallen into, took a deep breath, and exhaled heavily. "I'm sorry. I thought I saw someone I knew, but I was obviously mistaken."

"You mean, my brother? Tall, good-looking, denim jacket?"

"Who?" She still looked alarmed and a little dazed. "Oh. No, sorry. It was a woman. I looked out the window and was sure I saw an old friend from . . ." She inhaled deeply again and let it out. "Um . . . but it wasn't her. Sorry."

I wasn't entirely sure I believed her because I thought she'd been reacting to Jackson. But why would she lie? And where had Jackson disappeared to? "We can check outside to make sure."

"No, I already took a second look, and I was mistaken. But wow, what a shock. Sorry." She laughed ruefully. "That was weird."

"Yeah, you looked completely flabbergasted. I hope you're okay."

"I'm fine now, thanks." She linked her arm through mine, and we walked toward another aisle of photos. "These pictures are wonderful."

Clearly she wanted to get things back on track and so did I. But I was going to be talking to Jackson about this. And Derek. Most definitely Derek. "Aren't they cool? Robin took them."

"Robin?"

"Oh. Where'd she go?" I realized I hadn't had a chance to introduce them, so I glanced around but didn't see Robin or Austin anywhere. Frowning again, I said, "People seem to be disappearing right and left today. Anyway, you'll meet her tomorrow night if you'd like to join us for dinner."

"I'd love to," she said with enthusiasm. "You're so sweet to include me. I'm having such a good time."

"I'm glad." We spent another half hour at the exhibit before we both decided we were ready to go home.

Dinner at Arugula the following night was a blast. Elizabeth regaled us with stories of Trudy on a mission to find the best champagne-tasting venues in the region. "We drove for miles over the mountains toward Napa. There were so many treacherous hairpin turns, I didn't think we'd make it out alive."

"I hate that drive," Robin said. "I'd rather go twenty miles out of my way than go over the mountain."

"I'll never do it again," Elizabeth said. "Trudy was driving as well as could be expected, but still, it was scary. And then all of a sudden, in the middle of another turn, she slammed on the brakes and whipped into this driveway. The tires were screeching! I was clutching the dashboard for dear life. We were in the most remote area of the forest and, I swear, it looked like something out of a horror film. And then this tiny one-lane road opened, and suddenly we'd arrived at a beautiful little winery surrounded by acres of vineyards, where they served the most wonderful champagne."

"I've been to that place," Austin said, nodding. "It's really good, but you've gotta want to go there. Sometimes I think the owner makes it tough on purpose so he won't have to share his champagne."

"I don't blame him," she said, "but I'm glad we found it. Seriously, though, that road is awful. Is that how you get rid of tourists? You send them up the mountain?"

"Every chance we get," Austin said with a blasé wave of his hand, and everyone laughed.

Everyone but my brother Jackson, I thought with annoyance. He'd canceled on me at the last minute, and I was still miffed. Did he really believe I was trying to set him up with Elizabeth? Well, given her reaction to seeing him—or whomever she claimed to have seen—at the town hall yesterday, I didn't think he'd have to worry about her trying to finagle a date with him.

Elizabeth had looked absolutely horrified at the sight of him. She'd insisted she was looking at someone else she'd seen walking outside, but I had a feeling she was fibbing. After all, as soon as she made that face, Jackson completely disappeared from sight. Maybe he saw her first and took off running.

Why?

I might've been imagining the whole thing. Either way, I accepted that it was none of my business. But that didn't mean I wasn't going to find some answers. And it irritated me terribly that I'd completely forgotten to mention any of it to Derek. As soon as I got the chance to have a long talk with him, I was going to get his take on the situation.

I was curious. This was my brother and my new friend. My instincts told me that there was something going on there. Did they have some history between them? Maybe it had ended badly. Was there some way I could intervene—or was I playing with fire? I wasn't ready to do anything about it just yet, but I would if the right moment presented itself.

Since Derek had spent another afternoon dealing with the insufferable Noland Garrity, he was bushed by the time we got home from dinner. In spite of that, he went for an evening walk with me and Maggie before calling it a day and going off to bed. I spent a few minutes playing with Charlie and Maggie and checking my e-mail for any messages from my online group. There was nothing yet, but Claude had said to give him a few days, so I would have to be patient.

Since I was online anyway, I stopped by a few of my favorite rare-book sites to find values for comparable versions of *Journey to the Center of the Earth*. I wanted to be able to tell Robson what the book might be worth so he could make an informed decision on its fate.

The first American version of the book published in 1872 had just sold for forty thousand dollars. The description referred to it as "beyond rare," not only because of its age and its clean and bright condition, but mainly because no other copies of that edition had ever surfaced.

I made notes and moved on, searching for a French version published in the same year as my edition. I found one going for thirty-five thousand dollars and had to sit back and take a breath. High prices like this no longer astonished me, but neither did the fact that a book this rare and expensive was sometimes worth killing for.

Rather than dwell on that unhappy thought, I considered the story that the book told. I admit I'd never read *Journey to the Center of the Earth*, but I'd seen the old movie version. It had been one of my all-time favorites when I was young. I wondered again if young Anton Benoit and Jean Pierre Renaud had dreamed of traveling all those thousands of miles to find the cave that would lead them to the magical center of the earth. I believed they had had that dream, because what child hadn't? And I was especially convinced after I'd read the blood oath they'd written inside the book.

As I closed my notebook, shut down my computer, and turned off the lights, I thought how sad and oddly coincidental it was that the men's friendship had come to an end inside a cave so far away from their home. Had Anton known that Jean Pierre was dead? Was he the one who killed him? It was awful to think that anyone related to Guru Bob was capable of murder. But if it wasn't Anton, then who killed Jean Pierre Renaud?

I made sure Maggie was comfy and cozy in her bed in the den, then cuddled Charlie all the way to the bedroom, where I set her down in her little doughnut-shaped cat bed. My tiny kitten was growing up too fast. She was a few inches taller, and her pale fur was thicker and softer. Her face was just as adorable as ever, though, with tufts of light orange across her forehead and cheeks and big, inquisitive blue eyes. I gave her some light scratches behind her ears, and she purred as I gently admonished her to stay in bed. At home, she loved sleeping in her little doughnut bed, but since we'd been in Sonoma, she rarely stayed put all night. She hadn't ventured out of the bedroom and probably wouldn't, but I had found her curled up on the comfortable chintz rocking chair on more than a few occasions.

Derek woke up as soon as I climbed into bed, but he fell asleep almost as quickly after I kissed him good night. I chuckled to myself that Derek rarely went to bed this early in the city, but I guessed all this clean country air was wearing him out. Or more likely, the horrible Noland Garrity was simply exhausting to be around.

Sometime during the night, a low-pitched ringing woke me up. I blinked a few times, disoriented.

Derek sat up and grabbed his cell phone. I checked the alarm clock, saw that it was two forty-seven a.m., and almost groaned. Nothing good ever happened this late at night.

"I'll be right there," he said, and tapped the phone, ending the call.

"Who is it? What happened?" I had to shake my head back and forth to wake myself up. "Is somebody hurt?"

"Not yet," he said flatly. He was already out of bed, grabbing a shirt and pulling on a pair of jeans. "Someone tried to break into the storage cave."

Chapter 11

"I'm going with you." I threw on a sweater and jeans, then slipped my feet into a pair of loafers, and we were out of the house in three minutes.

"I'll bet it was Noland Garrity," I muttered as Derek drove the three miles to the winery.

"What makes you think it's him?" he asked.

"He's so arrogant. It just figures he would try to get away with something like this. I don't trust him as far as I can throw him."

"He's arrogant, but he's not stupid," Derek murmured. "Let's wait and see."

I sat back in my seat and tapped my feet anxiously until we turned onto the winery road. "Oh, hey, maybe it's Henri. He was angry enough to pull something like this."

"Perhaps, although he was on his best behavior during the tour of the cave." Derek turned into the lot and parked as close to the storage cave as we could. It was fifty yards away, and I could see some activity with Gabriel and his men, but I couldn't make out any faces.

Gabriel met us halfway.

"Did you arrest him?" I asked.

"Him?" he said, then shrugged. "Not yet. Thought I'd wait for Derek to get here before calling the cops. He's our interrogation specialist."

I looked up at Derek. "You are?"

He threw his arm around my shoulders and didn't bother to confirm or deny, which pretty much confirmed for me what Gabriel had said. "Let's go see what we've got here."

"A couple of clowns," Gabriel muttered, which made no sense, unless he was teasing Derek and me.

But as we got closer to the storage door and saw his men holding two people captive, I realized what he was talking about.

"Ma'am, please remove your ski cap," Gabriel said.

Ma'am? I watched the woman yank the ski cap off her head to reveal her shocking red hair.

"Darlene?" My gaze switched to the short man standing next to her. "Shawn? What're you guys doing here?"

"Uh, hi, Brooklyn. Hi, Derek." Shawn's voice was meek as he scratched his head. "This isn't what it looks like."

"He was using these when we got here." With the tips of his thumb and forefinger, Gabriel held out a small plastic case filled with a set of thin tools. I recognized them because Derek had a similar set. They were used specifically for picking locks.

"I can explain," Shawn said.

Darlene elbowed him. "You don't have to explain anything." She glared at me. "We're innocent."

"Carrying a set of lock picks and actually attempting to use them seems to indicate the contrary," Derek told her.

"And then there's this," Gabriel continued blithely, pointing to one of his men, who held up a crowbar in his gloved hand.

I scowled at Darlene. "You brought burglary tools and a crowbar, and you're telling me you're innocent?" I tried to block out the image of the fun-loving pair we'd met in the restaurant the other night. I needed to see them for what they were: petty thieves. "It looks to me like you were trying to break into our winery."

"That's crazy," Darlene said, trying to laugh. It sounded more like a harsh barking. "These guys have no sense of humor. We were just looking around. We wanted to get a close-up view of the whole area, the flora, the fauna, you know what I mean? It's our way of giving our readers the complete story."

"At three o'clock in the morning?" I said.

Gabriel and the others stood behind the guilty pair, arms folded across their chests as if they were all posing for the cover of *Dangerous Men* magazine, if only that were real. Gabriel was the only one who looked somewhat amused. I didn't see the slightest thing funny in any of this. I felt used.

"Well, yeah," Shawn said, his voice a little whiny as he hitched himself to Darlene's dumb story. "Late at night's the best time to experience the true sights and sounds of a place. No crowds around, no distractions. We're wordsmiths, Brooklyn. Creative people. This is how we soak up the ambience of a place. We marinate in the total atmosphere, becoming one with the setting. Our stories are better for it."

"What a bunch of bull," I muttered, feeling foolishly disillusioned and betrayed. But why? Did I really believe they were my new best friends because they'd bought us some wine? I needed to smack myself. I shook my finger at the security box in the wall by the doors. "Don't you get it? This place is locked up so tight, it squeaks. What were you thinking?"

Darlene wore a sly grin. "Shawn's got a knack for working his way around those pesky security devices."

I stared at her for a long moment, not quite believing what I'd heard her say. It was as much of an admission of guilt as anything would ever be. "Not tonight he doesn't."

Derek nodded at Gabriel. "Call the police."

"I'm so bummed." Now that it was just Derek and me in the car driving home, I was pouting. "I never expected to see those two being dragged away in handcuffs. I thought they were so friendly and quirky, you know? Turns out, they're just common criminals."

"Yes, they are." Derek kept his eyes on the road, but I could see his teeth were clenched. He was as angry as I was.

"It was creepy, wasn't it? The way she was smiling there at the end?" I sighed. "I guess I owe Noland an apology for assuming it was him."

Derek glanced over at me. "No you don't, darling."

"Good, because I couldn't stomach having to apologize to him. But I'm really bummed about Darlene and Shawn."

"I think you'd be wise to stay away from reporters from now on. You have a generous heart, and they'll take advantage of that. No matter how friendly they seem, they all have their own agendas."

"Isn't that the truth," I muttered. Really, I wasn't so much furious with the thieving twosome as I was disappointed in myself. I'd assumed the two bloggers were just as innocuous as they'd claimed to be, and I couldn't have been more wrong. What did that say about my judgment?

Derek reached for my hand and held it during the rest of the ride home. We were both exhausted, but I wasn't sure I'd be able to sleep after putting up with an hour of *The Darlene and Shawn Show.* They were grifters! I was still embarrassed that I'd fallen for their friendly act.

Honestly, with everything I'd seen in the last year or so, you would've thought my rose-colored glasses would be a little dim. Guess not. Derek was right. I planned to avoid all reporters from now on unless it was an official query related to the treasures found in the cave.

My mind wandered back to the conversation I'd had with China on Tuesday. Had she already introduced Josh to Annie? I hoped not. True, he seemed a lot more trustworthy than Darlene and Shawn, but he was only here to obtain information, and he would do it by any means necessary. And what if he turned out to be no better than Shawn and Darlene? I didn't want Annie to get hurt.

Once Derek and I got home and climbed back into bed, I found out I was wrong about sleeping, too. I drifted off within seconds of my head hitting the pillow.

I woke up hours later with a kitten sniffing around my face.

"Hello, little thing," I murmured, and she head-butted my cheek, purring softly. How could I resist such a wake-up call?

And how could I resist Derek when he had coffee and English muffins ready for me when I finally dragged myself out to the kitchen?

"My life is good," I said, setting Charlie on the floor, where she immediately pounced on Maggie, who didn't seem to mind a bit. I was growing to love the sweet old dog.

Leaning against Derek's back, I wrapped my arms around him.

"And so is mine," he said, squeezing my arms affectionately.

A minute later, I sat at the kitchen table. Derek kissed the top of my head before joining me. "What are your plans today?"

"I'm going to hide away in Abraham's studio and work on a few projects. How about you?"

"I'll be toiling in the fields with the menfolk."

It was a good thing I'd chewed and swallowed my bite of muffin because I burst out laughing.

"Why are you laughing at the thought of my doing an honest day's labor?"

"Because I think what you'll really be doing is drinking a lot of wine," I said, still giggling. "Not that I have anything against that sort of toiling. But mostly I'm laughing at the way you said it, with your upper-crust British accent, so erudite and sophisticated."

"Now why does that sound like an insult?" he asked, his lips twisting into a wry smile.

"You know it's not," I said, scooting my chair closer and touching his cheek. "Your erudite sophistication is just one more reason why I love you."

"You've managed to save yourself this time," he grumbled. "Pulling the 'I love you' card."

I rested my head against his arm. "It's my favorite card."

"Mine, too."

"So what's going on in the fields today? They're not starting the harvest yet, are they?"

"Not yet. We're going to walk the fields and check the grapes. Determine which area they'll harvest first."

"There will be wine, I know."

"It's part of the job." He stood, carried his dishes to the sink, and returned to the table. Taking hold of my hands, he lifted me from the chair and planted a delicious kiss on my lips. "I've got to be off. Think of me toiling under the hot sun, won't you?"

"I will. Mm, I can already picture you with your shirt off, all tanned and hot and sweaty and—"

"You have an evil streak," he whispered, effectively cutting me off as he kissed my neck and the back of my ear. Happy chills skittered through me as his lips made contact with my skin. I barely kept from melting into a puddle on the tile floor when he let me go.

I looked up and caught his self-satisfied smile. With a friendly stroke of my hair, he chuckled and walked out the door.

I brought Charlie with me to Abraham's studio to give her an intriguing new space in which to play. She prowled and sniffed every inch of the workshop while I set myself up at the center table, spreading out my tools before studying the job before me.

My friend Ian McCullough, the head curator at the Covington Library in San Francisco, had given me a three-volume set of medical books to refurbish. The subject matter was pathological anatomy, and this set was the first English edition, published in 1772. The cloth bindings were in bad shape with tearing along the edges of the spine and joints. The front covers were rubbed down to the boards. The gilded titles on the spine had faded completely.

The set wouldn't be put on display, but because it was historically significant to researchers, it would be available in the library. For that reason, Ian had asked me to replace the old cloth binding with sturdy leather.

I'd asked him to specify exactly how sturdy he wanted the leather to be, an important consideration when price was the main factor. Cowhide, for example, was generally the cheapest and most durable leather used in bookbinding, but it wasn't as pretty as goatskin or calfskin. It was also a little more difficult to work with because it wasn't quite as supple and thin as the more expensive hides. But again, because of the historical significance of the books, Ian chose to go with the high-quality, moderately priced navy blue morocco leather I'd suggested. With gold tooling on the spines, the books would be both handsome and somber, as befitted their subject matter.

Replacing cloth with leather was going to be a relatively simple job. The tricky part would be to make sure all three books remained a matched set when I was finished with the repair. The key was finding a piece of leather big enough for three books—or having two or more pieces with all the same characteristics dyed exactly the same color. Since the leather I'd chosen had come from one hide—and therefore been tanned and dyed at the same time—it wouldn't be an issue. I'd just have to make sure the gilding and binding were perfectly matched as well. I didn't foresee any problems.

Since volume three was the least damaged of the set, I decided to repair it first.

The cloth covering the spine was in sad shape, dangling by threads along the front joint. It was an easy job to cut away the rest of it and trim off the loose bits. I measured and cut a piece of thin cardboard to use as a spine liner, about the weight of a manila folder, and attached it to the spine with PVA glue. This would provide a more solid base for my raised bands than the original threadbare spine.

I had decided to add raised bands to the spine, even though there were none on the original clothbound book. These days, raised bands were mainly decorative unless the book was handmade, but I thought the addition would provide a bit more support to the spines of these books.

A raised band looked like a horizontal bump stretched across the spine of a book. Back in the old days, the cords used to sew the pages together were tied in knots and stretched across the spine. The leather binding was then stretched and molded around the cords. Once bookbinding became mechanized, the raised bands were no longer necessary to hide the cords, but the look was maintained because it was an attractive feature.

Once I had the spine liner in place and the glue had dried, I cut the individual bands from a long strip of leather, coated each piece with PVA glue, and attached them at evenly spaced intervals across the spine. Later, when the leather cover was completely finished, I would gild the book title, the author, and the volume number in separate spaces on the spine.

Now that the bands were in place, I began to strip away the old cloth cover. I used a razor, cutting it from the fore-edge and then pulling the cloth easily across the board.

I was happy to find that the boards were still in good condition so I wouldn't have to replace them.

"Meow."

I glanced down and saw Charlie gazing up at me, her little head cocked as though she were wondering what I was doing here since I wasn't playing with her.

"I'm sorry I haven't been playing with you, little one." I'd kept an eye on her all day, filled her water bowl, and made sure she didn't hurt herself. Mostly, she pushed her mouse around or napped in the rays of sunlight streaming through the windows along the south side of the studio.

"You've been very good all day," I said, checking my watch. "I think it's time to go home and see Derek."

"Meow."

"I'm glad you agree." Smiling, I picked her up and nuzzled her neck. She was the sweetest thing. I wondered if she would grow to ignore me someday, as cats sometimes did. I hoped not, because I was just tickled by her affection. I set her down and cleaned up my mess on the worktable, tossed the old book cloth into the trash can, gathered up my sleepy kitten, and walked up the hill.

Because of our middle-of-the-night sojourn to the caves the evening before, Derek and I had decided to spend a quiet evening at home. Thanks to Mom, we didn't have to make dinner. She'd prepared her famous taco casserole and had generously set aside a second smaller pan for us. It was an embarrassingly easy dish to make in the microwave, but I was still grateful that she'd done the work for us.

After dinner we took Maggie for another long walk along the ridge above my parents' home. We had both fallen for Maggie and talked about getting a dog when we returned to the city. If only we could find one just as sweet in one of the shelters around town. The only thing holding us back was that we lived in SoMA, a busy section south of Market Street in San Francisco. Would it be fair to keep a dog inside the apartment all day long except for the occasional walk down our crowded sidewalk? We did have a small park a block away, but was that enough? We decided to continue talking about it and see how we felt once we returned to our remodeled apartment.

Monday morning, Derek and I were having our second cup of coffee and laughing at Charlie's pitched battle with her new stuffed mouse. Maggie got in on the action, bumping the mouse with her nose and swatting it a few times across the floor, causing Charlie to skitter after it. It was as if they were playing mouse hockey.

I was halfway through my bowl of granola with fresh blueberries and bananas, and Derek had just finished his. He stood and checked the time on his watch. "I've got to join a conference call shortly. What are you up to today?"

"I'm spending the morning at Abraham's, working on my medical texts. I want to finish the first book today. Afterward, I thought I might swing by and say hello to Annie. Do you want to come with me?"

"If it's much later in the afternoon, yes. I have a meeting with Gabriel and his team directly after lunch."

"Is something wrong with the security?"

"No, and we want to keep it that way."

"Good."

He took his cereal bowl to the sink and rinsed it out. The subject of security reminded me of the other night.

"Have you heard from the sheriff about Darlene and Shawn?" I asked.

"Brace yourself," Derek said, taking a last sip of coffee. "They were released on bail yesterday."

I grimaced. "I figured they couldn't keep them for long."

"No. They didn't actually break into the caves, after all." He rinsed his mug and tucked it into the dishwasher.

"I know, but still," I groused. "I just hope they were smart enough to leave the area."

"They informed the deputy who processed them that they were headed directly back to San Francisco."

"They'd better be." I was still smarting over the fact that I'd fallen for their friendly act.

Derek, aware of my feelings, gave my shoulder a soft squeeze before picking up my empty bowl and sticking it in the dishwasher.

"Thanks." My cell phone rang, and I recognized the local area code but not the number. "Hello?"

"Good morning, Brooklyn. It's Trudy."

My mood brightened instantly. "Trudy, hi. What's up?"

"I have a surprise for you." Her voice was brimming with excitement. "I hope you can stop by sometime today."

"A surprise? Can you give me a hint?"

"No, because you're too smart. You'd guess it right away."

I chuckled. "I don't know how smart I am, but that's all right. I'll just have to wait." I glanced at the kitchen clock and gauged how long I would need to work on the first leather binding that morning. "Would three o'clock be too late to come by?"

"Three o'clock is perfect, dear," she said. "See you then."

"Okay. Bye." I ended the call and looked at Derek. "Looks like I'm going to Trudy's this afternoon."

Despite my commitment to Ian and the Covington to finish the three medical books, my heart was set on taking some time with the Jules Verne book. I spent a half hour using my gum eraser to carefully wipe along the top edge of the book where most dust and grime settled. The soft eraser was also helpful around the edges of each page where stains were often found. I never used it near the printed lines because there was always a chance that I might wipe away a word. That was never a good thing.

As I turned each page, I could see what other areas would need repairs or deeper cleaning, and made notes as I went from page to page.

From my set of travel tools, I found the short brush with the stiff bristles I used to sweep away any minute bits of dirt and grime that had been ground into the sewn centers. It was important to get rid of as many of the tiny abrasive grains as possible because they could damage the paper.

After my half hour was up, I put the Jules Verne

book aside to do the work I was paid to do. First, I cleaned off the table completely and washed my hands. Then I laid out the navy blue leather and, using the first medical book as my yardstick, I measured and cut the first piece, adding an extra inch to all four sides. After the piece was cut, the edges of the leather had to be pared, creating a beveled edge so the turndowns wouldn't be too bulky.

Paring leather wasn't quite the same as paring an apple. The first few dozen times I tried to pare leather had been complicated and scary moments for me. If I sliced away too much, I would ruin the entire piece and have to start over. I learned that the angle at which I held the knife was critical to my success—or failure. Learning what techniques and angles worked best took plenty of practice. And since I was left-handed, I couldn't always follow the person trying to train me. One great thing I'd done for myself was purchase an excellent left-handed paring knife.

I also sharpened my knife regularly using a whetstone and an old-fashioned leather strop. And I always pared my leather on a slab of marble. The harder the surface beneath the leather, the easier it was to do the job.

After I finished paring the new leather cover, I placed the piece on a large cookie sheet and added a thin layer of water to thoroughly moisten it. A few minutes later, I drained off the water and let it air-dry for a little while. I prepared my glue and applied it to the exposed side.

The moisture would make the leather more pliable and easier to stretch and mold to the boards. Since the leather would be moist, I wrapped the entire text block in wax paper, leaving only the front and back cover and spine free to work with. As every book lover in the world knew, moisture and paper did not play well together.

Once everything was ready to go, I balanced the book on its edge, spine side up. Picking up the sheet of leather, I draped it over the spine, adjusting it so that it was evenly centered, then used my hands to begin molding it to the spine and boards, stretching it as I went. I was working with high-quality morocco leather, so it had a bit of give, although it wasn't as stretchy as sheepskin. When I felt it staying, I began to trim the edges, being careful not to trim too close. It was always better to have too much leather than not enough.

Even though the glue would dry shortly, there was no need to rush the job. I just continued to smooth and press the leather evenly across all the surfaces in order to avoid air pockets. I returned to the spine every few minutes, using my thumbs and a bone folder to press and mold the leather against the raised bands.

"You're going to be beautiful," I murmured as I stretched the leather over onto the inside endpapers, creating the turndowns. I knew Ian would be happy with these books.

At the edges, I continued to stretch and press the leather until it overlapped onto the endpapers. I used scissors to trim away the excess and cut the corners, pinching them to make them fit together smoothly.

As the glue and leather dried, I could feel the leather shrinking a little, which was a good thing as long as I continued to smooth and press and tighten it around the folds. At the top and base of the spine, I used my thin, pointed bone folder to smooth and tuck the leather down into the spine so the headbands would show nicely.

I'd found that working with leather, even after hundreds of bookbinding jobs, was never an exact science. At this point in my career, the steps I took were instinctive; I knew what to do without much thought. I was incorporating years of skill and knowledge and experience—and adding a little touch of art.

And yet, every piece of leather was slightly different, so I was also applying a touch of science to each job. For instance, if a particular piece of leather got too stiff too quickly, I could moisten it with a damp sponge. I knew that wheat paste dried more slowly than PVA and absorbed more deeply, making for a more penetrating bond. But PVA was generally a faster surface adhesive, and I liked the way it worked along the edges of the turndowns. Each job brought its own new problems and solutions.

Unless I was attending a bookbinders' convention, there weren't a lot of people who cared to hear all these details, especially when it came to the intricacies of glue. I could go on for hours, but I usually stopped when I heard the snoring. My only consolation was that everyone could appreciate the beautiful finished product.

I took a break and ate the sandwich I'd brought with me. I used my phone to check messages, but there was nothing urgent. I was just waiting for the leather to dry. I walked outside and took a stroll around Abraham's pool and backyard area, then returned to the workshop to check my book.

The leather turndowns were dry enough, so I used my metal ruler and an X-Acto knife to trim them. They would ultimately be covered by new endpapers, so I wanted them to have a nice, even edge.

Finally, I cut two-inch-wide strips of wax paper and slipped them between the boards and endpapers to keep the leather from bleeding onto the paper.

After that, I slid the book into the wooden press until only the spine was showing, then tightened it enough to hold the book in place. I used my bone folder along the spine to further shape and emphasize the raised bands and the notches I'd made at the top and bottom of the joints near the headcaps.

I stretched my arms and rolled my shoulders a few times to get rid of the kinks and happened to look up at the clock.

"Oh rats!" I was going to be late to Trudy's if I didn't stop working right at that moment. With the book already in the press, my timing was perfect. I left it where it was, knowing that when I returned in the next day or so, the leather would be dried and the spine would be ready for gilding.

I cleaned up my work space, washed my glue brush, and raced home, where I took a quick shower and changed into a nicer pair of jeans and a sweater.

I'd managed to zone out while working on the medical book, but now I was curious all over again to know what Trudy's surprise could be. It had to have something to do with one of the art pieces in the cave. Unless it had to do with Elizabeth. Maybe she had decided to move here permanently. That would be a fun surprise.

"Doesn't do any good to speculate," I muttered as I locked up the house and jogged to my car.

I got lucky with traffic, and eight minutes later I was pulling to the curb in front of Trudy's place. I gazed at the pretty craftsman-style home and wondered if Amelia would be serving tea and cookies this afternoon. The thought made me snicker as I shut the car door and strolled up to the porch. Poor Amelia. Did she know how annoying she was? Probably not.

I climbed out of the car and glanced around Trudy's neighborhood. I'd been working inside for two days straight and hadn't been able to take advantage of the beautiful weather we'd been having lately. The air was clean, and the sky was a gorgeous shade of blue. I could smell hints of pine and newly mown grass in the light breeze. Someone must've lit a fire last night, I thought, because the smell of burning wood lingered in the air. It all reminded me of fall days when I was young, when school had just started and Halloween was right around the corner.

I smiled at the memory and climbed the steps up to Trudy's porch. I was about to knock, when a loud bang shattered the silence.

"What the—?"

That was a gunshot. I'd heard the sound before.

"Trudy!" I grabbed the door handle and found it unlocked, so I shoved the door open and ran inside.

Trudy lay on the marble hearth in front of the fireplace. My stomach pitched at the sight of blood pooling under her head. Amelia was sprawled awkwardly facedown across the nearest chair.

"What the hell?" Rushing over to Trudy, I fumbled in my purse to grab my phone. I needed to call 911.

"Oh my God. Please, please be alive," I murmured as I knelt down and felt Trudy's neck for a pulse. Her skin was warm. I almost fainted with relief when I felt her strong pulse.

The floorboard creaked behind me, and I started to turn around to check on Amelia. But before I could get a glimpse of her, something hard and heavy slammed into the side of my head. All I saw was a quick flash of light before everything turned black.

Chapter 12

"There's my girl," Derek murmured, his sexy English accent drawing me back to Earth when I wanted to drift off to never-never land. He stroked my cheek and brushed my hair with his fingers. "Come on, love. Stay with me."

"Uhhh." I was seeing three of him, not that I minded. Derek did have the most gorgeous face I'd ever seen on a man. But oh, my head. I tried to reach up to find out why my skull was throbbing as though ten sledgehammers were slamming against it, but he grabbed my hand.

"No, darling," Derek whispered, giving my hand a kiss and a soft, comforting squeeze. "Let the paramedics do their job first."

"Para . . ." I closed my eyes and pictured Trudy lying in a pool of blood. What happened after that? My hands were folded across my stomach, and I wondered why they felt so damp. Were they covered in blood? I sucked in several great gulps of air to fight back the sickness that thought brought. My eyes fluttered open, and I wondered why firemen were walking inside Trudy's house.

"Trudy?" I uttered.

"Trudy will be fine."

"Firemen."

"Yes," he said. "They arrived with the EMTs."

I held up my hand and struggled to say the word. "Blood?"

"No, love. There's no blood on your hands."

I inhaled and exhaled slowly. Okay then, I thought, as memories of what I'd found on entering Trudy's house began swarming through my mind. Professionals were here, taking care of things. Even better, Derek was here. And best of all, I was still breathing and, apparently, so was Trudy. The bad news? "Head hurts."

"I know, love."

"Blood?" I guess I was a little obsessed.

Derek's dark eyes narrowed with concern. "Yes, a bit."

I gulped and tried to breathe. I could barely tolerate the sight of someone else's blood. I had even fainted a few times in the past, so I squeezed my eyes shut to concentrate on staying awake and conscious—and not thinking about blood. Mine or Trudy's.

When I opened my eyes again, Derek was watching me intently, but then looked away to scan the room. He gave someone a curt nod and turned back to me. "The tech will be over here in just a minute."

I could tell he was angry. Something was very wrong, but since Trudy was all right, his anger was probably due to my being hurt. Unless . . .

"Gunshot," I murmured, recalling the last sound I had heard before passing out.

"Yes," he said through clenched teeth.

I tried to sit up. "Someone shot Trudy?"

He slipped his arms around me and eased me back to the floor. "Stay where you are until the techs are free."

"Someone shot . . . me?"

He touched my cheek again. "No, thank God."

I tried to think, tried to squeeze my eyes shut, but it hurt my head too much, so I watched his face. "Did Amelia shoot Trudy?"

"No, love," he said gently. "Just rest for a moment. We can talk about it later."

Amelia didn't shoot Trudy. Okay, good. But now I remembered what I'd seen when I first walked into the house. Trudy, bleeding on the floor by the fireplace.

Amelia, sprawled across the chair. I met Derek's gaze directly. "Amelia?"

His jaw tightened, and he swiped his hand across his mouth in helpless fury.

"Amelia?" I was confused. Neither Trudy nor I had been shot. That left Amelia. But why would someone shoot her?

I must've gotten hit harder than I thought, because I couldn't connect any dots. So I stopped trying and slipped back into dreamland.

When I woke up, I was strapped to a gurney and Derek was gone. I could barely move my head and became anxious, but relaxed a little when I was able to spot Derek standing a few feet away, near Trudy's kitchen door, talking quietly to Gabriel and Robson.

I was glad to see Gabriel here, but Robson shouldn't be here. There was too much blood.

No, no. I was the one who got sick over blood. Not Robson. Trudy was his cousin, his only living relative. Somebody shot her, so of course Robson had to be here.

Wait. Did somebody shoot Trudy or did they shoot Amelia? I couldn't remember. Did they shoot me? My head was throbbing as if two jackhammers were trying to drill through my skull. Was it from a bullet? I couldn't remember what Derek had told me.

Damn it, I needed to get up and find out what had happened here. I tried to roll onto my side, but I was restrained by the straps. Frustrated, I yelled out, but even that small effort made my head pound and the noise sounded more like a low moan.

I raised my head and tried yelling again. Strobe lights flashed in my eyes, and now my head felt like it might explode. So maybe this wasn't such a good idea. My head fell back against the gurney, and I was happy to keep it there for as long as it continued to spin.

At one point I thought I saw Detective Parrish from the sheriff's department staring down at me, but I might've been hallucinating. Was she saying something? Her lips were moving, but I couldn't hear anything. I closed my eyes and fell asleep.

"Brooklyn, darling," Derek crooned a few seconds later—or it could've been an hour—and he leaned over to kiss my cheek.

"Home," I whispered.

"Soon."

Instead, two paramedics wheeled the gurney—with me on it—out to a waiting ambulance. Derek walked along beside me, holding my hand.

"Is this necessary?" I mumbled, and heard Derek chuckle. The sound soothed me as the tech pricked my skin with a needle and I floated into unconsciousness.

I gradually woke up out of a drug-induced sleep and found myself alone in a white room.

It took a little while to figure out that it was only a white curtain and that I was obviously somewhere inside the local urgent care center. I could hear activity on the other side of the curtain, and I desperately wanted to be a part of it. The fog was lifting from my brain. I needed to know exactly what had happened to Trudy and Amelia. Were they all right? And was the person who hurt them—and me—already in custody? Who was it?

Elizabeth!

I'd forgotten all about her. Where was she? Was she the one who got shot?

I took a few deep breaths and tried to do a little mental triage. My head still ached, but it was a vague pain, thanks to whatever medication the techs had given me. It no longer felt as if my brain were going to spin off its axis, so that was reassuring. I checked my legs and arms, moving them slightly to make sure they were operational. Yes, they were fine. My stomach was good, too, as long as I didn't think too much about all that blood pooling under Trudy's head—and probably mine.

Nothing else hurt, so I figured I was okay to leave the room. I wanted to find Derek and get to the bottom of what had happened at Trudy's. I hated being left out of the loop.

I pushed myself up to a sitting position, and the world began to swerve. "Whoa," I whispered, clutching both edges of the narrow gurney. Maybe I would take things a little slower for the next few minutes.

"Isn't this perfect timing?" Derek said as he slipped through the curtain and into my space. "I thought you might try to make a move when I wasn't watching."

"Can we go? I'm fine, really."

"I saw your head wobbling just now," he countered.

"That'll pass." I hoped.

"Of course it will." He smiled grimly. "If you're sure you're ready, then let's go home. The doctor prescribed some pain medication to get you through the next few hours."

"I probably won't need it, but thanks." I started to slide off the table, and Derek grabbed me before my feet hit the floor. A good thing since I was pretty sure I would've kept going until my face was planted against the linoleum.

"Thanks again," I said, grateful to have him holding me up. "I'm going to be perfect any minute now."

"You're already perfect, love, just a tad unsteady." He had his arm securely fastened around my waist. "I'm not letting go of you, so as soon as you're fit to try walking, just say the word."

With the help of a wheelchair, we finally made it to Derek's car. It wasn't until I was buckled up safely inside the Bentley and we were driving home that I found out that Amelia was dead.

Derek carried me into the house and set me down on the couch with some extra pillows. I heard Maggie whine a little as she moved close and nosed my hand, then planted herself along the edge of the couch to guard me. Charlie jumped up onto the couch and curled up on my stomach. I wasn't sure I deserved so much wonderful treatment after the way I'd giggled and gossiped behind poor Amelia's back. And what must Trudy be going through, knowing that her companion had been killed inside her own home?

And where was Elizabeth?

After handing me a glass of water and one of the pills the doctors had sent home with me, Derek sat down at the foot of the couch and we talked about what had happened. I told him everything I could remember from the time I got out of my car in front of Trudy's until the moment when I lost consciousness.

"Do you know what else happened?" I asked. "Did you talk to Trudy?"

"We're piecing it together," he said. I reached out to rest my hand on his knee and felt calmer. "Trudy is still unconscious, but when she wakes up, we hope she'll be able to tell us exactly what occurred." He frowned and stood up, grabbed another pillow from one of the chairs, and shoved it behind my back so I could sit up a little straighter. He pulled my blanket up to my waist and tucked it under me. Charlie waited patiently until Derek was finished, then gingerly climbed on top of my stomach again.

"Is she too heavy for you?" Derek asked.

"No, she's perfect."

Derek adjusted the pillows again. He was nervous, I realized, fiddling with things while he figured out the best way to give me the bad news.

"Please, Derek. Just tell me what happened."

He sat on the heavy mission-style coffee table inches away from me and leaned forward, his elbows resting on his knees. "The best we can guess is that someone else was in the house with Trudy. They pulled a gun out and shot her, or tried to. We don't know why. Amelia ran over and pushed Trudy aside. The bullet grazed Trudy's shoulder and entered Amelia's chest, piercing her heart."

"Oh God." I pressed my hand to my own heart, appreciating its reassuring beat. It was painful to hear his words.

"When Trudy was pushed," he continued, "she hit her head against the tile fireplace and lost consciousness. Since you were close enough to hear the gunshot, I'm assuming the assailant was nearby as you ran inside. The minute you knelt down to help Trudy, he or she hit you with a vase filled with flowers that Trudy kept on the table by the front door."

"Are you kidding?" Now I realized why my hands and shirt had been so damp earlier. From the water in the vase. I hoped it wasn't something like a Ming vase. Of course, it would just figure that Trudy would own a Ming vase. But I was going off on another tangent and had to drag my brain back to the subject. "Poor Amelia. Poor Trudy. What did Robson say?"

"He's devastated." Derek shook his head. "It's too close to home for him. Nothing like this has ever happened here."

I nodded and felt the same disappointment and sorrow Robson must be feeling. It was as if Dharma had been living a charmed life since its beginning and now some of that innocence had been stripped away and would never come back. "That's true. Even the discovery of the body in the cave wasn't as shocking as this. Nobody knew Mr. Renaud, and he's been gone for seventy years. But Amelia . . . I just saw her the other day. She was scowling at me." I swallowed around the sudden lump in my throat. "Heck, when *wasn't* she scowling at me?"

Derek moved to the couch, picked up Charlie and set her down on my other side, and put his arms around me. Neither of us spoke for a while. It was enough for me to feel his solid warmth and the steady beat of his heart beneath my cheek.

A minute later, I suddenly sat up straight. "Wait. Where's Elizabeth? Is she okay?"

"We don't know," he said, his jaw tightening again. "She wasn't in the house when the police arrived, and we haven't heard from her."

"Oh my God. Do you think the killer took her?"

"We don't know, love. There was no sign of another struggle. As soon as Trudy wakes up, we hope she might know something."

I frowned. "Maybe she was out shopping. I hope she's okay."

"I do, too." He took my hand in his. "Can you tell me what happened when you arrived?"

"Oh yeah." I closed my eyes to organize my thoughts, then looked at him. "I was on the front porch when I heard the gunshot. I didn't even think twice, just pushed the door open and went inside. I saw Trudy in front of the fireplace, and Amelia passed out on the chair. I thought she was asleep or drunk or something. It never occurred to me that . . ."

"Why would it?" Derek said quietly. "Why would anyone expect this sort of violence to occur inside Trudy's home?"

"I feel so bad, though, because I sort of ignored Amelia and went straight to Trudy. I knelt down to check her pulse and grabbed my cell phone to call nine-one-one, and that was when I got hit from behind."

"Did you see or hear anything?" he asked. "Smell anything?"

I put myself back in the scene. "I did, but it won't help anything. All I heard was the floorboard creaking behind me. I thought maybe it was Amelia. Maybe she woke up. Stupid." I rubbed my eyes and inched down on the couch, exhausted from the recital.

"Sleep, love," Derek whispered, and pulled the blanket up to my chin.

Two hours later, I woke up to find Gabriel and

Robson seated at the dining room table with Derek. It was an oddly sweet picture to see these three powerful men sitting in the charming, old-world-style room. Lace café curtains framed the casement windows, and, outside, geraniums grew in profusion in window boxes. I loved the view from that room, but my head was still too achy to get up off the couch to join them. I did manage to overhear their conversation, though, despite its unhappy subject matter.

Guru Bob insisted on paying for Amelia's funeral.

"Does she have relatives in the area?" Derek asked.

"Trudy will know," Robson said. "As soon as she is able to speak, we will obtain the information and begin the preparations."

He sounded tired, but it was probably because he was so sad.

"I will attempt to persuade Trudy to move into my home," he continued. "There is plenty of room."

"You know she won't go for that," Gabriel said. "She's still feisty enough to fight you on it."

Guru Bob smiled, despite the lines of worry across his forehead. "Yes, I know. And I admire her lively spirit. But I am beside myself with worry, and I simply cannot bear the idea of her remaining in a home where such violence occurred. But if she insists, I would appreciate it if you would increase the security levels at her house."

"No problem."

"She knows her assailant," Derek said, not mincing words. "She saw the person aim the gun and kill Amelia. The killer knows this, so Trudy is in danger. However, I don't think moving her from her home would be the best thing for her. Especially not to your house, Robson. We don't want to endanger you, too."

He thought about that. "Then what can we do?"

"I'll move into her house," Gabriel said easily. "She's got an extra bedroom or two, and it'll only be for a few days, until she's well enough to tell us what happened."

I sat up on the couch and said, "I could move in with her. I could protect her."

Derek whipped around. "No."

Just *no*. What the heck? But the other men shook their heads in agreement with him.

"Sorry, babe," Gabriel said. "You're already on the injured list."

"I'll be fine by tomorrow."

Robson smiled. "I am grateful for your generous offer, Brooklyn, but I must agree with Derek. I will not jeopardize your health and safety any more than it already has been. And forgive me, but I have Trudy's safety to consider as well."

"I guess you're right. I wouldn't be much help in my current condition." But I glowered at Derek anyway.

Derek glared back until I raised my hands in surrender. "Okay, okay. You win."

Maybe he was right, but did he have to give me such a dirty look? I wanted to help. I knew I'd totally blown it when I arrived a few seconds too late to help Trudy or Amelia. Hell, I didn't even get a look at the killer. It was infuriating.

The front door swung open, and my mother and father charged into the room. Mom was carrying a heavy case.

Maggie jumped up and barked with delight. She ambled over and allowed Dad to pet her vigorously.

"Where is she?" Mom demanded as she whirled around, scanning the rooms. "Brooklyn? Oh, there you are. Thank Buddha."

Dad left Maggie and came to the couch, where he leaned over and gave me a light kiss on the good side of my head.

"Hi, Dad."

He sat down and held my hand as Mom set the briefcase she'd been carrying on the coffee table. She immediately pressed the back of her hand against my forehead.

"What're you doing, Mom?"

"Just checking that you don't have a fever."

"The killer didn't sneeze on me," I grumbled as I settled back against the pillows.

"Very funny." She pressed her hands to her stomach and breathed in and out. "You took ten years off my life, missy."

"Mine, too, kiddo," Dad said, sniffling a little.

They were obviously distraught, so I grabbed both of their hands and gave them a squeeze. "I'm sorry. But really, I'll be fine. I just got a little bump on the head."

Since my head was wrapped in yards of gauze and bandages, I didn't blame Mom for rolling her eyes at me.

"It looks worse than it is," I mumbled.

"Just stop talking," she advised, and opened her case to reveal a veritable pharmacopoeia of vials and potions and tinctures and God knew what else. Probably a tube of fairy dust and some eye of newt.

Heaven help me, the Grand Raven Mistress of the Celtic Goddess Coven was on a mission. And her mission was *me*.

Once upon a time, my mother would've dissolved into tears at the sight of my head bashed in. Now, though, Dad was the one tearing up while Mom was all business as she pulled out the ingredients to work one of her world-class healing and protection spells. As far as she was concerned, white magic would cure whatever ailed me.

Seriously. She believed it. The funny thing was, once in a while her crazy magic spells actually worked. But you wouldn't catch me saying that out loud.

I cast a pleading look at Derek, silently beseeching him to rescue me from Glinda the Good Witch. But Derek's eyes sparkled with laughter, and I knew I would get no support from him.

Robson gazed fondly at my mother as she prepared to terrorize me. So no help from him, either.

And forget Gabriel. Grinning shamelessly, he got up from the dining table, walked into the living room, and sat down to watch the show.

Mom pressed her fingers against the middle of my forehead—my third eye—and intoned, *"Om shanti . . . shanti . . . shanti."*

Peace.

I couldn't help but close my eyes and breathe. Repeated three times, the simple Sanskrit chant was meant to protect me from the three disturbances brought on by nature, the modern world, and one's own negativity.

I hoped it worked.

"I know you're in pain, so I'll keep it simple," Mom said, pressing two black tourmaline crystals into my hand. "Hold these. Visualize their power."

Black tourmaline. I'd seen Mom work with it before. According to her, the ancients had employed the stone as potent protection from demons and negative forces.

All black stones were protective by nature, but black tourmaline's power was further enhanced by its unique shape, a three-sided prism with vertical striations that acted as a strong deflector of negative energy.

Mom stood and closed her eyes. She reached out and touched my head with both of her hands, and began to chant:

"Goddess of Earth, Wind, Water, and Fire,
Grant me one wish I desire,
Protect my loved one from evil's spell,
Be ever watchful and guard her well.
Focus her power, make her strong,
Banish all that do her wrong.
My thanks and praise I offer thee
And as I mote, so shall it be."

A circle of white light surrounded me like mist in a forest. The black stones seemed to vibrate in my hands, sending waves of calming strength up my arms, across my shoulders, and down my spine. Glinda really did know her stuff. Within seconds, I fell sound asleep.

*   *   *

I woke up a while later, unsure how long I'd slept. It was evening, and the living room drapes had been pulled closed. There were no lights on, and the room was dark. Too dark. Almost depressing. I struggled to sit up, wondering where Derek was.

"Hello, gracious."

"Oh!" I jolted, and the sudden movement caused my head to ache. But I had to admit the pain wasn't as pronounced as it had been before my mother's visit, so go figure. "Hi, Robson."

He was still seated at the dining table a few yards away from me. "I apologize for frightening you."

"That's okay. I wasn't sure anyone was home."

"Derek drove to the pharmacy to obtain some instant ice packs and a heating pad for you."

"Oh, that sounds wonderful."

"Is there anything I can get you?" he asked.

It felt odd to be asking him for favors, but I plunged ahead. "Would you mind turning on some lights for me?"

"Of course not." He carried his chair over and set it down closer to the couch. After switching on several table lamps around the room, he sat and observed me. I figured I must've looked pretty bad to have him so concerned.

Maggie the dog shuffled over and settled at Guru Bob's feet while Charlie pounced against his shoe until he lifted her onto his lap. Ordinarily, Charlie would've been tucked up against me, but I had a feeling her instinctive kitty perception told her that Guru Bob was in more dire need of some affection.

"They love you," I said.

He smiled at Charlie as he stroked the kitten's back. "If only we humans could show one another as much pure love as animals do."

"If only," I murmured.

He returned his gaze to me. "I told Derek I would stay until he returned, in case there was anything you needed."

"That wasn't necessary, but thank you." I rearranged the pillows so I could sit upright and face him. "How is Trudy?"

"She is still unconscious, although the doctor indicated that she is recuperating nicely. She will stay in the hospital until she wakes up and is fully recovered. It could be a day or two." Even though his words were encouraging, he wore a worried frown.

I didn't want to sound like an alarmist and add to his worries, but I was suddenly nervous. "I hope they have someone watching her room. She's the only one who can identify Amelia's killer."

Guru Bob didn't respond right away. He was an expert at keeping his emotions in check, but the subject of Amelia and Trudy's assailant was testing his resolve. Finally he said, "It is such a blessing to have you and Derek staying in Dharma. Rest assured that he has already contacted his office to arrange a security detail and his people were quick to install a guard outside her hospital room."

"That's good." I gritted my teeth and confessed what I'd been considering for the last few hours. "I should probably move back to the city."

"Because you feel you have brought death to Dharma."

It was weird to be reminded that Guru Bob always seemed to know exactly what was going on in my head. Could he read my thoughts? Probably not, but he seemed to possess an uncanny empathic ability that most people lacked. Whatever his strengths, he blew my mind on a regular basis.

"We've talked about it before," I said, referring to my disconcerting habit of finding dead people. "But this time it's hitting too close to home. I don't want anyone else to be hurt. I feel awful about Amelia."

"And you blame yourself," he concluded.

"Well, yes." Did I? It sounded dumb to say it out loud. "Okay, I don't actually blame myself, but what the heck? I show up and somebody dies! It's creepy. If I were you or someone else, I would think twice about inviting *me* to dinner, if you know what I mean."

His smile broadened, lightening my mood despite my worries. "I used to get more sympathy from you," I grumbled.

He laughed, a deep melodic sound that was like music. "You know I have complete sympathy and concern for your feelings in this matter. I also am aware of your role in Amelia's life."

I sighed. "I didn't mean to be so antagonistic toward her, if that's what you mean. But she always seemed so annoyed to see me. I guess I let it get to me."

He sobered. "I misspoke. Let me rephrase my statement. I am aware of your role in Amelia's *death*."

"What?" It took me a few long moments to figure out what he was talking about, and I was afraid my face fell when I finally did. "Are you talking about that whole *Nemesis* thing?"

Nemesis was the name of an Agatha Christie novel in which Miss Marple received a letter from a man who'd recently died, in which he beseeched her to investigate the death of his son's fiancée. Guru Bob thought that, like Miss Marple, my destiny might somehow be wrapped up in seeking vengeance and justice for the dead who could no longer speak for themselves.

It was a little crazy, but how else could I explain my proclivity for finding dead bodies with such alarming regularity?

"Yes, gracious. I know that in your heart, you realize this, but let me make it extra clear: you are not to blame for Amelia's death. That blame goes directly to the person who killed her in cold blood."

"I know, but come on." I flailed my arms for emphasis. "Don't you think it's a little weird that I show up in Dharma and within days, there's a dead body? And then another one? What am I doing here? How will it end?"

"I cannot say how it will end," he admitted. "But I

repeat, those deaths have nothing to do with your being
here."

"But—"

"Whether you were here or not, we would have opened
the cave and found the body. I think that Amelia was
killed because of that discovery. In other words, it would
have happened anyway." He held up his hand to stop me
from interrupting again. "Your reason for being here is
clear. You are not the harbinger of doom, gracious. You
are the bringer of justice. You will find that justice for
Amelia. You will solve the puzzle of Monsieur Renaud's
death. And you will do all of this because you simply
cannot help yourself."

"I can't help myself." I thought about it and shook
my head. "That makes me sound pitiful. And even a
little ruthless."

"Not one bit," Guru Bob said with a tenacity I appreciated but didn't quite believe. "The last time we spoke
of such things, you told me that each time you have been
confronted with violent death, you've focused your mind
on the loved ones left behind. Their pain. Their ruined
lives. That is your motivation; that is your purpose in
delving so deeply into the mysteries of why such a thing
happened and who caused it. And that is neither ruthless
nor pitiable. It is a most admirable trait."

Admirable? Sometimes I wondered, but I had to
admit it felt good to know Robson's thoughts on all of
this. "But the police . . ."

"You have never hindered a police investigation."

"I've tried not to," I said, grinning sheepishly. "But
the police might disagree."

His smile was serene. "They are wrong."

Who was I to argue with a highly evolved conscious
being? Especially one who was trying his best to cajole
me out of my one-woman pity party? "Thank you."

"You are welcome." He bowed his head slightly.
"Perhaps you will grant me a favor or two?"

I sat up a little straighter on the couch. "Of course, Robson. Anything."

His eyes narrowed. "Stay in Dharma. Recuperate from this attack. Then work with Derek to track down the assailant who has brought this terrible evil to our community."

"Derek wouldn't want to hear you saying that."

"He wishes to protect you from yourself."

"Yes. Even though he's perfectly happy putting himself in danger to find the answers."

"In truth, he does this best when you are by his side."

I had to smile. Returning to the city right now had never really been an option anyway, I told myself. And to tell the truth, I wouldn't have wanted to leave until Dharma was once again its peaceful, normal self. But having Robson call it a personal favor pretty much sealed my decision.

"I'll stay," I said. "But I'm afraid you might have to answer to Derek if anything happens."

He pursed his lips thoughtfully. "Perhaps we ought to keep this between ourselves for now."

"Good idea," I said with a laugh.

Chapter 13

Despite my gauze-enshrouded head, I felt well enough the next morning to shower carefully and dress for the day. Over orange juice, a soft-boiled egg, and toast, Derek broke the news that Trudy remained in a coma. "But the doctors are hopeful she'll emerge within the next twenty-four hours."

"I pray they're right." I needed to ask a totally dumb question that had kept me awake for at least an hour in the middle of the night. "Did the vase break when the killer hit my head?"

Derek smiled in sympathy. "No. Whoever swung it wasn't able to do permanent damage to either your head or the vase itself."

"Small favors," I whispered. I would take them wherever I could find them. "I imagined I'd broken a Ming vase with my head."

"If it had been a Ming, you probably would've broken it. But sadly, it was harder than your delicate little head."

I chuckled. I finished my egg and toast, but lingered over my juice. "I feel like I've been out of it for a week. Is there any news? Was someone arrested? Have you seen Elizabeth? How's Trudy doing? Is Amelia being autopsied?"

"It all happened yesterday, so you haven't missed much." Derek smiled but turned somber as he began to answer my questions. "Amelia's autopsy is being performed today. I don't expect any grand revelations. And no one's been arrested. The detectives are questioning everyone they can find."

"Do they want to talk to me?"

"I called Detective Parrish to relate everything you told me yesterday, but they'll want to hear it from you eventually. I assured her that we would contact them as soon as you're up to it."

"Any other updates on Trudy's condition?"

"As of last night at eight o'clock, there was no change. I'll call Robson after breakfast and find out how she's coming along."

There was no more news to report, so we read the paper and finished the last bits of breakfast in amiable silence. Afterward, I stayed seated at the table while Derek washed the dishes, dried them, and put them away. I knew he had to leave in a little while to chaperone the odious Noland Garrity into the caves in order to view the artwork once again.

"I'm not completely incapacitated," I insisted, trying not to sound too whiny. "I could go with you."

He gave me a look over his shoulder, then shut off the water and returned to the table. "Darling, less than twenty-four hours ago you were coshed in the head and came away with a bloody bad gash and a concussion. One woman is dead and the other is in a coma. The only reason you escaped a hospital stay is because I swore I would wake you up every two hours to make sure you weren't seeing double and slurring your words. So, while the doctor has given you a clean bill of health, I think you should stay close to home today. Rest. Take a nap, read a book."

"Sounds so boring."

"You'd honestly rather spend the day with Noland Garrity?"

"Ugh. Maybe you're right. But I hate knowing you'll have to deal with him alone."

"So do I."

"Can't we make him go away?"

He laughed and folded the dish towel, hanging it on the small rack under the sink. "It won't be a pleasant day, but I'll survive him."

"I hope so. I'll miss you if you go to jail for throttling him."

He chuckled. "I won't throttle him, I promise."

I felt a sudden throbbing and rubbed my head. "I was thinking I might have lunch with China, but I'd better not push it yet." Saying it out loud reminded me of my last lunch in town. "And you didn't say whether anyone's heard from Elizabeth yet."

Derek scowled. "I don't know. I'll give Detective Parrish a call to see if she's heard anything."

"You don't think she could've . . ."

He gazed at me for a long moment. "I don't, no. But it's suspicious, her being gone like this."

I didn't know what to think. I liked Elizabeth and couldn't imagine her doing anything that would hurt Trudy. But then, what did we really know about her? Almost nothing, except what she'd told me. And who was to say she'd told me the truth? But recalling what she'd said about her beloved grandma Reenie, I couldn't believe she'd been lying. It made my stomach hurt to think about it.

"Before you leave," I said, changing the subject, "can we call and find out how Trudy's doing?"

"Funny you should say that, darling, because I was just going to call Robson to find out that very thing."

"I hope she's awake."

He sat down beside me at the kitchen table and made the call on his cell phone. When Robson answered, Derek pressed the Speaker button so I could listen in.

"I am at the hospital now," Robson said, "and it is very good news. Trudy is awake and seems to be doing well despite her ordeal."

"That's wonderful," I said.

Derek agreed. "Please give her our best."

"Yes, we're looking forward to seeing her soon," I said.

"Thank you both for your kind thoughts. She will be pleased that you called." Robson hesitated, then said, "May I ask you to hold on for a moment?"

"Of course," Derek said.

It was a full minute before he came back on the line. "I am sorry I kept you waiting. I wanted to step outside Trudy's room to give you the rest of the news."

I glanced at Derek. We could both hear the tension in his voice.

"What's wrong?" I asked. "Is she really okay?"

"Trudy is fine physically," he assured us. "There is a problem, though. She does not remember a thing."

After calling to reschedule his morning meeting with Garrity, Derek drove us to the hospital. Guru Bob's news had been a shock, and there was no way I was going to sit around waiting for updates. We both wanted to see Trudy, even if her memory was temporarily gone.

And as long as I was at the hospital, I was determined to have this headful of gauze and bandages removed. I was pretty sure a simple, small bandage would do the job. I didn't want to scare poor Trudy half to death by walking into her room looking like the Invisible Woman.

"Poor Guru Bob," I said to Derek as he drove down Shakespeare Lane toward Ridge Road. "He's the one who's always being called on to comfort the sick and troubled. So who comforts him when he's suffering?"

"Looks like it's you and me," Derek said.

I nodded. "I guess we'll do what we have to do."

Derek took hold of my hand as he drove, and we talked for another minute or two, until the gentle movement of the car made me drowsy and I closed my eyes. The good news about sneaking a little car nap was that it would help in my healing process. The bad news was that Derek was probably regretting taking me along while I was still a little wobbly on my feet. The sooner I was completely back to my normal self, the sooner I could start figuring out who the hell had killed Amelia. Because if Trudy couldn't remember anything that happened yesterday, we were still at ground zero.

I woke up as we pulled into the hospital parking lot. Derek agreed to go with me to the clinic to have my bandages removed. It only took a few minutes, and I was looking and feeling much better after the new dressing and small bandage were applied.

We took the elevator up to Trudy's floor, and I was happy to see an armed guard stationed outside her door. I was even more gratified to see her looking so well. Someone had come by and fixed her hair. She was sitting up in bed, and Guru Bob was seated in the chair beside her.

"Oh, how sweet you are to come by," she said, holding out her arms to greet us. When she saw my small bandage, she faltered. "What is this? Were you hurt?"

I gave Guru Bob a quick glance, and he shook his head. So he hadn't told her anything yet? I could hardly scold him. He looked so upset, it broke my heart.

"I had a little accident," I said lamely. Derek, meanwhile, had brought two more chairs into the room and set them down on the opposite side of the bed from Guru Bob.

"We could be having a party," she said.

I smiled. "Trudy, do you remember what happened? Why you're in the hospital?"

"I can't remember a thing. The doctor says my memory is temporarily missing because I hit my head." She laughed lightly. "But I can't even remember doing that."

Derek closed the door to the room, and I moved my chair closer to Trudy's side. "It's not good news. I'm sorry."

Guru Bob reached over and took her hand in his.

"Oh dear. You all look very serious." She tried to smile. "Am I dying of some rare disease?"

I leaned in and held on to her other hand. "I came to

your house to see you yesterday because you said you had a surprise for me. Do you remember what that was?"

She gazed at me blankly. "I have no idea."

"When I arrived, I heard a loud noise, like a gunshot. I ran into your house, and you were lying near the fireplace."

I glanced at Derek, who continued the story. "Someone was in your home, Trudy, and they had a gun pointed at you. As they pulled the trigger, Amelia ran over and shoved you out of the way. The bullet went through your shoulder and hit her in the chest. I'm sorry, Trudy, but Amelia died yesterday."

I gripped her hand as she gasped. She glanced from Derek to Robson to me, gasped again, and then couldn't seem to catch her breath. "No. No. No. No."

"I'm so sorry," I said.

Her eyes filled with tears, and she shook her head. "It's not possible. It can't be true. Robson, tell me the truth."

"Oh, Trudy." Robson stood up, leaned over, and pressed his cheek to the top of her head. He couldn't lift her up and hold her because her shoulder was bandaged.

I kept my hand locked on hers and felt her squeezing it so tightly, I could barely feel my fingers. I didn't care.

Derek walked out into the hall to find a nurse. I knew we'd dealt a crushing blow to Trudy's spirits. She would probably need a tranquilizer, and I wondered if she'd be able to come home as early as they'd said.

But almost as upsetting was seeing how distraught Guru Bob was. I'd never seen him like this before. It was perfectly understandable, of course, but I'd always known him to be so strong. He seemed to have aged overnight.

I had a feeling the best thing for Guru Bob—and everyone else—would be for Trudy to regain her memory and fully recover from this awful experience. But who knew how soon that would happen?

"Tell me everything," Trudy said abruptly, letting go of my hand and grabbing the remote control to bring her hospital bed to a fully upright position. "I want to hear it all, no matter how horrible. I'm heartsick and my head can barely accept what you're saying, but if you tell me the whole story, I might be able to remember something."

"All right," I said, thrilled that she was willing to act, not just sit back and worry.

Robson sat down just as Derek walked back into the room with a nurse, but Trudy waved her away. "Thank you, Lynette, but I don't want any shots or sleeping pills right now." She trembled and sniffled twice before her eyes narrowed in on Derek. "I want you to find the person who did this, and you can only do that if I can recall what happened. And dozing off for the next three days won't help."

Guru Bob's concerns for his beloved cousin seemed to dissipate slowly as Trudy spoke. He scooted his chair closer and took hold of her hand again. It seemed to comfort him as much as it did her.

Derek leaned against the wall facing her. "Can you think back to the last thing you do remember?"

Trudy stared at him for a moment, then said, "Dinner. Wednesday night. Amelia served my favorite, chicken stew with dumplings." She frowned. "After that, nothing."

For some reason, that filled me with sadness. Wednesday was the night before Amelia was killed. So she remembered nothing about Thursday.

I continued telling her what had happened. "When I saw you lying on the floor, I ran over to help you. I vaguely registered that Amelia was sprawled on the chair, but I was more worried about you. I didn't even think . . ."

"That she might be in worse shape than I was?"

"Yes. I'm sorry. My concern was with you. I felt your pulse and knew you were alive, so I pulled out my phone to call nine-one-one."

Derek added, "And she was attacked from behind by the killer, who hit her over the head with a vase."

Trudy's eyes were wide as she realized I'd been injured, too. "Dear God. Brooklyn, I'm so sorry."

"None of this is your fault," I insisted. "And I'll be fine. I've got a hard head."

She gave me a weak smile. "So much damage. Why? What in the world happened?" She took another glance at each of us. "I'm the only one who knows. And I can't remember."

"But you will," Robson said, squeezing her hand for encouragement. "Your memory will return shortly, and you will be able to tell us who did this horrible deed."

She nodded. "I will. I promise." Her eyelids fluttered closed. "I'm so tired."

I thought about asking her if she knew where Elizabeth was, but Trudy had been through enough trauma today. I didn't want to compound it by suggesting that her new friend had disappeared.

Lynette, the nurse, must've been hovering at the door, because she walked into the room just then. "I'd like you to let her sleep. She's been devastated by the news. Sleep will help her get her strength back and, in turn, it'll help with her memory."

"Yes, we'd better go," Derek said, looking at me as though he thought I could use some sleep, too. Frankly, he was right. I was exhausted.

"I will stay for a few more minutes," Robson said. "I would rather she have someone here in case she wakes up."

I walked to the other side of the bed and gave him a hug. "She's going to be all right."

"Thank you, gracious," he said.

Derek and I walked out of the room, just as another security guard approached. I was surprised to see that it was George from Derek's office. He had been undercover security when I worked on a television show several months earlier.

I looked at Derek. "I forgot that Robson told me you hired your own team for Trudy."

"Gabriel's men are busy at the caves, so it made sense to recruit a few of my own people. George is in charge of the security detail for as long as Trudy's hospitalized. He's doing a great job."

"Of course he is." I had complete confidence in George's abilities and knew Trudy was in good hands. It didn't surprise me a bit that Derek had gone the extra mile on this. But it did make me love him even more.

Smiling at his boss's words, George greeted me with a hug. We talked for a moment, then turned to leave, just as a woman dashed up the hall toward us in a state of complete panic.

I did a double take. "Elizabeth?"

She skidded to a stop. "Brooklyn?" She whipped her head around, looking for something. "Where's Trudy? I have to see her."

I stood my ground, unwilling to let her pass. "Where have you been for the past thirty hours?"

She seemed taken aback. "I was . . . I was out of town for a few days. Trudy knew I was going away. I was supposed to return tomorrow but . . ."

"But you're here now."

She shook her head as though confused. "Yes, because I happened to check my voice mail and heard a cryptic message from a police detective that something had happened. I rushed back home to Trudy's and saw the crime scene tape and called the detective back. She refused to tell me where Trudy was, so I tried to contact you, but there was no answer. So I called your mother."

"My mother?" I was getting dizzy from the twists and turns of her story. Frankly, I hadn't checked my messages since the attack occurred, so I rifled through my purse for my phone. Sure enough, there was a missed call. "Okay, it looks like you tried to call me. But where were you? When did you leave? How did you get my mother's number?"

"From, um, your sister Savannah."

"Savannah?" That was weird, but possible, I supposed. She'd met Savannah when we all had dinner at her restaurant the other night. "And my mother told you what happened?"

"She just told me that Trudy was in the hospital, so I raced over here as fast as I could. Will she be all right? I want to see her. What happened?"

"She was shot," I said bluntly. "Why did you disappear?"

She shook her head a few times as though she hadn't heard me correctly. "Brooklyn, I didn't just *disappear.* I've been out of town since Saturday. What in the world happened while I was gone?"

"Somebody shot Trudy and killed Amelia," Derek said. "Can you confirm where you were on Monday?" He was being blunt, too.

"Monday?" Elizabeth swallowed nervously. "You mean yesterday?" Her gaze was diverted to something behind us. I turned and saw Robson standing at the door to Trudy's room, listening to every word she said.

Elizabeth blinked and looked back at Derek. "I—I was out of town. I told you."

"Can you be more specific?"

She scowled. "No."

"So that's all you have to say?" he asked.

"Yes. Are you accusing me of something?"

"Not yet. I'm simply gathering information. Can anyone corroborate your story?"

"You mean, do I have an alibi?"

"Yes."

She stared at the floor for a long moment, then glared up at Derek. "It's none of your business where I've been or who might've seen me. I don't have to tell you anything. You have no authority over me."

I almost sputtered. The man had *authority* written all over him. And as far as the town of Dharma went, Robson Benedict was the supreme authority, although the Sonoma County Sheriff's Department might've balked at that description.

"True," Derek said mildly. "You don't have to tell me a thing. But you will have to tell the police." He pulled out his cell phone and made the call.

Derek dropped me off at the house and drove off to keep his rescheduled appointment with Noland Garrity. After all the excitement at the hospital, I spent the rest of the day sleeping and recuperating. I barely managed to do much else but sip from a bowl of soup that night.

The following afternoon, Derek returned home from yet another meeting with Garrity. As he fixed a pot of tea, we returned to the topic of Elizabeth's brief disappearance and her reluctance to tell us anything.

"She was right, of course," Derek said as he pulled two teacups out of the cupboard. "We can't force her to talk to us. But we weren't exactly interrogating her. We just wished to know where she's been for the past few days."

"I'm glad you called the sheriff." I was still miffed that Elizabeth wasn't willing to tell us where she'd gone. I'd been so worried, but now I was just suspicious.

"I'm confident they'll obtain more information from her than I was able to get."

"I really hate to think that she killed Amelia. I mean, she did go to the trouble of showing up at the hospital yesterday. I suppose that's a mark in her favor. And she did call the local police to find out what happened at Trudy's. If she was the killer, she would've just kept running, wouldn't she?"

"Would she?" Derek's gaze narrowed. "Perhaps she believed that coming back, showing concern, taking all those steps, would make her look innocent. I don't buy that angle. Until she's willing to tell us where she's been, I have to assume the worst."

We were silent for a full minute while he filled a

small plate with a half dozen of his favorite English biscuits. Normally at this time of day, we might've been sipping a glass of wine and munching on cheese and crackers. But with my head injury, Derek had automatically switched to tea and biscuits. Just one more reason to love him. As he poured tea, I thought about Elizabeth and her lack of an alibi. Why wouldn't the woman talk? What was she hiding? And why?

It was all too confusing and depressing to think about, so I changed the subject. "The good news is that Trudy is feeling better every day." I picked up my teacup and took a cautious sip, then frowned. "My head is a little fuzzy still. I don't suppose you'd like to get a pizza delivered and hang out at home tonight."

"I would love to. It's my favorite way to spend an evening."

"Mine, too." He led the way into the living room, and we sat together on the couch. After taking a bite of a biscuit, he remarked, "You didn't even ask me how my day went with Noland Garrity."

"Oh no." My shoulders drooped. "I must have been so out of it, I forgot completely. How did it go?"

"I survived," he said wryly. "But I've come to the realization that he has somehow obtained access to the caves from someone besides me."

That got me sitting up straight. "What? No way. You're the only one he's allowed to go in there with."

"Yes, and I thought I made that very clear. But he was quite eager to let me know that he didn't have to kowtow to me. He has other means of access."

"He's lying."

"I would've thought so, but there were items out of place since the last time I took him into the caves."

I froze. "Out of place? Or missing altogether?"

"There were three silver candlesticks missing from the first cave. Originally they were standing on top of the large ormolu dresser."

"I remember them."

We both sipped our tea. It was a strong, dark blend and I marveled at the difference between this and the insipid tea bags I'd grown up with.

"I finally found them in the back cave," he said. "Behind some of the rolled artwork."

"On the floor?"

"Yes."

"That's just weird," I said, resting my elbows on the table. "Did you ask Garrity if he moved them?"

"He insisted that he didn't."

"He must be lying," I repeated. "Who else would move stuff around? The only person I can think of would be Robson. Or maybe Gabriel. Did you ask either of them?"

"I phoned Gabriel. He said he never would've given the fellow access, first of all, and second, he would never move anything. I didn't have a chance to ask Robson when we saw him at the hospital today."

"It wasn't a good time to ask, anyway."

"No."

"Maybe it was one of Gabriel's men."

"Possibly." Derek was frowning now and so was I. I didn't like to think about people coming and going from those caves.

"Gabriel assured me he would talk to his entire security team. And he insisted that no one could breach the doors without him being aware of it. So who knows? I'll discuss it with Robson when the time is right, and we'll get to the bottom of it. In any case, Garrity will be gone within the week."

"Thank God," I groused. "Because I am really sick of Noland Garrity."

"I'll admit he does wear on a person." Derek reached for another biscuit. "He was in rare form yesterday."

"I'm sorry," I said, sympathizing, but quickly added, "Do tell me everything he did and said. All the dirty little details."

Derek smiled, but the emotion didn't reach his eyes. "He tried to convince me that someone in Dharma has stolen something from the cave."

My own eyes widened. "He's right, sort of. I took the Jules Verne book, remember? And Trudy took her bird sculpture."

"Both of those items were already gone when Garrity arrived, so he's not referring to them." Derek shifted on the couch, turning to face me more directly. "He's insisting that one of the paintings is missing. The Renoir 'facsimile,' as he puts it."

"The man refuses to suggest that it might be a genuine Renoir." I shook my head. "He's probably right, but I would love it if he were wrong."

"I'll admit he's not working under the most ideal circumstances, but I'm not willing to let him take anything out of the caves. I don't trust him. And Robson must agree; otherwise, he might've arranged for him to work in a more spacious, well-lighted studio somewhere."

"Do you think the painting is actually missing? It might've been moved to a different place. Like the candlesticks."

"I'll keep looking," Derek said, but he didn't look optimistic.

So we had thieves as well as a murderer in Dharma. Someone who had access to the caves? It didn't seem possible. How could they have gotten inside with no one noticing, let alone bring out a valuable painting?

"I hate to mention a sore subject," I said, "but what about one of the Frenchmen? You toured the cave with them last week, right? Could one of them have slipped the canvas under his shirt?"

"I was watching them closely. Then again, if we're willing to believe that one of the Frenchmen could get away with it, then so could Garrity. Although I always watch him closely as well."

"Good. I don't trust him, either." I gave in and reached for one of the sweet biscuits. "What if Garrity stole the painting," I theorized, "and now he's making a stink over it because he wants to appear above the fray while at the same time throwing suspicion elsewhere?"

As theories went, it wasn't a bad one. Especially given Noland Garrity's generally foul attitude.

"It's possible," Derek admitted casually, although I knew better than to think he was as relaxed as he sounded. "Perhaps the reason he calls the Renoir a facsimile is to draw less attention to it. If it truly is a Renoir, the fact that it's missing would be a massive scandal."

"I don't remember seeing a Renoir listed on any of the families' inventories, so chances are, it's not an original."

"Good point, darling."

"But it's still missing." An idea was bubbling inside my head, and I had to talk it out. "What if Garrity met Trudy somewhere in town and charmed her—I know it's hard to fathom, but humor me. He's not a bad-looking guy as long as he keeps his mouth shut. Anyway, he talks Trudy into asking Gabriel or Robson to let her into the cave to visit some of her own family's treasures. Garrity sneaks in after her. And then maybe later, she invites him to her house to show off some of her own pieces of art. And while they're talking, he tells her he needs to go back into the caves, but this time she refuses to help him. Maybe she's getting suspicious."

Derek jumped in. "So he pulls out a gun and shoots her, killing Amelia? Do you honestly believe he's capable of that?"

"I think he's pretty awful." But I thought it over and came to a sad conclusion. "But no, I guess not. Even though he's a bully, he doesn't seem to have a killer instinct. Cold-blooded maybe, and cowardly, but not a killer."

Derek rose and walked to the kitchen, returning with the teapot. He sat and poured more tea into each cup before continuing. "I don't see any evidence telling me that Garrity has ever met Trudy."

"Thanks for the tea." I took a bite of my biscuit. "We should ask Trudy about him, just to be sure, but you're probably right. If she'd asked Gabriel or Robson to let her back into the cave, I think they would've mentioned it. Especially after she was shot."

"True."

As I sipped my tea, something else occurred to me. "Wait. What if it wasn't Trudy? What if Amelia was the one who met him in town? Those two sourpusses would have plenty in common. He flirts with her to get closer to Trudy. She invites him over to the house for lunch and . . . I don't know. Something happens. She catches him going through Trudy's purse, trying to find the key. Or something. She screams bloody murder."

"So he pulled out a gun and killed her?"

I mulled it over. "Okay, what if he was aiming the gun at Amelia, but then Trudy ran into the room to intervene and Amelia pushed her away? What if his original target was actually Amelia?"

"But why, darling? What could Amelia have said or done that would cause him to react so violently? I know you dislike him. I do, as well. But I can't see a motive."

"I know, I know." I slumped back in the couch. "It's all ridiculously far-fetched."

"I'm not discounting it completely. Garrity could very well have stolen the Renoir. And since we have nothing concrete to go on so far, any thoughts or theories are welcome."

I pushed myself off the couch and found my purse. Pulling out a little notepad and pen, I began to jot down names.

"What have you got there?" he asked after swallowing another sip of tea.

I grinned. "A suspect list. So far we've got Elizabeth Trent and Noland Garrity. Any or all of the Frenchmen, but especially Henri. And I'd love to add Darlene and Shawn, but I have a feeling they're long gone. But I'm adding Josh Atherton because he asks too many questions and he's probably going to go out with Annie. So of course, we need to investigate him."

"Of course," he said, smiling.

"Darlene and Shawn are the perfect suspects," I said sentimentally. "Alias Smith and Jones. Even their name sounds criminal."

"And they're quite friendly," Derek remarked. "They could easily have struck up an acquaintance with Trudy and finagled an invitation into her home."

"Wow, that's true."

"But they're so easily recognized with all that bright red hair," he said. "They'd be taking a big chance showing their faces in Dharma again."

"It could be worth it to them."

Derek's mouth twisted into a frown. "And they did have all those lock-picking tools. Although, truth be told, they couldn't have broken into the caves with those tools. Gabriel would've been after them in a heartbeat."

"But somebody got into the caves, right? Maybe they snuck in while the door was open. Could one of the winery workers have gone in there and left the door open for a minute or two?"

"Anything's possible," Derek said. "But Robson announced that the caves were off-limits, so I can't imagine anyone in Dharma going against his edict. Although it's conceivable that an employee would have to go in there for some legitimate reason. Even if they were locked and secured."

Something occurred to me. "My brothers probably have the security codes to the doors."

"And it's quite possible that they've gone inside once or twice in the last week or so."

"And if some felonious critter has been watching the doors, he could sneak in behind them."

Derek smiled at my words, but he quickly sobered. "That might indeed be the way Garrity obtained entry."

"Sneaky bastard," I muttered, and stared at my list

of names. "Does Gabriel's security system make a note each time the doors are opened and closed?"

"Yes, of course," he said, contemplating the possibilities. "And the closed-circuit cameras record everything. It all shows up on an elaborate printout."

"Can we get a look at it? I'd like to create a timeline for all these suspects and add the security information to it."

"Excellent idea, darling." He pulled out his cell phone. "I'll set up a meeting with Gabriel first thing tomorrow morning."

Chapter 14

Bright and early Thursday morning I followed my doctor's advice and took the last of my bandages off. I was giddy with relief that I could finally take a real shower and wash my hair. By the time we left for our meeting with Gabriel at eight o'clock at his house, I felt as fluffed and fresh as a pretty flower.

Derek drove for a full mile up a winding road high in the hills above Dharma. When he came to a stop, I was mystified. I hadn't even known this place existed until that moment. I'd grown up in Dharma and was familiar with most of the town's nooks and crannies and hideaways, but I'd never realized there was a beautiful home tucked away at the tip-top crest of Dragon Valley Road.

As I gazed down one side of Gabriel's steep mountain, the view was of green terraced vineyards with grapevines that seemed to spread out forever. On the other side of the hill, I could see the ocean in the far distance as the marine layer was beginning to break up.

His home was a modified log cabin, similar to Austin and Robin's alpine home, only bigger. There was a pool in back with a good-sized patio deck, and along the side of the house were three large satellite dishes. These were the really big ones, the kind found at television studios and around airports.

What in the world? Maybe Gabriel really loved television, but this was ridiculous. Then I remembered how he talked about his drones and wondered if there was a connection between the drones and these dishes.

"Brooklyn," Derek said, "are you coming?"

"Yes, but did you see those dishes? They're huge."

"Gabriel does a lot of communicating by satellite."

"Oh." I didn't even know what that meant.

Gabriel met us at the door, looking impossibly sexy in a black T-shirt and stonewashed jeans. "Hey, babe," he said, giving me a hug. He smelled delicious and made me wonder how a simple citrus-and-spicy scent could be so dangerous.

Derek smiled indulgently, secure in the knowledge that I considered him even more dangerously handsome than our dashing friend. He shook Gabriel's hand. "Thanks for meeting us on short notice."

"No problem," Gabriel said, and led the way down a wide hallway and into a small conference room next door to his office. On the wall was a giant map of the world with lots of little pins stuck in certain spots. There was also a map of the oceans and the sky. I was afraid to ask what all those little pins signified.

A full coffee service along with an inviting basket of croissants and scones was laid out on the credenza under the window. The view out the bay window was of the pool and spa.

"Your home is beautiful," I said. "I didn't realize you'd moved to Dharma permanently."

"It's permanent for now," he said, grinning as he glanced out the window. "I like it here. And being at the top of the mountain has its advantages."

"I'll say. Your views are spectacular." I could think of other advantages that probably had something to do with those satellite dishes.

"Can I get you some coffee or tea?" he asked.

"I'd love some tea, but I can take care of it."

"Okay. Help yourself to the goodies, too."

"Thanks." I took a blueberry scone and a cup of tea. Even though the coffee smelled delicious, my system wasn't quite ready for it yet.

Derek poured coffee for himself, and we sat at the conference table.

Gabriel handed us a thick printout of the security system log and pointed out that he'd arranged it so that the top three pages listed the activity at the doors to the storage cave. The hours were listed in military time. As soon as I solved that little puzzle, I was able to read the information more comprehensively.

I pulled my desk calendar out of my satchel and opened it to the first week we'd moved to Dharma. I angled it on the table so that both men could see it. Pointing to Monday of that week, I said, "This was the day we excavated and discovered the first cave and the body of Jean Pierre Renaud. The police investigators were in and out numerous times, but you didn't have your security up and running yet. Later that day, I found the note in the book, and on Tuesday, Derek and I found the second cave. Wednesday we spoke to Trudy and showed her the cave. That night, we all met with Robson at my parents' house, and he asked you to beef up security for the caves."

"Right," Gabriel said, "and the following morning, Thursday, my team was installing new alarm systems on the cave doors." He used a pencil to point to the first line of data on his sheet. "This first log-in time corresponds to that moment. We were testing the systems all day, so you can see a series of notations. They aren't as important as the times on the next page."

"That's the same morning I started my inventory list."

Derek consulted his phone calendar. "And later that day, we had lunch with the Frenchmen."

"That feels like such a long time ago," I marveled, "but it's barely been three and a half weeks."

"A lot has happened since then," Derek said.

"I'll say."

We went through all of our calendars and tried to match up our visits to the cave with the corresponding times on Gabriel's security log.

"I've got seven entries logged that first weekend," Gabriel said.

"We were in and out of the caves those first few days," I recalled. "I was still doing the inventory and you and Derek were setting up light trees to help illuminate everything. And the police were there a couple more times, weren't they?"

"Yes," Derek said. "And Robson brought a few members of the commune board over to see what we were up to. Everyone was quite excited."

"I get that," Gabriel said.

"It took me three days to complete the inventory, working a few hours each day." I went through my calendar and told Gabriel which days I was in the caves. He checked off the corresponding log entries.

"If my notes are correct," Derek said, staring at his phone screen, "that following Tuesday, Robson called us over to request that we talk to the press. He had heard from the town mayor back in France, and he'd already hired the art appraiser. Word of the discovery had spread around the world."

"Yeah, I've got that on my calendar, too," Gabriel muttered.

"And Mom did a cleansing ritual the next day, Wednesday morning."

"Can't leave that out," Gabriel said, smiling. "And it's indicated right here on the chart."

"Now it gets tricky," I said. "Because Wednesday afternoon, Derek went to see the Frenchmen to set up a tour of the caves for them. And Trudy heard from Elizabeth for the first time. It doesn't have much to do with the caves, but I mention both incidents because all of them are suspects as far as I'm concerned."

"How did Elizabeth contact Trudy?" Gabriel asked.

"Elizabeth called her out of the blue," I said. "She's the granddaughter of an old friend of Trudy's. I guess that part's true enough, although we should probably double-check. Elizabeth told Trudy that she'd seen something about the cave discovery in her local paper, and she asked Trudy if she wouldn't mind having a visitor for a week. Trudy was thrilled."

"Sounds reasonable so far," Gabriel said.

I glanced at Derek. "By the way, it was during that same visit with Trudy that she gave me the letter that I wanted translated. I contacted my online group that night."

"Busy day," Derek said.

"And for the next three or four days, we were preparing for the photo exhibit. Robin and I were in and out of the caves, taking pictures, while Mom was setting up volunteers and such."

"Can you pin down the number of times you and Robin were there?"

I thought about it. "Okay, twice on that Thursday, once on Friday for four hours, and once on Saturday, but just for about a half hour."

Gabriel checked off a number of items on his sheet. "Okay, got 'em. Except there's another entry on Saturday afternoon."

"That was the tour I gave the French families," Derek noted.

"When did Elizabeth arrive in town?" Gabriel asked.

"The following Wednesday." I frowned, remembering something else. "Now that I think about it, Trudy waited until Amelia was out of the room before she told us about Elizabeth's visit. I wonder if Amelia was suspicious of Elizabeth from the very start."

"Interesting," Gabriel murmured.

"On the other hand," I said with a shrug, "Amelia never liked having anyone around, so maybe Trudy just waited until she was out of earshot to save herself the aggravation of an argument."

"That's the more likely scenario," Derek admitted, having met Amelia himself.

"I guess so." I checked my notes. "But wait. Before Elizabeth arrived, the horrible Noland Garrity showed up. He came on Monday, two days before the exhibit opened."

"What day did you go to lunch with Elizabeth?" Derek asked.

"That was Thursday, the day after the exhibit opened."

Gabriel leaned forward in his chair. "Were you able to learn anything about her?"

"She told me she lives in some dinky town in Wisconsin. No, sorry. It's in Michigan. She didn't give me the name of the town, but it's somewhere on the Upper Peninsula. She was lamenting that there aren't any good Mexican restaurants in the area. She's a navy brat. Spent some time in Sicily. None of this is helpful, is it?"

Derek chuckled. "It's a start, love."

"You'd be surprised what we can find out from that little bit of intel," Gabriel said, winking at me.

I was smiling back at him when I suddenly realized something and jumped from my chair. "Oh my God," I cried, pacing the floor. "Oh my God, I completely forgot to tell you this part." I stopped and pressed my palms against my forehead. "How could I have forgotten?"

Derek stood and put his arms around me. "What part, love?" He clearly thought I needed comforting, and maybe I did.

"I'm so sorry. I think this might be significant, but I have no idea why." My head was starting to spin from the exertion. Derek helped me back into the chair as though I were an invalid.

"I feel so silly forgetting to tell you, but there's been a lot going on."

"That's putting it mildly," Derek said, taking another moment to rub my back.

"Sorry to be such a drama queen," I said, feeling

even dumber for causing that little scene, "and it's probably not even important."

"Tell us and we'll help you figure out what it means," Gabriel said.

"Okay. After we had lunch, I took Elizabeth over to the town hall to show her the photograph exhibit. Her attention was immediately drawn to the alleged Renoir painting. She forgot all about me and just stood there staring at that photograph. So I wandered around for a while, ran into the odious Mr. Garrity and exchanged a few insults, and after he left, I saw Robin. She was there to show off her photos to Austin and Jackson."

"I'm with you so far," Gabriel said.

"So I stopped to talk to those guys, and then Robin and Austin walked away to check out the exhibit. Jackson stayed with me, and I invited him to dinner the next night at Savannah's restaurant. I wanted to introduce a bunch of people to Elizabeth because Trudy's hoping if she makes enough friends, maybe she'll move here."

"That's the dinner I had to turn down," Gabriel said. "Sorry about that."

"I know you were busy," I said, smiling. "We'll do it again sometime." I frowned. "If Elizabeth doesn't turn out to be a psychopathic killer."

Derek pointed to the calendar. "That dinner was Friday night, so your conversation with everyone at the exhibit would've been Thursday."

"Right," I said. "Same day as my lunch with Elizabeth. So there I am, talking to Jackson, and he agrees to go to dinner with us, and suddenly I hear this big gasping sound behind me. I turn and see Elizabeth, who looks like she's seen a ghost. She can't breathe. And now I'm worried, so I turn back to Jackson for help. And he's gone. Vanished."

"Where'd he go?" Gabriel asked.

"I have no idea. It was like he vanished in a cloud of smoke."

"What did Elizabeth say?"

I rolled my eyes. "She made up this story about how she thought she saw some woman she used to know. I told her we should go find the woman, but Elizabeth insisted that it wasn't that woman, after all. She got over it pretty quickly."

"Sounds bogus," Gabriel said.

"I thought so, too. And then Jackson didn't show up for dinner the next night."

"Yep, definitely bogus," Gabriel said.

"I totally agree."

"So you believe they knew each other," Derek said.

"Doesn't it sound that way to you?"

"Yes, it does," he said. "I think we should have a talk with Jackson after we finish up here."

"Can you get me a photograph of Elizabeth?" Gabriel asked.

"I'll take care of it," Derek murmured as he typed a note into his calendar.

I'd watched *NCIS* enough times to know that Derek could submit Elizabeth's photograph to a facial recognition program and find out who she really was within minutes. Hopefully she wasn't some sort of criminal mastermind, but you never knew.

"Let's get back to the caves," Gabriel said. "Since last Thursday, the day of your lunch with Elizabeth, and up until yesterday, I've got log entries once each day and twice on Saturday, Sunday, and Tuesday."

Derek checked his calendar and frowned. "I had time scheduled with Garrity every day but Saturday."

I sat back in my chair. "So Saturday there were two entries and neither of them were yours?"

"That's right. Along with one extra entry on Sunday and Tuesday." He thought for a moment. "No, Garrity and I only entered the caves once on those days."

"What times? Do you remember?"

Derek told him the times he met Garrity and Gabriel

checked off the applicable entries. "So we've got a question mark for Saturday morning, Saturday afternoon, Sunday morning, and Tuesday morning."

"Were they all the same times in the morning?"

"Different times," Gabriel said.

"I tried to meet Garrity in the mornings," Derek said, "Usually around ten. But there were a few afternoons, as well."

"I think I've noted them all." Gabriel double-checked his log-in list. "So we've got four entries unaccounted for."

"That's disturbing," Derek said.

Gabriel shrugged. "It could be completely innocent. Maybe Robson stopped by to check on something."

"Or an employee had a valid excuse to go in there." Derek's eyes narrowed in concern. "Brooklyn and I were discussing the possibility that the appraiser or one of the reporters was able to cajole someone into letting them inside the cave. Even Trudy might've asked Robson if she could take a look. After she opened the door, someone could've snuck inside. This is all conjecture, but it's worth considering."

I had stopped listening and simply stared at my calendar page until my eyes went blurry. "Oh no. Oh my God. This time it really is all my fault."

"What is it, love?" Derek said, taking hold of my arm. "What's wrong?"

I jabbed my finger on the calendar note. "My chat room! I sent them all the first paragraph of the letter that Guru Bob's grandmother sent to her sister. It was in some medieval language, remember? And I described the watermark on the paper. I told them the letter came from a storage box in a friend's house. It wouldn't be hard to track it down. It must be connected."

"Not necessarily, darling," Derek said in his most soothing tone. Usually it worked to calm me down, but not this time.

"Something else is going on here," I said, growing

more agitated. "Look at the timeline, Derek. My online communication about that letter might've set everything in motion. What if something in that ancient language triggered some kind of reaction in cyberspace? What if someone connected to my chat room killed Amelia?"

An hour later, after an extended rant on my part combined with Derek's lightning-fast skill at pointing out the obvious flaws in my hypothesis, I managed to compose myself. But though I'd stopped sharing my ideas on this, my brain kept racing. Had I brought all of this trouble to Dharma? Was it my fault Amelia was dead?

Gabriel sat back and enjoyed the show until Derek and I were finished with our little discussion. Then he poured himself another cup of coffee and said, "Let's go back to some more realistic possibilities. Like, Elizabeth."

I sighed and let go of my careening thoughts. After all, I had to admit it would be better if Elizabeth was at the bottom of all this, rather than my longtime chat group filled with book geeks like me. They'd been my virtual friends for years.

"Fine," I said.

Gabriel pointed to my calendar. "So she first called Trudy on Wednesday, ten days after the artwork and furnishings in the caves were discovered. She said she'd read about the treasures in her local paper and that reminded her that Trudy lived in the area. So now she wants to come visit. Out of the blue. That right there raises a red flag, wouldn't you agree?"

"Absolutely," Derek said.

Gabriel nodded. "Seven days later, she arrives in Dharma. And five days after that, Trudy is in a coma and her companion is dead."

"That's fairly compelling," Derek said.

It was. I glanced from one man to the other. "So you don't believe I could've sent a paragraph written in some obscure, ancient French-Coptic-Aramaic language out to the inter-webs, and set in motion a hundred-year curse on the Benoit family?"

Gabriel grinned. "It's a cool theory, babe, but it's straight out of science fiction."

"Damn," I grumbled. "It was a very cool theory." But if Gabriel and Derek were right, then I wasn't to blame for Amelia's death, and that was even cooler.

Of course, I wasn't ready to let go of my little notion quite yet. But I let the conversation return to the suspects who were actually in town and involved in some way or another with the cave discoveries. I had zoned out for a few minutes, but I tuned back in just as Gabriel began to talk about his drones.

"We've already programmed one of them to activate whenever there's any kind of motion near the cave doors. It'll record everything it sees and hears. If you'd like something more invasive, we can add more motion-detection lights and cameras."

"That's an excellent idea," Derek said. "Because you know they'll be back. If they've gotten away with stealing one painting, they'll want to return for more. And if they've gotten away with it once, they're familiar with the positions of the cameras. They won't be expecting any additional ones. We could also beef up the locks."

Gabriel stared at his notes and shook his head. "I'm just afraid it might be an inside job."

"I refuse to believe that," I said, not caring if I sounded like a Pollyanna. "If someone from Dharma is allowing the thief access, it's got to be inadvertent. Nobody who knows Robson would do it deliberately. This means too much to him."

"I'd like to think you're right," Derek said.

"But here's the big question," I said, gnawing at my lip as I tried to figure it all out. "How is the theft of the painting connected to the murder at Trudy's house?"

"Maybe there's no connection," Gabriel said off-handedly. "Maybe it's all just a weird coincidence."

"You don't honestly believe that," Derek said.

"No," Gabriel said with a crooked grin. "Just throwing it out there for us to munch on."

As much as I hated being a magnet for dead bodies, experience had taught me that there was always a *reason*.

"Anything's possible," I said, "but it's crazy to think it's not all connected, don't you think?"

"Sure," Gabriel said lightly. "But if you seriously believe the theft and the murder are connected, then you have to ask yourself what the connection is."

"Something tells me you've already done that," I said. "So what do you think the connection is?"

His smile was resolute. "It's Robson Benedict."

After the intense morning at Gabriel's, my head was pounding, so I spent the afternoon resting on the couch. Derek had gone back to the caves to do a little investigating because we theorized that whoever stole the Renoir—*alleged* Renoir—might've left a clue somewhere. Chances were slim, but we both thought it was worth following up.

I had finally found a comfortable sleeping niche and was dozing off when someone knocked on the front door. I groaned out loud and waited a few seconds, thinking they might go away. But then I realized it was probably my mom, and she wasn't going to go anywhere.

I shuffled across the room and swung the door open without first peeking to see who it was. That was something I had to stop doing, given that someone had tried to kill me in the last forty-eight hours. Luckily, I saw that gorgeous head full of dark curly hair and knew it was a friendly visitor.

"Hey, you," I said, grabbing Annie in a hug. "Come in. I'm so glad you came by."

"Since you've refused to visit me, I thought I'd better."

"I'm sorry," I said, leading the way into the living room and returning to my comfy corner of the couch.

"I've been meaning to get into the store to see you. It's been a little crazy lately."

"Yeah, I've heard."

Annie's real name was Anandalla, and she was the daughter that my mentor Abraham Karastovsky never knew. Her mother never told him she was pregnant after she moved back to her hometown of Seattle, where Annie was raised. It wasn't until her mother was dying that Annie had learned the truth. Her father was alive and well and living in Dharma. She and Abraham met for the first time only days before he was murdered.

Annie was petite, adorable, and in her midtwenties, all qualities I'd held against her when we first met. She'd been a goth princess back then, all kohl-rimmed eyes, skull earrings, and black leather vests. These days, however, she was clean-scrubbed and tie-dyed, pure Dharma right down to her Birkenstocks.

Several months after she'd moved to town, she'd opened her kitchenware store and named the shop *Anandalla!* The exclamation point fitted Annie's personality and the Hindu-inspired name suited Dharma perfectly. The store was very popular with locals and visitors alike.

She sat down in the chair opposite me and took her time looking me over. Taking in my disheveled appearance, she said, "You know, you didn't have to go to all this trouble just to avoid me."

I chuckled. "Very funny."

"Seriously, though, I'm sorry. I heard about Amelia and Trudy." She shook her head in sadness and disbelief. "Amelia was in the shop just three days ago. She used to come in at least once a week, and she could easily spend an entire afternoon in one aisle. I can't believe she's gone."

"It's sad, isn't it?" I was surprised to hear that Amelia had taken such an interest in kitchenware, but it made sense since the kitchen seemed to be her realm at Trudy's.

"She was a sweet lady," Annie said.

"Was she? I'm glad to hear it, because she didn't seem to like me at all."

Annie grinned. "Did I mention she had good taste?"

"Ha ha." I bit back a smile. "I forget how funny you are when I don't see you for a while."

"It's a gift." But then she frowned. "I know Amelia was an oddball, but she loved to cook and bake, so we got along well."

"I think you and Trudy might've been the closest thing she had to friends."

"That's entirely possible. She wasn't exactly the most outgoing woman in the world." Annie stood and asked for some water. I told her to help herself, pointing the way to the kitchen. She walked out of the living room and was back in her chair a minute later, gulping down a glass of water. "Ah, much better, thanks. So how are you feeling, really?"

I sighed. "The pain comes and goes, but mainly I'm going crazy here. I need to be doing something."

She got up, came over to the couch, and peered more closely at my head where the wound was still healing. "It doesn't look too bad, but I guess they nailed you good."

"Yeah. I'm lucky to be alive."

"I'd say so." She sat down, and I scooted back so I could sit up straighter.

"So, what's new with you, Annie?" I asked, anxious to change the subject away from my head wound. "I haven't seen you in at least two months. How's business? Do you still love it here? Do you have a boyfriend?"

She thought for a moment. "Um, nothing much. Great. Yes. And none of your business."

I laughed. "None of my business? You know this is a small town, right? All I have to do is ask my mother. She'll tell me everything about your love life."

Annie rolled her eyes. "Unfortunately, that's not a joke. That woman knows everything about everyone in town."

"Yeah, we've all given up trying to keep secrets from her."

She smiled fondly. "Your mom is the best."

"She loves you, too."

She stared out the window at the beautiful blue sky and the line of pine and oak trees that covered the ridge. "I was so lucky to find this place."

"Lucky?" I said. "If memory serves, I was the one who introduced you to Dharma."

It was her turn to laugh. "You just keep believing that."

I gave her a smile. "It's really good to see you."

"You, too." She glanced at her watch. "But I'd better leave you to rest. I've got to go meet someone in a little while."

"Hot date?"

She shot me a suspicious glare. "Since you'll find out anyway, I might as well tell you that I'm meeting that reporter for coffee. Your sister set me up."

"Reporter?" I frowned before remembering my conversation with China. "You mean Josh Atherton?"

"Yeah. Oh, I guess you must've met him since he's here to research the caves. China wouldn't tell me anything about him. Well, only that he's nice and cute."

"He's perfectly pleasant and very cute," I agreed with a nod. I hesitated, then added, "Just please don't forget that he's a, you know, a reporter. Watch what you tell him."

"Don't worry," she said. "He won't get anything out of me."

"Good." I grinned. "Have fun."

"Always." She gave me a quick hug and took off, leaving me to contemplate Josh Atherton. Annie was a lot more confident in her ability to resist his interrogation techniques than I was. I could only wonder what sort of information he would try to wangle out of Annie.

Friday morning, I washed dishes while Derek finished up a phone call with our contractor, who assured him that the work was moving along and everything was on schedule. Our home would be ready and looking beautiful within a month. Derek let him know that he planned to be in the city next week and would stop by to inspect everything done so far.

After the phone call, we drove to the supermarket to stock up on groceries and incidentals for the week.

On the drive home, we got more news, this time from Gabriel, who announced that Trudy had come home. As Gabriel had predicted, Trudy had refused to leave her home for the sake of her own safety, so he was in the process of moving into her spare bedroom. Trudy had only weakly protested his presence, and now it was clear that she was happy to have him there, especially since Elizabeth would be visiting for only a few more days.

If she wasn't arrested for murder first.

We drove by the house to welcome Trudy home but stayed just a short while. I had to endure Elizabeth's hugs while she expressed the hope that she and I could get together for lunch soon. But how could she possibly think I would want to get together with her when I didn't even know if she was guilty of killing Amelia or not? She carried on as if nothing had happened, and I made some lame excuse about being too busy this week to go to lunch.

Derek sensed my unease, and we left as quickly as we could, leaving Gabriel to watch Elizabeth's every move and keep Trudy safe. If anyone could multitask under those circumstances, it was him.

Amelia's memorial service took place the following day in the tiered theater side of the town hall, opposite the exhibit hall.

Robson had been hoping that Trudy's memory would return by then, but the poor woman was still at a loss as to what had happened to her companion and friend. But since the sheriff had released Amelia's body and the funeral home had gone ahead and performed the quiet burial—with just Trudy, Robson, Elizabeth, Gabriel, Derek, me, and my parents in attendance—Robson decided not to wait any longer to hold the larger memorial service.

It wasn't a religious ceremony but a simple and sweet memorial to a woman who was known by very few of us but who nevertheless had left an indelible mark on Dharma. There were several lovely short speeches, including a few words from Annie. A string quartet played in the background.

At the last minute, we had tried to track down any possible relatives of Amelia's. Trudy was unaware of any and expressed the belief that the woman was alone in the world. Amelia had been an only child, she said, and Trudy was fairly certain that both of her parents had been as well.

"I never saw her write a letter to anyone," Trudy had said. "She never called any family."

It was sad to think that the woman had no one who would care that she was alive or dead. But that wasn't really true. She had Trudy. And I was pretty sure that Trudy was the reason why most of the town had gathered together to give her friend a decent send-off.

"She died a hero, saving Trudy's life," Robson stated in his eulogy.

It was true. There was no better way to say it. But as I listened to his words, guilt rained down on my soul. I had been so ambivalent toward the woman. She was finicky and judgmental and always scowling at me, and I had no idea why. Was she jealous of Trudy's time or affection? Or was she just a sourpuss? I guessed it was both.

Glancing around the tiered assembly room, I spotted Trudy sitting in the first row and found Elizabeth in the seat next to her. A quick chill tickled my spine at that sight, but then I spied Gabriel seated directly behind the two women. He was clearly taking very seriously his job of guarding Trudy. Mom and Dad were sitting with my two brothers and Robin a few rows down and over from me and Derek. China and Savannah were seated together nearby.

Seeing my brother Jackson reminded me of his odd disappearance that day at the exhibit hall when I was about to introduce him to Elizabeth.

I leaned over and whispered to Derek, "We need to talk to Jackson."

He nodded. "As soon as this is over."

I smiled, glanced around, and found myself staring right at Detective Hannah Parrish from the Sonoma County Sheriff's Department. Her smile was a lot less friendly than the last time I'd seen her and I quickly looked away. Then I had to try and remember exactly when I'd seen her last. I recalled seeing her at the press conference, but I also had a vague recollection of seeing her at Trudy's house the day Amelia was killed.

Was she annoyed with me? Did I say something strange while under the influence of painkillers? I would have to make a point to talk to her after the service. I didn't need a local cop focusing her anger on me.

I continued to wonder why she was so annoyed. Though to be fair, I seemed to have that effect on police officers.

"Ms. Wainwright."

I turned and looked directly into the eyes of Detective Parrish. Again.

"Hello, Detective. Can I offer you some crudité? Or something a little heartier?"

We were standing in the attached dining hall where an abundance of savory food and delectable desserts was always served after events.

"No, thanks." She looked around. "Everything looks great."

"We know how to throw a party, even when it's a sad occasion."

She seemed uncomfortable, but I didn't know if it was the surroundings or me, specifically. "I'd like to ask you a few questions about the day you were attacked."

"I remember seeing you there. It's a very foggy memory, I'm afraid."

"I can understand. I'm sorry you were hurt."

"Mine was the least of the injuries that day."

"Indeed. I was hoping to hear from you before now."

"Oh. I thought you got all my information from Derek. Derek Stone."

"I asked him to have you call me."

"He might've said something, but I was probably still out of it and didn't follow through. I apologize."

She seemed to relax a little as she reached for a carrot stick and took a bite. "No worries. Can you tell me what happened?"

I related everything exactly as I remembered it, and exactly as I'd told Derek before. She listened and nodded and crunched on her carrot stick.

"Mr. Stone said that you heard the floor creak?"

"That was my only warning. I thought it was Amelia, but it wasn't."

She nodded again. "I appreciate your help. I may call you again to ask more questions, if you don't mind." She pulled a business card from her jacket pocket. "And if you remember anything else, please feel free to call me."

"Thank you. I will. I'm sorry again that I got my wires crossed."

Detective Parrish smiled and walked away. I stared after her, wondering where she'd received her training. The cops in San Francisco never would've been so polite or nonjudgmental. I always felt as if I were being put through the wringer with the city cops, and right now, I almost missed the feeling. *Almost.*

I was crossing the hall to get a glass of juice, when I caught a glimpse of Annie bringing in another tray of desserts. I detoured over to help her.

"Hi," she said, setting the tray down and spreading

the individual tart plates across the table. "You're looking a lot better than you did the last time I saw you."

"Thanks," I said, laughing. "That was a whole two days ago."

"Hey, you were wearing pajamas."

"I clean up well." I helped her move plates around so she could fit all the tarts on the table. "These look so good."

"I've had two of the apricot tarts, so I can promise they're fabulous."

"How have you been?" I asked.

She glanced around the crowded room, gave me a look, and whispered, "You mean, 'How was your date?'"

I laughed. "Well, now that you mention it, yeah. How was it?"

"You're such a bozo," she said, shaking her head. "I didn't think I would like him because of you."

"What do you mean? I told you he was pleasant."

"You made him sound like a snoop. Like he might go prying into my underwear drawer or something."

"I never meant that."

She laughed. "I know you didn't. And I realize he's a reporter, but you're right—he's really pleasant and very attractive and seems pretty interested in me." She smiled shyly. "We're going out again tomorrow night."

"I'm glad," I said, and meant it. "I want you to be happy. And as I already said, I like him. It's just that . . ."

"I know, I know." She rolled her eyes. "He's a reporter."

I grinned. "Exactly."

"Don't worry," she said, picking up the empty tray. "I won't divulge any of your deep, dark secrets."

I smiled indulgently. "If only I had any."

Later that afternoon, once the memorial service and reception were over, Derek and I tried to find Jackson, but he had disappeared again. We swung by the vineyard offices, but he hadn't checked in. We even made the long drive up to his house, but he wasn't home.

Giving up the search for now, we decided to stop by Trudy's to visit and commiserate. Robson had arrived a few minutes before us, and shortly after we got there, my mom and dad walked in. Mom was carrying her briefcase, so I had a feeling we'd be witnessing another purification ceremony at some point. I had no problem with that. It would be fun to see her work her magic on someone besides me. And any little ritual that would help Trudy cope with the loss of Amelia was okay with me.

I was happy to see Elizabeth doting on Trudy. I had to admit I liked the woman, although my suspicions prohibited me from getting close to her. I seriously hoped she had nothing to do with the attack, but we wouldn't know for sure until Derek's facial recognition people were able to figure out if she was anyone other than who she claimed to be.

Derek had managed to take a good picture of her during the memorial reception earlier and had instantly texted it to his assistant at his office in San Francisco. She would forward it to their London office, and he was certain we would hear back from them within a few hours.

Mom and Dad had brought some of the leftover desserts and several bottles of wine from the reception, so we had a little commemorative party in Amelia's honor. Mom worked her magic, conducting a wonderfully bizarre cleansing ceremony that made Trudy laugh and cry, declaring it the most life-altering thrill ride she'd ever experienced.

But none of it shook up Trudy's memory, and I wondered if she would ever recall the face of the person who'd tried to kill her. Or even if she should try. Because maybe, just maybe, her amnesia was all that was keeping her alive.

Chapter 15

The first thing I saw on my phone the next morning was a message from Claude from my chat room. He included his translation of the first paragraph of Marie's letter and apologized for taking so long.

"If you send me the rest," he wrote, "I can probably get it done within a day or two. Last week you caught me in the middle of a three-day continuing education class. OMG! Boring!"

Claude went on to explain that the language was exactly as he'd thought, mainly a combination of school-girl medieval French and Chouadit, the long-extinct Jewish language he had mentioned in our first chat room talk.

I wrote down what he'd translated. The first few sentences were the usual chitchat and news sent to a friend concerning different family members, the weather, and her health.

As I looked at the original letter, I was reminded that it was written by Marie, Guru Bob's grandmother, to Camille, who was Marie's sister-in-law and Trudy's mother. I hadn't paid much attention to the date when I first saw the letter, but now I did. It read *4 April 1946*, and I realized its significance.

Jean Pierre Renaud's ticket for passage on the ocean

liner was dated April 12, 1946. So this letter was written the week before.

I assumed that both women were living in Sonoma with their husbands. According to Trudy, they and their families had all moved here from France during the war. They probably didn't have telephones at the time, but they couldn't have lived far from each other. Why didn't Marie simply ride her bike over for a visit? Was there something in the letter that couldn't be said out loud?

The last sentence Claude translated was troubling: "Oh, Camille, I have witnessed something so terrible that I'm almost afraid to tell you about it, but I must get it off my chest."

I wanted to know what Marie had seen. What was so terrible that she had felt the need for a confession of the soul?

I showed the translation to Derek and voiced my thoughts.

He sipped his coffee. "There must be something in this letter about Monsieur Renaud."

"Shall I send Claude the rest of the letter?"

"Absolutely," he said. My face must've betrayed my fears, because he put his cup down and wrapped his arms around me. "Are you afraid your friend Claude might be Amelia's killer?"

Derek really did know me much too well. Yes, my brain had actually considered that very idea before dismissing it.

"No, of course not," I said. "And when you say it out loud, it sounds even more ridiculous." I pressed my cheek against his chest. "But the timing is still disconcerting."

He leaned back and tilted my chin up to meet my gaze. "If it means anything, I am absolutely certain that your chat room friends are not responsible for Amelia's death."

"I know you're right," I said, pouting a little. "Claude

lives in Indiana and can barely afford to take the bus, let alone fly out to California to go on a killing spree."

"There, you see?" He smiled, but then sobered up to add, "I hope it hasn't escaped your attention that if someone in the chat room did kill Amelia, you would be in even more danger now."

I thought about that for a few seconds. "But I've never seen any of them in person."

"But they would know you," he reasoned. "They would have to get rid of you because of the chat room connection. You would be a threat to them."

"I suppose that's true." I shook my head in defeat. "Luckily it's too ridiculous and convoluted to contemplate, which means you were right in the first place."

"I never tire of hearing that."

"Fine, I'll say it once more. You were right. It was a ridiculous theory. But it was a fun one."

"Oh, fun. Absolutely." I had a feeling he was trying not to laugh. "If you want my opinion, I say you should go ahead and send Claude the rest of the letter and find out its contents. If nothing else comes of it, it'll be an interesting bit of ephemera for Robson's library."

I smiled at his use of my bookbinding and conservation terms. "Good plan. I'm going to scan the letter and send it to Claude. Then I'll join you for breakfast."

"My heart awaits your presence."

"Such a funny man."

His handsome grin was so rakish, I might've sighed a little as I hurried off to take care of sending the letter to Claude.

Talking about Monsieur Renaud reminded me that I still hadn't dealt with the ownership issue of *Journey to the Center of the Earth*. So after breakfast, I took a quick drive over to Robson's home to show it to him. Since it was his grandfather Anton who'd written the pledge on the back flyleaf, I figured the book belonged to Guru Bob as much as to anyone. I wanted to ask him if he would like me to rebind it or simply refurbish it and leave it as close to the original as possible.

I had a feeling I knew what his choice would be, and I was right. He preferred to have it spruced up, but he wanted it to remain in the same basic condition as when his grandfather read it as a boy. I promised I would simply clean the gutters, tighten the text block, and replace the flattened bands on the spine. The endpapers were still beautiful, and the flyleaf with its remarkable pledge in his grandfather's blood would naturally stay as I'd found it.

An hour later, I was home, packing up my satchel in anticipation of spending the day in Abraham's workshop. I wanted to take Charlie with me, but since Derek was working from home today, I left her to play with him and Maggie.

As I strolled down the hill to the workshop, I marveled at how quickly I had grown to love the darling creature. And by that I meant Charlie, not Derek. Although he was darling as well, and I loved him more than I thought possible. They were both awesome and wonderful. My little family. And if I daydreamed about adding Maggie to the group, it was only because she was such a sweetie pie with so much love to give. The Quinlans were lucky to have her.

I walked into Abraham's workshop and sniffed the familiar scents, and felt at home once again. Now that I had Robson's approval to work on the *Journey*, I wanted to get it done right away. I pulled it out of my satchel and, setting it on the worktable with my tools, felt a wave of sadness because of what had happened to those two young boys who'd signed their blood pledge all those years ago.

At the same time, I was relieved that the book hadn't been the cause of the tragedy that took Jean Pierre's life. I'd worked on too many valuable, rare books for which people had willingly lied, cheated, stolen, or killed. This wasn't one of those.

I took a quick minute to check on my medical books. Volume one was still in the book press where I'd left it a few days ago. Its leather cover was completely dried and looked fantastic if I did say so myself. The spine was ready to be gilded, but I wasn't sure I'd have time to do it today.

Back at my worktable, I pulled out my brush to continue cleaning the pages. But first, I grabbed my magnifying glass to give the Jules Verne book another close-up look. Even though the book had been battered by the boys who'd read it over and over again, Robson didn't want a new cover. I would eventually apply some high-quality leather rub and leave it at that. But first I would remove the leather and replace the six raised bands on the spine that had gone flat. Once I had the leather cover pasted back on the boards, I would gild the titles again and fill in where the gilding on the spine and covers had faded. I could also spruce up the tattered crown and foot of the spine where it was splitting from that front hinge.

Beyond that, a thorough sweeping of all the pages would finish the job. Then it would be Robson's to do with what he wanted.

I took another look at the back flyleaf where the boys had written and dated their pledge in blood. I felt a twinge, wondering if they had bled for each other on more than one occasion. I was sad to think that their friendship had ended in that cave with Jean Pierre's death. Had Anton mourned him always? Was he the one who walled off the cave? Would we ever find out the truth?

I hoped Claude would be able to translate Marie's letter quickly, because the suspense was killing me. I had a feeling it might hold some answers to my questions.

I stared one last time at the faded rust-colored ink and shivered again. "Blood," I muttered. "Boys are gross."

And thinking about gross little boys reminded me that we hadn't tracked down Jackson yet. There was no time like the present, so I pulled out my cell phone and pushed his number.

"Hey, sis," Jackson said upon answering. "What's up?"

"I was wondering if you'd be around sometime tonight. Derek and I wanted to ask you a question or two."

I used Derek's name in case he was inclined to balk. It was a sisterly thing to do.

"What's this all about?" he asked, sounding ready to balk regardless.

I could've lied and told him it was something to do with the vineyards, but he wouldn't have believed me anyway, so I told him the truth. "We're wondering if you know anything about Elizabeth. That woman who's visiting Trudy?"

"Why would I know anything about her?"

So male, really. He didn't answer; he just asked another question. Which told me that my brother knew something he didn't want to talk about.

"Well, you were acting weird last week when I was about to introduce her to you. Remember how you disappeared? And then you canceled dinner? And now we have a situation. . . ."

"A situation?"

It was just as well that he stopped me, because I was blathering, digging myself into a hole. "Yeah. So will you be around tonight?"

Jackson didn't answer right away, and I thought maybe he'd hung up on me. He was an elusive guy, so I never knew quite how to deal with him. But he was my brother and I loved him, so I was prepared to pester the heck out of him until I got an answer.

"Hello?" I said. "Are you there?"

"Yeah, I'm here."

I breathed a sigh of relief, although I could hear the annoyance in his tone. I didn't care. I'd heard that tone in his voice all my life.

"Listen," he said finally, "how about if you guys come by the winery tonight around eight? We're having a barrel tasting this afternoon, and I'll just be finishing up then. We can have a glass of wine and talk."

"That would be perfect." Better than perfect, I thought, because there would be wine. "Thanks, Jackson."

"See you then."

He ended the call, and I immediately telephoned Derek to let him know what we were doing that night.

I spent the rest of the afternoon sweeping the gutters of each page of the *Journey* and then bringing new life back to the raised bands on its spine. I reattached the leather cover and rubbed it with leather cleaner until it was gleaming.

Before I was ready to quit for the day, I took a half hour to cut and pare down the leather for the next medical text cover. I also wrapped the text block in wax paper and then packed up my bags to go home.

When I arrived, I found Derek working in the office with Maggie asleep at his feet.

I gave Derek a smooch on the lips and asked, "Where's Charlie?"

"She's dozing in my lap," he said, wrapping his arm around my waist. "Otherwise I'd have you sitting there."

I laughed. "I'll have to wait my turn."

He glanced back at his computer screen. "I'm just waiting for one more e-mail before I quit for the day. Then we can grab a bite to eat and go meet your brother."

We decided on Chinese food and drove a mile outside of Dharma to the best Asian fusion restaurant in the world—or in Sonoma, at least.

At eight o'clock, Derek parked in the winery's lot, and we walked into its cavernous bowels, looking for Jackson. The place was empty and the lights were dimmed. It was obvious that the barrel tasting had been over for some time.

"Hello?" I called. "Jackson?"

"I'm over here," my brother shouted from the other side of the warehouse-sized barrel room.

The room was kept cool, and I suppressed a shiver as we walked past a dozen massive stainless steel vats that held thousands of gallons of wine. We found Jackson standing against the far wall at a wine-barrel table surrounded by three stools.

"Hey, Derek," he said, and the two shook hands.

I gave him a hug and took a seat at the table.

Jackson grabbed the bottle. "I'll pour you some of the reserve Meritage we were tasting earlier."

"Wonderful," Derek said, straddling the stool next to me.

As he poured, Jackson gave a short lecture on the Meritage concept. The word was applied when at least two grape varieties were blended together, as long as none of the varieties made up more than ninety percent of the final merging. So it was a true blend, and it usually included cabernet sauvignon and merlot grapes.

Meritage was actually the name of an association formed by local winemakers in the Napa Valley back in the day, after many of them voiced frustration with the U.S. labeling requirements and decided to form their own brand. They combined the words *merit* and *heritage* to create a name for both their new alliance and their new blending style.

"There's more to it," Jackson said, "but that's enough for tonight. Let's taste it."

I took my first sip, rolling the dark red liquid around my mouth and tongue. "It's yummy."

"That's a technical term," Jackson explained to Derek, who chuckled.

"It's yummy indeed," Derek said after his first taste. "It has a nice spiciness to it. Also a hint of blackberry and . . ." He paused. "Mocha?"

"Yes!" Jackson said. "I get that, too. That's probably from the barrel, but it may be left over from the fermentation process." He pondered the question as he took another taste and gazed at the legs streaking down the side of the glass.

"It's mellow, but spicy, too," I said, taking another small sip. "Plummy. Herby. Nice tannins. And I'm getting a little toasted oak, definitely from the barrel."

"What do you think of that?" Jackson asked, always looking for opinions on barrel fermentation.

"You know me," I said. "I love an oaky red."

We continued the wine talk for another ten minutes. Jackson estimated how many days were left until the harvest, and Derek expressed his interest in taking part in the event.

"We'll welcome every able-bodied human we can find," Jackson assured him. "And you've already proven yourself to be an excellent field-worker."

"High praise," Derek said. "I appreciate it."

Finally, I met my brother's gaze and said, "So."

"So?" he said coolly in response.

There was no soft and easy way to introduce the subject, so I got right to the point. "Last week in the exhibit hall, you disappeared the moment I tried to introduce you to Elizabeth. So, do you know her? Why did you run away? What's the story? Do you think she's dangerous? She's living in a house where a murder took place. Do you think she did it? Is Trudy in danger?"

"Slow down, speedy," he said. "Nobody's in danger from . . . What did you say her name was?"

"Elizabeth."

He raised an eyebrow. "Right. I . . . know her. No, she's not dangerous." He frowned and added, "Well, at least not to Trudy."

"But you ran away that day. What was that about?"

"Is that important, love?" Derek asked softly.

I looked at him. "Well, maybe not in the larger scheme of things, but I want to know if my brother is hiding from the law or something."

Jackson snorted, and I turned back to him. "Well then, what's up with that? Why did you leave?"

"None of your business, squirt."

"I'm thirty-three years old," I said through gritted teeth. "Stop calling me that."

"All right, punkin'."

"And that." Another dreaded childhood nickname. "Just grow up and answer the question." Brothers, no matter how old and mature they grew to be, always retained a talent for obnoxious behavior.

"Okay, okay," he said with a stiff laugh. "Look, this is not something I'm prepared to discuss with anyone."

I could see Derek studying him more closely than usual, and I wondered what he was thinking.

"Fine," I said. "We don't have to talk about it anymore. But look, if there's a problem or if you're in some kind of trouble . . ."

"There's no trouble," he assured me.

"Okay," I said, stifling a smile. "But if she turns out to be your probation officer, all bets are off."

"Very funny," he said, not laughing. "Look, just accept the fact that Elizabeth didn't have anything to do with Trudy's attack and Amelia's murder, and let's change the subject."

Derek's gaze focused in on him. "Are you her alibi?"

"Damn it," Jackson swore, and clawed his fingers through his hair in frustration.

"Wait a minute," I said, the light dawning. "You're her alibi? She was with you those couple of days when she was gone from Trudy's?"

He sighed. "Yes. And that's all you have to know."

"But how do you know her?" I frowned. And all of a sudden the pieces fell together. "Wait. She didn't come here to see Trudy. She came to see you. But why? Where did you meet? I'm more confused than ever."

"So just let it go," Jackson insisted, but then couldn't help but add, "And she didn't come to see me. She was just as shocked to see me as I was to see her."

"Fascinating," I murmured.

"Overseas," Derek guessed. "Africa? The Middle

East?" He thought for another few seconds. "Of course. Southeast Asia."

"I'm not saying anything else." Jackson glared at Derek. "You, of all people, should know that."

My eyes widened, and I stared from Derek to Jackson. "Oh no. Not you, too. What are you, CIA? Military intelligence?" I waved the question away. "Never mind. Don't tell me. You'll just have to kill me, right?"

Suddenly Jackson was grinning. "Yeah, I'll have to kill you, so stop asking questions."

"All right, all right," I muttered. "But what about Elizabeth, *if* that's really her name. What is she? Some supersecret spy you met while rapelling down some treacherous cliff in Burma?"

"Maybe, in your own warped mind." He was laughing at me now, but he still wasn't spilling the beans. And why did that not surprise me? Jackson had always been the stoic one in the family, quietly going about his business. He'd been great at keeping secrets, like the time he caught me behind the school gym, kissing Richie Kirk. Back then, I was shocked that he hadn't told my parents about it. There were other incidents as well.

So I guess I didn't care if he told me the whole story. For now. It was enough to know that much of Jackson's past was truly secret. I would honor that. And I was glad to know that Elizabeth—or whatever her name was— was innocent of harming Trudy or Amelia.

Which meant that I could take her off my suspect list. And we would have to look elsewhere for the killer.

The three of us walked out to the dark parking lot together, and Derek and I waved good-bye to Jackson.

"That was fun and educational, too," I said as we watched Jackson drive his truck out of the lot.

"The wine was very good, too," Derek said, smiling broadly as he unlocked the car and held my door open for me.

"Always." I turned to look at him. "Do you believe

Jackson was telling the truth when he said he didn't know Elizabeth would be here?"

Derek's expression sobered. "I do. He has no reason to lie to us, other than evading other details of his past. But I don't hold that against him."

"I guess you're right." I shut my door and watched Derek circle the car and climb into the driver's seat.

"I should've known he was in intelligence," Derek muttered a moment later as he glanced in his rearview mirror.

"I'm surprised you didn't," I said lightly. "You people seem to have a built-in radar when it comes to detecting that aspect of one another."

"And I missed the signs with Elizabeth, too." His frown deepened.

"I don't blame you for that. She's a whole different story. She told me the reason I wasn't able to place her accent was because she was a navy brat and had traveled all over the world. Now I wonder if she just said stuff like that so I wouldn't realize that she's a German spy or something."

"I doubt that she's German," Derek said, chuckling.

"You've probably figured out what she really is."

"Mossad, I imagine," he murmured.

I stared at him. "You think she's Israeli?"

"Not positive, but it's an educated guess," Derek said, checking his rearview mirror again. "Mossad has a discreet relationship with Thailand's intelligence community."

"Okay. So what's the connection?"

He glanced at me. "The tattoo on Jackson's left arm is a Thai phrase."

I stared at him in disbelief. "What tattoo? My brother has a tattoo?"

Derek grinned. "You'd know about the tattoo if you had toiled in the fields like I do."

I laughed. "Oh great. So what's the word?"

He pronounced the phrase using a sharp, guttural tone, sounding completely unlike himself.

"Wow. What does that mean?"

"Tranquility."

I thought about it. "That suits him. But couldn't he have gotten it anywhere?"

"It's possible, but not likely. Thailand is made up of hundreds of communities, each with its own language and colloquialisms. The phrase tattooed on Jackson's arm is from an obscure area in northern Thailand. I doubt he could've gotten it anywhere else in the world."

"How do you know so much about Thailand? Did you work there, too?"

"Yes, briefly. I had to take immersion courses in languages and customs in order to complete the mission." He glanced in the rearview mirror once again.

I could tell he was distracted, so I relaxed and enjoyed the ride. Two seconds later, I gasped and turned to him. "Wait a minute. If she's Mossad, she could be looking for artwork stolen from the Jews. That's brilliant, Derek. It has nothing to do with Thailand, but it's brilliant."

"Thailand simply provides a possible connection between Jackson and Elizabeth."

"Right. There are so many different threads to this situation, I can't keep them all straight." I thought of the rest of Elizabeth's backstory. "Is she really the granddaughter of a friend of Trudy's?"

"We'll have to ask her." He pulled over to the side of the road.

"What're you doing? Is something wrong with the car?"

"No. I saw someone sneaking over the hill back there."

"It's so dark out, how could you see them?"

"They had a flashlight turned on for a moment. They were headed in the direction of the caves."

"Damn it! We've got to stop them." I shoved my door open and had one foot on the ground before Derek grabbed my arm.

"Brooklyn, wait," he ordered, yanking me back. "Close the door, please. The interior light might alert them."

"Oh crap." I scrambled back into the car and tried to shut the door quietly. "I'm sorry. That was stupid."

"Never mind," he said more calmly. "I believe we're far enough away that they didn't notice the light through the tinted windows. But I don't want you charging off without a plan."

I thought about the last time I had charged in without a plan. I had gotten bashed in the head. "Okay. Sorry." I took a few deep breaths to chill out. "With all the trauma we've been through, my first thought was to hunt them down and throttle them."

"Perhaps you'll get your chance." He glanced up at the sky through the windshield and then scanned the landscape in four directions. The moon was a sliver and the sky was cloudy, so there was almost no light shining down on the nearby vineyards and surrounding countryside.

"How did you see him?" I asked.

"I saw his silhouette—that is, I assume it's a man, but it could be a woman—when he or she skulked across the fire lane that runs parallel to the cabernet vineyard."

"That was lucky. It's the only spot around that isn't covered in vines or thicket."

"Yes, lucky indeed." He looked at me, frowning. "I don't suppose you'll wait in the car."

"Not a chance," I said, buttoning up my jacket. I was glad I'd gone with a dark wardrobe tonight. "But I promise I won't get in your way."

"Damn straight you won't." He reached across me, unlocked the glove compartment, and pulled out his scary-looking gun.

"I suppose that's necessary," I said, basically to myself.

"Yes, it is."

"Fine." I pulled my cell phone from my purse. "But do you mind if I call Gabriel so you have some real backup?"

Derek checked his rearview mirror. "He knows we're here."

"He does? How?"

"One of his drones is hovering above our car."

"You've got to be kidding."

He grinned, took another look out the windshield, and waved up at whatever was above us. "I've got to get one of those."

"You guys scare me. You really do."

He reached for his door handle. "Ready to go?"

"Yes."

"Stay behind me." Derek opened the car door and was out in three seconds. I tried to duplicate his moves, but I wasn't quite as smooth or fast as he was. We snuck across the road and hiked up the shallow hill above the lighted parking lot. Here there were rows of graceful birch trees lining the ridge along the bottom of the vineyard acreage.

I stopped behind one tree and looked up at the terraced hill above us. It was really dark out here tonight. The storage cave was fifty yards in front of us, so we continued following the line of trees, staying in the safe shadows as long as we could.

Derek held up his hand, and I stopped immediately. He pointed to something in the bushes at the end of the tree line. I had to squint to try and see what he was looking at, but I couldn't see a thing.

"Stay here," he whispered, barely loud enough for me to hear.

I nodded, and he took off toward whatever he was seeing. I waited. I had no interest in getting in the way of his gun. After a few moments, I had a sudden attack of cowardice. Did I really want to see what he'd found? It was a lot easier to be brave while sitting inside the luxurious Bentley. But out here in the elements, with some bad guy skulking around? Not so much.

"Brooklyn," Derek said aloud, breaking the silence of the dark night. "Get Gabriel on the phone. Tell him to call the sheriff and get an ambulance over here."

I forgot my fears and went running over to his side. "What happened?"

He pointed to the ground behind the bushes. "It's Noland Garrity."

"I knew it!" I leaned over and looked down at Garrity's body, sprawled motionless on the dirt and hidden by the hedgerow. "You caught him."

"No, someone else did," he said grimly, "and left him for dead."

"Just to be clear," Gabriel said, "nobody entered the caves tonight."

"Good," I said, pacing the room, trying to shake off the nerves and fear I'd felt out there in the dark.

After the ambulance had whisked Noland Garrity away and the police had finished asking their questions, Gabriel, Derek, and I had returned to our house. The two men were seated at the dining table, munching on pretzels while I continued to pace around the room.

"Garrity must've been trying to sneak inside, right? Did you find a key in his pocket? Anything?"

"No key," Derek said. "More likely, he was planning to meet someone else who had the key."

"He definitely met someone," I muttered, "and they beat the heck out of him. Two fractured ribs and a broken nose, plus bruises everywhere." I shivered. "I mean, I can't stand the guy, but I'm sorry he was so badly injured."

Derek sat back in his chair. "He'll be able to tell us who did it when he's awake and talking again."

"Maybe." But I frowned. It had been pitch-black out there on the hill, so I was doubtful that Garrity even saw who had attacked him. With Trudy's memory not yet recovered, we were still completely in the dark.

The ambulance had arrived in record time, followed by the local police. Within minutes, Garrity had been rushed to the hospital. The police had stayed around and cordoned off the area behind the bushes where we'd found Garrity unconscious. I figured we would see the sheriff's detectives sometime tomorrow.

"This is really disturbing," I said, continuing to pace. "Since we talked to Jackson and decided that Elizabeth is in the clear, I had Garrity pegged for the most likely suspect. Not so much for the murder of Amelia but most definitely for the theft of that Renoir."

"Yes," Derek said, nodding. "He was certainly the most likely candidate."

"So who is it we're not suspecting that we should be suspecting?" Gabriel and Derek looked at each other, then at me.

I sighed and pulled my notepad out of my purse. "I guess we'd better go back over the list."

The next morning, I stopped at Trudy's to see how she was doing. Gabriel answered the door, grinning like the devil as he let me into the house.

Trudy sat on the couch and waved a small handheld computer tablet over her head. "Look at this, Brooklyn. I can open and lock my front door from my tablet."

"What if I decided to break in?"

She smiled broadly. "I have an app for that. It's a panic button."

I looked at Gabriel. "She has an app for that?"

Gabriel chuckled. He was having fun while looking hot at the same time. Go figure.

I was thrilled and grateful that Gabriel had set up this elaborate security system and had taught Trudy how to operate it directly from her tablet. So she could work the sophisticated, computerized system, but she still couldn't remember who had tried to shoot her.

I was also grateful that Elizabeth wasn't a suspect anymore, but now I felt guilty for putting her at the top of my list. I knew I'd get over it and maybe we'd laugh about it someday, but right now, I watched her surreptitiously as she cleaned the breakfast dishes off the dining room table. I knew she was beautiful, but I'd never noticed her almond-shaped eyes. I'd thought her exotic looks were from her Italian father, but now I realized it was entirely possible that she was Israeli. Of course, I'd seen Israelis with blond hair, so what did I know?

She glanced up and saw me watching her and smiled. I knew then that Jackson must've told her what he'd said to us the other night. She had to know I'd suspected her of killing Amelia, but she didn't look angry and I appreciated that. I guessed the next step was mine if I wanted to repair our fledgling friendship.

As I'd made a habit of doing, I gently quizzed Trudy again, asking if she remembered the surprise she wanted to show me.

"No, Brooklyn. I'm so sorry. I wish I could."

"You will," I said, keeping my tone upbeat and positive. "Do you mind if I keep asking you?"

"Not at all! I want to remember."

"You will," I repeated. "In the meantime, I hope I'll see everyone at the Pre-Harvest celebration on Saturday."

"I'm looking forward to it," Elizabeth said.

Trudy beamed. "Wouldn't miss it for the world."

I believed her, just as I believed she would get her memory back. I wanted *her* to believe it, too. I just wished it would happen *now*.

Somewhere inside her mind, she was holding some vital, dangerous information, and for that reason, even though Gabriel and Elizabeth were here with her every day, I was determined to visit as often as I could. Trudy needed all the protection she could get.

Chapter 16

Two days later on Wednesday, we held the first official gathering of Robin and her girlfriends to help plan her wedding. With Robin's permission, I'd invited my new friend and neighbor, Alex Monroe. Derek and I had become good friends with her after she helped me fight off some really bad guys a few months back. Alex was a gorgeous, tall, high-powered businesswoman with the best wardrobe in the world. She was also an expert at Krav Maga and other defensive disciplines. I had introduced her to Robin and Austin a month ago at a dinner party Derek and I had thrown, and my two friends had hit it off nicely.

My sister London had driven down from Calistoga to join us, along with China, Savannah, Annie, and Barb, another old friend Robin and I had gone to school with. The eight of us spent an hour chatting and giggling foolishly about every little thing before settling down to plan Robin's wedding of the century. It helped to have a few true experts at the table, namely Alex, the cupcake and wardrobe queen; China, the textiles maven; Savannah, the gourmet goddess; and Annie, who knew everything about kitchenware. Much to Annie's delight, Robin would be registering at her store. The rest of us fell into the general know-it-all category and blithely added our homegrown expertise to the conversation as often as we could.

After lunch, I spent a half hour in the parking lot, chatting and catching up with Alex. She filled me in on how well the construction was moving along and assured me that our new loft was going to be fantastic. We made plans to meet for dinner and then Alex took off to check in to one of the spa hotels in town.

When I arrived home, I felt much more relaxed than I had in a while.

Part of my feeling of calm came from knowing that Elizabeth hadn't killed Amelia. But as I walked into the house, I suddenly wondered if she was the one who'd taken the Renoir. She'd been obsessed with the photograph of the painting at the town hall photo exhibit. Could the painting have belonged to a Jewish family before World War II began? Had Elizabeth been assigned by Mossad to look for it? Had she somehow gotten into the cave and taken it? Had Jackson given her the key?

"Impossible," I muttered. My brother would never allow that to happen.

Not only that, but I couldn't see Elizabeth sneaking in and stealing it. If she had found evidence that a piece of artwork in the cave was once owned by a Jewish family, it would be a simple matter of alerting the local authorities and starting an investigation. She was welcome to do so, as far as I was concerned.

But knowing the history of how this artwork had made it from a village in France to a wine cave in Sonoma, I didn't see how any of our treasures could be what she was looking for.

That evening, Derek and I took Alex to dinner at Arugula. She had already given me the highlights earlier, but now she elaborated, filling us in on all the news going on in our building. Our new space was beyond wonderful, she assured us. Derek and I planned to drive into town next weekend to see it for ourselves. And Vinnie and Suzie's little girl, Lily, was growing so fast, she reported.

It was during dessert that Gabriel stopped by the table. "Hello."

We greeted him enthusiastically and introduced him to Alex. I watched his face as she spoke to him and it reminded me that Gabriel was very good at hiding his reactions. But I did see one of his eyebrows lift appraisingly and that told me a lot. It was easy to see why he would find Alex attractive. She was simply beautiful. Tall and confident with a good sense of humor. What was there not to like? But unfortunately for Gabriel, Alex would never get involved with him because as a super-high-powered woman, she preferred the attentions of more passive men. She called them beta types, as opposed to alphas like Gabriel.

Of course, knowing Gabriel, I doubted that he'd give up after just one meeting. I couldn't wait to talk to Alex about him, but she was unusually quiet once we were in the car.

After dropping Alex off at the inn, we drove home. I did a quick check of my e-mail and found a message from Claude. He had translated the letter completely. I thanked him profusely, but he turned around and thanked me instead.

"You lead a much more interesting life than I do, Brooklyn," he wrote. "This was the biggest thrill I've had in months. Normally, the only excitement I ever experience is when I read it in the pages of a book."

I smiled at that, since much of my excitement came from books, too. Sometimes, though, it was a little *too much* excitement.

I printed out Claude's translation and found Derek at the kitchen table, scanning his phone for messages while waiting for me to finish. He glanced up. "Are you ready for some news?" he asked.

"I was about to ask you the same thing."

"You go first," he said.

"No, mine will take some time."

"All right then. I just heard back from the London office." He read from his phone screen. "'Elisheba Asimov, known as Elise, is a high-ranking Mossad agent in charge of tracking down artwork stolen from the Jews during the Second World War.'"

"Wow, just as you suspected. I was right. You are brilliant."

He smiled. "It was a good guess."

"And Elisheba," I said. "That's an interesting name."

"It's the Hebrew version of Elizabeth, according to Corinne."

"Corinne knows everything," I said, smiling at the picture of Derek's delightful assistant. She had followed Derek over from his London office last year, and she and her husband had fallen in love with San Francisco.

"Yes, she does," he agreed.

"So I guess the name Elizabeth wasn't far from her real name."

"No." He set his phone down on the table. "What is your news, love?"

"Claude sent me his translation."

"Excellent," he said, pulling out a chair. "Sit and read it to me."

"I already read you that first paragraph, remember? But I'll start it there so we can get the full picture." I began to read Marie's words from Claude's translation.

"Dear sister,

"Oh, Camille, I have witnessed something so terrible that I'm almost afraid to tell you about it, but I must get it off my chest.

"First I must say how wonderful it has been having Jean Pierre visit. Anton was so happy to have his best childhood friend here! He's been so

carefree, like the boy I met and fell in love with so many years ago. But in the last two days, the two men have been like strangers to each other, avoiding each other and casting dark looks. Anton refused to tell me what was wrong.

"Then late last night, he rose silently, got dressed, and left the bedroom. I was nervous and decided to follow him. He walked across the vineyards to the cave where they store the wine barrels. I hid outside the entry, afraid that if I went inside, he would see me. I heard someone walking in the brush and ducked down to escape detection. It was Jean Pierre! They were meeting in the cave. Oddly, he carried a suitcase and was dressed for traveling. At three o'clock in the morning!

"I ventured a few feet inside the cave and hid in an alcove near the entry. Anton and Jean Pierre were too wrapped up in an argument to notice me.

"Jean Pierre insisted that he had to give everything back. But Anton ... Oh, Camille, you know how he can be. His mind is no longer right. Every day he grows more afraid that the Nazis will arrive in California and kill us and take our possessions. It isn't reasonable, of course, but somehow he believes his dark dreams more than he believes the newspapers and news reports. I'm terrified that the war has taken a grave toll on Anton that he will never recover from.

"But back to the argument. Jean Pierre kept shouting at Anton, telling him he couldn't keep those things; they didn't belong to him.

"And Anton was shouting back, telling Jean Pierre that he had shared the secret with his beloved childhood friend and no one else. He trusted Jean Pierre. And now he was threatening to betray him.

"At first, I didn't understand what they were talking about. Then Anton promised he would give the precious treasures back after the war was over. Jean Pierre shouted that the war was over and it was time to return everything. But Anton swore that the Nazis were poised to attack again at any moment.

"They continued to talk back and forth about the Nazis, the villagers' belongings, the artwork and cherished bits of silver that they had entrusted us with.

"Anton told me he had already sent everything back to the village. But instead he hid it all away, thinking the Nazis would track him down and take it if he didn't. He lied to me, Camille. Did he think I would turn him over to the Nazis or something equally evil? Does he not trust his own wife? Is he so sick in his mind that he believes his own words? I was praying that with Jean Pierre's arrival, things would be straightened out and poor Anton would come to his senses. But instead they argued incessantly. Jean Pierre knew my husband better than anyone in the world, and instead of helping him, instead of understanding his sickness, he accused Anton of stealing and lying about it.

"'I have packed my bag,' Jean Pierre said, 'and I'm taking with me the one thing from your home that always meant the most to both of us.'

"'Not the book,' Anton shouted. 'Give it to me.'

"'No. You are breaking the blood bond we've had from the age of seven. You are no longer my blood brother.'

"'You are the one breaking it! But I will always be your blood brother, and you will be mine, no matter what you say.'

"'I wash my hands of you.'

"'No!' Anton screamed the word. 'You have to help me. I'm so afraid.'

"*I could hear Anton sobbing, Camille. The
sound stabbed at my heart. My poor broken
husband.*

"'*I can't help you, Anton,' Jean Pierre said.
'You've lied to everyone. I've only come back to
the cave to salvage what little I can and return it
to our friends.'*

"*I crept closer until I could see Anton and Jean
Pierre. They were in another alcove at the back of
the larger cave. The ceiling hung down so low that
I could see only Jean Pierre's hands as he began
to gather up small items from the dressers and
bookshelves. Jewelry, several pieces of gold, a
precious kitten sculpted from marble.*

"*Anton fought with him over every piece. He
shouted at him again, trying to persuade him to
stay, to change his mind. They could become
partners. Jean Pierre would not bend. Anton was
beside himself, and he lashed out. Jean Pierre
shoved him, and Anton fell, hitting his head. I was
afraid he was knocked unconscious, but he
stumbled back onto his feet. And then—I hesitate
to write this down, but I must—Anton pulled out
a gun and shot Jean Pierre!*"

I swallowed hard, looked up at Derek, and saw the
same grim resignation I felt carved into his features.
After a moment, I began reading again.

"*I ran from the cave, no longer caring if Anton
saw me or not. He didn't, though. And over the
next few days, he banned the workers from the
storage cave. I watched him push a heavy wheel-
barrow back and forth from one of the supply
barns to the cave. It was filled with bricks and
stones. A week later, Anton was called into town
on business, and I ventured back into the cave. He
had plastered over the entire alcove! The small*

*inner cave where he'd hidden all of our friends'
treasures was completely concealed behind a wall
of brick and cement.*

*"And suddenly I wondered if Jean Pierre's body
as well was hidden forever behind that wall. We
will never know, because as you know, Camille,
Jean Pierre's mother and father passed away
during the war. He has no brothers or sisters, no
family left to question where he disappeared to.
No one will inquire why he has not returned home
to France. I thought to myself, if only your Luc had
been home during Jean Pierre's visit. Of all times
for him and Jacques to go fishing! Now no one will
mourn the poor man's departure. Except me. And
perhaps Anton, in those moments when his mind
is clear.*

*"Anton seems happier now that the cave is closed
off. He goes about his days, working in the fields
and pressing the grapes. But I can't look at him
without thinking of poor Jean Pierre. They were
best friends, Camille. I know you must remember
what great comrades they were when we were all
in day school together. I yearn for those carefree
times.*

*"I don't know if I will mail you this letter,
knowing my words will betray my husband. But
if I do, please remember that he was a good man,
Camille. Never forget that, I beg of you.*

*"I feel relieved to have written down my story,
and I pray that my dear Anton will find peace
someday. I am not sure I ever will.*

> *"With much love,*
> *Marie."*

Speechless, I looked up at Derek and shook my head.
It was unbelievable.

He placed his hand over mine and squeezed. "I can
tell by your expression that you're thinking of Robson."

"I feel awful. I'm going to have to give this to him and watch him read it."

"I'll go with you when you do."

"Please. I'm dreading it."

He stood up and went to the refrigerator to pour each of us a glass of ice water. He handed a glass to me and remained standing as he drank his. "You probably need this after all that reading."

"I'm parched," I admitted. "Thanks." After taking several long sips of water, I said, "I don't believe Marie ever mailed the letter. So no one else ever knew."

"I think you're right." Derek leaned back against the kitchen counter. "Now we have to ask ourselves if Anton was essentially a good man or if he had some underlying need to steal from his friends."

"I seriously doubt that. It sounds like the war and the fear of the Nazis drove him crazy."

"Probably so. But can we honestly believe that he kept all of those things hidden inside that cave, that he killed his best friend because of some sort of post-Nazi stress disorder? Did he truly slide down into madness, or was that Marie's excuse for his behavior?"

"She didn't sound as if she was making excuses for him. She sounded heartbroken. It was much worse to lose her husband than to lose a painting or a fancy dressing table."

I took a quick sip of water and added, "Frankly, Derek, the world still suffers from post-Nazi stress disorder. To this day. Look at Trudy. She remembers the tragedy at Oradour-sur-Glane as if it happened yesterday. Millions of people suffered and died, and we're still dealing with the aftermath."

He nodded. "It was a devastating time."

We sat in silence for a minute or two. My mind was reeling from Marie's letter. I couldn't imagine having to witness one's own husband killing his best friend. I sighed. "Did I tell you what Guru Bob said that day we met the Frenchmen?"

Derek thought for a moment. "I don't recall your telling me."

"He talked about his grandfather and wondered if Anton's purpose was altruistic or not. If he was a thief, why didn't he sell off the pieces or display them in his own home as if they were his? But he never did. That must mean something."

"It must," Derek agreed, "but who's to say what?"

"We'll never know." I frowned at Derek. "I hate that."

I stood up. He met me halfway and we hugged each other. "I'll call Robson in the morning," he said, "and arrange a time to meet. He should know as soon as possible, for his own sake."

"Yes, he should. I remember telling him that there was absolutely no way his grandfather could've killed that man in the cave, but Guru Bob wasn't so sure. He said he didn't have my confidence simply because he never met his grandfather. I mean, I never met the guy, either, but I couldn't imagine Guru Bob would be related to someone who would do something so . . . well. I guess he was right to withhold judgment. Even of his own flesh and blood."

We sat quietly with our thoughts for a minute; then Derek said, "The letter does answer a question I had about the cave itself. Why did Anton build a second chamber? What was the purpose?"

"It sounds like the small, inner chamber was already there," I said.

"Yes. He filled it to capacity with the rarest artwork and silver, plus a few pieces of furniture. The big furniture and other items remained in the larger storage-cave area."

"That makes sense, especially if he believed he'd be sending things back to France eventually."

"Yes, but he never did. He was completely mad by the time Jean Pierre showed up. Marie's letter says that in so many words. And once Jean Pierre was killed, Anton had to single-handedly wall up the area in front of the small chamber, creating a second cave with his friend inside.

"He did a darn good job with that wall," I said, trying to lighten the mood.

"Indeed," Derek said. "None of us, not even the excavation team, suspected there was anything behind it except a mountain of rock and packed dirt."

I rested my head on Derek's shoulder, and he rubbed my back. "Let's go to bed, love," he said. "Tomorrow's going to be another busy day."

Upon reading the translated letter, Guru Bob was overwhelmed.

"I'm so sorry," I said.

"I appreciate that, gracious." He took hold of my hand. "You have been so good and kind throughout this ordeal. I wish there was some way to relieve the pain you are feeling at having to deliver this unfortunate news to me."

"My pain?" Shaken, I glanced at Derek and then back at Guru Bob. "No, Robson, I'm not the one in pain. I'm worried about you and your pain."

He smiled. "You have such a beautiful heart. I know you were not prepared to discover the truth about my grandfather, while I have had years to prepare myself for this inevitability."

"You have?"

"Yes." He sat back in his chair, calmer than he had been a minute ago. "I have been struggling with how to deal with the news if it was bad, and now I know. As reparation for my grandfather's deed, I plan to build a museum of tolerance and justice in Dharma. It will be a serene space where people can come to celebrate mankind's goodness while never forgetting that it coexists with evil. What do you think?"

I smiled and blinked away my tears. "I think it's a dandy idea."

"Dandy." He grinned. "I like that."

*   *   *

Derek and I split up after our meeting with Guru Bob. I drove into town to meet China for lunch and follow up on some official bridesmaids' duties while Derek drove over to Frenchman's Hill to discuss the delivery of the inventoried items. I tried not to worry about him having to confront Henri, but I knew he could take care of himself. And if worse came to worst, he did have that big, badass gun in his glove compartment.

Derek had insisted that Henri had been on his best behavior since our first meeting, so I figured the only weapon he would have to use was his innate charm.

I parked on the Lane near Annie's shop. Since I was early, I decided to stop in to say hello.

"Hey, you," she said as she gathered a red-and-white-checkered tablecloth into a decorative knot. She surrounded it with all sorts of pastas and jars of red sauce. On the table display were pasta makers and bright red bowls and utensils for stirring and mixing sauces. "Wish I could meet you guys for lunch, but I'm manning the store this afternoon."

"Don't worry, I'll take notes on everything."

"Okay. Just let me know what you need me to do."

"I will, thanks." My gaze settled on the jar of rich, thick red sauce filled with basil and mushrooms and onions. "Wow, this display is making me hungry for pasta. That hardly ever happens."

She laughed. "Only every other minute, right?"

"Right. I could pretty much eat it every day."

"Mm. Me, too."

I looked at the red bowls and decided on the spot to buy them for the Quinlans. They would look cheerful and bright in their glass-fronted kitchen cabinet. Then I picked up one of the cellophane-wrapped bags of pasta and the jar of red sauce. The perfect meal. Now if only I could boil water. But maybe Derek would handle that part.

"You just made a sale," I said, holding up the bowls, the bag of pasta, and the jar of sauce.

She laughed again. "Hurray."

"You're awfully chipper. How's it going?"

"It's going great. Life is good."

"That's so nice to hear. Oh, hey. How was your date?"

"It started out great, but then Josh had to cut it short. He got some message about a deadline."

"That's too bad. What time did you get home?"

"Around nine o'clock. Maybe nine thirty."

"Do you know what he was working on?"

Annie gave me a frown. "What is this, twenty questions?"

"Sorry, just wondering. No big deal."

But Derek had seen Noland Garrity sneaking up to the storage cave around that time, and then he'd been attacked. The timing was about right, if Josh Atherton left Annie and drove to the winery.

I was grasping at straws again. Josh Atherton specialized in antiquities, so he was researching the cave discoveries and maybe even the caves themselves. He seemed like a really smart guy. Would he honestly care enough to get caught stealing a Renoir? And what could possibly connect him to Trudy? I was only suspicious of him because I was protective of Annie, and that wasn't fair. So I brushed those thoughts away, paid for my pasta, and went to meet China for lunch.

On Saturday the winery held its big Pre-Harvest celebration of the fall season. We had made plans to take Trudy with us, but then Elizabeth wanted to go, too. And since Gabriel refused to let Trudy out of his sight, he was in, too. He drove the two ladies, and Derek and I met them all in the parking lot.

I waved at Annie, who had arrived with Josh. They did indeed make a cute couple, and I felt a twinge of guilt for discouraging her about him. When we walked into the tasting room, Robin and Austin were both at work at the bar along with Jackson and Dad. Mom joined us five minutes later, and it was officially a party.

We'd been tasting wine for fifteen minutes, laughing and chitchatting about everything under the sun—but mostly about wine and the attack on Noland Garrity. Robin noted that some of the winery employees were a little nervous about it, but Derek and Gabriel assured her that the attack was an isolated incident and they had nothing to worry about.

It was interesting to watch Jackson with Elizabeth. There was definitely sexual tension ringing between them, although they barely made eye contact. I took a quick trip to the ladies' room, where Robin cornered me.

"What's going on between Jackson and Miss Universe?"

I laughed at her title for Elizabeth. It fit the statuesque woman, but she was so much more than a beauty queen. I couldn't say too much, but I managed to tweak her interest. "Apparently they knew each other in a past life, so there's some residual smoldering."

"Smoldering," she said, nodding slowly. "Good word. Darn, I've got to get back, but we need to do lunch."

"Absolutely. We've got a lot to catch up on."

"Yippee."

As we walked back into the tasting room, the heavy French doors swung open and a well-dressed couple walked in. I was taken aback as I recognized Monsieur Cloutier and his charming wife, Solange, from Frenchman's Hill. We'd had lunch at their home with Guru Bob that first day when we went there to tell them about the cave discovery.

Seconds behind them, Henri and his wife, Sophie, entered, followed by Felix, the old man who had the habit of smacking Henri to keep him in line.

"Bonjour," I said, greeting them all politely since they had been civil with Derek the other day when he went to talk to them.

"Bonjour," Solange said, and her husband nodded. The others greeted me in a friendly way, and I felt the beginnings of a rapprochement. The thought made me smile.

"Welcome," Austin said jovially, and set five wine-glasses on the bar in front of the visitors. "Your tastings are on the house today, compliments of Robson Benedict."

"No, no, that is not necessary," Henri protested.

I walked over to Henri and gave him a big smile. "Please, we insist. You are our honored guests."

Felix smacked his arm. *"Imbécile.* When someone offers you free wine, you take it."

Everyone laughed, including Henri, and I figured this had to be their regular routine.

As I walked back to the bar, Annie stopped me. "Josh and I were just talking about you."

"Me? What's up?"

"I think we should all go out some night this week."

I glanced at Josh, who was biting back a grin. The action only made his dimples more prominent. "It wasn't my idea," he said.

I gave him the benefit of the doubt, especially since he seemed to make Annie happy. "Okay, I'll see what Derek's schedule looks like and I'll call you."

"Super," Annie said.

I started to walk away, when Josh pulled me aside. Pointing at Trudy, he said, "Is that the woman who was attacked last week?"

I frowned. "Yes."

"Please don't think I'm being crass, but do you think she would be willing to talk to me?"

"As a reporter?" My frown grew deeper.

"Well, yeah," he said, shoving his hands into his

pockets. "I mean, that's my job. I won't push her, but she's been inside the caves, right? I'm trying to paint a complete picture of your discovery, and she would be a good one to talk to."

Paint a complete picture, I thought. It sounded like the same blathering nonsense I'd heard from Darlene and Shawn when we caught them by the storage cave that night. Were they all in cahoots? I tried not to think about it as I glanced at Trudy and then back at Josh. "She's not quite ready to talk yet."

"I understand," he said, backing off instantly. "And I didn't mean to bother you. I'd like us all to be friends."

Over his shoulder I saw Annie looking tentative. I hated to cause her worry, so I nodded and smiled. "No problem."

I returned to Derek and Trudy just as Robin was pouring us the first glass, a wonderful muscadet that Dharma was famous for. It was light-bodied and mineral-edged, with a hint of apples. But it wasn't sweet at all, just crisp and refreshing.

"Oh, this is a favorite of mine," Trudy said after her first sip. She looked so healthy and happy to be out among friends, I almost forgot she'd been viciously attacked only days ago and that Amelia's killer was still on the loose. The fact that Trudy was in her seventies was another fact I tended to forget, but in that moment I felt a new resolve to protect her.

"It's lovely, isn't it?" Elizabeth said, swirling her glass.

Out of the corner of my eye, I could see Jackson watching her, and I wondered idly if she might stay in town for a while.

Elizabeth took a step forward to avoid bumping into a new group of people coming into the room. A fellow behind her moved even closer, and Elizabeth's glass bobbled in her hand. I tried to grab it, but it fell and shattered on the concrete floor.

She pressed her hands over her mouth in embarrassment. "I'm so sorry."

"It's my fault," the fellow insisted, and stooped down to pick up the broken stem. On his way back up, his gaze scanned her entire body, ending at her gorgeous waterfall of black hair streaming down her back.

He looked dazed.

As a way to get Elizabeth's attention, it was doomed to fail. I caught a glimpse of Robin, who studiously ignored the fellow and pushed a new wineglass over to Elizabeth. "No worries, occupational hazard," she said with a wink, and poured her another few ounces of white wine.

Jackson walked around the bar and came over to sop up the spilled wine and pick up the pieces of glass. When he stood, his muscled chest created a wall between Elizabeth and the clod who had bumped into her. She didn't mind Jackson's closeness at all.

I took another taste of muscadet and was marveling at the speed at which the broken glass was cleared away, when Trudy began to sway next to me.

"Oh my," she said, pressing a hand to her head.

"Trudy, are you all right?" I asked.

Derek grabbed her arm and braced her.

"What's wrong?" Gabriel demanded, taking hold of her other arm. "Let's go outside."

"No. No, I'm fine." She blinked a few times, trying to regain her equilibrium, and then she stared at me. "Oh, Brooklyn. Oh my. I had a surprise for you."

"You remembered?" I whispered.

"Yes." She inhaled and let her breath out slowly, glancing around as she did so. "My goodness. It must've been the broken glass. He broke a glass that day."

"He did what?" Gabriel asked in a low voice.

"Who?" I demanded quietly. "Who broke the glass, Trudy?"

Derek closed ranks, shielding Trudy from the crowd.

Gabriel remained close beside her, and Elizabeth's entire personality changed in a heartbeat. All of a sudden, she looked taller, stronger, like Wonder Woman with her hands clenched into fists, ready to do battle.

Jackson morphed into the powerful soldier he'd obviously been once upon a time. His shoulders rose and his muscles tightened. I seemed to be shrinking next to all of them, but I managed to maintain a cool, calm exterior. I also imagined that Derek would laugh at me for painting that picture of myself.

Trudy scanned the crowd for a few seconds. "Yes, there he is. He's the one. He came to my house to interview me. He stole my quail sculpture, and he killed Amelia."

"Who?" I asked again.

She pointed at Josh Atherton. "Him."

I watched Josh as he realized what was happening and his eyes turned cold.

"Annie, run!" I shouted, but it was too late.

Josh had pulled out a gun and grabbed Annie.

Someone screamed.

"I'll kill her," he said, his voice flat and deadly. "Don't think I won't."

Annie looked absolutely terrified and confused. Her fear radiated right into me. I made eye contact with her, and she kept her gaze on me. When I glanced up at Derek, she did, too.

Yes, keep watching Derek, I thought, hoping she could read my mind. *He'll get you out of this.*

"Don't do it, Josh," Derek said, his tone composed yet urgent. "I can speak to the sheriff. It's not too late to work out a deal."

I prayed that his cool, calm British accent would lull Josh into a false sense of security. Otherwise, someone was going to get hurt. I glanced around. Gabriel had disappeared.

"You're lying," Josh said angrily, clutching Annie's arm and waving the gun. "Just back off, let me out of here, and nobody gets hurt."

Who was lying now?

Behind Josh and Annie, the doors swung open, and Gabriel strolled into the room behind them. How had the man moved so quickly? He had to have snuck back into the fermentation room and raced around to the front of the building.

"Hey y'all, what's happening?" Gabriel said loudly. "Can I get a drink around here?"

Distracted by the newcomer, Josh whirled, dragging Annie with him.

Annie cried out, and the sound made me hurt inside. But now Josh had his back to us.

Before I could mutter, "Get him," Derek took three strides forward and snatched the gun from Josh's hand.

"Hey!" Josh shouted, and twisted to grab the gun away.

Derek popped him on the forehead with the butt of the weapon, and he wobbled. Elizabeth sprang forward and grabbed him in a light choke hold.

Annie was about to crumple and faint dead away, when Jackson jumped out and swooped her up in his arms.

The Frenchmen began to applaud and whistle.

I glanced at Trudy, who was shaking her head in amazement. "I am surrounded by heroes," she said.

I looked over at Robin and started to laugh.

"I love this family," she cried.

"Me, too," I said fondly as I watched everyone in action. All we needed now was for Mom to come in and shake burning sage over Josh's head. For once I wasn't the one being threatened or rescued at the last possible minute, and I really preferred it that way.

It was a phenomenal show. And other than the shattered glass that had brought Trudy's memory back to her, not a thing was broken or lost. Except Josh Atherton's freedom.

Once the cops carted Atherton off to jail and the paramedics gave Annie a clean bill of health along with a mild sedative, Guru Bob arrived, and we gathered chairs together in the fermentation room and listened to Trudy's story.

"I met him at the photo exhibit," Trudy said, clutching Guru Bob's hand tightly. "He was such a sweet young man, so interested in what I had to say. He had attended the press conference and was interested in writing some more in-depth articles. He told me he wanted to feature me. Said I was living history." She glanced around the room and sighed. "I think he meant I was old, but I was foolish enough to be flattered."

"You are beautiful inside and out," Robson said.

Trudy leaned over and squeezed his hand. "Thank you, dear. I didn't see any harm in agreeing to an interview. He came by the house the same day I called you, Brooklyn."

I simply nodded.

"Amelia didn't like him at all. In this case, her instincts were correct." She sniffled, then said, "In any event, I left him sitting in the living room and went to help Amelia with the tea and cookies. She was in a mood because he didn't want tea but preferred to have a glass of water. I can remember her muttering, calling him a heathen. She was so funny."

I had to marvel at Trudy's kind impression of her curmudgeonly friend.

"A minute later," she continued, "I returned to talk to him, and that was when I noticed that my quail sculpture was gone."

"Was he holding it?" I wondered aloud.

"No. He'd brought a briefcase with him, and he probably hid it in there. I didn't think anything of his carrying a briefcase. He's a professional journalist after all." She sighed. "Perhaps he thought that with the abundant objets d'art I have in my house, I wouldn't notice one missing, but my quail is my pride and joy."

"What did you say to him?" Elizabeth asked.

"I looked right at him and shook my finger. 'What have you done with my quail?' I said."

"Did he admit he'd taken it?" I asked. "What did he say?"

"He didn't say a word. He just pulled out a gun. I believe I gasped, and that was when Amelia walked into the room. She saw the gun and dropped the tray. Cookies went flying, and his water glass shattered on the wood floor just as she shoved me out of the way. The gun went off, and I hit my head. And that was it. My memory was gone."

I looked at Derek. "I never even thought about checking for missing items after that. If I'd noticed the quail was missing, we might've been able to track it down more quickly."

Trudy waved my comment away. "Don't blame yourself, Brooklyn. I didn't notice it was gone, either. I have so much stuff in that house, he must've thought I'd never notice." She shrugged helplessly. "I suppose he was right."

"But you did notice," I reminded her. "You noticed right away."

She considered that and smiled. "That's true." Her smile faded. "I wish I hadn't noticed. Amelia would still be alive if I'd kept my mouth shut."

We were all silent for a minute. It must've been hard for Trudy to relive the moments leading up to Amelia's death, but she was handling it like a trooper. In that moment, I felt sorry for Annie, too, who was curled up with a blanket on one of the benches in the room.

And that was when I recalled that she'd mentioned that Josh cut short their date the other night. That was the night Noland Garrity was attacked. Had he left Annie and gone off to meet Noland? Had the two been in cahoots together? Probably not in the beginning, but once they got to know each other, maybe they figured they could do each other a favor. And what about Darlene and Shawn? Had the four of them recognized a familiar streak of larceny in one another?

Annie was dozing, but I suspected she was listening off and on to Trudy's story. I glanced at my mom, who was sitting on the bench, stroking Annie's hair. I knew she considered Annie one of her own daughters, and I was happy that Annie had someone in her life like my mom.

I couldn't predict the future, exactly, but I could foresee a rollicking good cleansing ceremony in Annie's future.

Elizabeth cleared her throat. "While the police were cleaning things up a little while ago, I ran a quick survey of Josh Atherton's last four years of articles. He wrote feature stories from archaeological digs, museum events, and art gallery events from around the world. And with each article he wrote, there was a corresponding story in various local newspapers noting that a small item of significance was found missing sometime after the event concluded." She glanced down and read from her phone screen. "'Items missing included a shard of pottery, a book, a ring, a length of cloth, a small bell.'"

"Tokens," Gabriel murmured.

Elizabeth looked up. "Yes, tokens. Souvenirs. Each newspaper story mentioned that the particular item was small and not an essential part of the event, but historically important nonetheless."

"Like my quail sculpture," Trudy said.

Elizabeth's jaw tightened. "Yes, like your sculpture."

"Why was he never caught?" I asked.

"The items were insignificant. They wouldn't have been missed right away."

Annie dragged herself up to a sitting position for the first time. "Knowing Josh, he probably arranged for someone else to look guiltier than himself."

Mom frowned. "Why would you say that?"

Annie looked straight at me. "He was already talking about how that appraiser you guys hired . . ."

"Noland Garrity," I said.

"Yeah," Annie said, nodding. "Josh told me that he saw Garrity sneaking into the storage cave. When I asked Josh why he didn't report the guy to the police, he said that as an investigative journalist, he often worked undercover with the police."

"What a crock," Jackson muttered.

"He told me the police had asked him to keep an eye on Garrity, get to know him, and see what made him tick. They suspected him of stealing the artwork he was hired to appraise."

"So Josh was setting you up to point the finger at Garrity," I surmised. "Much later, of course, after he and Garrity were gone and we finally discovered something missing."

"That's horrible," Mom said.

I sucked in a breath and stared at Derek. "The Renoir. Did he take that, too?"

"No," Elizabeth said.

At the same time, Jackson said, "It's safe."

"Yes, it is," Derek confirmed.

I gazed from one to the other, shaking my head, then looked back to Derek. "I think there's a story here."

"I found it hidden behind the false wall of the wardrobe," Derek said to me. "It was just the other day, when I went back to investigate further."

"You never told me," I said.

He took my hand and squeezed it. "We've had a lot going on," he said, then glanced at Jackson and Elizabeth. "I'd like to hear your take on it."

"When I saw the photograph of the painting at the town hall," Elizabeth said, "I was sure it was the Renoir we've been looking for. The Nazis stole it from a wealthy family living near Oradour-sur-Glane shortly after the massacre. I asked Jackson to get me into the caves to study it up close."

"And then you hid it?"

"No. I found it in the wardrobe, right where Derek

found it. I have two theories. One is that Garrity planned to steal it, but he couldn't get it out of the cave without Derek catching him, so he hid it in the wardrobe until he could sneak back in and steal it for good."

"What's your other theory?"

"That someone in La Croix Saint-Just was a master forger. The painting in the cave was a remarkable likeness of the original, but it was fake. I wonder if one of your local Frenchmen tried to hide the painting so as to avoid bringing shame to his ancestor."

"Clever," I said. "So when the wardrobe was delivered to Frenchman's Hill, the painting would go with it."

"I believe your second theory is correct," Derek said. "And I know exactly who it was who tried to hide the evidence of forgery."

It had to be one of the people from Frenchman's Hill. I knew better than to ask Derek in front of the whole crowd, but I knew he'd tell me later. For now, I was happy to change the subject. "So Noland Garrity was only guilty of being a total jerk and not a crook."

"True, gracious," Robson said. "He is not a crook."

"But he is a jerk," I insisted, although I tried to say it lightly. "Why do you work with him?"

Robson smiled. "I appreciate Noland for his ability to force me to consciously work against negative emotions."

I shook my head. "I failed that test."

"It is not your test to fail, gracious. You are perfect just as you are."

I laughed at that one and noticed Mom and Dad snickering, too. I was pretty sure Derek was biting his tongue.

I looked at Elizabeth and said what I hadn't been able to say before this. "So you hunt down stolen treasures? Are you really the granddaughter of Trudy's old friend?"

"Of course not, dear," Trudy said. "Elizabeth is a highly trained secret agent specializing in stolen artwork. We made up that granddaughter story so that she'd be able to slip into town and do her work without anyone suspecting."

I felt my mouth gaping. "Trudy?" I blinked a few times, completely bowled over. "You knew all along?"

"It was my idea," she said, and couldn't keep from flashing a proud grin. "As soon as I saw all those treasures in the cave, I worried that there would be some hanky-panky. So I called an old friend of a friend, who recommended another friend, and Elizabeth called me back." She gazed fondly at Elizabeth. "I think we worked very well together."

Elizabeth's eyes glistened with unshed tears. "I think you are the bravest woman I know."

"I agree," Robson said.

When I was over the worst of my shock, I said, "Wow. Good job, you two."

Robson held up his wineglass. "A toast, to all the brave women we know."

"Hear, hear," Dad said, giving Mom's shoulder a light squeeze.

As I watched Trudy take a slow sip of wine, I was reminded of something else. "Trudy, you said you remembered what the surprise was."

She brightened. "Oh, Brooklyn! Yes, I wanted to give you my bookends."

I frowned at her. "Your kitten and quail?"

"No, no. I would never give up my darling kitten and quail. They were gifts from my father. No, the bookends I had for you are two lovely brass angels. Your mother always says you need a guardian angel to watch over you because you're always finding . . ." She blinked. "Oh dear."

She didn't have to say it. I was always finding dead bodies. Trudy was probably stammering because she realized I'd done just that when I'd run in and found Amelia lying dead in her living room.

"Well," Trudy said, a little flustered as she fluffed over that detail. "I decided that morning that I wanted you to have the angels because when I talked to Robson, he called you an angel. And it's true. You are."

"Oh."

Derek handed me a tissue before I asked for it. He knew me, knew that tears were already welling up in my eyes.

"And that day before the young man arrived," Trudy went on, "I was straightening up my mantel to make more room for my marble bookends. That was when I saw the angels and was reminded of you. So I wanted you to have them."

"That's so sweet." I gave her a big hug. "Thank you, Trudy."

"I wish I had them to give you right now."

"That's okay. I'll get them next time I'm at your house."

"Oh, wait!" She laughed. "I took a picture of them with my phone that day. Just like the kids do." She fished her phone out of her purse, found the photo, and passed it to me.

My eyes widened as I stared at the photograph of one of the angels she planned to give me. One angel was bent over, comforting a child, and the other had a sword raised above his head. The avenging angel. I handed the phone to Derek, who studied the picture for a long moment.

He passed the phone back to me, and I could tell from the bemused look on his face that we were thinking precisely the same thing: Trudy's angels looked exactly like something sculpted by Rodin. We had both done a bit of research when we were wondering who might've sculpted Trudy's kitten and quail.

We stared at each other and began to laugh. So it was possible that Trudy really did have a pair of Rodin bookends. Or they could be wonderful forgeries. It didn't matter one bit.

"Thank you, Trudy," I said, handing back her phone. "They're beautiful. I will cherish them and the thought behind them always."

Robson leaned over and kissed Trudy's cheek. Then he turned to the small crowd and held up his wineglass. "I would like to propose another toast."

"Hear, hear," Dad repeated, and winked at me as he lifted his glass with enthusiasm.

"To the angels among us," Robson said, his affectionate gaze touching all of us in the room. "May they always guard our treasures, great and small."

Epilogue

Two months later, on a gloriously sunny day in Sonoma, at the top of a terraced hillside overlooking the beautiful green valley, my best friend Robin married my brother Austin, surrounded by several hundred family and friends.

The food was fantastic, the wine was delightful, and the dancing continued late into the night. I was thrilled to be able to call Robin my sister every chance I could, mostly because she was brought to tears every time I said it. But more important, because we had been sisters of the soul since we were in third grade. I loved her as much as, or maybe a little more than, my own sisters. She had lived in my house for months at a time, and my parents considered her the fourth daughter—or was she the fifth?—they always wanted.

I finally took a break from dancing to rest my feet. I rarely wore heels, preferring to wear Birkenstocks when I worked in my studio—shoes that Robin referred to as "Hobbit wear." Needless to say, my feet were feeling the stress.

The party had been going on for six hours now, and I was more than ready to leave. But as maid of honor, I felt it was my duty to stay until the bride and groom left. As soon as they were gone, though, I would be dashing out of there.

It wasn't just the dancing that had exhausted me. No, it was something much more insidious. It was my mother's girlfriends. They were on some kind of mission. Frankly, if I had a nickel for every time one of them had asked me when Derek and I were going to tie the knot, I'd have ended up with a great big pocketful of change.

Besides being a rude, clichéd question to ask, it was embarrassing for me. None of them seemed to care, though. A few of my mother's friends had even asked me the question right in front of Derek. He had smiled politely, uttered some charming bit of fluff about me being the love of his life, and then extricated himself as quickly as possible. I didn't have that luxury, since my mother would find out if I'd been impolite to her girlfriends. No, I had to stand there and smile and make excuses. It was weird. I should've come up with something funny to say, but those women caught me off guard every time.

I brushed those thoughts away and concentrated on all the wonderful parts of the day. Several of the Frenchman's Hill families had been invited to the wedding, and it had been so much fun to see them enjoying themselves. I hadn't seen them since Robson had rented a massive truck and a few of us had driven over to Frenchman's Hill to deliver the heirlooms and treasure back to their rightful owners. That was a day I would never forget. And now we were all celebrating together as friendly neighbors. It was a lovely thing to see.

I watched Elizabeth slow dancing with Jackson on the dance floor. Those two looked awfully lovey-dovey, even though they continued to insist they'd never known each other in a past life. I wondered again if she might ever consider moving here. I knew that Trudy would love it if she did, and I would, too. Elizabeth and I had become good friends again, but it was more than that. If she made Jackson happy, we would all love her forever.

"Darling, are you ready to go?" Derek whispered in my ear.

I turned and wrapped my arms around him. "Almost. Where are Robin and Austin?"

"They left a half hour ago."

"Oh. Darn." I looked up at him and laughed. "We could've been out of here a lot sooner."

"You were still dancing."

"And my feet will kill me tomorrow." I laid my head on his shoulder. "I'm glad Robin escaped without too much fanfare. She was afraid everyone would make a fuss."

"They snuck away soon after the cake was served. I overheard your mother suggesting to Robin that they get out 'while the getting was good,' as she put it."

"Smart woman."

"The party appears to be winding down," Derek said, "although the caterers and bartenders are still on duty."

"Robin asked them to stay until midnight. But if she's already gone, then as maid of honor, my work here is done. Let's go."

We walked arm in arm to the car, and just as Derek opened the passenger door for me, I noticed two people standing in the shadows nearby, under an oak tree.

"Who's that over there?" I asked quietly, trying to see in the dark.

"Some neighbors, perhaps."

"Wait. No, that dress looks familiar." I looked closer. "Are they arguing?"

"It's none of our business, love." He tugged at my arm.

I gazed up at him. "You know that's not true. We introduced them."

"Let's go." He gently shoved me into the car and jogged around to the driver's side.

"Why were Alex and Gabriel arguing?" I asked myself.

"None of our business," Derek reiterated as he pulled out into the narrow lane and headed down the hill.

"He can't possibly be interested in her."

"Why not?" he asked. "She's a lovely woman and very accomplished."

"But she's a dominant, remember? She likes submissive males."

Derek laughed. "How could I forget? I was rudely informed of that news many months ago."

"Oh, right." I felt myself blush as I recalled an old, slightly crazy conversation from months ago, about handcuffs and masking tape. "But that's just it. Gabriel is the second most alpha man I know. They'll never get along."

"That doesn't mean they can't be friends," Derek said reasonably.

"This is terrible."

"Darling, don't take it so hard."

"No, it's terrible because Alex is leaving for a business trip in New York," I whined. "I'll have to wait a whole week before I can get any news or gossip from her."

"One week without gossip," he said with a laugh. "That is a terrible shame." As he drove, he reached for my hand, slowly lifted it to his lips, and kissed my palm.

I smiled. "I knew you'd understand the problem. That's why I love you."

"And I love you, darling. Perhaps we simply ought to make our own news instead of waiting to hear from others."

"What do you mean?"

He pulled the car to the side of the road and stopped. I watched, mystified, as he reached over to the glove compartment, removed a small box, opened it, and held it in front of me. "Marry me, Brooklyn."

Read on for an excerpt from Kate Carlisle's
next Bibliophile Mystery,

Books of a Feather

Coming in June 2016 from Obsidian.

The air inside the old bookshop was thick with the heady scents of aged vellum and rich old leathers. Heaven. I breathed in the lovely pulpy odors as I climbed the precarious rolling ladder up to the crowded top shelf to start cataloguing books.

The aisles of the shop were narrow, barely three feet wide, which meant I could reach out and touch the volumes on both sides of the aisle—if I was willing to let go of the wobbly handrail, which I wasn't.

I had spent the last week helping my friend Genevieve Taylor conduct an inventory of the thousands of books that had been crammed onto these shelves over the last forty years. It was a dirty, back-straining, mind-numbing job, yet I didn't mind too much. It was fun to visit with Genevieve, plus I was surrounded by old books. How could that be bad?

I hadn't been back to visit Taylor's Fine Books since Genevieve's father was murdered here almost a year ago. I hated to think of that moment when I found his body, tucked in a corner behind one of the brocade wingback chairs in the antiquarian book room. His neck had been slashed with a type of knife used in papermaking and bookbinding. Naturally, there was blood. A horrifying amount of blood. I'm a pathetic wimp when it comes to blood and tend to faint dead away. I managed to keep it together, but it was a close call. Not something I was proud of.

Recalling that image, I had to clutch the ladder rail, feeling woozy all over again at the thought of all that blood seeping into the faded Oriental carpet beneath poor Joe Taylor's body. I'd always hated the sight of blood. With all the dead bodies I'd come across over the past two years, I liked to think I'd matured enough to now handle the sight of blood oozing from an unfortunate victim. But it was still touch and go for me.

"I just found another first edition," Genevieve announced from the next aisle over.

I was grateful for the distraction. "What is it?"

"Bram Stoker's *Dracula*. Printed in 1897. Boards are slightly soiled, but the hinges are intact. Slight foxing. Spine's a little faded."

She said the words as though she were reading from a bookseller's brochure.

"A faded spine's to be expected," I said philosophically. "If it's in good condition otherwise, it's still probably worth ten thousand."

"Oh, wait," she said. "The pages are untrimmed."

"And the price just shot up to fifteen thousand."

She laughed. "That's what I like to hear."

"So that makes what?" I wondered aloud. "At least a dozen first editions we've found just today."

"Fourteen by my count," she said, and I could hear her "tsk-tsking" in dismay. "I'm excited to find them all, but I'm also a little flipped out that they were just sitting here on the shelves. I love my dad, but he had a real humdinger of a filing system."

I smiled. "At least he kept the books in alphabetical order. Sort of."

"Sort of," she muttered. "I found *Dracula* in with a bunch of paperback Charles Dickens novels."

"Well, they all start with 'D.' Sort of."

She laughed, but I detected a bittersweet tone, and I couldn't blame her. It had to be difficult going to work every day in the same shop where her father had died. But Genevieve was determined to carry on her dad's legacy as the premier antiquarian and rare bookseller in San Francisco. And given the dearth of good neighborhood bookstores out there, I wanted to support her in any way I could.

All day long, customers came and went while we kept working. They usually took their time, perusing the shelves and picking out a book or two. Some quietly minded their own business while others chatted away with Genevieve or her assistant, Billy.

I continued to write down titles on the inventory form Genevieve had created for the task. Besides the book title, she wanted the author's name and the aisle and shelf numbers. The work was slow but steady, and when I finished with one shelf, I climbed a few steps up to work on the next one. I knew I'd reached the top shelf when my head skimmed the ceiling. I felt a little sorry for these books on the top shelves. A reader would have to be willing to risk a sudden onset of acrophobia to explore all the way up here.

Hours later, I checked my watch and realized how late it was getting. "I'd better call it a day," I announced, and started to descend the ladder—but stopped when I spotted something on the opposite shelf. With one arm looped around the ladder's edge for safety's sake, I leaned over and reached for the book, easing it out of its cramped spot. It was the title and splashy dust jacket that had caught my attention.

One Flew Over the Cuckoo's Nest. It was one of my mother's favorite books. After taking a minute to admire the almost pristine condition of the dust jacket, I looked inside and found the author's flamboyant signature scribbled in blue marker on the front free endpaper. Was it for real? I turned to the copyright page. 1962.

"I think I found another first edition," I murmured, feeling a tingle of excitement at the find. Call me a weirdo, but books could do that to me.

"Cool," Gen said from the next aisle over. "What is it?"

"*One Flew Over the Cuckoo's Nest.* And guess what. It's signed."

"Are you kidding?" she asked, her voice rising two octaves.

"Nope. The author's signature is right here on the flyleaf."

"Is the book a mess?"

"No, it's in beautiful condition except for a small rip in the dust jacket, but that can be fixed."

"It's got to be worth ten thousand dollars."

"Ten or twelve thousand for sure." I closed the book and turned it around to study it from all angles. "I mean, it's in really good shape."

"Will you fix the rip?"

"Sure." Was she kidding? I would kill to work on this book! Even if it was something as simple as fixing a measly little rip in the jacket.

Instead of sliding the *Cuckoo's Nest* back onto the shelf, I scurried down the ladder and placed it on the short stack of books destined for the antiquarian room. That was where Genevieve, like her father before her, showcased the pricier volumes that would appeal to collectors and other booksellers.

Before I left for the day, Genevieve went to the computer and ran some comps on the seventeen first editions and various other gems we'd found that day. We both took guesses as to which book we thought was the most valuable—and we were both wrong. It turned out that a copy of *The Maltese Falcon* she'd discovered earlier that morning was similar to one that had sold recently for ninety-five thousand dollars.

"I'm beyond thrilled," Genevieve exclaimed, tossing her long, dark braid off her shoulder. "Can you imagine all these beautiful books were buried in the stacks? Thanks, Brooklyn."

"I'm having fun," I said, giving her a hug.

As I walked to my car, I had to admit I was pretty

thrilled to be walking out with eight wonderful books to refurbish, including a battered copy of *The Grapes of Wrath*, a charming hardcover edition of *The Merry Adventures of Robin Hood of Great Renown*, the signed *Cuckoo's Nest, Dracula*, and *The Maltese Falcon*. It was a win-win for both me and Gen and a nice reward for all my hard work.

It was a minor miracle that I was actually pulling into my apartment garage a half hour later. Driving from the Sunset District across town at this hour of the day when traffic was at its worst should've taken much longer, but I wasn't going to argue about my good luck. I parked the car and took the freight elevator up to the sixth floor. The noisy old wood-planked elevator was one of the holdovers from the 1900s when this building had been a flourishing corset factory. It had sat empty for decades until recently when it was refurbished and converted to trendy artists' loft-style apartments. The smart builders had kept the elevator intact, along with the original brick walls, the beautiful hardwood floors, and the large reinforced wire windows.

Officially it was located in the area of San Francisco known as SOMA, or South of Market, but since we were only a few blocks from AT&T Park, where the Giants played baseball, some people considered the area more China Basin–adjacent than SOMA. I wasn't too picky, but San Franciscans took their neighborhood differentiations very seriously.

As soon as I closed and locked my front door, I sagged in relief. I usually worked at home, so being gone all day was unusual for me. But after a moment, I perked up, knowing Derek was already there; I'd seen his car parked in the space next to mine.

Derek Stone was my fiancé and . . .

Fiancé. It was still odd to say the word out loud, let alone think it, but it was true. It was real. We were getting married, and how crazy was that? The two of us had almost nothing in common. I'd been raised in a peace-love-and-happiness artistic commune in the wine country and wore Birkenstocks to work. Derek had been a highly trained operative with England's military intelligence, and he carried a gun. Think James Bond but more dangerous, more handsome, more everything. I was crazy in love with him. I figured that the old adage that opposites attract had to be true because he loved me right back.

He had proposed two months ago, the night my friend Robin married my brother Austin. Of course I said yes. Duh! Since then, we'd barely had a chance to talk about a wedding or anything else related to getting married. We'd been living temporarily in Sonoma, and Derek had been commuting back and forth to the city while our apartment in town was being remodeled. And that was happening because months ago, Derek had purchased the smaller apartment next door to mine, and we decided to join the two places together.

We had been back in town only a week. Our place was still in a state of flux, to put it mildly. We'd been rearranging furniture and picking out new stuff and doing all those things you did when you suddenly had two extra bedrooms and a much bigger living room. It was fun and time-consuming and a little bit mind-boggling. I occasionally had to stop and pinch myself.

So no, there hadn't been much time to discuss wedding plans. We'd get around to it one of these days.

With a happy sigh, I slid the case that held my bookbinding tools under my worktable and set my satchel on the counter.

"Derek, I'm home," I called, even though he probably knew it already. He was preternaturally aware of everything that went on around us. Besides, our freight elevator tended to shake the entire building when it rose up from the basement parking garage, thus acting as an early-warning signal. I liked to think it made things more difficult for bad guys to sneak up on us, and yet they still tried it every so often.

"We are in here, darling," he called from somewhere in the vicinity of the kitchen.

We?

I heard a burst of male laughter, confirming that Derek was not alone. So much for showing him my stack of fabulous books from Genevieve's shop. I hung up my peacoat in the small closet by the door, trying to recall if we had made plans to see friends tonight. I was pretty sure we hadn't.

Not that I was paranoid, but I had to find a place to hide the books. Okay, maybe I was paranoid. I'd taken elaborate precautions before leaving Genevieve's shop, tucking the books away in a zippered compartment inside my satchel, which I had worn strapped across my torso and clutched all the way to my car. I never took chances with books. Especially rare, valuable books. Our home had been broken into on more than one occasion by unscrupulous people who were determined to steal a book from me.

"I'll be right there," I called out, and turned in a circle, scanning my workshop for a long moment, looking for a good hiding place. There were lots of them. Besides my worktable in the center of the room, I had three walls of cupboards and counters that held all sorts of equipment and supplies. At the end of one counter was my built-in desk.

I grabbed my satchel and pulled out the eight books— the eight rare, extremely valuable books that I'd been entrusted with—and carefully slipped them into the deep bottom drawer of my desk and locked it. I would've preferred to stash them all inside the steel-lined safe in the hall closet near our bedroom, but this would have to do for now.

I felt almost silly for taking such precautions. It shouldn't have been necessary since I was inside my

own house. I wondered if I was being overly suspicious.
But the answer was no, absolutely not. I was all too
aware that there were people in the world who would
lie, cheat, steal, or kill for a book. *So better to be safe
than sorry*, I thought, and was about to rush out to greet
Derek and whoever was visiting us when I spied a fluffy
bundle of fur clawing at the old sandals I wore for work
and kept under my desk.

"Hello, my little peanut," I said, and reached down
to pick her up. "You're getting so big." I lifted her into
my arms and rubbed my nose against her soft furry
coat. It made me a little sad to realize that Charlie, our
beautiful little kitten, was growing up.

"Who's visiting us?" I whispered. She simply purred,
and I hoped that meant that our visitor was friendly. I
held on to her as I walked through the archway that led
from my office workshop into our living room.

Derek stood by the bar that separated the kitchen
from the living area, pouring red wine into three glasses.
Another man, wearing a beautiful navy suit, had his back
to me. Though I couldn't see his face, I could see he had
straight black hair and was nearly as tall as Derek. He
had just said something that caused Derek to laugh. I
stopped and listened to that deep, sexy sound.

"And there she is," Derek said, spying me at last.
"Darling, come meet Crane, one of my oldest friends."

"I'm not that old," the other man joked as he turned
and stared at me. "Ah, how delightful."

If I'd been walking, I might've stumbled. The man
was Asian and spoke with a British accent and he was
simply . . . beautiful. Not as dashing or as blatantly masculine and tough as Derek, but then, who was? Still,
Crane's smile was brilliant and his dark eyes twinkled
with humor. He moved with a natural ease and confidence that made him even more attractive. *No man
should be that pretty*, I thought vaguely.

It was a bit overwhelming to have two such gorgeous
men smiling at me, but I decided I could endure it. I

hurried over to the bar to give Derek a quick hug and kiss, then turned to our guest and extended my hand.

"Hello, Crane. I'm Brooklyn."

His smile grew as he gripped my hand warmly. "It's a pleasure to finally meet you, Brooklyn. I've heard so many wonderful things about you."

I glanced at Derek. He'd never said one word to me about his friend Crane before. And yet the man knew all about me? Hmm.

Derek bit back a grin, clearly reading my mind. "Darling, Crane and I were in school together. We haven't seen each other in at least five years."

"Closer to six," his friend admitted. "Although we chat on the phone occasionally."

Derek set the wine bottle down. "It's a good thing. I'm always wondering if you've ended up in a federal penitentiary somewhere."

Crane laughed. "And I always figured you'd be the one to wind up on the wrong side of the law." He shook his head in mock dismay. "Instead, you joined forces with the good guys."

"Considering our misspent youth, it's surprising we both turned out this well."

Crane nodded at me. "It was always a competition to see which of us could cause the most havoc in school."

"You won in the end," Derek admitted, handing each of us a wineglass. "But only through a technicality."

I gazed at Crane. "How did you win?"

"He cheated," Derek said dryly. "He came into his inheritance, and nothing was the same after that."

"It's true. Money changes everything," Crane admitted with a worldly sigh. "It's not as much fun getting into trouble when you know you can simply bribe your way out of a jam."

Derek chuckled. "I, for one, am grateful for a few of those bribes."

I looked from one man to the other. "I'd love to hear stories of Derek causing havoc."

Crane leaned close. "I'll tell you everything, but first"—straightening, he held up his glass—"a toast, to old friends and new."

We clinked glasses and took our initial sips of the excellent Pinot Noir Derek had poured.

"And as long as we're toasting," Crane added, "I understand congratulations and best wishes are in order." He raised an eyebrow. "You're a lucky man, Stone."

"I know," Derek said, and kissed my cheek.

Happily flustered, I moved into the kitchen and quickly put together a cheese platter along with a bowl of crackers and some olives. Derek ushered Crane over to the living room, where we all sat to talk.

Crane leaned forward with his elbows resting on his knees. "Derek tells me you work with rare books."

A flash of guilt made me hesitate. I'd hidden all my pricey books earlier, unsure whether our guest was trustworthy or not. Now that we'd officially met and I knew he was one of Derek's oldest friends, I felt a bit silly for having hidden them from him. Still, the books were valuable, so I refused to feel bad for being cautious. "Yes, I'm a bookbinder. I take books apart and clean them up and put them back together again."

"She's being modest," Derek said. "Brooklyn has a unique gift for repairing the rarest of books. Almost like a skilled surgeon."

"Without all the blood," I murmured.

"But she's also an artist," he continued. "She's designed some fantastic book art."

I felt my cheeks heating up. I knew Derek appreciated my work, but all this lavish praise was going straight to my heart.

He touched my knee. "Darling, Crane has an impressive art collection. I think he would enjoy seeing your work."

"I would indeed," Crane said, helping himself to a cracker. "I collect all sorts of art, including books. I'd like to see your work sometime."

"You're welcome to join us tomorrow night at the Covington Library. They're having a big party to celebrate the opening of a new exhibit featuring Audubon's massive book of bird illustrations. It's a real masterpiece."

Crane blinked, clearly surprised by my invitation. But then he flashed me a spectacular smile. "Thank you for the invitation. I'd love to join you."

"And while we're there, I'd be happy to show you some of the books I've worked on." I started to take a sip of wine, but stopped. "That is, if you're not otherwise engaged."

Crane flashed me a spectacular smile. "I'm not. I'd be delighted to see everything you can show me."

"Good," Derek said. "It's settled, then." He put his arm around my shoulder. "You should be aware that the place also has a sentimental meaning for Brooklyn and me. It's where we first met."

"Now I'm truly intrigued," Crane said.

I almost laughed at the way Derek made it sound so romantic. True, we'd met at the Covington Library, but it was only because my mentor was killed that night and I found the body. Derek, in his role of security expert for the priceless antiquarian book collection on display, had found me with blood on my hands and immediately accused me of murder. Not the most starry-eyed way to start a relationship, but we'd managed to overcome those first few bumps in the road.

"And just think," I said, gazing up at Derek, "this time there won't be any dead bodies to worry about."

Crane seemed amused, but Derek was no longer smiling. In fact, he was staring at me as though he might've wanted to check me into the nearest loony bin. That was when I realized I had just tempted fate in the worst possible way. Right then and there, I began to pray that my words wouldn't come back to haunt me.

The Bibliophile Mystery Series

FROM

Kate Carlisle

Meet Brooklyn Wainwright, rare book expert—
and crime solver.

Homicide in Hardcover

If Books Could Kill

The Lies That Bind

Murder Under Cover

Pages of Sin
(Ebook Novella)

One Book in the Grave

Peril in Paperback

A Cookbook Conspiracy

The Book Stops Here

Ripped from the Pages

**"Brooklyn is my kind of detective! She loves
books, wine, chocolate—and solving mysteries."**
—*USA Today* bestselling author Maureen Child

Available wherever books are sold or at
penguin.com

Also from
New York Times bestselling author

Kate Carlisle

The Book Stops Here
A Bibliophile Mystery

Brooklyn Wainwright is thrilled to appear on the hit
television show This Old Attic as a rare book expert and
appraiser. Her first subject is a valuable first edition of the
classic children's story *The Secret Garden*, owned
by a flower vendor named Vera.

But soon, Vera's ownership is contested by an angry thug,
and the show's host is threatened. And when Vera is found
dead, Brooklyn must enlist the help of her security-expert
boyfriend and her cupcake-baking new neighbor to find a
clever killer—or her big chance in prime time may be
cancelled permanently.

Available wherever books are sold or at
penguin.com

facebook.com/TheCrimeSceneBooks

OM0131